Copyright © 2023 Sarah Demens

ALL RIGHTS RESERVED

The characters and events portrayed in this book are fictitious. Any similarity to real persons, living or dead, is coincidental and not intended by the author.

No part of this book may be reproduced, or stored in a retrieval system, or transmitted in any form or by any means, electronic, mechanical, photocopying, recording, or otherwise, without express written permission of the publisher.

ISBN (paperback)
979-8-89074-876-8

ISBN (hardback)
979-8-89074-940-6

Cover design by: Hannah Bailey

For all the believers and outcasts...
this story is for you

✦✦ CHAPTERS ✦✦

Prologue: An Unsettling Beginning . . . 1
Chapter One: The Beckhart Estate . . . 2
Chapter Two: PineTimes . . . 12
Chapter Three: Hitting The Town . . . 20
Chapter Four: Conversion . . . 27
Chapter Five: A Chilling Return . . . 37
Chapter Six: Words Unspoken . . . 42
Chapter Seven: Going Out On A Lim . . . 55
Chapter Eight: Pained Memories . . . 66
Chapter Nine: Red Sky In The Morning . . . 71
Chapter Ten: Talbot's Den . . . 79
Chapter Eleven: An Unseen Threat . . . 83
Chapter Twelve: Consultant . . . 88
Chapter Thirteen: Resonance . . . 99
Chapter Fourteen: Strength In Numbers . . . 107
Chapter Fifteen: Together We Stand . . . 117
Chapter Sixteen: The Tapes . . . 127
Chapter Seventeen: Fender Bender . . . 137
Chapter Eighteen: Secrets Of A Small Town . . . 145
Chapter Nineteen: Emotional Response . . . 153

Chapter Twenty: When The Dust Settles . . . 161
Chapter Twenty One: A Warning . . . 171
Chapter Twenty Two: Blood Feud . . . 181
Chapter Twenty Three: A Long Night Ahead . . . 190
Chapter Twenty Four: Surrealism . . . 196
Chapter Twenty Five: Turn A Blind Eye . . . 208
Chapter Twenty Six: Reformation . . . 223
Chapter Twenty Seven: Witness Protection . . . 237
Chapter Twenty Eight: Supply & Demand . . . 242
Chapter Twenty Nine: Vulnerable . . . 255
Chapter Thirty: Target . . . 259
Chapter Thirty One: Fish On A Hook . . . 266
Chapter Thirty Two: Improvised . . . 272
Chapter Thirty Three: Some Assembly Required . . . 277
Chapter Thirty Four: Snare Of The Fowler . . . 285
Chapter Thirty Five: Leap Of Faith . . . 294
Epilogue: Come Back Soon . . . 305

PROLOGUE
✦ AN UNSETTLING BEGINNING ✦

The air was hot, the atmosphere cluttered with fog.
She charged through the cloudy darkness ahead of her blindly and as quickly as possible... despite her exhaustion... despite the pain she felt in her lungs, stinging with every heaving breath she took.

Her breath was on a cross between panting and whimpering. She dared not look back... for the thing chasing her would further induce panic.

She needed to run. Keep running.
Don't stop. Never stop.

She needed help.
She couldn't do this alone. She couldn't run anymore.

She pushed, she cried and she stumbled as fresh hot tears ran down her face; the way already foggy, her vision now blurred.

That's when things took an unfortunate turn, when creation is simply, clearly, *not* on your side.

She tripped. She fell, a*nd she screamed.*

CHAPTER 1
✦ THE BECKHART ESTATE ✦

In the quiet town of Hollowgrove, there rode a slick black limousine... one of which was traveling straight from the airport, on the way through a dismal forest. Despite the light coming from above, the pathways within the wooded area were blanketed by shadow. The winding road ahead of the Beckhart siblings... the very same riding the vessel... almost made the two carsick.

Audrey Beckhart, the younger, was the age of 21... a natural beauty with long brown hair streaked with black, donning large expressive eyes that sparkled in the sunlight. She was dressed in a soft lavender coat and knee high brown boots, a sky blue beanie atop her head. She was beautiful and everyone knew so. Of course, she was a member of one of the richest and most popular families in town.

She stared out, maintaining the same deadpan serious expression for a quarter mile now... something obviously on her mind, though she wouldn't say.

Seated next to her was her brother, Gabriel, aged 22... a rather classy young man with slick brown hair that actively covered over his bright eyes, with a buttoned up suit and an aqua green scarf wrapped around his neck. His pleasant, expensive cologne spread through the car's interior and filled everyone's senses.

With a cell phone in hand, he tapped the device against the edge of his car door, biting his lip nervously as he stared out his own window. He had just finished talking with the pair's mother and father... though his facial expression indicated that the conversation did not go so well.

His eyes slowly turned to his sister, who remained silent the entire ride. His reluctance was made obvious.

"Audrey..."

"Let me guess."

She didn't even bother to look at him.

"...Not home after all."

He scrunched up his face in a manner that indicated he wasn't surprised that she wasn't surprised.

"...Pretty much."

He cleared his throat, preparing to mimic their parentals.

"Hey son, welcome home. Sorry, but we're actually out of town right now and won't be back for awhile.

Don't worry, you have the whole house to yourselves-- card's on the counter, treat yourself to a homecoming party, have over all the friends you want, see you when we see you!"

Audrey rolled her eyes.

"Great, not so much as an 'I love you'... why did they even have us?"

The last part was said in more of a whisper, as not to necessarily be answered aloud.

But Gabriel took it upon himself to do it anyway.

"I've concluded we were both mistakes spanning one year apart."

She chuckled softly.

"That makes sense..."

The driver made several turns on the way to the Beckhart residence, which resided deep in the woods, far from the town itself.

The three kept silent the rest of the way until they finally reached their destination. A lavish mansion with a wide open courtyard which the limo turned into, winding around a fountain in the middle of the area, which then parked in front of the house.

Behind the mansion was nothing but woods. The mansion itself was a surprisingly plain white with dark red trimmings and solid black double doors.

Both the Beckharts pressed against Audrey's window to gaze upon their home. A home of which apparently withstood four solid generations of Beckharts. Naturally, it had many remodels and improvements to survive being such a lavish and modern residence. Just looking at it, however, you could tell it had a great deal of history. Sheltering so much of their family, for so long a time.

The Beckhart family had been around since the beginning of Hollowgrove, so they were told. Which eventually earned them quite a bit of wealth and respect. The house before them, though it was *their* house, seemed as foreign as though they were just discovering it. Coming home from college was like visiting as two strangers.

Every time they would return on their breaks, of course, their parents just happened to be away on another vacation of their own and never awaiting their arrival.

That really didn't mean much in itself, of course, as they were hardly ever around with their children to begin with. Too much concern about other matters that required a wealthy individual's attention. Due to this... the relationship between them and their parents was... saddening, to say the least.

Both the Beckhart siblings climbed through and stepped out of the vehicle gracefully. Audrey's eyes were glued to their estranged estate the whole time, though Gabriel's were more attentive to the sky above them: a solid white canvas hovering over the world below.

Audrey cut her eyes at her brother, curiously and silently seeking out an explanation as to why he was so concerned above them.

Though Gabriel soon said aloud his reasoning.

"Is it supposed to rain, Henson? That sure is an awful overcast." Henson, the driver, stepped out himself and nearly strained his neck trying to look up as well.

"The sky has been getting like that a lot lately, sir. Hardly ever get a sunny day anymore."

He shut his door and lowered his head, shaking it in a strange manner.

"...There always seems to be a storm coming..."

Gabriel and Audrey glanced at one another, pondering on this.

Welcome to Hollowgrove

Gabe shook away the hair that was crawling over his glasses and sighed, clearing his dry throat.

"Still standing, I see..."

Audrey knew he was referring to the house. Indeed, it looked untouched.

She turned her whole body towards it and stared at it, as if attempting to reacquaint herself with it. She slightly shivered from the chilly Autumn air. Holding both sides of her coat together, she shrugged her shoulders, clicking her heels together.

"No place like home..."

Gabriel stood next to her, placing his hands in his pockets as he faced the estate with little to no interest whatsoever.

"At least we have a home, I guess."

"...Still... it'd be nice not to arrive in a limo."

Movement behind Gabe caught his attention, and he turned to see that Henson was opening the trunk and beginning to pull their bags out.

"That's alright, Henson, we'll get them."

Henson stood upright fast, as if shocked by what he heard, and blinked several times in outright confusion.

"I'm sorry?"

"We can get them, Henson."

Gabriel advanced towards the tall, well built middle aged man in a dark suit, who wore a professional little cap that Audrey found to almost be a part of him now.

Audrey herself joined her brother and the two pulled out their luggage from the back of the trunk.

"Are you sure, sir? I really don't mind."

"No, Hen..." Audrey spoke.

"You just get home to your family. I'm sure they're missing you terribly."

Henson was at a loss.

"Oh, but your parents specifically instructed me to-"

"Please, we're not in any need of a chauffeur or bodyguard. We grew up in this town, we're big kids. Go home already."

Audrey smiled at him. Gabriel did the same.

Henson was reluctant at first, but he eventually smiled back, nodding his cap at them.

"Thank you, Mr. and Miss Beck-"

"Pleeaassseee, you've known us forever!"

Henson chuckled at Audrey.

"Alright... Gabriel... Audrey... thank you. I greatly appreciate it." Gabe moved the bags onto the gravel ground, just as Henson advanced for the driver door and began to climb inside.

"You have a lovely vacation, you hear?"

"You too." The siblings sung at once. The humble driver, who had been serving the family for many years, started his engine and drove off, leaving the two alone on their property.

Audrey let out a breath, scratching her neck. "Here goes..."
Gabe handed her her luggage and the two advanced for the door. The Beckhart siblings stepped onto the welcome mat in front of the door. Audrey had to set her bags down in order to pull out the house key from her warm pocket.

She at first had difficulty jiggling the small object into the tiny keyhole, as her hands were freezing and in need of the gloves she forgot to put on. She at last got it and turned the brass knob, the black door creaking open, so loudly and unpleasantly that the two grit their teeth.

The siblings sighed and cleared their throats, taking a deep breath before they stepped into the safety of their expensive domain.

Gabe shut and locked the door behind them, setting his bags down. Audrey did the same and took a long look at the interior of their estate, taking note of all the changes they made, despite their parents hardly ever being in the home itself.

"...I swear, they have this place decorated different every single time we come home."

Gabriel shook his head in disdain as he put a finger to his lips and typed in the code to the security pad. After he turned from doing so, he and his sister left their bags behind to venture deeper into the house.

"Geez, it's freezing." Audrey acknowledged as she hurried to the fireplace, rubbing her hands together.

"Let's get the fire started. Be sure to turn that heat up, too. I am not turning into a popsicle my first night home."

Gabriel adjusted the thermostat before removing his coat and tossing it on the side of the couch. He sighed upon noticing it and blandly turned back around, facing the kitchen.

"They got a new couch."

"Figures."

He, too, rubbed his hands together as he studied around the mostly white, modern looking living room. He dropped this after a few seconds, falling into boredom very easily, then made for the fridge.

"Audy, I'm starving. What are you in the mood for?"

Audrey chucked in a fresh set of logs into the fireplace, setting them ablaze shortly before poking them with a firm grip.

"I'd eat anything at this point. As long as it's not expired."

Gabriel wasn't in the mood for the food located inside the fridge, therefore stepped back and approached the counter in the middle of the kitchen. It was glass with many chairs surrounding it and a glistening marble full of lights that shined from the bottom of the table itself.

Sure enough, his parents had indeed left one of their many credit cards on the table for them to blow money on whatever they chose. He took it and stuffed it inside his back pocket.

"They left us the card."

"Joy. Lord knows we're short of those."

Audrey fixed herself back up and slipped off her hat and coat, sighing tiredly as she threw them over a chair, revealing a cottony baby blue sweater.

She ran her fingers gently through her dark brown curls, trying to take out the tiny tangles. That's when she heard a yelp. She gasped as before she knew it, an animal had surprise attacked her and was jumping up her leg, showering her hands in tiny wet kisses, shaking so much that it barely could contain itself.

"Scrooge, baby!!"

She giggled as she got on her knees and held the tiny dog in her arms, his licks transferring from her hands to her face.

"Hiii, pretty puppy!" She exclaimed with glee, her voice reaching one that you only ever use for a dog.

"Oh my goodness, baby, you missed me almost as much as I missed you!"

Gabe grinned at the sight of their dog, appreciating the smiles that it brought Audrey. There was a deep sadness that had settled in her for quite some time now, and it was rare for her to genuinely display true happiness anymore...

After the greeting, she picked up the small dog and made for a glass table sitting in the living room. She studied the contents atop of it that had caught her eye: a picture of her and Gabriel's parents.

She took hold of the frame and held it in front of her. Their father, a successful and abundantly wealthy banker. Their mother, a beautiful and famed actress. They stood in each other's arms at an event in Casper City, which closely neighbored the quiet town of Hollowgrove.

The two were well respected and adored by the people of both the town and the city, and were always pulled from the family for their work there. Not that they minded... they had never put their children first, not even once.

Gabriel walked to her side and stared at their picture, his jaw tightening. "Look at them..."
Audrey noticed.

"...They look so happy."
After a few minutes, she finally found it necessary to set the frame down.

"...Funny, I was almost starting to forget what they looked like." Gabe looked down, searching for other frames.

"There's only one of us. The one from my 18th birthday, remember?"

"No need to sound like a narrator, dummy." She corrected as she smiled teasingly.
"...Except you're getting to be an old man. It was your *16th*."
He frowned. "...Oh..."

She chuckled and approached him, staring down at the photo.

"...I remember it clearly, because I was 15 and Carl Lanley, my humongous high school crush, was there. I was too embarrassed to be seen by him because of my accursed braces that they forced on me. But you kept telling me, you needed one last shot of us since you were afraid they were sending you to a school overseas. And you'd hardly ever see me again… you were begging me."

She touched the frame, in deep remembrance.

"I felt too guilty to say no. So right in front of him, I grabbed you and had our friends snap the picture. I didn't even care if he saw me at that point, as long as you were happy. To this day, it's my favorite of us."

Indeed, a teenage Audrey had her brother dragged into an embrace, her hair pulled into a loose ponytail, her wide beaming smile laced with metal. Gabriel's partially longer and untamed hair fell over his eyes as he smiled in his sister's company, the two seated at a bowling alley.

"That was the most normal birthday I'd ever had."

He stuck his hands into his pockets.

"They don't even have a picture of all of us. What does that tell you?"

"That we haven't had a photo together in a long freaking time." Audrey sighed, clearing her throat and bowing her head as her fingers gently stroked the fur of Scrooge's ears. "Well..."

She took a deep breath and turned around.

"Pointless to be thinking about all that and getting ourselves depressed. Let's eat something."

She moved away, advancing for the coffee table, where she picked up the remote and turned on the TV using the old fashioned power button, as opposed to the fancy voice-activated feature her parents installed. She insisted on doing everything as normally as possible, of course, with *as much* as possible.

Gabriel turned towards the television, folding his arms, the channel currently being set on the news.

"Well I'm certainly in no mood for a party."

He went to sit down, as Audrey had made for the kitchen, where she smiled and peeked at him.

"So, another quiet, relaxing night of old monster movie marathons and pizza?"

Gabriel smirked.

"Must be psychic, cause you read my mind."

Audrey smirked back.

"Well, Mom and Dad said they were gonna be gone for awhile, so that probably gives us the week to ourselves. Why don't we hit the town later? Maybe the library? Give you a chance to work on your book!"

Gabriel sighed, however, shifting uncomfortably.

"I've hit a block."

She chuckled as she poured milk into a cup and put it inside the microwave for cocoa.

"That's the whole point of visiting the town. Get those so-called creative juices flowing."

"I just don't like how the idea's coming out. It doesn't feel quite... *me*... you know?"

Audrey turned as her brother fell into an awkward silence, and she stared at the back of his head as she stood next to the heating cocoa. Scrooge was currently laying on the couch, sighing

Uncanny

contently at his masters being home.

"You'll get it, Gabe. The idea will come... I know it."

Gabriel stared at the floor, taking a deep and saddened breath.

"At least someone does."

Audrey didn't hear him; she was too preoccupied with getting out the whipped cream and cinnamon.

Gabriel fell completely silent, as he usually does... until something caught his attention. His eyes darted for the TV, his mouth running agape.

"It's been two days, and young Melony Martin, aged 16, is *still* missing."

Gabe leaned forward with intrigue.

"She was last seen near her family's home in Crooked Creak road late Thursday night. Witnesses say at the time of her disappearance, a bright light occurred and quote... 'a powerful and violent thunder sound' came from the sky, which was then followed by reports that an unidentified aircraft 'zipped' through the sky. Said witnesses were separate individuals... a hunter, Harold Roland, and a family of campers, the Zeplins, all of whom have claimed that young Miss Martin was undoubtedly... *abducted by aliens*."

"Hey Gabe, when should I order the-"

"SHHH!" He exclaimed, halting his sister behind him, who then turned her attention to the television.

"This is the seventh abduction report... and the 12th missing person overall since June. Local authorities have urged residents to be cautious as they try to find the one, or ones, responsible. When asked for clarity on the situation, our very own mayor, Ripley Ravenwood, has stated that despite the disheartening number of missing individuals, there is nothing for his citizens to worry about, and encourages us to get back to 'business as usual'. This is his fifth overall statement on the matter since the cases began in June, the residents themselves desperate to get answers... on just *where* their loved ones are."

Gabriel turned in his seat and looked up at his sister, Scrooge perking his head as he sensed something was up. Audrey simultaneously looked to him and the two Beckharts gained the same look of pure and utter shock.

"Audrey... what's happening here?"

CHAPTER II
✦ PINE TIMES ✦

The clock struck **12:15 pm,** which initiated an obnoxiously loud blaring to come from an alarm clock.

A thin, nail-bitten hand reached in and smacked it into silence, which then limply slid off the device and retreated back into the blanketed covers of the body attached to it. A soft groan came from the body. There occurred some movement as the body stirred, yawned and finally started to rise, kicking off the covers.

A young woman with red hair emerged from her slumber and yawned increasingly as she stumbled from her bed, reaching in tiredly for her glasses sitting upon the nightstand. With groggy eyes she looked around, putting on her lenses, her sight adjusting to her room.

After a deep breath and a moment to reflect on her day's agenda, she made for her bathroom. There, she gazed into the mirror, did a quick hygiene test, and proceeded to brush her teeth. She wasn't the most elegant to handle her self-care, but she got the job done and looked and smelled pretty decent. Once done, she made her way back to her nightstand and put on her forest green beanie.

Upon doing so, she immediately went to the mini fridge sitting in her room and pulled out an energy drink. Snapping the can open and taking a few swigs, the girl was ready to take on the day's challenges. She grabbed hold of a small USB on her nightstand, then seated at her desk. Opening her laptop, she inserted the USB, visited her desired web address on the internet browser, and finally awaited as it loaded.

After a good yawn, she rolled over to a squeaking cage, where she tapped the tiny bars.

"Morning, Porky. You hungry, babe?"

Out of a little magenta hut emerged a tiny tan gerbil that sniffed its nose at its mama. With a smile, the girl reached into a bag of gerbil food, then extended her hand into the cage to dump the small handful into a tiny bowl. Porky walked over to it immediately and began eating his breakfast.

Welcome to Hollowgrove

After this, the girl rolled back to her laptop and cracked her wrists, immediately proceeding to check the news sites. Her eyes ciphered through the different articles she saw. She tried to avoid the big news sites. Too many cover-ups... too many non-believers. The smaller ones, the journalists, the tiny stories to be found that no one believed... that was where it was at.

She checked the local news site, and that's when she saw the update. She bit her lip and swallowed. After reading the full article and taking all the information she could... she went back to her blog:

The PineTimes.

After a glance at the ceiling and a deep breath, she started typing.

~

The time reached to 2:05 pm.

Gabriel and Audrey both got busy unpacking. Their rooms were thankfully just as they left them, so it was easy to get back into the groove of things.

But something was troubling the two Beckharts. The news report. The missing girl. The missing *people*. Something was going on in their town. And the abductions? Alien abductions? That was just a tip of the iceberg.

Strange things had always been plaguing the town. Always affecting everyone... had them on edge... but this was different. They both knew it; things were getting out of control.

It drove them crazy trying to figure out why no one was doing anything about it. This was not what they wanted to come back on vacation to.

"What do you think?" Audrey questioned.

"About what?"

"About the missing girl?"

Gabriel paused from folding his clothes, and his head slowly turned to her.

"...I think it's terrible."

She sighed heavily, dropped the clothes on her old bed, and swung her body around to face him, giving him a most undeniably sassy glare.

"You know what I mean."

He frowned and his face turned away once more, looking back at the clothes. "I think... something's happening."

She swallowed. "With the case?"

"...With the town."

He looked back at her.

"Hollowgrove... Casper... all of it... it's as if this place is... cursed."

Audrey crinkled her face at this. "...Cursed?"

"I know... it sounds ridiculous... but seriously, why else would this place be so weird? Is my theory really *that* crazy?"

She thought of this for a second before turning her head away.

"...No."

Gabriel looked back at his clothes.

"... Let's just make it through the night. Then, maybe tomorrow, we can do something."

"Do what??"

Gabriel had to try and figure it out first.

"I don't know... we'll see... I'll tell you later."

Audrey and Gabriel both looked away from one another, and Gabriel zipped up his suitcase.

"It's going to be weird, having separate rooms."

"Yeah..."

Audrey sat down on the bed she had spent her teenage years sleeping in that had always been across the room from Gabriel.

When they went to college, they requested to be roommates and had spent all that time sleeping in the same room, as they did when they were children. Now Audrey was moving into her own room, and this almost made her feel vulnerable.

"If you want, you can sleep here for the night."

"That's okay... unless you want me to."

Her head bowed. "Kinda..."

He smirked, shaking his head.

Sharing the same room was never really a thing about privacy for the two siblings. Their parents insisted they have separate rooms, but the two, as close as they had always been, wanted otherwise.

When Audrey was a little girl, she had extreme fear and anxiety problems that were only remedied when her brother was near. Being around him made her feel safer. The two would talk for endless hours, late into the night.

Despite being 21, Audrey still struggled with her anxiety, and tried to conquer her fear. It's harder than it sounds; age does not automatically kill off your struggles. Sometimes you have to force them out... and sometimes... they're justified.

He turned around and approached her, laying both his hands on her shoulders.

"You going to be okay without me?"

She smiled and shook her head at his question.

"Of course I am... I'm a big girl now, remember?"

Gabriel's eyes briefly glanced to the ceiling.

"Three nights ago, you were hiding under the covers, cuddling Snoofer, after reading those god-awful online horror chat stories."

Audrey crinkled her eyes and gestured at her stuffed plush wolf sitting on her pillow. "You leave Snoofer out of this... and those god-awful horror chat stories are freaking *terrifying*!"

"Riiighhtt." He smiled teasingly and turned away.

"Well... tomorrow night, I better not be bolting up from you sneaking in, after Angelica learns that her texting boyfriend is actually a homicidal impostor coming after *her* next."

"Oh god, I'm never dating anyone again."

He rolled his eyes. "Please don't tell me there's actually been a plot revolving around that."

She turned her head away, innocently.

"You are pathetic." He laughed.

"*Shush*!"

Audrey threw a pillow at him.

~

The time struck 7:25 p.m.

Audrey and Gabriel, now roosted on the couch, surrounded themselves with snacks and soda, sharing a large tub of popcorn as they watched a marathon of old classic monster movies.

Scrooge, their adorable little old man of a Pomsky, was now curled up next to Audrey. Wrapped in his favorite blanket, being fed popcorn every so often, he was just as invested in the movie as the Beckharts.

"I missed little Scrooge... and nights like this."

She stroked the dog's thick fluffy fur, behind the ears.

Gabriel smiled, stuffing popcorn in his mouth. "Me, too."

He reached in and scratched Scrooge's forehead, who was adoring the attention. The way he closed his eyes and smiled through a pant, his little wet tongue hanging out happily, would make anyone melt.

Despite his name implying he was an overall unhappy dog, the name came from when they were younger, where Scrooge would get snappy at anyone other than the two siblings. Even though it was just a phase, and his demeanor was now that of an angel, the name remained. It still made the two laugh to see such a happy and laid-back dog have such an old grouchy name.

The two went back to the movie, the fire crackling from the fireplace, the living room and kitchen in the background having low lighting that added to the cozy atmosphere.

In the midst of the ideal Autumn night, however... something caught Scrooge's attention.

His head instinctively snapped to the glass doors to his right, it being almost pitch black outside. His happy demeanor turned to one of alarm, his tongue whipping back into his mouth. Then he let out a soft growl that at first went unnoticed by the two humans... until he let out another, this time louder.

Audrey looked down at him.

"Scrooge, what's wrong?"

Gabriel's attention was grabbed.

"What is it?"

"Scrooge, he's growling at something."

Her eyes lifted to the glass doors.

"He's looking outside."

Gabriel cut his eyes at the two, as he turned his attention to the same direction.

"...Might just be a deer or something."

Audrey was unsettled.

"...Can we go check?"

Gabriel frowned. "Audrey..."

"*Please?*"

His eyes moved to her face and hers to his.

"With what's been going on, I'm spooked out, okay? Just please, let's check."

Gabriel was thankfully a reasonably understanding person. He nodded. He was willing to do anything for Audrey, to make sure she not only felt safe, but *was* safe.

"Okay... go ahead and pause it."

She grabbed the remote, putting the movie on hold, and gathered Scrooge into her arms, who was shaking far too much to pretend to be brave. The two siblings walked over to the glass doors, with a hint of caution, not being able to see a thing due to the zero percentage of light.

Gabriel took a few short glances at the outside before flipping a switch to turn on the backyard lights. A mesmerizing white glow popped up in small pockets all throughout the back, and from the pool. Which for some reason was bubbling, despite the jacuzzi setting being turned off.

Both the curious humans expected a wild beast to pop out or a mindless serial killer with a machete, to attack the unsuspecting double. But nothing appeared. It was tranquil... even though Scrooge was growling, and shaking. The darkness was awaiting from the other side of the glass, almost beckoning them to come out and venture beyond it.

Gabriel and Audrey both settled, laying out a deep breath of relief as the fear turned out to be for nothing.

"It's nothing... Scrooge is just jumping at shadows."
Audrey glared down at the dog, before turning her gaze back up to her brother. "Yeah, but... what if something is there... watching *us*?"

Gabriel gave his sister such a look of criticism, that she instantly felt shame and wanted to retreat from his gaze. He shook his head and started to turn.

"I think you two have watched enough monster movies."
She exhaled in a frustrated manner, falling right behind him, while Scrooge grumbled in her arms.

"Gabriel, I'm not a child. I know when something doesn't feel right!"

"Well, you and your feelings need to calm down."
She groaned, "You're doing it again!"

"Audrey, please. Let's just get back to the movie. Like you said... what's going on has gotten you spooked. It's okay though, we're safe."

Audrey huffed. She plumped back down on the couch and bitterly stroked Scrooge's fur as she peered through the television screen with a tightened jaw. The last thing she saw, however, was a monster chasing after the female lead... before she unwillingly

Uncanny

drifted off to sleep not even half an hour later. Scrooge was not far behind, the two huddled close together.

Gabriel's eyes peeked from his diligent viewing of the film climax to the sleeping lady and dog. He saw his chance. He pulled out his phone and bent over, immediately loading up his browser. He kept glancing at the two to make sure they were staying asleep. When he found it safe to breathe again, he visited it.

The search results. For Hollowgrove news.

There, it only appeared to be worse than what the television had led on. There wasn't just abductions... there were countless monster sightings. Attacks. What wasn't an abduction was a complete and total mystery, with zero leads. The television can only let on so much of the weird activity that had been taking place more and more as of late.

It unsettled Gabriel just how riddled with supernatural forces the town had become. So much that he felt... sick. Something was undoubtedly strange and otherworldly. Real monster activity or not.

Gabriel didn't know what to make of it. It was so peculiar. So insane. So uncanny. And no one was doing anything about it.

One thing, however... one thing did certainly catch his attention... a spark of familiarity. He spotted an article. Done by a blog titled PineTimes.

He clicked on it.

"It's day two. The most recent abduction? A 16 year old girl named Melony Martin. Melony happens to be a friend of mine. Not a close one, but this news has hit home. We're a small town, but not everyone knows everyone. In this case, the abductees have been so random, so completely different from one another, that someone is hurting somewhere. They're missing their friend, father, mother, child, sister, brother, spouse... and the local authorities are doing nothing to fix it.
The police have no idea what to do. And the mayor keeps telling everyone there's nothing to worry about. No one is really helping these people. We need to stop them. They're taking us for God knows what. Next thing you know, they'll be taking children. And then the line will truly be crossed for this town. Hollowgrove is in serious danger. It's been this way for over a year. Who's willing to

help us?"

Gabriel's eyes lifted and he breathed a heavy exhale.

"Amelia"

CHAPTER III
✦ HITTING THE TOWN ✦

Morning came almost as quickly as it left. A gentle ray of light glimmered upon Audrey's soft porcelain face, and her eyes began to flutter open into two narrowed slits. She was sitting up on the couch in the same spot she remembered passing out in.

The soft sound of sizzling and sweet aroma of food, as well as an infrequent tapping noise, further brought her back to consciousness. The only thing that was different from the night before was that a soft plush blanket was thrown over her up to her chin.

She smiled warmly as she began to rise, noticing that the fireplace was no longer lit ablaze and instead was a lifeless pit of ashes as dark as the night time previously was. All life seemed to be standing still ahead of her, causing her to look to her right.

Outside, the sun was shining through the trees and the distinct sound of birds singing could be heard even through the glass. She watched the mesmerizing sight of nature as she sat up, taking her time to recover from such a deep sleep. Until her eyes finally gravitated to the source of the tranquil sounds of cooking.

She found none other than Gabriel in the kitchen, a towel over his shoulder, whipping some eggs in a glass bowl as bacon sizzled in a pan on the stove. He quickly caught a glimpse of her and nudged his head in acknowledgment,

"Morning, dear sister of mine."
He poured the eggs into a separate pan, the yellow goo instantly forming into a round peculiar shape. "Sweet dreams, I trust?"

She moved from the couch to slowly advance toward the kitchen counter, where she sat up on the stool across from him.

"Hardly... it was a rather dark, empty sleep. Never envisioned anything at all."

Gabe frowned. "That's unfortunate."
She briefly raised her brows.

"Well... look at you. Breakfast and tucking me in? You're going to make some girl a very lucky wife someday."
Gabriel chuckled nervously. "If that day ever comes."

He stepped towards Audrey, setting down a plate where he then took a spatula and slid two fluffy, buttery and greasy pancakes on to the dish.

Audrey's eyes sparked with delight at the sight of food and she leaned in, reaching for a few slices of bacon.

"Thank you so much, I'm starving."

"Great, cause there's plenty."

Audrey began ungracefully stuffing her mouth, not even caring if there was another soul around.

"So..." She spouted out between chews. "What's on the agenda for today, Mr. Beckhart? Have you decided?"

It took Gabriel a moment to reflect on his answer. It had been eating on him all night, keeping him awake, his mind reeling with questions.

Something in him had awakened... something unethical. Unrealistic. But here it was... an unsettling feeling of enlightenment. A truth he didn't even want to know. A truth unclear and vague, but he felt it so strongly.

He finally turned to his sister, inhaling and exhaling deeply as he leaned against the counter, his eyes trailing to the outside.

"I was thinking about maybe hitting the town."

His sister's interest became piqued as she perked up. 'Hitting the town' seemed a little too informal of a term for Gabriel to use, being so literary and all. It made her question his mental state... but before she could even utter a single word, he abruptly dropped his phone in front of her, causing her to flinch.

Her eyes briefly widened at him before she leaned over and squinted at the tiny screen. "...What in the... Gabriel... what is-"

"It's Hollowgrove. Complete layout of all the strange occurrences of the town."

She reluctantly picked up the small device and began to scroll through the various search engine results. "All of this?"

"Yes. I was up all night, thinking about it. The news yesterday made me realize... Hollowgrove isn't just some abnormal town. This place has been unsettling from the start. Something... I don't know... supernatural."

Her eyes cut to him. "...Gabe."

Her voice was teeming with a serious tone that insinuated she was growing concerned. He knew very well how it was sounding; like he had lost his mind. The odd part was, however...

he didn't care.

"I started piecing it together, Audrey. I went and looked at every single article I could find. Missing people, strange sightings... did you know all this has been going on for years? The local news, the police, they've been investigating it for decades and we haven't even noticed. I mean, if you even knew the things I read from Amelia-"

"*Amelia?*"

Her eyes lifted. He tensed.

Slowly, she sat the phone down and began to lace her fingers together, her gaze honed on her brother like a predator honed on its prey.

"Amelia *Pine?*"

His eyes darted away.

"...Yes..."

Her teeth clenched.

"You're not seriously taking that girl's word seriously, are you? Do you know how many people she turned against me? How many rumors she started? All because she was jealous and vengeful against me?!"

"She's *your* enemy, Audrey, not mine."

"I'm well aware how close you two are."

She settled a bit as she took her mug and brought it to her lips.

"Or *were*..."

Gabriel shook his head as she drank in that moment and he clenched his fists. "It's been years since then. We grew apart, and it's been a long time since she said all those things about you. Bury the hatchet already. We're not teenagers anymore."

"Oh, you just got a soft spot for her because she's always had a crush on you."

"No, she didn't."

"OH, yes she did. She followed you around like a puppy."

He groaned.

"Whatever, it doesn't matter. Point is, she knows things."

"She's a crackpot!"

"She is not!"

He shifted his glasses, as he thought about it a moment.

"Okay, she *is* a little eccentric... but you have to give her credit. She's passionate about what she believes and you at *least* need to

respect her for that. She's trying to warn people."
"You're starting to scare me with all this."
"Good. We should be scared."
Her eyebrows furrowed.
"When did you talk to Amelia?"
"I haven't... not yet. I read her blog, and it is filled to the brim with articles about what's really going on here. And the crazy part is? It all makes sense. You can see it yourself something is wrong."
"Yeah, but... Amelia isn't exactly the most reliable person for monster info. She'd do or say anything to get people to believe. She's desperate."
"Amelia is many things, but she isn't a liar. And she's our best source right now… besides being a friend I owe a visit to."
Her eyes enlarged and she shot up out of her stool.
"*Visit?*"
Gabriel rose his eyebrows with a hint of a sly smile.
"Get dressed. I'll go set up a chauffeur."
Audrey nearly melted into the counter as her face fell into her hands, and she internally screamed at what her brother was now making her do.
"Oh my dear god, kill me now."

~

Fall was upon the town just as heavily as it was the Beckhart estate. This wasn't enough to mask the eerie feeling settling in Audrey and Gabriel's stomachs. Their ride arrived quickly, and the two were soon arriving on the streets, past the forest.
They had abandoned their syrup-saturated pancakes and cold bacon in favor of their hometown, a dreary overcast hovering over them. It looked as if it might storm at any minute, but the weather promised otherwise... not that anyone can really trust the weather system.
The townspeople were either preparing for seasonal purposes or festive purposes, despite Halloween being almost a month away.
The people themselves did not seem to change one bit. Among the decorative flares of autumn and holiday cheer laid their peculiar obsession with the local folklore.
The supernatural... much of which was the source of the problem with Hollowgrove. Aliens, monsters, dark beings that

Uncanny

ruled the night. There were countless residents who had reported a monster encounter. In fact, there were very few who hadn't reported something. Seen and heard things that could only be located in nightmares. Something the Beckhart siblings had never really found important, until now.

Growing up, there was a layer of both doubt and an open mindedness in the two that it all may be true. Now, it just seemed to click that there was something truly significant about the cases. About monsters.

People were going missing... what next? What would they wind up finding? When would the madness cease? These were the questions the two were afraid to find the answers on... but nevertheless needed to, all the same. They did not want casualties. They wanted solutions. For the town to have some peace. They didn't know how they were going to achieve this... but they were determined to do so regardless.

As they passed the streets they knew all too well, many a resident stopped in their tracks in the midst of their routine just to wave happily at the well-known siblings, with delighted expressions and enthusiastic greetings. So many familiar faces they had known for so long. So many old friends from their child and teenage years.

One after the other, the people of Hollowgrove smiled, waved and warmly welcomed the pair. As if nothing terrible at all was happening in their town. Perhaps they had just grown used to it. Like scabbing over a wound.

They recognized the residents with each building they passed... residents such as Mr. Coyle, their old principle, climbing into his car.

Wallace Bane, the owner of the town attractions shop, who was nailing a new sign up.

Professor Elias Lurch, formerly of Oxford University, who tipped his hat at them, books in hand.

Ed Jones, who was an agitated and reclusive farm owner, nodding at the two with a sack of seed over his shoulder.

Emma Gull, a bright young librarian who always kept herself as plain as possible, as if intentionally.

Jerelyn Jackson, the spicy and fully southern-hearted local diner owner, who had promised the two a free milkshake on the house upon returning home.

    Then there was Agatha Mourie, a former cheerleader turned news journalist, whom Gabriel once had a flame for. Audrey wanted to poke fun at him once a gleaming Agatha passed by, whipping her long curly red hair in the wind... but the timing did not seem appropriate. Especially when Gabriel sunk so very sadly upon laying eyes on her once more. He never got the stomach to speak to her... and he missed his chance. Now, he fully regretted it.

    After driving a bit more, Audrey bit her lip as she slowly returned her gaze to her brother. He was being so quiet the whole ride... it made her uncomfortable. "...Gabriel?"
He didn't look at her directly. But he was listening.

    "...Last night worried me. I swear to god, something was there."
Gabe didn't have any more patience to lie any longer.

    "I know... me too."
She perked.

    "You said it was nothing."

    "I was trying to keep you calm. I could feel something watching us."
Her eyes fluttered at the window. "...An animal?"

    Gabriel couldn't find it in himself to speak in anything more than a whisper. "...I hope so."
He looked down at the paper in his hand, which held an address. A patch of houses was nearby of which caught the attention of Audrey.

    "If memory does me justice, her new house is over there, right?"
Her brother brought the paper closer to his eyesight, squinting through his glasses to read his rather sloppy handwriting as a result of a late night.

    45 Bluebird Drive.
His eyes drifted upwards and he could see it clearly... these houses were a far cry from the luxurious estate the Beckharts resided in. The neighborhood wasn't an outright trailer park, but it wasn't fancy by any means. A rather aged brown building laid before them, in desperate need of TLC. It seemed so sad, it didn't even seem possible for anyone to occupy it. Nevertheless, there was a small blueberry colored beetle sitting in the front with many

peculiar stickers plastered on the windows.

The address matched the numbers hanging over the door. As the car parked, the two looked to one another, almost wondering if they should turn back or not.

"Are you sure you want to do this?"
Gabriel's eyes instinctively drifted to the house at his sister's question. He tightened his jaw and inhaled deeply.

"I'm sure."

Her expression eased and she turned her head away, having the answer she already expected. In many ways, she was both surprised and proud at what Gabriel had decided to do. And in many ways, she was prepared to help him go through with it. Even if it meant having to face seeing Amelia again.

"Okay then."
With that, she opened her car door and stepped out into the chilly Autumn air.

Gabriel watched as she started off without him. Something in him felt the overstimulating rush that things were changing in that moment, and he didn't know what to make of it. He was terrified, fascinated and ecstatic all at the same time.

Why he felt so strongly about this, he didn't know. He couldn't put it into words. It was as if something beyond his understanding was pulling him into doing this. A force too powerful for him to fight or argue against. Therefore... he succumbed to it.

He adjusted his glasses, stuffed the paper into his pocket... and he stepped out to join his sister's side.

CHAPTER IV
✦ CONVERSION ✦

The two arrived at the front door. They cleared their throats, exchanging uneasy glances. Gabriel straightened his jacket before he ran his fingers through his hair with a fidgety hand. Audrey chuckled to herself... maybe that crush Amelia had on him wasn't just one sided after all.

Taking his fist, he knocked three rapid times. They awaited an answer... but were only met with silence. An eerie, uncomfortable silence. A few moments passed, before Gabriel knocked again. Even more time passed. Still no answer. Audrey grew impatient. She leapt forward and rang the doorbell several times before jumping back.

Gabriel rose his hand up in confusion, but she stood stone-faced while rolling her eyes innocently to the sky, not prepared to give him a word of explanation.

The two abruptly jerked as the door was finally opened, by a slender young woman. Copper red hair slithered out of her kelly green beanie in two ponytails. She peered at them through thick-trimmed black glasses, donning a white t-shirt with a flower-crowned alien head, cut-off blue denim shorts, striped tights and brown ugg boots.

Her mouth filled with liquid, a bottle of soda in hand, her eyes shifted between the two, her face frozen as she saw who was on the other side of the door. She at last swallowed. Then with a gaping mouth, her eyes enlarged.

"No... heckin'... *way*."
She frantically opened the door, her head dashing back and forth from him to her. "Gabriel?!"

Her eyes fell on Audrey. "....*You!*"
Audrey's face ached from how much she was having to fake a smile.

"'You'... interesting that I don't have a name anymore..."
Gabriel ignored his sister, proceeding to smile warmly at Pine.

"Hey Amelia... been awhile."

"Awhile? Try *years*."

Uncanny

The siblings glared at one another with a hint of guilt. Pine's face was brimming with confused excitement, looking all around.
"What are you guys doing here?! At *my* house... I mean, you got the right house, right?"

"Yeah, we do." Audrey uttered with a shift.
Amelia gestured.

"Are you here for my dad?"

"Why on earth would we be here for your dad??"

"Okay, are you lost then? Need directions to like... the casino? Hollywood?"

"Oh my god, Amelia, we're here for *you*."
Amelia rose a brow. "Why though?"

"Obviously to talk to you!"

Gabriel shook his head at his sister's rude impulses towards their old friend. Pine seemed to skim over it, however.

"When did you even get back in town?"
Gabe stepped in, "Yesterday. We're on vacation."

"Uhhh, okay... guess richies don't get the same vacation schedules as the rest of us."

"We completed our classes **early**."
Audrey grit her teeth in irritation.

Amelia breathed heavily at this and her eyes slightly drifted at the female Beckhart.

"Well, I suppose I won't be going on a date any time soon with Audrey back in town."

Audrey bit her tongue. She wanted to call out Amelia so badly on the fact that she wouldn't get dates anyway, with her reputation, even without her interference. But she had to hold back... she knew Gabriel was already growing frustrated with her unfiltered comments at their strange companion.

Gabriel sighed, shaking his head, while trying to keep a respectable composure. "Amelia, this is actually important."

"I'm sure it is, with you two knocking on an alien nut's door... speaking of me, Audrey, there's a certain guy I've had my eyes on and he happens to have a slightly mutual interest in me, so I would appreciate you leaving that one for me."

"Good god, woman, I don't date *every* single guy!"

"Just about!"
Audrey charged forward. "This is important, you little freak!"

"Waiting to hear the importance, kitten, cuz if not, I have work to get back to!"

"HA, work?! You mean being an absolute-"

"OKAY-"

Gabriel jumped in and shoved his arm down between the two, making both flinch backwards.

"You lionesses can fight over the gazelle *later*. If you two can't get along, then Audrey can stay in the car. With or without her, I have things to discuss with you, and I don't have time for you to be at each other's throats."

Amelia and Audrey both simultaneously sighed as they retracted from their offensive stances. Pine rolled her eyes to the ceiling.

"Whatta ya want from me, Beckhart?"

Gabriel opened his mouth, stuffing his hands in his pockets as he tried to collect his thoughts.

"We need your help... your expertise... on supernatural activity."

Amelia's mouth dropped as her eyes landed upon him once more.

"The kind that's affecting this town. The aliens, the creatures, the strange forces from the beyond, we want to know about it all."

What he just said could not be fully processed through the mind of the redhaired strangeling before him. She stood with her mouth still hanging open, her eyes unable to blink, her body as still as a statue. It made Audrey wonder if her brother gave Pine a straight up heart attack on the spot.

"...I must be dreaming."

Her eyes fell.

"Or I'm being featured on that one Ashton Kutcher show."

"I swear to you, Amelia, this is not a trick."

"YOU two... die hard skeptics... are coming to ME about the supernatural?"

She pointed at the pair.

"That right there is the most unbelievable thing I've ever heard."

Audrey wanted to strangle her at this point.

"Amelia! We had something stalking us last night! We came home to a bunch of people missing without a single explanation! This isn't a stupid joke! We really are trying to figure out what is freaking going on in this town!"

Gabe cut his eyes at his sister before returning them to Amelia. Who, meanwhile, was narrowing her gaze at the Beckhart girl in a heavily suspicious and fierce manner. They stood there for a very prolonged moment, making the Beckharts shift uncomfortably. The silence was growing heavy on the two.

"...Can we please come inside, it's cold..."

Pine finally budged. She folded her arms, raising a brow at the two.

"...C'mon. We got business in my office."

The short girl spun on her heels and headed back into the house. Gabriel rose his brows as he glanced over at his sister.

"...She's got an office."

Audrey watched as he disappeared inside, hurrying after Pine. She sighed in a most frustrated manner.

"I'm already regretting this."

~

Amelia led the siblings up a set of stairs into her domain. The house itself was full of silence and unfortunately was just as cold as it was outside, but the interior was humble as Amelia's father was constantly at work and the Pine girl's time mostly consisted of dwelling in her room.

As they arrived inside the strangeling's quarters, their eyes enlarged, their pace slowing. Despite the curtains being drawn, they could see the décor quite clearly. Quirky imagery, newspaper clippings, photographs of blurred objects, UFOs and cryptozoological accessories and stickers were placed all about the walls. Topped with these was a spaceship painted on the wall that had a starry mountain night sky as the background.

Audrey couldn't believe she was saying this, but here it was coming out of her mouth:

"Your room is actually, surprisingly, really cute..."

Pine only glared her way like something was terribly wrong with her, not even bothering to respond to that. Instead, she turned her attention to her laptop, where she pulled up her site and gestured at the two with her opposite hand, plopping atop her spinning chair.

"Have a seat."

There was no other seat in the room to sit upon other than her bed and a giant red beanie chair. Gabe found it inappropriate to sit on her bed, therefore planted himself upon the plush blob which immediately sunk underneath him, leaving him practically slouching against the floor. Audrey softly leaned against the mattress, crossing her legs. She felt as though she were about to fall, which she prevented by holding onto the edges with her fingertips.

"Now..." Amelia spoke, still typing away. "I'm still convinced a prank's being played on me and you two are in on it... but I'll humor you."

Her shoulders straightened and she turned back around, placing her hands on her hips. "Now class... are we paying attention?"

The siblings exchanged glances.

Audrey blinked with little to no emotion. "There's only two of us."

"Cool, then let's get started."

The Beckhart girl breathed in deeply before pulling out her phone and quickly typed. Gabriel's side suddenly buzzed and he pulled out his

phone, only to read a text sent by Audrey.

"You owe me all the years of your life for this torture."

He snickered at her, mocking her inner pain, and she narrowed her eyes darkly at him. Their humorous exchange was interrupted by Amelia clapping her hands together loudly and facing them as if she were a strict teacher from their college.

"*Okay*, where to begin... what do you two know *so far*?"

They each looked away, a slight feeling of guilt overtaking them. Pine's gaze widened with disapproval and she puffed her chest, inflating like a threatened puffer fish.

"K, let's just assume you know nothing... alright, what's your official opinion about them?"

"Slightly acknowledging." Uttered Gabe.

"To be determined." Said Audrey.

Amelia's fingers turned into immediate claws as she grit her teeth towards the floor. "Yes, but what's your *attitude* about them?"

"...Meaning what?"

"What do you think is wrong: the crimes or the creatures?"

They paused a moment, giving her a peculiar gaze. She gestured in disbelief. "Y'all not dumb, right?"

They didn't respond, which she found quite annoying, and she shook her head.

"If you're like most people, which we've established you are, you would say it's the creatures... or as they are often called... 'monsters'."

She pointed at the images on her walls.

"Society has demonized them for not just years, but *generations*. Look at monster movies, science fiction, ghost stories, things that go bump in the night. We have been turning creatures that are different from us into outright murderous freaks for as long as time has existed. What we fear, what we don't understand, we attack it. We turn ourselves into the protagonists and them the antagonists."

Audrey cocked her head, "Pretty much like witch hunts?"

"In many ways, yes... for instance, look at how an animal attacks someone. Even today... if a kid or adult gets attacked, humans hunt down that animal and not only kill *them*, but as many of its kind as possible. Humans have committed countless genocides and persecuted anything they deem unnatural or unpleasant. If humans see it as a threat in any way... they destroy it."

"But here's the thing..." Gabe cut in. "...They supposedly HAVE attacked and killed people. They *are* dangerous."

"As we are to believe... but lemme ask you something. What's the difference between them doing it and say... a shark... tiger... bear... crocodile... sliding on over and doing the same thing? These creatures are just as much animal as a turkey or lion. It's their world, too. Their territory. *We're* the invaders. We like to think we own everything on this planet... but we come into *their* home, drive them out, and tick them off."

She handed the two a stack of newspaper articles of various monster attacks and historical occurrences regarding the supernatural.

"There has been legitimate reports of scenarios where animals have been attacked or their young have been killed and they have struck back in retaliation. They have attacked livestock and threatened all those who have come on their property. They are products of nature, who need food and have to provide for their children. They know full well we're a dangerous and hostile species who have driven them to the point of extinction. They've grown to fear us, considering we've been hunting them for years. And we're taking their homes away, their barrier, their safety. That line separating us is being erased. We do it every day when we tear down the forests and the country that they hide in. What do humans expect? We're driving them out. If we get hostile, if we attack or kill them... they will strike back. Animals are far more clever than we give them credit for."

Audrey shifted, "So you think they're just animals? No offense, but... if they were just animals, why haven't we gotten any good shots of them?"

"That is an excellent question, preppy miss. And I answer back with... how many people do you know who've taken these shots? Think about an animal you've seen. A deer, for instance. I've never seen deer in person. Say I see it, though, that could be right in front of me, but I don't have a camera. Or I don't get it out in time. It's already gone. You come back to the same spot later, it's not there. Animals move, and they're fast to boot."

She pointed at a random photograph. "And really, if you saw something that dangerous, that terrifying... would you really be sticking around to take that photo? And if you do... would you really live past that encounter?"

Audrey swallowed.

"...What if they're taken?"

Amelia cut her eyes at Gabriel. He lowered his chin.

"The creatures... what if someone takes them?"

She grinned from ear to ear.

"Careful... now you're thinking like a conspiracy nut."

She walked back to her laptop.

"Sometimes all you have to go on is a person's account of things... for some reason, we're totally trusting of a person's funny story or dramatic encounter which could be straight up garbage. But when a person claims they've seen a cryptid? They're deemed insane or looking for attention."

"A crypde?"

Pine sighed.

"Cryptids. X-creatures, hidden creatures, spookables, whatever you wanna call 'em. Cryptozoologists are the ones that study them... now you know me. I lean more towards ufology myself, but that doesn't mean I don't study and believe it all. It's all a part of the same picture. You'll find that everything in the universe is connected somehow, in some way."

Audrey shifted, "What's the picture?"

Amelia rose her brows. "What's really out there."

With a wag of her finger, she ushered the two to join her. They rose and walked to either side of her. There, they all three peered at her laptop, and their jaws dropped.

Displayed were all the countless cases taking place inside Hollowgrove, so many of which were just in the past year... all unsolved.

"That being said... even I'm terrified of what's happening." Audrey's hand gravitated to her mouth, "Oh my god..."

There were a total of 80+ unsolved cases just in that year, each involving creature attacks and missing person reports.
Amy pointed.

"The amount of cases, the close timelines and proximity of locations... the attacks, sightings and people..."

She rushed over to her map, that was littered with strands of yarn and pins, with notes written in magic marker stating the dates, times, attacks and creature sightings.

"Look at it." She pointed.
They approached the map and studied the lines that seemed to almost conjoin with one another.

"In all my years of studying, I've never seen a location in America more concentrated with cryptid encounters and sightings than Hollowgrove. To the point where... we have practically become a monster town." She turned her head to look at the two.

"...Tell me that's not weird."
Audrey drew a shaky breath, where Gabriel appeared almost as pale as a ghost.

"Okay... I'm a believer."
His sister crossed her shivering arms that were secretly littered with goosebumps. "Undeniably same."
She shook her head. "They're everywhere... how have we not seen them running around town?"
 Amelia looked at the Beckharts in a rather grim manner.

"Typically speaking... some of the most dangerous predators are nocturnal hunters."
 The Beckhart girl's spine was pulsing with chills.
Amelia shifted her glasses,

"You guys wanna tell me about last night?"
Gabriel leaned against the wall, staring up at the map.

"Last night... Scrooge was barking at something... it was dark and we couldn't see anything, but... it felt as though something was watching us."

"Well that's no wonder. You guys are smack-dab in the middle of the woods. That's cryptid territory 101."

"Oh Amelia, I swear to god, I was better not knowing this!!" Audrey hid her face. Pine shook her head.

"They're getting bolder. These attacks... it's almost as if something is like... *driving* them to come here. And... I don't know." She turned her head away, but Gabriel laid a hand on her shoulder, causing her to flinch. "What, Amelia? Go on." Her eyes slowly returned to him.

"... Almost as if... they're retaliating." The Beckharts glared at each other.

"But it's not just creatures..." Audrey breathed. "It's aliens. And other supernatural stuff happening. People are seeing things beyond anyone's imagination!" Amelia nodded in agreement.

Gabriel's head lifted. "We need to talk with the survivors. The ones who have seen these things, had encounters with them."

"That would be refreshing on their part, since pretty much everyone who has spoken to them think they're nuts or just publicity hounds." Audrey suddenly perked up, her face brimming with enlightenment.

"A girl..." She turned.

"I saw an article about a girl..." She hurried towards Amelia's laptop and bent down to scroll through the blog.

"Where??" Questioned Amelia.

"On your site."

"*When*?" Pressured Gabriel.

"You're not the only one who decided to look up this stuff." She located the article at last and stepped back, putting her hands on her hips. Pine and the Beckhart boy joined her side and looked at what she had to show.

Amelia breathed. "...**Ivy**." She took hold of the device and held it up, where the siblings gathered round.

"Who is this? Why does she look familiar?" Gabriel questioned. Pine cleared her throat, licking her dry lips.

"Seven year old Ivy Rein... she was found months ago in the

middle of the night by police. She was shaken and terrified, on the verge of hysteria, the only living creature with her being a disheveled German Shepherd who was extremely protective of the girl. No one came to claim her, therefore she has no known family members and thus has been put into the foster system. She's been put with a family who has claimed... that SHE claimed... she was attacked by a monster."

Gabriel leaned back, adjusting his glasses in an intrigued fashion. "She sounds like a suitable candidate. Let's go talk with her."

"Oh, and uh... here's the fun part."
Amelia slapped her laptop closed and turned her head at the siblings. The smirk she gave them was unsettling and rather devious.

"...She's mute."

CHAPTER V
✦ A CHILLING RETURN ✦

The Beckharts left Amelia's residence with nothing further to say. They returned home, entering with fresh doses of paranoia they did not wield the day before. All around them now seemed to be a danger ground. As if they were somewhat lucky to have made it this far.

Pine had surely opened a new world of fears for the two, but it was all justified. Seeing the number of reports and sightings would make anyone suddenly feel unsafe.

The paranoia truly hit them, however, when they stepped through their threshold and an instant spark of chills ran down their spines. The house was freezing cold. So cold, they could see their breaths turn into tiny puffs floating through the air.

Audrey instinctively tucked her hands into her sleeves and brought them up to her mouth to breathe into them.

"Why is it so cold?! Did you touch the thermostat?!"

"I didn't, I swear!"

Gabriel ran to check what temperature it was set for, but seeing the numbers baffled him. "Go check on Scrooge, poor thing's probably freezing!"

Audrey hurried into the living room and looked around, calling their beloved dog's name. With no reply, she moved on to their bedrooms.

"Scrooge! Baby, where are you?!"

She scrambled over to the beds and rummaged through the blankets.

She started to become frantic until she heard a swift yelp come from underneath the covers. She gasped and quickly moved the blanket away to reveal a tiny trembling canine, who she snatched and brought close to her chest. "Oh, Scrooge!"

She took the blanket and wrapped it around his small body as she rocked him back and forth atop the bed. "You poor little thing!"

Still shaking, but content now that his mother had returned, the tiny dog was soon showered with kisses and an endlessly warm embrace.

Meanwhile, Gabe was busy adjusting the thermostat to a reasonable number... at least more reasonable than being 16°... while simultaneously tightening his jacket and scarf, stuffing his free hand into his pocket.

One feature he appreciated now from his rich parents was that the thermostat kept a log of when it was changed. He looked at the time of when he and Audrey were last there, between the time they returned. Normally, he would expect to find nothing and be content. Now, he was on edge, and rightfully so. For as he looked upon the log and saw a most unnerving sight, his body began to tense.

The temperature was altered 30 minutes ago.
He looked all around. "...Audrey?!"

She came out from the bedroom and peeked at her brother, her face etched with concern. "What's wrong?"

Gabriel turned around, his eyes focused on Scrooge.

"...Did you set the alarm for the house?"

"...Yeah?"

"...Set all locks?"

"Yeah, why?"

He looked away. Audrey tilted her head in a way that indicated she knew something was wrong. "Gabe, what'd you see?"

He didn't answer her. He began to make for the alarm system.

"Gabriel, talk to me, what's going on?"

He still didn't answer her. He hastily checked the alarm to make sure it was set and... he swallowed hard. It had been disarmed.

Gabriel turned to her.

"Audrey... please tell me those doors were locked..."

"They were, I swear, last night freaked me out enough to double check!"

Gabe flicked his head towards the back door. "Check again."

She let out a breath of frustration, but still charged toward it, knowing for sure it would be locked nice and tight. She reached in, grabbed the handle and yanked. It would naturally have made a clicking sound as the locking mechanism would seize it from going any further. Only, Audrey was sent flying as the door took her all the way. A gust of wind blew past her, stealing her breath.

She stood as still as a statue as she stared with a widened, terrified gaze at the wooded environment beyond their luxurious backyard. She and her brother tried their hardest to remain calm. But... now... it was growing impossible.

"Someone was here." Gabriel uttered, breaking the eerie silence that rested within their residence.

His statement was enough to snap Audrey out of her petrified state, and she immediately slammed the door shut, locking it as securely as she could make it.

"Call them *right now*."

"Who?!"

She ran for the kitchen. "Who do you think?!"

It clicked. Their parents. He got out his phone and tapped on one of his parents' icons. His instantaneous choice was their father, since he was more likely to answer the phone than their too-busy-to-function actress mother.

He waited as the phone rang loudly in his ear, while he watched his sister abruptly grab a kitchen knife. This made him gawk, especially when she began frantically darting in and out of every corner of the house, opening closet doors, looking underneath furniture and searching for any other sign of tampering from their unwelcome visitor.

His observance of her was cut short when his father's voice came on,

"Helllooo?"

"Dad!"

"Gabriel? Why are you calling, son?"

"Dad, please tell me you and Mom were just here!"

"Hey hey, quit shouting, you're going to make me deaf."

"Please just answer!"

"Easy-- no, your mom's busy shooting for a commercial right now. And I've been at the office all morning. Why, what's going on?"

Gabriel hesitated.

He gulped as he tried to come up with a reason behind his phone call, to not sound so suspicious. He shook his head.

"Nothing, I thought... I thought maybe you guys were coming soon, that's all. We miss you."

"Aw, son, that's nice... but no, we won't be back for awhile. We talked about this, remember? Your mom and I are very busy."

He nodded. "Yeah... well... bye then. Sorry to bother you."

"Right. Bye." His father hung up.

Gabe slowly withdrew the phone from his ear, temporarily taken back by his father's emotionless interaction. If only he could have had a father who didn't treat him like a business deal...

Gabe shook his head and pocketed his phone. His eyes lifted to see Audrey return to him, her eyes wild with paranoia.

"What'd they say, were they here?"

He swallowed. Ever so softly, he shook his head. "It wasn't them..." Audrey's face became as pale as a ghost.

"I knew it... something came in here... it *was* watching us."

"We don't know for sure, Audrey..."

"Gabriel! You literally said-"

"I mean for it to be some*thing*."

He sat down on the couch.

"It could have been a burglar."

"A burglar who comes in, changes the thermostat and disables the alarms for no reason?"

He perked.

"...Nothing's missing?"

She sat down on the couch next to him.

"*Nothing*. I checked our safe, Mom's jewels, everything of any value. Nothing was taken."

She tensed her muscles. "But they *were* looking for something..."

His eyes drifted to her. "What?"

"...They were looking through *our* things. Our clothes were all thrown out of our drawers. My notebooks are scattered all over the place. So are your's."

He had to think of this for a minute. "...What about-"

"Mom and Dad's room wasn't even touched."

Gabriel turned his head away, as he contemplated this revelation.

"...Weird coincidence."

"What?"

"We go to Amelia's and learn about this stuff... and now we come home to this."

His eyes flickered for a second to his sister before closing them and shaking his head. "Put the knife down, Audrey."

She realized now she was still holding the blade tightly, to which she instantly set it on the coffee table. Albeit a little reluctantly.

"Whoever it was is gone now." Her brother assured.

Audrey shifted, holding Scrooge tighter.

"...Do you think they broke in just to mess with us?"

Gabriel buried his hands into his face in total despair, his mind not believing that he was actually living through this type of situation.

"I don't know... maybe... maybe to spook us."

"Maybe to let us know he's here and he's watching."

She glared at the back doors, of which weren't providing any privacy in the slightest and making her feel all the more vulnerable.

"We need to invest in curtains."

"I agree." Gabe muttered, leaning back against the couch.

Audrey sat there for a few moments as her mind raced with various panicked thoughts. She shook her head and shot up.

"I'm calling Amelia."

Gabriel perked once again.

"...I'm sorry? Come again? Did I just hear *you* say... you're calling *Amelia*?"

"*Yes.*"

She grabbed her brother's phone and sifted through the numbers he had saved, one of them being Miss Pine's. As she clicked on her name to call her, Gabriel shook his head in further disbelief of what was happening.

"That does it, it's the end times."

Audrey turned as Amelia came on the line and she spoke in a quieted voice, hurrying into the hallway.

Gabe lifted his head back,

"Tell her the Antichrist is here and God's coming back!"

CHAPTER VI
✦ WORDS UNSPOKEN ✦

Amelia Pine stood outside her car, rapping the bottom of her shoe against the front tire, her hands stuffed into her pants' pockets.

Her eyes wandered the neighborhood she awaited in, Pine herself always remaining watchful and extremely observant to details. This often distracted her from conversations held right in front of her, as her attention was ever pulled by the events around her.

She watched people. Not because she necessarily enjoyed it, and not just because she didn't trust them. But because she saw things that others didn't in them. Things that most people miss.

For instance, the boy delivering papers on his bike. A person you overlook half the time. He threw the papers religiously at each address with concentrated precision. Donning a dark blue cap and a muddy green backpack strapped securely around him.

No one would have noticed that the boy had worn a cap to hide the bruises on his face, the black eye he was trying to lower his head to conceal. His clothes being worn and run down and his right leg performing poorly compared to his left, which made him wince every so often, indicated an injury.

This made her wonder: bullies or abuse?

Next was the lady peeking from her window. You could just make out her face appearing from the slit in her curtain. Most people would think her a nosy neighbor, but this was put aside when the boy passed her house and she made for the door.

A few seconds later, she slightly opened the entrance only to hurriedly reach in and grab her paper, quickly slamming the door shut behind her.

This made her wonder: agoraphobia or perhaps on high alert from someone she fears?

Amelia's head rotated to a small group of teen boys walking the sidewalk behind her. They were laughing amongst themselves, whispering inaudibly one to the other. A group of teens might seem harmless... but the longer Pine watched them, she saw them begin to point towards the houses and whisper even quieter, while another took pictures on their phone and smiled a bit too smugly for Amelia's liking.

This made her wonder: wanna-be social media stars or marking homes for future break-ins?

Amelia was observant. She was suspicious, and she saw more than others gave her credit for. Pine's eyes returned to the concrete ground below her and she took a deep, calculating inhale.

She gave her phone a quick check on the time. It had been 40 minutes since Audrey called her and told her they wanted to meet ASAP to speak with Ivy Rein.

By the sound of Audrey's voice, she was shaken, but she didn't give Amelia enough information on what had happened. This frustrated her, naturally, as she was desperate to know everything.

She stood in front of the Chapman's residence, the current home of Ivy. Lucky for the Beckharts, she was able to get them a last minute interview with the seven year old survivor, after she had just told them she would be able to maybe set something up later on in the week. Kathryn Chapman was thankfully a sweetheart and very eager for others to believe young Ivy.

She was half tempted to proceed on her own to wait inside for the siblings, as it was growing even more bitterly cold. But it wasn't long after she had this thought that a limo abruptly pulled next to her, immediately catching her eye. She perked up as it parked and the doors were soon opened by Audrey, Gabriel jumping right out with her.

Pine rose a brow at the siblings. A limo in a suburban neighborhood. Truly never a dull moment knowing the Beckharts. On top of that, Audrey was holding her dog, Scrooge, who was wrapped tightly in a blanket like a completely coddled little barking pillow.

Gabriel leaned in and thanked the driver before closing the door and watched a few seconds as it drove off. Amelia eyed its exit just for a moment before shaking her head softly and sighing.

"Y'all are unreal."

They turned to her, looking a bit disheveled.

"What do you mean?" The Beckhart boy questioned innocently. But she waved her hand.

"Whatever. Your phone call made things sound a bit urgent, fill me in. And include the dog." She stared at Scrooge as she once again stuffed her hands in her pockets; wondering very reasonably why Audrey was carrying her dog to an interview.

Audrey gave Amelia an offended glare.

"I couldn't just leave him there after what happened."

"You don't bring dogs to investigations." Amelia shot back, as-a-matter-of-factly.

"Unless they're the talking kind." Gabe joked.

She rolled her eyes. "All I'm saying is, you don't see me toting around my gerbil to an interview."

Pine turned her back, in which Audrey took the chance to scowl viciously at her. Gabriel sighed, sensing the growing tension between the two once again start to interfere with their goal. But all Audrey was focusing on was the question of whether or not she would start to train their dog to bite annoying redheads on sight.

"So why were you two so eager for the interview? Andddd why didn't you call the police again?"

She rose her hands. "I mean, don't get me wrong, I'm flattered you chose me over lads of the law, ya know, public defenders of this beautifully strange town of our's... but I think it's pretty dang idiotic not to report a break-in."

"We didn't think it was necessarily police-worthy considering they didn't take anything."

"And because we wanted your expertise on the matter first." Pine pursed her lips. "See, *that's* what makes things look suspicious, when you *wait*..."

The Beckharts stood side-by-side, eyeing the Pine girl with worry.

"What do you think it could have been, Amelia?" Audrey uttered, her naturally soft but raspy voice still trembling.

Amelia wanted to laugh, but she decided against it. The question was a serious one, but still seemed wildly ridiculous.

"Well, I've never heard of a monster that specifically disables security systems just to change the thermostat and pick through clothes and notebooks, but anything's possible."

The siblings groaned at her mocking tone. She only smirked.

"But I think you were right... I think they broke in to mess with you. Spook you."

"Could it have been looking for something?" Audrey uttered. Gabe's eyes flickered to his sister.

"Why do you keep saying *it*?"

"Now Gabe, rule four of being a believer is, never ridicule another believer's handling or wording of a situation. Let them believe in their own way. If Audrey here thinks it's an 'it', then she has every right to believe that."

Audrey's eyes widened a second. Never in all her years of life did she ever in her wildest dreams expect to be pegged alongside the word 'believer'.

"Believer, I just... Gabe's right, this is the end times."
Amelia smiled in an unsettling manner and laid her hand on Audrey's shoulder. Their eyes met in a way that made the Beckhart girl want to ugly cry.

"Welcome to the freak show, kitten."
The Pine girl left Audrey internally screaming while her brother betrayed her by leaving her side when all she wanted to do was hide.

The Beckharts really had no idea what they were getting into. Not even Pine knew... and this scared them. But it was becoming clear... they needed to know. They needed to pursue this. Because no one else was willing to.

Amelia decided to avert their talks of monsters for a second and lighten the mood.

"So... welcome to the cold and breezy outdoors! What's it like, hanging about a suburban neighborhood? Not often y'all get to experience that adventure!"

"Why you want to know?" Audrey questioned with suspicion. Pine smirked and leaned her head in,

"Writing an article about spoiled rich kids stepping outside their mansion to explore the homelands of the less fortunate."

Audrey was now triggered, "Oh really, cool! I'm writing an article too, about freakish little outsiders being so full of bitterness and insecurity that that's literally *all* they think about!"

Gabe held his forehead in his hand. "I swear to God, I'm going to have to start carrying a spray bottle for you two. **Behave**."

The girls looked away, already wound up with contempt for the other. The only one not agitated was Scrooge, who looked around excitedly with his tiny tongue hanging out happily.

The Beckharts looked upon the house of the Chapmans. It was quite lovely and much more down to earth compared to their ridiculous mansion. Something they appreciated.

"This is so nice and homey..." Audrey whispered to her brother.

"Yeah, some foster homes are like that, I guess." Amelia said aloud, hearing her clearly.

The female Beckhart shifted Scrooge in her arms.

"At least Ivy isn't in a dirty, volatile environment."

Amy bit the inside of her cheek, to keep from saying something smart.

"...Yeah..."

She gestured with a woolly, finger-less gloved hand. "Well... shall we?"

They nodded and began to walk up the brick path leading to the house. The three positioned themselves at the door step, shifting coldly and nervously. Gabriel took a deep shaky breath, where the two girls glanced at him to do the honors.

He looked at them with a hint of unease. "...*Me*?"

"Yes." Amelia answered crisply and a little too quickly.

"You're the man. Do the thing."

Feeling targeted, the Beckhart boy puffed his chest, but inevitably had to fight off the need to protest and caved in to the women. He sighed and reached in, ringing the doorbell.

"COMING!"

The three instantly jerked backward at the violently loud voice coming from the other side. Before they had a chance to utter a word, the door was thrown open making Pine widen her eyes, for Audrey to tighten her hold around her dog, and for Gabriel to retract his hand in fear.

A young teenage girl stood before them. She had soft blonde hair, a baby blue short sleeve shirt and a pair of white shorts that were inconceivable to wear in this type of weather.

She gave them a raised brow, her expression teeming with toxic levels of attitude, "*What*? Who are you?"

"We're, um, uh, here to see, er, Ivy?" Audrey hesitated. She felt like an imbecile. Being intimidated by a teenager was not her proudest moment.

The girl only squinted at her, her mouth hanging so far down, it could catch flies. Despite the overwhelming urge to punch this girl, Amelia stepped in and faked a very convincing smile.

"Hi! Yes, my name's Amelia Pine, I investigate cryptids and extraterrestrial phenomena. These are two of my very fresh-out-of-the-crib believer associates, Gabriel and Audrey Beckhart. I spoke with your mom on the phone about coming to see your new foster sister, **Ivy Rein**? We have some questions about her previous experiences. We believe they might be connected to an on-going case, so it's kind of a big deal, so it would be *fantastic* if you could lead the way."

Audrey and Gabriel stood impressed. There was no wonder now why she was such a good blogger and researcher. She was driven and pushed past any barriers before her... even if that meant having to gently handle socially disagreeable individuals she otherwise wanted to physically assault.

The girl tapped all her fingers against the door and lifted her chin.

"So in other words... you guys are nut jobs."

Pine pressed her tongue against her cheek, a clear indication now of her growing frustration. Something that started to diminish her already steadily declining smile.

The girl groaned and stepped back a hair.

"One, she's not my mom. Just some chick I'm staying with until they dump me with someone else, cuz I got no basic human rights until I'm 18. And two... the kid's weird. But I'm sure you three won't have a problem with that."

She gave them a sarcastic smile, which Amelia forced one back in reply, before the girl opened the door the rest of the way.

"Come on in, I'll tell Kathryn you freaks are here."

She walked off, as the three gradually began to enter.

"*Thank you.*" Amelia grit through her teeth.

Her proceeding to let out her frustrations by angrily wiping her shoes against the welcome mat made the Beckharts almost choke. This girl was an absolute spitfire.

They stepped through the Chapman residence, their eyes wandering the inside of the neat, modern design of the environment. It was evident why it was kept so clean and lacking any real distinguishable characteristics, as so many kids came in and out of the home and were no doubt destructive to the property. Also logical to take into account that one child out of all the good ones would decide to steal anything valuable.

At the same time, the neat and clean area didn't exactly harbor the homey feeling the exterior exhibited for the guests, and that was rather a disappointment. It made Amelia in particular make a face, as her own room was cluttered with personalization.

"I imagine your home is still as lifeless as this?"

They gave her a look that visually acknowledged her, but verbally ignored her, which in itself spoke volumes that she needed to keep her mouth shut already. They had learned over the years to grow a thick skin from others attacking their wealth and higher reputation. But for some reason, when Amelia attacked them, it struck a cord. Making them feel quite horrid about themselves.

However, they thought, in her defense... perhaps she had only gotten to this point since so many people had no doubt attacked her endlessly about her own beliefs and status. And now she was just in a constant state of insecurity, filled with the need to get back at others. It made them pity the strangeling, really.

Footsteps began to approach them. Their attention turned to a lovely looking woman. Her face had soft features and she held an instantly warm presence, while her attire was modest and simplistic.

She greeted them with a warm smile.

"Amelia Pine and the Beckhart siblings?"

Audrey smiled back and extended her hand.

"You must be Kathryn Chapman."

Kathryn took her hand and shook it gently. "That I am."

She nodded, "Welcome to our home... I see you've met Whitney."

The girl that allowed them entry stepped next to her foster mother, her arms crossed and looking uncomfortable.

"Yep, we met... and I'm heading out."

Kathryn's smile instantly fell and she looked at the girl with a worn and dreading expression.

"With whom?"

"Does it matter, Kat?"

Whitney then crudely shoved herself past the four, pulling her phone out of her pocket, and headed out the door.

Kathryn shook her head, sighing deeply, before she remembered that she had guests and needed to put on her game face. She smiled once again, but this time, it was obviously fake.

"I'm sorry, Whitney's rather... angry. More than usual."

Gabriel tilted his head. "How come, if I may ask?"

Kathryn's eyes drifted toward the wall.

"She's... had a rough life. I don't blame her at all for being upset. And now they're considering moving her again, to another state. She's... well, not taking things very well."

She turned and stepped away a short distance.

"Don't get me wrong, I love my kids. They're each unique, special... coming in with a brand new set of challenges and we get through it, together. Whitney isn't my first angry kid. I've had my share."

"How long have you been doing this, Mrs. Chapman?" Inquired Audrey.

"20 years. Started young, at 25. Came from an abusive household myself. Looked after my siblings until I could provide us a better home. So, looking after others and being a maternal figure has just always been a part of my life."

"That's young to be a foster mom, taking on such a responsibility." Pine noted. Kat nodded.

"The required age is even younger than that. Thankfully I was able to grow up fast, even earlier than that, knowing what I wanted and who I was."

Kathryn cleared her throat and folded her arms.

"Most of these kids... they have their own anger, fears, depression, anxieties... it comes with the territory of being an orphan or a kid whose parent or parents just up and decides one day that their existence means absolutely *nothing* to them. After awhile, it's going to mess up your mental health in some way."

She turned her head to them as she led them on.

"I've had all sorts of kids of different colors, shapes, conditions... that's why I try to use this place as some sort of structure. A tidy, tight-knit atmosphere. Their life is already a mess. I just don't want to confuse them with a bunch of personal items from my side or the town's. Being trapped in a cluttered atmosphere. Can't really design it the way I want, anyway... the social worker I work with strongly advised me to keep things neat and clean. So... sorry it's a bit... you know."

Pine wondered when they were getting to Ivy, as Kathryn seemed like a bit of a talker. Especially when it came to over-explaining herself. But the Beckharts were genuinely intrigued by her and wanted to learn more.

"Are you married, Mrs. Chapman?" Audrey asked.
Gabriel thought that perhaps she was just separated and kept her name the same. Though her response debunked this,

"Yes I am. But my husband is always working and our hours clash, so I barely get to see him."

Her face grew a bit tired and dismal at mentioning her husband, in a rather sad way. Gabriel's eyes wandered the hallways they passed, wondering how it works out that you can find someone to love and marry, and yet still wind up apart and lonely. A fear he held in the back of his mind for his own future. Next to the fear of becoming like his parents.

"That must be hard."
Kathryn swallowed. "It is."

She spun the wedding ring resting on her finger as she pondered on this. Something in her broke her own thoughts, however, and she gently rattled her head to her right senses.

"I'm so sorry, I've been going on and on."

They stopped in front of a room and she exhaled, as if preparing herself. The door held a few drawings that were not very clear in the faint darkness of the hallway. She looked to the three.

"First, I want to thank you for coming and listening to us. You must understand... she's a very incredible child. Gifted and intricate in everything she does. I've never seen anyone like her... but... she has immense trauma. When I heard about her and what she went through, I couldn't let her suffer alone, and I had to take her. But I had no idea how fragile her mind actually was... nor how unique."
She swallowed, thinking for a moment.

"...I've had child prodigies... children with various syndromes and disabilities... but never before have I had anyone as smart, nor as complex as her."
Kathryn took hold of the knob and gave them one final, stern stare.

"She knows more than I do about this town and she's only seven years old."
Audrey lifted her chin, "If she's mute, Mrs. Chapman, then how do you know this?"

Amelia had been wondering the same thing as that is what Kathryn had reported to the police and officials, but never explained how or why. Kathryn, however, did not answer. She merely opened the door.

On the other side was a room made for a child... the standard furniture for a typical playroom decorated to be kid friendly, but there were obviously things that did not originate in the decorating process. Such as the drawings... drawings that were placed *everywhere*. Drawings on the walls, furniture and all over the floor. It combined with papers, scattered with words, that the three could not make out from that far. But the drawings... the drawings were another matter entirely.

Audrey held her mouth. The drawings displayed a terrifying creature with tentacles... chasing a small and defenseless child in a wooded area. Their eyes followed the drawings to the most intriguing object in the room. A little girl.

She sat on the floor in front of a small table, her back turned to them.

The next object in the room took them by surprise: a German Shepherd curled up, sleeping next to the child. Scrooge started to quietly growl at the large animal before them, but Audrey held him tighter and whispered in his ear to calm him down.

The little girl was busy drawing, not even bothering to look back at the four as they entered. Kathryn led them around the table, which made the dog perk up in alarm, but Mrs. Chapman eased him with a gesture of the hand. He stared them down, even so, his large face etched with fierce intensity. Something in his eyes had violent intentions and sent chills down their spines.

It was worth it, however, as they now saw the little girl up close. Her long dark brown hair fell over her tiny face. They could still make out her youthfully pretty features.

"Ivy..." Said Kathryn, which failed to grab the little girl's attention, though she never expected it to.

"...Meet Miss Pine and the Beckharts. Miss Pine and Beckharts, meet young Ivy Rein."

She was emotionless as they stared right at her. Amelia glared over at her drawings, still disturbed and physically ill at the sight of them.

"...She's quite the artist..."
Kathryn couldn't deny her talent. "Yes, she is… she draws almost all the time."

Gabriel looked down at the floor and bent down to pick up one of the papers, which had words lined up neatly and held surprisingly perfect penmanship and grammar.

"Not to sound like a total buffoon, but did Ivy write this?" The answer was obvious, but he had to be sure.

"Yes, she did..." Kathryn held her hands. "She keeps this diary, of sorts... but she rips the pages out when she doesn't need them anymore. She also uses it to communicate with us, and discards those pages when we've already read what she's said. She writes down answers to questions you ask her, things she wants, needs..."

Audrey turned her attention to the woman,

"So that's the only way she communicates, is through writing?" Kathryn nodded.

"I've been trying to teach her ASL... you know, sign language. To communicate quicker with others, in case of emergency. But she still insists on using pen and paper."

She sat down, watching Ivy delicately.

"She knows things she shouldn't even know about this town... and its creatures... its secrets."

Amelia jumped, getting just a bit too excited at the word 'secret'.

"What *kind* of secrets?!"

Audrey and Gabriel quietly judged the girl with a single glare to one another. Kathryn's eyes gravitated elsewhere.

"I'd rather not say... they're explicit. Confidential. That girl has seen and heard things that would no doubt get her into trouble... my duty is to protect her, and that's what I will continue to do."

Gabriel looked around at the various drawings, noticing that Ivy had depicted more creatures in her art.

"Are these..."

Kathryn looked at what he was looking at. She shifted, uncomfortably.

"Local legends... monsters that go bump in the night. For some strange reason, I think she's somehow seen them. She... feels things."

The three shared uneasy glances. Amelia gestured at the main drawings of the creature with tentacles.

"...Is that the thing she encountered, Mrs. Chapman?"

Kat raised her brows.

"If it is, she hasn't pointed it out. To be honest, I have tried not to pay too much attention to her drawings. Too disturbing to me... I've left that to her therapist."

Amelia's attention turned to Ivy, but she soon jolted and elbowed the other two, as she realized the girl had been staring at them for an unknown amount of time. Her gaze was screaming at them that they were intruding. Pine's eyes widened as she stared down at the peculiar child... though Audrey felt something when she saw the girl before her, looking back into her soft brown eyes. Almost a connection, of some kind, that she couldn't shake. She smiled tenderly at the child and knelt down in front of the table, to Ivy's level.

"Hi..." She whispered in a sweet tone. "My name's Audrey... and your name's Ivy, right? That's a pretty name."

Her eyes flickered to the art Ivy was currently working on.

"Can you tell me what you're drawing?"

Beckhart's attempts were wasted. Ivy only continued to stare at her, her marker-wielding hand hovering over the paper. Audrey swallowed and rose back up, turning to the others. She drew closer, before speaking in a hushed voice,

"Mrs. Chapman...do you know if Ivy was able to speak at all before this incident? Or has she always been..."

Amelia jumped in, "Kids, even adults, upon experiencing trauma often resort to an extreme state of depression, anxiety, and even go through a period of not talking for a long time. So it's entirely likely she knew how to speak before."

Kathryn nodded, "We're hoping after feeling safe and enough time has passed, she'll get out of this stage... but it's also entirely possible for her to remain mute. No one knows for sure."

Her muscles tensed as she stared down at Ivy for a moment, "I should mention...she does make sounds. Screaming out of her sleep... crying from nightmares... sometimes I just find her wandering aimlessly around the house late at night. It's clear she experiences episodes of PTSD... even at such a young age. It's heartbreaking."

Gabriel's eyes found themselves on the German Shepherd. "I take it that's the dog she was found with?"

"Magnus." Kathryn smiled. "He follows her everywhere. And I mean *everywhere*. Growls at anyone who tries to rip them apart. The agency suggested it be best not to separate them. Regardless, in light of everything they've been through, I wouldn't have the heart anyway, to take them away from each other."

"It wasn't her dog, was it?" Audrey acknowledged.
Kathryn shook her head.

"No, she said he came out of no where and protected her. Scared the monster off. Hasn't left her side since."

"No tags?"

"Nothing. I wondered if maybe he was a police dog who just lost his collar, with how dutiful and fiercely protective he is, but you would think they would have claimed him by now..."

Gabriel leaned against the wall. "That's a loyal animal."
Kat nodded with a laugh,

"Don't be deceived by his appearance, he's sweet. Only time he's aggressive is if you threaten to separate them. So I just leave them alone."

"Did *she* name him?" Pine inquired.
Mrs. Chapman shook her head, "Said he told her that was his name."

The three looked at her with confusion.
She glanced. "I told you... she knows things she shouldn't."

As exhilarating as the whole experience was... Amelia knew they couldn't keep this going forever.

"Mrs. Chapman, we don't wish to overstay our welcome... but would it be okay if we came back tomorrow?"
Kathryn perked at this.

"Oh, of course. Thank you... thank you so much for believing in her. She's... she's so extraordinary."

Audrey's eyes fell on the child, and she found herself smiling.

"...Yes, she is..."

Gabriel found himself not wanting to leave the girl. A strange pull on his heart screamed for him to stay and talk to her... but naturally, he couldn't. It wasn't his place.

But there was one question he had to get out. He turned to Mrs. Chapman and approached her.

"Just one thing I need to know, ma'am... why is she telling you all this? Why does she draw these things?"

Kathryn glanced at the floor a moment, as if in contemplation... before sniffing, lifting her head up and swallowing hard.

"She wants to find them... and she wants to save them."

CHAPTER VII
◆ GOING OUT ON A LIM ◆

Pine and the Beckharts exited out from the Chapman residence, the day pressing close to evening. Amelia recognized it was almost dinner time, as her stomach was nearly eating itself. She turned to the siblings, hands in her pockets.

"Say, Beckharts, you ever been to the Pizza Shack?"
They perked. "Pizza Shack? The one next to the beach?"
"The same."
"I've been there once." Gabe revealed, though this caused Audrey to make a face.
"I haven't."
"Well, it's the most popular food place in Hollowgrove. You gotta try it!" She pulled her keys out and rattled them in her open palm.
"Here, I'll make ya a deal. Buy dinner for us and I'll personally escort you two richies home."
It was a rather tempting offer; a normal night out and a normal ride home. Just like real people.
Gabriel nodded his head, as Audrey gave her brother a glance to signal her okay. "Yeah, sure, why not?"
Amelia smirked, "Perfect. Hope you kids got a leash for the pooch though, cuz he isn't accompanying us indoors."
Audrey rolled her eyes at this since it was a no brainer... until she realized she did not, in fact, have a leash for Scrooge.
"Um... we'll need to make a stop."

~

The three, after a short detour, made their way for the Shack. It took them roughly 10 to 15 minutes, driving past the buildings, past all the trees, past the bridge that hovered over a rushing river, to a bizarre environment that seemed foreign to the rest of the town.
Gabriel and Audrey peaked out their window as they saw the immense arena of sand ahead, a blue crisp ocean just beyond. Just before that was the road and a wide strip of gravel that divided between the concrete and sand. As the car rolled on top of this new material, they shook and rattled, making the siblings'

teeth grit. The car at last halted as Pine parked next to a small, but rather nostalgic looking shack.

Amelia unbuckled her seat belt, turning the car off, and she looked back at the siblings with a grin. "Cute, huh?"

Audrey cocked her head. "Why is it so far out, away from everything else?"

"It's for the beach goers." Gabriel explained. "He also sells other things for surfing, and some knit knacks he found while traveling."

"*He?*"

"Troy Brooke." Pine answered with delight. "Just about the *coolest* guy you'll ever meet."

Gabe whispered in Audrey's ear, "He's very laid back and care-free."

Audrey raised her brows.

"How long has this place even been here?"

"Few years, I believe, right Pine?"

"Yee-yep. He's from Florida."

"I thought it was California?"

"No, it's Florida. Him and I are pals."

"Oh god, a Floridian." Audrey buried her face in her hands.

"No no, don't be like that. He's extremely chill and sweet!" Pine climbed out and opened the door for the siblings, to which both crawled out, Audrey being a little more reluctant.

"If that place has a distinct odor, I'm bolting the other way." Pine made a face, "Why would it--- hey now, no stereotyping or you can stay outside with Stooge!"

"*Scrooge.*"

"Whatever."

Pine shut the door behind them and locked the car, the loud beeping making Scrooge yelp. Gabriel guided the small dog to what Audrey now noticed was a small section against the wall designed for dogs, with a few canines already happily interacting with one another.

Gabe knelt down as he attached Scrooge's leash to a pole, pointing to a bowl of water. "Here you go, buddy, you got some friends and some water."

He reached in to a box ahead that was full of dog treats, making him smile at how thoroughly thought out this section was. He

tossed a biscuit to the small creature before standing back up.
"Play nice."
Scrooge made a content noise, while his whole body shook from excitement, the other three curiously approaching him and sniffing his tiny fluffy ears.

The three entered inside, with Audrey's eyes widening at the décor within. Classic 80's music blasted from a vintage jukebox, setting an eerily retro mood. Various people from the age of 25 and under seated before them, each minding their own business as they laughed and chatted. The aroma of sweet greasy bread and oozing cheese instantly overtook their senses, and hunger hit just a little bit harder.

"It's cleaner than I expected." Audrey acknowledged.
She took notice of the wall design, the various artworks placed upon the brown layer of paint. One of an alien throwing up a piece sign as he held a piece of pizza... another of a werewolf with a whole pizza hanging from its jaws... another of a pizza that straight up *was* a monster... a UFO beaming up a pizza delivery car... and little drawings of creatures and aliens crudely etched next to the booths, as if done by children.

"I take it he's got a thing for monsters?" She asked quietly. Her head turned to Amelia, who was glancing at her phone, but upon Beckhart looking at her, she quickly put it away.

"What are you doing?" Beckhart questioned, in suspicion. Pine's further behavior of smiling and perking up now had her on edge. "Nothing! Yes, he is, he's very out there, but he's totally harmless, shall we get a table?"

The siblings glared at each other as Pine led the way. Gabriel started to sit down at an empty table near the entrance, "How about here?"

"NO, too bright."
The siblings perked.

"He won't- I mean, I don't like it. Let's try another one."
Amelia charged towards a table with two booths. She slid her small backpack in as the Beckharts approached. Gabriel went in for his, expecting Audrey to sit next to him, but as she tried, Pine made a sound that resembled that of a trilling bird.

"Over here!" She pointed next to her.
Audrey tensed. "Why the heck for?!"

Uncanny

"Just do it, richie."

The Beckhart girl growled under her breath and moved towards her. She hesitated for a second, "I don't like being cornered."

"Well I have a weak bladder."

Audrey rolled her eyes and slid in to place. Pine sat next to her with a plop. She smiled brightly towards Gabriel, as she laced her fingers together. "Isn't this lovely?" Her shoulders bounced. "So cozy?"

Gabriel's eyes trailed off suspiciously as he shifted his glasses. "Yeahhhh."

The Beckhart boy leaned in to look at the menu before him. Audrey took hold of hers to do the same, after tying her hair in a loose ponytail. However, her eyes were soon pulled to Pine once more as the redheaded girl was peaking once again at her phone, to what appeared to be a conversation with someone.

"...Amelia, what are you up to?"

The Pine girl, who was biting on her finger, serving as a nervous tic, quickly withdrew her hand and dropped her phone onto the table, retracting her body instantly. "Absolutely nothing."

Gabe shifted in his seat. "Is it a reporter?"

Her eyes grew in size, tensing her body. "No."

"Is it a contact of some sort?"

Amelia curled her lips back, "You can say that."

The Beckhart girl suddenly perked. "Oh, I know! It's that guy you like, right? The one you mentioned before?"

"Holy heck, *no*, what is wrong with you?!"

"Well you're obviously talking to some-"

In that instant, someone had approached the table rather speedily and had set himself right next to Gabriel, both the Beckharts jumping at the unexpected fourth party member. They stared at him with eyes widened, as he nodded at Amelia, a slight smile traced on his lips.

"*Hi.*"

He stopped and gave Gabriel a look of acknowledgment, who was still staring wide-eyed, before the strange man looked to Audrey, then finally his menu. His movements reminded the two of a fidgety bird or lizard and it was almost humorous... but they were still confused as to who it was.

"Um...hi." Gabriel spoke politely, albeit a little hesitant.

He looked over at Pine, as their visitor went on to his business, not speaking a word, and Gabe leaned in. "Amelia... who is this?"

Audrey raised a brow towards the guy, mentally asking the same question. The young man straightened back up and looked to the siblings, adjusting his glasses.

"**Quinton Lim**." He eyed both intensely. "-And you two are the Beckhart siblings."

Audrey cleared her throat, shifting the menu in her hand. "Yes..." Quinton, who had spiked jet black hair, dressed in a classy black jacket, turtle neck and dress pants, moved his head about while he talked, something that they noticed he just *did* and didn't know why.

"Couple of richies who just got back into town and finally opened their eyes that their town is messed up, and are finally willing to do something about it. Yes, I know, no, you won't know me, nobody does."

He looked back at his menu. The Beckharts eyed each other as Audrey shivered.

"I see you've been spending too much time with Amelia."

"Oh no." Quinton looked back up...

"We all think that." ...Before looking back down again.
She narrowed her gaze. Gabriel made a rather painfully inquisitive expression as he stared down at the table.

"Okay.....so... is no one going to tell us *why* you're here?" Pine smiled nervously, "I invited him."

"Clearly." Audrey spoke a little loudly, her eyes focused on the menu.

"She invited me."

"Yes, we established that." Audrey shot back.
Quinton shuddered, "I'm sensing tension, so I'm going to just, yeah, I'm a student at Casper Community College, second in my class even though I should be first, I love film and horror fascinates me, bright environments make me nauseous, people not sitting in gendered pairs makes me light-headed which yes, is why Amelia put you where you are now, I don't like looking at people directly for too long a period because direct eye contact terrifies me, my family immigrated from Korea when I was 4, and I'm an amateur filmmaker, *next*."

His head fell back to his menu. His words left the siblings

stunned, while Amelia nodded her head slowly, smiling deviously.

Quin perked back up... "Oh! And I believe in monsters, too." ...Back down again.

Gabriel's head cocked, "Can you not keep your head up for more than 3 seconds?"

"Gabriel, he just said he doesn't like looking at people for too long, *honestly*!" Pine's playful scold made his mind whirl.

Audrey looked between the two, smiling nervously. "You two are very... spastic." She pointed first at Pine, "You a little less so, but *you*-" She pointed next at Quinton, who looked up at her and gave her a slightly vague, slightly annoyed expression.

"...Wow. I mean that in a good way! It's just... you're very... high energy and... jittery."

Quin's brows rose as his head fidgeted about more,

"Oh, well, that could account for my obsessive compulsive disorder, my social anxiety, which has spawned panic attacks, incoherent speech, intense migraines, blurred vision, seizures and psychotic episodes, which I have to take extensive medication for to keep my mind straight, and the only real negative effects I have are rapid speech, short attention span and a body that can't seem to sit still, but yeah, you're right, I'm really high energy and jittery."

His eyes returned to the menu.

Audrey's eyes widened, to which she gravitated towards Pine. Quinton was the fastest and yet most precise talker she ever met, and it took her mind places she didn't know it could go.

Pine smiled, licking her lips. "...See, I met Quin when we parted ways, so, we're pals now thanks to you."

Hearing this made the Beckhart girl feel guilt, and suddenly she realized that her treatment and behavior towards Quinton actually came out quite rude. Which made her feel further guilt from *that*... so she extended her hand across the table. "It's nice to meet you, Quin..."

Gabriel was proud of Audrey for taking that step. He made an appealing smile and turned to Lim, taking his hand after the strange young man shook Audrey's. "Yeah, it's a pleasure."

Quin gave the two a look, now donning the smile he had upon walking in.

"Well... it's not every day here in Hollowgrove that you get to sit at a pizza place with the Beckhart siblings... so I guess I'm a bit star-struck."

Audrey chuckled as she shifted in her seat and cleared her throat,
"Hm, yeah... you lived in *Korea*?"

He nodded, adjusting his glasses. Her face lit up in excitement.
"What was that like, do you remember at all?"

"I actually do, yeah."

"Okay, but like, uh, before we get to... Korea..." Pine sat up and turned to the others. "There's something I want to discuss with you..." She looked back at Quinton. "Quin knows... but... it's the reason why I brought him here."

The Beckharts glared. Her hands held each other, anxiously.

"You two... seem really interested in finding out about all these mysteries, right?"

They nodded.

"And, ya know... helping Ivy and all that. Well... me and Quin have been talking about this for a long time, we just... haven't gotten around to it yet."

"Gotten around to what?" Gabriel set his menu down.

This didn't sound good. Pine looked to Quin, whose eyes lifted and drifted to the Beckharts.

"We think the four of us should start a group."

"Like a band?" Audrey said, in a deadpan tone.

Amelia's face drooped in irritation.

"No, dummy. Like a private investigating agency."

"Like a sleuth assembly?" Gabriel joked.

But Pine took it to heart and dashed her head towards him,

"OH MY GOSH, THAT'S GOOD. Sleuth Assembly, we can be the Sleuth Assembly!"

Audrey did not seem wildly enthusiastic, but Gabriel had his attention held by the notion. Pine leaned forward in excitement.

"Look, we could really use this to our advantage. People might take us as a more legit deal if there's a larger group of us than just three or two or whatever, and then we can use it for our benefit. We can investigate the town and its secrets and maybe, I don't know, get a name for ourselves. So people trust us."

"She's right, you know, I mean... typically a group of people is taken more seriously, as individuals on the other side of those beliefs view them as a collected mind and are presented as the example of those ideals, so... non-believers might just be a little

Uncanny

more swayed by seeing a group of believers banding together."

"See, I knew it was a band." Audrey poked. The other three made a face at her. She smiled, wickedly.

"You know, actually, this sounds like it could work. Not so much the... *believer* idea, but just... forming a group and getting out there. Having different viewpoints and backgrounds, it could actually give us the advantage. Maybe one of us will see something the other doesn't."

"*Exactly*!" Pine exclaimed.

Gabriel was shocked that the two girls were actually agreeing on something. His brows raised as he leaned back against the booth.

"Well... maybe we should consider bringing in Troy."

Just as Pine and Quin got excited about the idea, Audrey tilted her head, confusion emanating from her face.

"Why would we bring pizza man into this?"

Quin leaned in towards Gabriel, his hand hovering over his mouth as he whispered. "You didn't tell her the most important part about Brooke?"

Pine smiled as she looked towards Audrey. "He's uhhhh... he's had monster encounters."

The Beckhart girl immediately turned her whole body towards Amelia, who looked away innocently.

"Oh my god, you're telling me he's one of *those*?"

"It's not what you think, Audy." Gabe assured.

"He's had various encounters across the country and even outside the country, and it made him a believer."

"Speaking of this man, is he here or does he have employees? Because I'm starving and no one has approached us."

"It's just him, but he's probably surfing right now."

"Dear god, how does he keep a business?"

"No no, he got help, remember Pine?"

Pine pointed at Quin in remembrance. "Oh yeahhhhh, Spike!"

"*Spike*?!" Audrey exclaimed.

"HOW'S everyone doing tonight, huh?!" An obnoxiously loud and extravagant individual greeted as he came from no where, holding a notepad in hand, a dirty apron wrapped around his waist. His colored green and red hair was styled into a mohawk, wearing a raggedy black tank top, spiked combat boots and holey faded blue jeans.

Audrey's jaw fell, as her face filled with horror. She prayed with all her might to God that Spike would not look down at her, but she nearly had a heart attack when he, for sure and for certain, lowered his chin, instantly locking eyes with the first person his sight came into contact with.

"Holy cow, AUDREY?!"

Kill me now... Audrey pleaded, to the same higher power she felt betrayed by.

Pine grinned with a slight laugh, "You two know each other?"

"Know her, dude, we dated for like, a WEEK, back in middle school!"

He grinned wide, nodding his head at Audrey with a rather intimate flare. "Best week of my life, bro. Audrey's a real one."

"A real one, wow." Pine reveled in Audrey's torment, grinning at the girl who wanted to slide below the table.

"So I was correct in my assumption that you DO in fact date everyone!"

Audrey held her mouth as she quickly looked away. She wanted to die and she wanted to die right there.

"Wow, Audrey, babe, how is it?! It almost felt like you were avoiding me all these years, zipping in and out of town!"

Audrey's voice almost broke as it did indeed crack,

"We want food."

"Oh, I see..." Spike grinned as he looked down at his notepad, pulling the pen from behind his ear. "She's bashful. So many good memories."

The Beckhart girl almost screamed. Gabriel held his mouth for a brief moment to keep from busting out laughing. He didn't wish to embarrass her anymore than she already was.

"Sorry about the delay, my dudes, I was putting a pizza into the oven and it caught on fire."

The bluntness in delivery of Spike's words that made it seem like a pizza catching on fire was just a natural part of life made it more humorous than it actually was.

Gabe's regained composure turned to visible and darkly hilarious concern, his eyes widened at the table, trying to determine if he actually heard what he just heard. He shifted.

"Uh, should we be worried?"

"Not at all. Happens all the time."

So pizza catching on fire really *was* a natural part of life.

"So..." Spike said, as he jotted down in his notepad. "Pine, I'm guessing you want your usual. Large, stuffed crust, extra cheese, with a Pepsi cola."

Amelia gave him a silent thumbs up.

"Quin, my man, you want a small, extra cheese, with pineapples and a water?"

Quinton jiggled his head as he scribbled on a napkin, his face practically touching the table. Audrey narrowed her eyes at Quin as she heard the word 'pineapple'.

"You're one of *those*..." She whispered, venomously. She then eyed Pine, "And what is it with you guys and extra cheese?"

Pine seemed a little shocked, "You mean you *don't* always order pizza with extra cheese?"

"It... just about comes out the same..."

"Audrey, babe, what'll it be for ya?"

"Um, just, cheese? Large, I'll share it with Gabe."

"-With extra cheese."

"Not you, too!"

Gabriel grinned.

"K, large, extra cheese, anything to drink?"

"Water." The siblings said in unison.

Spike laughed, "Ya sure you guys ain't twins?"

They didn't respond. He nodded his head, grooving to a beat of his own. "Say, Audrey, you seeing anybody right now?"

Audrey was too stunned to come out with words. Spike ripped off a paper he had been scribbling on and set it down on the middle of the table. A paper containing a phone number, next to a crudely drawn heart.

"Gimme me a call some time." He winked before he swaggered away. It didn't take Pine long after his departure before she burst out in laughter, wheezing like a broken dog toy.

"HOLY COW, YOU AND SPIKE, I CAN'T!"

Audrey hastily tried to defend her honor,

"Look, he wasn't, that is totally not... *ugh*."

"No, he really was, Audy."

Audrey looked to her brother in absolute betrayal.

"That was the only reason she went out with him for a week, was because it was a favor for a friend of hers, and a favor alone."

He leaned in to whisper to Quin, who wasn't even appearing to be paying much attention. "He's the brother of one of her old friends. He had a huge crush on her, and she was trying to be nice."

"And now he thinks you two are soul mates!" Pine sung mockingly, waving her arms like the story was an interpretive dance.

Audrey held her face in dismay and absolute humiliation.

"Literally all we did was go to the arcade and skating rink. He never wanted to do anything else."

"Yes, but didn't he buy you a milkshake and chilly dog?"

"Correction: he had his *friend* buy me a milkshake and chilly dog, cause he was dead broke. He didn't want me to know though, it was kind've adorable... in an odd, juvenile sort of way."

Quin flipped his napkin over, not bothering to lift his head up.

"Of course, he was taking out one of the richest and prettiest girls in town, he had to make an impression."

Pine was too busy delighting herself in the pain of the wealthy girl sitting next to her to even pay attention to what was being said.

"How come I didn't know about this?"

"Because I specifically avoided telling you." Replied Audrey in a grueling tone. She then looked away, back towards the monster paintings, attempting to change the subject. "Did Troy do these himself?"

"Nope. Random citizens came and decorated it for him."
Pine played with the menu in front of her. The Beckhart girl pressed her tongue against the inside of her cheek.

"Sooo... will we be meeting Troy today?"

"Probably not. But, if we're seriously considering recruiting him, then we should just come back tomorrow after our meet up with Ivy." Pine glared at the Beckharts. "Unless you two decide upon waking, that you're really not into this after all, and back out."

"Not a chance. We'll be there."
She smiled at Gabe, who truly seemed determined about all this.

"Alright then."
She leaned back, resting an arm across the back of the booth.

"Tomorrow it is."

CHAPTER VIII
✦ PAINED MEMORIES ✦

It was late by the time the four finished eating and bid good-night to Quinton. Amelia was yawning and rolling her neck, obviously tired from the exciting day, but she was alert enough to get the Beckharts home.

Audrey leaned against the door with her chin resting upon her arm, staring out her window, as her mind started to drift off. Scrooge had fallen asleep, snuggled close to her chest, as the silence of the drive eased any anxiousness the two might have had.

The trees blurred by, as the sky was overtaken by darkness. The only light existing now was from the headlights, which wasn't the best, but served its purpose well enough.

The atmosphere they had entered somewhat made the three paranoid now, with everything that had been discussed that day. And now, with someone breaking in, the Beckharts were rather dreading what they were coming back to.

Gabriel, in particular, was troubled. His mind went over a million things that he hadn't mentioned to the girls. Things that, now as a growing believer, made sense. And it terrified him.

With these things potentially being real... could that mean monsters that lived under your bed were real all along? Could fear of darkness be justified? The possibility of something stealing him away and no one having any idea how it happened, nor where it had taken him, made his blood run cold. There were so many things to now fear. And perhaps, this was the reason why so many people had denied the existence of the supernatural. They just wouldn't be able to handle the truth.

Then there was the matter of Ivy. Ivy... his mind kept coming back to that poor girl. A girl whose childhood was being robbed from her. Her innocence, her dreams, her happiness. She was just a child and she had to face so many horrors too soon.

He couldn't shake the feeling that he had to keep close tabs on her. He had to know where she was and how she was doing. Something instinctive. Audrey felt it, too.

Gabe took a deep breath and rested the side of his face against the car door, folding his cold arms into his chest. There was so much out there, unknown, secrets waiting to be revealed. In his half-tired, half-racing mind... he felt that fear from before... but also... the most strange thing of all... he was actually anticipating it.

Familiar ground was crossed. They soon arrived past the woods and around the fountain, Amelia parking next to the gleaming estate. It looked a bit different at night, the glowing marble lights shining from the exterior. One could see its lights hovering hauntingly in the sky above, merging with the stars.

Pine leaned over to look at the home, the lights glimmering off of her glasses. "Wowzers. So much bigger than I remembered."

The Beckharts stirred from the backseat, groggy and ready for bed. Scrooge was still crashed out, dreaming peacefully, to which Audrey held him tight and gently got out of the car, trying to avoid waking him. Gabriel crawled out, stuffing his hands in his pockets, as he walked around the car.

Both were welcomed with freezing temperatures that made their faces numb and fingers feel like icicles. The Beckhart girl scrambled to the door to unlock it, while Gabe stood still a moment, hesitating. He thought, for a minute, about Amelia. Something in him now had to ask her, or else it would eat on him.

He turned back around and walked to her door, where she rolled down her window.

"I thought you were going to just leave without saying goodbye. That'd be hurtful."

She smirked as she poked her arm out, but Gabe held on to the roof and leaned in a little. "Amelia... you think you should spend the night?"

Pine's face dropped.

"I mean... it's late and it's a long way back to town. You're already exhausted and I... I would hate for something to happen." His eyes briefly drifted to his sister, who had already opened and barreled through the front door.

"Besides... Audrey wouldn't admit it, but I doubt she wants to spend tonight alone with just the two of us. Not after what happened. It would be nice to have a friend."

Pine shifted, considering it a second, as she displayed obvious signs of flattery and reluctance. "I mean... if it's okay with you, I...

okay... sure."

Gabriel smiled and bowed his head, respectfully. "Alright. We have extra blankets and pillows inside, just come in when you're ready."

"Okay." She replied, a little too sweetly for her taste. Gabriel had that effect on her, however. He had always been such a gentleman, full of charm and kindness, no matter what state their friendship was in. He never treated Amelia like a freak... for once, she felt respected, when she was with him.

But she shook her schoolgirl crush out of her mind, putting those thoughts to rest. This was a friendly, professional courtesy. They were going to practically be business partners soon. She had to try to get her mind off of Gabriel for good...
-

Pine sat in the middle of the room, the fire lit up as bright as a Christmas tree. After a thorough inspection, the Beckharts concluded that there wasn't a secondary break-in. The alarms were still set, the doors all locked tight and nothing appeared to be tampered with. This brought them at least *some* peace of mind. Even more so with Amelia here. Having a monster fanatic in the same room with them seemed almost like having a monster in itself. Maybe she would be a repellent.

Audrey laid on the couch, opposite the one Gabriel was to sit in, as she stroked the soft fur of the still sleeping canine. Both the siblings had decided that the three might as well have a sleepover of sorts.

To celebrate, Gabriel returned to the girls with cups of hot chocolate, which made the two beam with childlike delight. Amelia took her cup with both hands as she took a long sip, shifting comfortably, with a blanket wrapped around her.

Gabe sat back down and the three relaxed in the silence, peacefully watching the fire burn and crackle. Pine sighed deeply, with content. "...This brings back memories."

She looked back at the Beckharts, her eyes twinkling. "When we were young... having those sleepovers?"

Audrey sniffed a laugh as her eyes fell. "Yeah, having those movie marathons or playing those ridiculous games."

She chuckled. "Remember when we would play truth or dare and I dared you to shave Gabriel's head bald, and you were ACTUALLY going to do it?"

The three burst into laughter as the image of Amelia chasing Gabriel with a buzzer flashed back to their minds.

Audrey giggled a moment,

"We had gotten so bold and insane that summer, right before..." Her voice trailed off as she remembered. And this memory caught on to the other two, a shadow of sadness casting itself over them.

"...Before we went separate ways." Gabriel tried to close off the subject, quietly sipping his drink, but Amelia's mood had been too dampened. She moved her head away, drinking her cocoa once more.

Audrey bit her tongue, digging her nails into her palm. She did it again. Said something that upset Amelia. All because of her bitterness. Bitterness over something that happened so long ago. But it hurt. The incident still hurt. And it ruined other friendships... all because of what Amelia did. And that was something she didn't know if she could forgive. Besides... Pine seemed perfectly content on hating her anyway. So there was no point in even trying.

She shook her head and started to turn on her side.

"I'm going to sleep... goodnight."

"Night, Audy." Gabriel said gently, his eyes focused on the back of Amelia's head.

He felt terrible for the Pine girl... she seemed so confident most of the time, and then times like that night... there was so much in her she refused to show to others. So much pain and loneliness.

She was fiercely proud of who she was and what she believed in... but at the same time... it just seemed like she still wanted to be accepted.

With Audrey now asleep... the two couldn't really talk. And besides... what was there to talk about, anyway? He didn't feel quite as comfortable as he felt he should have been with Amelia yet. They, after all, had just seen each other again after years. Resuming their friendship so quickly would have seemed suspicious and misleading, perhaps something Pine wouldn't appreciate. She in many ways hated the Beckharts, and didn't necessarily trust them. So this was just something he had to accept.

He rested his head against the back of the couch and sighed

deeply. "Goodnight, Amelia..."

Amelia moved her head only slightly. "Night, Gabriel..."

Her voice was cracking... whispering so softly, but so solemnly...

Gabriel fell asleep...

Audrey was asleep...

leaving her sitting alone, with nothing but her thoughts.

Her memories.

Her chin lowered, her arms hugging her knees and she removed her glasses, setting her cup down. As much as she tried to hold it back... she buried her face, and silently cried.

CHAPTER IX
◆ RED SKY IN THE MORNING ◆

*T*he forest seemed darker and more menacing than he had ever seen it. The sky, which had been drastically growing dimmer and more ominous as time went on, looked as though it had a collection of rain trapped inside of it... but no rain came.

It was accompanied with a rustling forest, the trees swaying sporadically with the wild winds sent from above. The air smelled heavy of a stench he could not figure out. Where had he smelled this before... where had he felt this type of dread before? And what was more... how did he even get here?

Gabriel took a step forward, his movements in almost a slow and cautious motion. His mind reeled with questions, as his eyes scanned around him.

What was this place?

Had he seen it before?

Something in him felt as though he did. But it was no recent memory, if it was. He did know, however... this place made him feel sick. A feeling that twisted his stomach and brought a pain in his heart and mind, that he couldn't describe even if he wanted to.

His eyes traveled up to the sky above, where a funnel began to form from the clouds, as if attempting to mutate into a tornado. He experienced chills he hadn't felt as an adult. Fear. Genuine fear. Fear that caused him to become paralyzed.

His attention was broken from the sky and now turned back to the forest. Something resided in the trees. Something he could not bring himself to investigate. He was frozen in place, his legs almost solidifying into statues. Something prevented him from going further. A knowledge of a terrifying truth.

At that moment, Gabriel could hear the oddly familiar sounds of a car approaching. He turned his head to see it...

A gray, relatively ancient model, that was rolling up fast towards him. Seeing the vehicle brought him another feeling he couldn't describe. It was even worse than what the forest did to him.

The car stopped only a short distance away from him. He anticipated whoever was driving to get out, so he may see their *identity... but another part of him knew he should run. Run for his life. Yet he remained incapable of controlling his own body.*

A sense of duty overtook him, as his eyes glued to the driver's side. Like his mind was trying to force him to see who it was. What it was. Why he was here. He needed answers, he needed to figure out why his subconscious brought him here.

This was no ordinary dream. This wasn't a nightmare. This was almost... a repression.

Just as the car door began to open, and Gabriel's breath was locked inside his throat, a force began to pull him. Pull his body from the car, from the forest, from the sky. He suddenly found himself spiraling backward, into the concrete road that at once turned into an all-consuming ocean of scrambled memories, that evolved into an empty void of dark space.

His name echoed through that void as he watched the face from the driver ripple and distort before him, Gabriel's body plummeting through the hole. He was left silently screaming as he fell further and further and further until--

"G a b r i e l , w a k e u p!"
-

Gabriel jolted upwards in an abrupt gasp, his body springing so fast, it gave him whiplash. It took him a few moments to realize he was now awake, and it had reached morning time in the physical realm. But as to who called his name remained a mystery, as he saw to his right that both Audrey and Amelia were still asleep.

His face scrunched in quiet confusion; if there was no one else awake, and he knew for sure it was a female calling to him, then who or *what* awakened him? He held his head as the images of the dream faded too fast for him to keep safe. He was already forgetting all the details of it, the only thing remaining from the world he had just visited being the sickening sensation deep in his stomach. He needed to get himself under control, however, and brush off whatever it was.

He sat up straight and took calm, slow breaths to ease his inflamed nerves. He reached for his glasses, and then for his phone. The time read 6:45. There was a dark overcast coming from the window, so it made sense.

The fire was out, causing the girls to tighten their covers and curl their bodies into fetal position. Gabriel rubbed his still tired eyes beneath his spectacles and scratched through his shaggy hair, before rising from the couch and quietly stalking past his sleeping sister and friend.

He made his way into the kitchen, where traces of hot chocolate still hung in the air and captured his senses. The aroma made him hungry, thirsty and longing for good feelings after what he just experienced.

The only real answer was to put his hands to work. Doing something would distract his thoughts from returning to that dark place, and onto pleasant things. Things that had nothing to do with whatever his mind was trying to put him through. He didn't want to remember anymore. He wanted to forget.

-

Quinton, who often only slept a few unhealthy hours, busily tinkered in his room on a small malfunctioning camcorder. His room was shrouded in darkness, despite it being morning outside, due to his black curtains and there being no lamps turned on. The only trace of light to be found was his black light, which he had multiple uses for with his work, and the red light resonating from his arachnid terrarium.

On the other side of the room was the fish tank home to his pet dragonfish, a 3 inch deep sea creature, which he had found stranded on the shoreline several months prior. Quin tightened the screws to the camera as he finished up repairs, before grabbing his phone and dialing in a number. He waited as it rang a few seconds, before hanging up and trying again.

He was a rather impatient fellow and expected the phone to be immediately answered, or else the silence would set him off in a bad way.

He called again. This time, whoever it was he was attempting to reach, picked right up.

"Hello?"

The voice was tired and a bit emotionally distant.

Quinton used both hands to drive a screw in, as he put the phone on speaker. "Beckhart. You're awake."

"You're lucky I am...... wait, who is this?"

"Me."

"Fascinating. Totally been waiting for your call. We go way

back. *Who* is me?"

"Me me."

"I'm hanging up, man."

"Quinton Lim, weird guy you met yesterday, where's Amelia?"

"How in the... how'd you get my number?"

"You do remember being popular and rich, right?"

"Audrey and I are unlisted, try again."

"Pine."

"She gave you my-- *ugh*!"

"Where's Pine, I need her."

"She's sleeping."

"So? She's always sleeping; wake her up, I need her."

"Dude, you talk *way* too fast. And I'm not waking her up, she gets cranky if that happens."

"How would you know?"

"I was friends with her longer than you, Quinty."

"*Quinty*?"

"As soon as she wakes, I'll have her call you, chill."

"Don't call me Quinty."

"We're seeing Ivy after we eat, see you then."

"Do not hang up on-"

The line went dead.

Quinton's back straightened, and he was left staring blankly at the wall, as he dropped his screwdriver.
-

Audrey began to stir, her body temperature too comfortable to leave the warmth of her covers... but alas, she needed to awaken. Her eyes opened only half way, as she began to poke her face from her blankets. With a single finger, she brushed the hair from her eyes and looked around at whatever activity awaited her.

It didn't take her long to get up all the way, and she tossed the blanket from her, craning her legs around to stand up. Scrooge had apparently nestled inside the blankets with her, which her departure disturbed his sleep and he was soon crawling out from his hiding place. His head emerged, poking his nose at her hand to sniff and lick it. Due to his high temperature from his time beneath the covers, his tiny tongue was warm and dry. Audrey turned her head to him and gave him a few head scratches, before her eyes gravitated to Amelia.

The Pine girl was still deep asleep, her face completely buried under the enormous material. A part of Audrey wanted to wake her, while the other wanted to enjoy the few brief moments of silence before Pine's excessive talking ensued.

She scooped Scrooge into her arms and walked over to Gabriel, who she for the second day in a row found cooking in the kitchen. She noticed he was only working with one hand and due to the lack of any greeting towards her, she assumed he was most likely on the phone. As he turned, she saw she was correct.

"As soon as she wakes, I'll have her call you, chill."
She perked. She? Could he have meant Audrey?
Gabriel flipped a piece of French Toast onto a plate.
"We're seeing Ivy after we eat, see you then."
He then clicked his phone off and slipped it into his back pocket. His eyes lifted to his sister. "Hey, morning."

"Who was that?"
She sat on a stool, where Gabriel glanced at her a minute, before rolling his shoulders and putting another piece of toast on to the plate.

"That Quinton guy. He wants Amelia to call him."
Her brother stood back, his eyes adjusting to Amelia's direction.
"Maybe I should wake her."

"She's fine." Audrey uttered a bit too quickly, as she slid the plate towards her and began serving herself, pouring syrup onto her food.

It caught Gabe's attention and he darted his eyes to her.
"What was that last night, anyway?"
Audrey glared. "What do you--"
"With Amelia." He shook his head as he straightened himself up, rubbing his eyebrow in quiet frustration.
"If you didn't want Amelia here last night, then-"
"It's fine. I don't care."
"Don't be like that."
"I'm not being like any way, I'm just saying... I don't care. It's whatever."
"Audrey, I-"
"I smell food."
The two Beckharts hushed up instantly, as the Pine girl emerged from her mental cave and stumbled into the kitchen.

Audrey softly groaned and held her forehead, as Pine sat at the stool next to her, the large blanket still engulfing her by the shoulders. Scrooge wanted to greet her, but Audrey kept her dog at bay, her eyebrows scrunched up in irritation and slight jealousy.

Amelia's eyes weren't even opened, as her body remained motionless sitting upon the stool, holding the blanket close to her chest. Her hair was atrociously ruined by bed head, as if it hadn't been brushed in six months, and her glasses weren't even adjusted correctly, resting crookedly on her face and serving no real useful purpose.

Audrey took another quick bite of her toast as she examined Pine up and down, next reaching for her glass of milk to wash the sugar down. "Nice hair."

"My life is in shambles."
Amelia shook her head and unexpectedly face-planted the counter. Both the Beckharts stared with disdain, even Scrooge.

"Er..." Gabe slid a plate of toast towards Amelia's head, which he next poked with a reluctant finger. "Ey..."

The redhead immediately perked up. "Mm?"

"That Lim guy called. He needed you for something."

"Ugh."

"Ugh?"

"Yes, ugh."

She reached into her pocket and pulled out her phone.

"He texted me last night about Ivy."
The siblings glared. "What about Ivy?"

"He was looking up details about her case, and any possible leads to her identity."

"And?" Audrey pressed.
Pine hovered her milk in front of her lips. "Zilch."

Gabe stood up straight, "Man... that makes me feel so terrible for her... no family... no one looking for her."

"That we know of." Amelia cut up a piece of toast, after pouring some more syrup and powdered sugar. "She no doubt gave us a fake last name, to protect her real identity. She could have very well been taken and dropped off here, too. We don't know for sure what it exactly was that took her, or was sent to retrieve her. Not even *she* seems to know these things."

"Unless she's lying."

Pine and Audrey's brother glanced at her; Audrey shifted.

"She could be just telling us certain things to throw us off. There's things she knows about this town she really shouldn't, right? Maybe she's just trying to protect herself by giving false information or lack thereof, for that matter."

"She *is* precocious." Gabriel examined. "And there's something about her that makes me think Audrey's right... there is definitely more to this kid than meets the eye."

A sudden chirp made Scrooge perk and twist his head to Amelia, who upon receiving the chirp abruptly jolted and widen her eyes, as she shakily set her cup back down. The Beckharts looked rightfully alarmed.

"Amelia, what's wrong?"

Her mouth fell open as she stared at her phone, softly shaking her head.

"What is it?" Audrey was growing impatient.

Pine's eyes drifted to the two at last, as she contemplated on what she should tell them.

"...It.... it's.......... nothing."

She at once set the phone down. The two were baffled.

"Amelia! You literally looked shocked!" Gabe grabbed the phone and tried to sign in, "It CAN'T be nothing!"

She snatched it right back. "It IS nothing! Back off!"

But Audrey was less than gracious about the matter and snatched it from her grasp, soon tracing her security pattern within seconds that granted her instant access.

Amelia's mouth dropped. "HOW?!"

"Are you kidding, I hacked into your phone all the time as a kid. You never change the pattern."

Pine was appalled, but what could she do? The Beckhart girl was already in, and seeing what Amelia had seen. Her eyebrows furrowed instantly.

"Amelia… what is this?" She looked up at her, her back arching.

"This is… this is your room." She scrolled to the next photo.

"This is your house!"

Amelia tried to stay calm, but it was proving to be very difficult.

"Ok... somebody was in my house. Someone who's been texting me..."

"For how long?!" Gabriel exclaimed, immediately concerned

about the situation.

"...For a few weeks." Pine tightened her fists. "I tried telling the police... but they couldn't trace it. I've blocked the number multiple times. He still gets through."

Audrey was already freaked out, but when she got to the next photos..... she jumped out of her chair. Her hand clamped over her mouth, as her eyes widened wildly.

It was the Beckhart Estate.

"OH MY GOD." She uttered through her fingers. "IT'S OUR HOUSE."

With a shaky breath, she swiped to the next. It was here, she dropped the phone.

"HEY!" Pine exclaimed, as it clattered against the floor. Audrey was already speeding to the couches and grabbing blankets. Blankets of which she raced towards the glass doors, and hung up over the rails to cover such open views.

"What is wrong with you two?!" Gabriel yelled, before Amelia herself gasped loudly and dropped her phone all over again.

"Oh, for goodness sake!" Gabe raced to the poor mishandled phone and picked it up...but his spine instantly experienced chills that ran through his entire body. His breathing at once became irrational.

It was a photo of the three. Asleep in the living room.
Taken last night.

CHAPTER X
✦ TALBOT'S DEN ✦

In the heart of Talbot's Den, a humble supply store frequented by campers and hunters, business was gradually increasing due to the intensifying news reports playing out over the course of only a few days.

The amount of customers was rather a discomfort for the loner Russell Talbot, who just so happened to be the owner of the store. Because of this, he had been taking refuge in the solitary corner behind the counter, busying himself with bullet organization and key-making.

His young and naïve hired help, Lycan, was an edgy sort, but nonetheless reliable and well-mannered. He had been an extraordinarily relieving addition to the store since he started as a young boy, help of course being a rather taboo topic Talbot was uncertain about. For the good 20 years of owning the store, he had almost always handled it on his own.

Now that the town was falling apart, it seemed, the store's business had increased, with the townsfolk rushing in to stock up on supplies. Everything from steaks to silver bullets, rifles to bows & arrows. People were taking all the precautions possible to fight against monsters.

Young Lycan was better at customer service than Talbot. The older man wasn't necessarily terrible with how he communicated with others, but his social skills were that of an awkward preteen, and thus he felt more comfortable with having someone of a bit more friendlier and manageable nature to handle such tasks.

The rusty man avoided eye contact with the browsing customers, as he kept his gaze down on the key machine. His bald head glinted under the troffer light, as he wore his standard button-up, faded blue shirt and raggedy dark old jeans.

The moment arrived, however, that he dreaded having to face. Poor Lycan was having to juggle with three different sets of customers across the relatively small store, leaving the fourth set being forced to speak to Russell himself. His body clenched as the woman's voice managed to rise above the incredibly loud rumble of the key machine, and he squeezed his face in dread, facing the opposite direction. He needed to talk to her. Didn't mean he had to like it, though.

He sighed quietly to himself and turned around, nodding at the woman with a forced smile. She stood next to presumably her boyfriend; they were a young couple, by the look of it...which made complete sense.

"Hi there, sorry to bother you..." She started off, displaying manners that surprised him. She sat down her expensive looking pink purse, that matched the rest of her gaudy outfit, and whipped back her shiny brown hair with a freshly manicured hand.

"Me and my boyfriend were looking for some bottles of holy water, and I noticed you didn't carry any? Are they kept in the back?"

Ugh... the holy water question again... couple of young fools. He wanted to shake his head, but he knew he had to be careful. His eyes fell.

"Fraid I don't, but... if it's holy water you're looking for... grab a cup or bottle of water... get it blessed by Pastor Poe at the local church... and you should be set."

She nodded understandably. "You know where I can get bottles?"

He wasn't entirely sure if that was a real question.

"....Dollar store? But uh... grocery stores... also... carry bottles... with water..."

She narrowed her eyes suspiciously.

"Do you know where I can *get* the water?"

His eyes slowly shifted to her boyfriend, as if unsure how to answer.

"Please don't answer that." Her boyfriend pleaded, slowly shaking his head. She gestured in confusion, "What, honey, I don't know how this stuff works. I wanna do it right!"

She turned her head to him, "Sorry, we're new here. My brain's a little frazzled from everything we've been finding out about the town. You know... its monster problem?"

"We're from Casper City, clearly." The boyfriend explained, as if trying to repair their dignity.

Talbot grinned, shaking his head.

"You're all good, man... tell ya what. Since you're new, and no doubt unfamiliar with the area, I'll go ahead and write down Poe's address. Plus, head to the grocery store across the street and get a whole case of bottled water free on me. Tell 'em Russell sent you."

He grabbed the pencil tucked behind his ear and wrote down the address to the church. The two smiled at his kind gesture.

"Thank you so much, sir!" She chirped with delight.

He nodded as he took a quick glance at what they were setting down. A couple of hunting knives and some matches.

"That all for you today?"

The man nodded. "Yes, sir... we're going to the drive-in theater tonight and wanted to be prepared."

That wouldn't do squat, but he decided to keep his mouth shut.

"Well in that case... I'll give ya a discount, since you picked 'em humbly. Give ya more money for your date."

The generosity of Talbot made the two grin from ear to ear and thank him up and down, while he rang them up. He nodded and gave his farewell, but his eyes quickly left the two, however, as his attention was drawn to the television hanging from the ceiling a ways off.

The continued reports of the missing people and all of that day's monster sightings were for two very brief seconds paused, as it was announced that the Beckhart siblings were back in town. All the noise in the store immediately silenced in his head as he stared at the screen, with his mouth hanging open. When the Beckhart children's faces popped up, he felt himself hum with a hopeful sensation.

"Well son of a gun... they're back."

Lycan's hands were finally freed, giving Russell the opportunity to speak with him.

"Lycan!"

The boy's head popped up.

"You know the Beckhart kids?"

Lycan's eyes drifted to the television.

"Are you kidding? The most popular kids in town? Yes, sir, everyone knows them."

Talbot ran his finger along his bottom lip.

"...I want ya to talk to them."

Lycan's eyes enlarged, as if the man just requested him to jump into a volcano. "Tal--ta--- TALK to them?! *Talk* to them?! You'd have better luck asking me to jump in front of incoming traffic! *No one* talks to the Beckharts, they're like... freaking celebrities!"

Russell pointed right at him with an authority that intimidated the boy, like a father scolding his child. "Attempt it and I'll give you a raise!"

He instantaneously straightened right up, saluting in all the ways that brought him shame. "YES, SIR!"

CHAPTER XI
✦ AN UNSEEN THREAT ✦

Gabriel fell into a chair, trying to keep himself from entering a state of sheer panic. All the while Audrey and Amelia were both pacing frantically, doing very little to keep themselves calm.

"I can't believe someone's following us and sneaking in to our homes, like... god, this is crazy!"

"What did that message say, Amelia?!" Audrey exclaimed.

"Every word!"

Pine pulled out her phone and examined the messages, gulping loudly and forcibly.

"I-it says stuff like… *you're saying too much... you know too much... I'm warning you, Amelia Pine... don't go down this route…* uhh... *some old friends of your's came into town, I see... don't talk to them… if you do, there will be consequences…* gosh..... *you shouldn't have done that... now face the consequences.*"

Amelia tried to keep her head, but she was failing. She bent over and held her breath, closing her eyes. "Oh gosh, I can't..."

Audrey, however, swiped the phone from her hand, as Pine was recovering from her own panic. The Beckhart girl held the phone up to her eye level.

"*You're a fool and you all will be made an example of. I'm in your house. I'm in **their** house. Sleeping angels. Last time of peace, I assure you. House is beautiful. Nice car. Dog's no good. This will be your last warning, stay away. Do not speak to young Ivy R-*"

Audrey had enough.

"Oh, no, I don't think so."

She lowered the phone and began to do something.

Gabriel shot up and ran to see what it was, "What are you-"

"I'm putting an end to this crap."

She scrolled over to the description of the sender and worked some magic. She then typed in the number into a people search. An *expensive* people search. From one of Audrey's many 'people-in-high-places' level of connections.

"Seriously… what are you doing?!" Pine exclaimed, inching closer to see.

"Finding this pervy little troll."

It was then she brought up the results. She smiled through her shaken state. "Got you..." She returned to the anonymous sender and began typing as quickly as her fingers could go.

"Nice try, creep.... let's see what the police… will say... about your little game."

She hit send.

Pine held her head. "What the-- ARE YOU CRAZY?!" Gabriel shot his arm up toward his sister.

"Are you trying to get us killed?! You just activated his murder button, Audrey!!"

"Not likely."

"Really..." Pine spoke, in doubt. "Explain to us how that is." Audrey turned.

"Look... we're going monster hunting, right? So obviously, they're just a little more dangerous than some creep with a phone, yeah? If we have any hope of facing against their level of threat, then we really shouldn't be so squeamish about this guy. Monsters aren't scared of cops. *He* is. He's playing us."

Amelia rose a brow, as she stared at Audrey in disbelief.

"You flopping from actress to lawyer now?"

"Nope. Just too many crime shows."

Gabriel turned to his sister.

"This guy obviously has it out for us, Audrey, I really think we should stand down."

"Stand down? HA!" She bent down and gathered Scrooge into her arms. "Look, I know, it's disturbing he was able to get in, but he's trying to scare us off. Well, it's not gonna work on me! I'm doing this freaking thing and for all I care, that freak can just kiss Scrooge on the lips!"

Gabriel made a face, as he glanced down at their clueless dog's furry black mouth.

Audrey began to turn, "Just let him try to mess with us. You and I got weapons, and I'm sure Amelia does, too! The police will nail him in no time."

Pine smiled in sarcasm, as she crossed her arms.

"I am truly moved by the level of patriotic trust Audrey has for the police force, but all due respect, they kinda got their hands full *not* solving the monster and missing person cases. They don't have time for a rich girl's woes and worries about a stalker."

"Even if it was you, Amelia?"

"*Especially* if it's me. Commoners are expendable."

"No wait, hold on..." The Beckhart boy held up his finger. "Hold on.... Audrey actually has something here...." He looked back and forth at the girls, his eyes constricting in thought. "...We could use this. What if.... this could be used as a cautionary tale? Like... what if things like this is how people are going missing?"

Amelia rose her brows in surprise of the notion, while Gabriel's sister stared at him with a tilted head. He shrugged. "...They'll listen then, right?"

Pine thought about it for a moment, before shrugging right along with him. "I mean... yeah… Gabe's right… especially if you tell them the strange ways of how this guy got in."

"Oh my god... I forgot about that..." Audrey squeezed Scrooge's fluffy body.

The three shuddered at the thought of the stalker's unsettling methods of slipping in and out unnoticed.

"That settles it, then..." Audrey turned back to the two. "I'm going to the cops." She hurried over to the safe and started rummaging through it as soon as she opened it.

"Good, we'll go with you." Gabe agreed.

"No, you two keep our appointment with Ivy. I've got this."

"Excuse me, you are not going on your own. This guy could-"

"Not with this, he's not."

Audrey walked back to them with a glistening glock 38, a peculiar thing to wield with a small furry dog in one's opposite arm. It was almost like Dorothy Gale had taken it up a notch against the witches and monkeys.

Gabe rose his arms up in defeat. "Okay, you win."

Amelia's eyes widened. "Audrey with a gun???? Am I dreaming?"

"Nope. Sis was top of her class in firearms training. You should have seen her shooting targets..."

"Oof... I'd rather not see yet another thing Audrey is perfect at to extend my insecurities, thank you."

He smirked. "Well, I can't have you outshining me, so I guess I'll grab a piece, too." He grabbed a taser from a nearby drawer.

"This is nonsense. You two have no business being rich, popular

AND ridiculously cool."

Audrey and Gabriel both smirked, as they equipped their trinkets to their sides. "We only learned from you, Amelia."

Gabriel's comment made Pine's face instantly flush.

"And you have no right to say things like THAT!" She quickly turned in embarrassment. Oh, how she hated the Beckharts. Only ones to make her lose all, but one single ounce of her dignity... and it certainly would not be the last time.

-

The main doors to the Beckhart estate were opened. A beanie-covered head popped out and looked both ways. Amelia's eyes were filled with caution and paranoia.

"...I think it's clear."

"Would you move? You're letting the cold in."

Audrey bumped Pine forward, which made the skinny girl stagger to catch herself. The Beckharts closed the door behind them, where Amelia looked their way.

"Why don't you guys have a car of your own? It would make things a whole lot easier."

"Agreed, but that would imply we were staying longer than a simple vacation."

Gabriel buttoned up his jacket to his neck, tightening his scarf. Pine's face sagged.

"Oh yeah... you guys are going back... forgot about that."

"Don't look so disappointed." Audrey remarked. "You know you hate us being here."

The strange girl's eyes averted to the ground, unable to respond to that. "So... what was that creep's name?"

Audrey smiled halfway, as she walked to the car and looked at her phone. "Hm... Nelson Blum... 27... total criminal record."

"You hack into the police records?"

"Uh, no. Multiple articles about this guy. He's a hacker to boot. Makes sense." Audrey turned her head and began to speak obnoxiously loud. "AND he lives in *THIRTEEN* WEST-BREW-STREET."

The others tried to keep from smiling. They didn't know for sure if the creeper was still around, but it was a good way to make him panic, given what they were about to do.

They checked the back of the car, making sure there were no

unwanted visitors. They then climbed inside and buckled up, Amelia at the wheel.

"So… police station, right?"

"Yep. Drop me off there and I'll try to get a ride to Ivy's pronto. It shouldn't take long."

Amelia nodded. "Copy that."

She started the engine, and they were on their way.

. . .

The car drove away down the path leading into the forest. But as soon as they departed, and the air fell silent... out of the trees, into the open, emerged a figure. A figure of which watched after them intently, a fire burning inside him.

Soon, this fire burned too intensely. Too much that he let go. Dropped his phone to the ground... and crushed it with a single stamp.

CHAPTER XII
✦ CONSULTANT ✦

Quinton sat as patient as he was able, waiting for the others to arrive, as he was parked in front of the Chapman residence. He repeatedly looked at the clock, sighing every so often in anticipation of their arrival.

He hadn't heard from Amelia, as Gabriel had claimed he would when she awoke. Which made him believe either Gabriel had lied, or Amelia simply forgot about him. Either way, he was a bit aggravated. And now they were taking forever to get there.

The team was off to a scrambled start, judging by the communication skills-- or rather lack thereof. Quinton, however, was usually not one to engage in arguments, or outwardly confront people about such grievances, unless it was to make a quick comment or sparkle of temporary attitude.

Quin was much more prone to keeping a notepad nearby that he would focus his frustrations on and write down everything that upset, angered or otherwise concerned him. Once written, he felt satisfied to get it out somewhere, and not allow it to become trapped in his head. He was now jotting down four pages worth of material.

His eyes lifted as he heard the distant sound of a car engine, and sure enough, it was Pine. Quinton jolted up and hurried out of his car. As soon as Amelia parked, he was already advancing towards her small blue car, his pad in hand. Having no intention of showing her what he wrote, he still waved it at her, squinting his eyes with a tamed level of fury.

She stepped out and gave him a look that indicated she was already wiping clean all evidence of her sins and playing it innocent.

"3 hours... 3 hours I've been waiting for you!"

"Excuse?"

"You were supposed to text me forever ago, Pine."

"Whatever, stop whining. Things came up. Look at your texts." Lim delayed her statement and pointed at Gabriel.

"Where's the female version of *him*?"

"She's at the police station. **Look at your texts**." Pine growled. Lim took out his phone and looked down at it, scrolling to Amelia's chat head. "...Oh."

"Oh." Pine proceeded to head-slap him for his imbecile-like behavior. His brows furrowed as he cut his eyes to her briefly, pushing her glasses back. "Stalker issues, huh? Never had those. Lucky. So we doing this?"

Gabriel looked over at Amelia, with a hint of frustration. "Are we sure we don't want to wait for Audrey?"

"I'm sure she'll be fine." Pine excused, shrugging the matter off casually. She jerked her head at Lim, "You got your camera?"

"Always." Replied Quinton, nearly insulted by her suggestion of otherwise.

Gabe rose a finger, "I'm sorry... *camera*? Isn't that an invasion of her privacy? She's a *little girl*, she's been through enough."

"Just a precaution in case Kathryn gives us the okay. We need to keep track of her behavior and responses. Don't worry, it's not for media purposes, only us."

"Okay, but still... feels wrong exploiting her."

Gabriel shrugged uneasily as he followed behind Amelia, who was treating the matter with little to no care. Naturally, he felt strange about doing all of this to begin with and yes, this was truly Amelia's field and not his... it just seemed wrong to even be dragging Ivy into all of this in general.

Truth be told, however... she was already a part of it. She, indeed, stated the previous day that she wanted to help find the creatures. Maybe this wasn't as big a deal as he felt it was...

Quinton walked behind Gabe, his camcorder in hand, and the three advanced towards the front door. Amelia cleared her throat and rapped a few quick knocks against the hunk of wood.

It was soon answered by Kathryn, thankfully, as the last one to greet them wasn't exactly the house's warmest of welcoming committees. Kathryn's face had a hint of relief and satisfaction at seeing the group, and she smiled a gentle, tranquil smile.

"Oh, I'm so happy you came back. Ivy's been waiting for you all day."

Gabriel rose his brows, "Really?"

"Oh yes, she's been anticipating your return."

Her facial expression, however, fluctuated when she noticed

something. "Oh... your friend... the woman, she's not with you?"

Pine puffed up, trying to keep from screaming at yet another person doting on Audrey. "We're not sure if she can make it today. I'm afraid she's held up with a police matter right now."

She gently pushed past. "How's Ivy, Mrs. Chapman?"

"Good, good..." Kathryn spoke quietly, as she let her and the boys through. Pine remembered about Quinton at that moment,

"Oh yeah, this is my friend and colleague, Quinton Lim. We were actually both wondering if it would be alright to record or take photos of Ivy, due to her case being one we're greatly interested in taking on, and need photographic material for our research."

Kathryn nodded slowly, as she tried to shake Quin's hand, but was walked right past by the strange spiky-haired fellow. Her eyes blinked repeatedly, unsure what to make of it. "Uhh... yes. Of course. Whatever you need." She turned and made for the hallway. "If you'll all follow me, please "

They walked for only a moment, before she looked back. "And you mentioned police matter... I hope everything's alright."

"Well, actually-" Gabriel cut in. "We had a bit of an incident with a break-in."

Kathryn turned her head, alarmed.

"Break-in?! Oh dear goodness, I hope everything's alright!"

"Oh, yes..." Gabe shrugged off, his hands stuffed in his pockets.

"They didn't take anything... I'm rather convinced it's a possibly obsessed fan, or disgruntled ex-employee."

"You poor children have to tolerate such things and not even enjoy your vacation... saddening." Mrs. Chapman shook her head, solemnly.

Amelia almost wanted to laugh at Kathryn's compassion over two richies, who were perfectly fine and insured. But then again... maybe Pine was being unfair. Maybe it was a bad thing, no matter what your status is, and is no laughing matter. Maybe Kathryn just more easily looked past such prejudices, and not hold on to jealousy or stereotypes like others.

"Thank you for that, I appreciate it." Gabe spoke softly, making Amelia feel a bit guilty. Kathryn led them to the back of the house, down the hall, where Ivy's room awaited them. She turned her head and smiled at them.

"I truly appreciate your coming here again... you've no idea how much it means to us both."

Amelia and Gabriel smiled warmly back at her, while Quin simply stared up at the ceiling, hands in his pockets, looking rather bored and uninterested in the small talk.

Kathryn nodded to herself as she held her hands together. "Well... Ivy requested she speak with you on her own, as there are questions she has she just... doesn't feel comfortable asking around me. She'll be able to write them down, but I was simply curious... do any of you know how to do ASL?"

"I can." Quin immediately responded, purposely keeping his gaze elsewhere. Amelia and Gabriel smirked at Quin's abrasive behavior. Mrs. Chapman let out a sigh of relief.

"Wonderful... thank you." She began to walk past them. "If you need me, I'll be in the kitchen."

"Thank you, Mrs. Chapman." Gabriel said, graciously, hanging behind the two, who appeared more than ready to kick open the door to Ivy's room. "Remember, gentle... she's just a kid..."

Amelia and Quin cut their eyes at him, a sprinkle of irritability in their facial expressions. "You don't control us or our lives." Pine shot back. Until she turned her head back to Quinton.

"But no, seriously, don't scare her by being yourself, Quin, she's but a wee innocent babe."

Lim nodded it off, not really caring, and readied his camera. Pine cleared her throat and took a deep breath, before reaching in and swinging the door open. But upon it opening, the three widened their eyes at what they saw.

Brand new drawings they had not seen yesterday were in every single inch of the room. Drawings of which depicted the most terrifying and horrendous creatures they had ever seen, posted on the floor, the walls, the windows, and even the ceiling.

Sitting in the middle of the floor was a cross-legged Ivy, head bowed, her brown hair hanging over her face. Her face of which, upon hearing the three enter, she slowly lifted up and made direct eye contact with the trio, in the darkest way a child had ever looked at them.

And at this, Amelia gulped. "...Or maybe not."

. . .

It wasn't long after Audrey was dropped off by Amelia and

Gabriel that the Beckhart girl marched into the precinct. She had obviously not made a habit of coming to the police station, given the fact that all legal matters had always been taken care of by her parents... *and* the fact that she wasn't a criminal needing to be arrested. But something inside told her she would soon be visiting such a place more than she had the desire to.

As she walked in, she was immediately finding herself in need to channel out the many gasps from the force, and a few catcalls from the arrested delinquents. She rolled her eyes, as she ran straight for the officer at the front desk, only stopping to throw a smile, and to greet back a kind veteran officer she knew when she was just a child. Other than that... she was a stone wall.

She arrived at the desk, causing the officer's eyes to lift to her. He looked incredibly bored, and in need of excitement in his life. Even seeing Audrey didn't seem to satisfy him. Something she appreciated.

"Hello..." She read his name-tag. "...Officer Martinez?"
His brow twitched in minor enthusiasm. She faked a smile.

"Hi...I...um...need to file a report, if that's okay?"
Wow, she was struggling. How does one even go about doing such things?

"Report?" He said, dryly, suddenly popping a slice of dried pineapple in his mouth. She nodded one single time. "...Yes."

It was prolonged, but he eventually got to turning around and fetching a book. He hovered it in the air, making his way back to the counter and dropping it before him, making Audrey flinch. It was a heavy gray binder, with just about a million pages stuffed inside, each page marked with a colored tab. He slid his finger in and flipped the book open, the other side landing with a tiny thud.

Her brows furrowed, as she watched him meticulously flick through the yellow pages, countless reports residing within them. Audrey was able to catch sight of a few key details as he turned the pages. She took note that most of these cases... were strangely unsolved. He cleared his throat, as he finally came to a blank page and reached for a pen. He attempted to write down the date, but was stopped by the lack of ink dispensing from the tip. A good little shake of the tool got the juices to flow once more.

Audrey leaned in a bit, "Uh, the name's Audrey--"
"Beckhart, yeah, I know who you are."

He finishing writing down her name, before moving on to writing down other information. "You held hands with my brother in middle school at one point. Wouldn't shut up about it. Happiest moment of his life."

Audrey wanted to die. She needed to move. Where absolutely no one knew her. She licked her lips, flooded with embarrassment, lowering her eyes to the floor.

"Uh, I uh... yeah... your brother, wow... how's he doing?"

"Prison."

"*Great.*"

She smiled with all the shame she was capable of feeling, wanting to die all over.

"I know, you don't remember him, it's fine. I envy you. I'm blood, I'm sentenced to remember him."

He sighed heavily, obviously hating his life and everything in it. His gaze moved up to hers.

"What would you like to report about?"

Beckhart cleared her throat, feeling as if she was at the DMV and not the homebase of the town's law enforcement.

"Well, I have a stalker..."

It took her a minute to realize after saying this that Martinez was staring at her, completely deadpan. And her blood ran cold.

"Wow... no way... never would have guessed that ever happening."

She blinked.

He shook his head with a groan, getting back to work regardless.

"So someone leave you love notes or snap a few cute pics of you?"

"Uh, well, if you'd call sending threatening messages to my friend, and sneaking into our homes while we were sleeping last night, taking pictures of us, and I'm pretty sure he was in mine and my brother's home even earlier than that, using means we're not entirely sure of, 'love notes' and 'cute pics', then yeah totally."

Martinez's head shot back up.

"Would your friend, by chance, be Amelia Pine?"

Her brow twitched.

"Yes... I believe she mentioned she attempted to report the messages prior to this and you were unable to help her."

"Yeah... hit a dead end. Couldn't trace it."

"Well, I did." She set her phone down and slid it towards him. He peeked at it, his eyes squinting.

"His name is Nelson Blum. Criminal record. Hacker. Bad news. Lives not far from here. You're welcome."

Martinez straightened his back and stared at Audrey with the utmost confusion. "Nelson Blum?"

"Yes."

"*Nelson Blum* is your stalker?"

"*Yes*." Audrey forced, her eyes narrowing.

He looked away, his tongue running along the inside of his cheek.

"....Huh, come with me."

She sighed and grabbed her phone, as he pivoted his lazy body and walked away from the counter, soon leading her down a hall that was frequently passed by officers on duty. She cocked her head, as he stopped at an interrogation room and opened the door. He stepped aside for her to look. She peeked within, and her eyes became saucers.

There sat Nelson in a chair, being grilled by an officer, both of whom paused to look towards the two. She expected the officer to perk and excitedly acknowledge her presence. What she did not expect was for Blum to do the same. He seemed genuinely ecstatic, in fact. "Oh my gosh... Audrey Beckhart!! What the actual-- WOW!" His cuffed hand clamped over his mouth to hide the squeal waiting to burst through.

She looked over at Officer Martinez and leaned in.

"...Deputy, are you psychic? That was ridiculously fast work..."

"Uh...'fraid not. There's a hole to your little conclusion."

Audrey gained a look of offense. She swung back around.

"Okay, idiot, jig's up. Caught you red-handed. You're obviously running around and breaking into houses and playing a dumb game, well you're too late now, aren't you? They got you."

Nelson's face changed from one of excitement, to one of gradual shock. "Uhh... I'm sorry?"

She waggled a finger at him. "Don't play stupid; you broke into the Beckhart and Pine homes!"

A shrill escaped his mouth that was inhuman.

"WHOA! WHOA! Back up, man! I didn't break into any homes! Okay, not recently..."

"Quit lying!!"

"Dude, I'm seriously not lying! I couldn't have! I mean, I'm flattered you're that confident in my criminal skills, but--"

"Oh god, *save* it." She groaned, starting to turn, but Blum stopped her in her tracks.

"It's TRUE, man, I've been here for *two* days!!"

She froze. Her eyes lingered on him for several painful seconds, as her brain slowly tried to process what he just said.

She looked to Martinez, who rose his brows in an unsurprised fashion, then at the officer interrogating Blum, who nodded.

"It's true. He's been locked up the whole time. Couldn't be him." Audrey's eyes rolled to the floor, as she felt her body start to lose oxygen, her blood pressure rising by the second. All she could do was suck in one single breath, and dart away,

"Thankyouforyourtime."

She ran. As fast and as far as her legs could go.

. . .

Gabriel, Amelia and Quinton all stood before Ivy, who was watching them intently as they slowly entered the room in a cautious and perplexed manner. It almost felt as if they were approaching a wild animal, using such slow and careful movements.

Pine smiled, as she walked towards Ivy and let her pack slide down her arm to the floor, before she sat in front of the girl, crossing her own legs and settling in a comfortable position.

"Hey Ivy... remember me?"

Ivy's eyes were as brown as her hair, but intense and calculating.

Amelia felt analyzed as she faced the child, but she kept her composure and handled her with poise. "My name is--"

Ivy suddenly signed something.

Pine stopped and bit her lip. Her eyes briefly cut to Quin, who had stood next to her and was fiddling with his camera.

"Quin, a little help."

Her friend lifted his eyes and took notice, as Ivy signed again. His brows flexed.

"She says 'I know who you are. Amelia Pine'."

Amelia looked back at her, her face teeming with intrigue, and she shrugged her shoulders, "How?"

Ivy began signing again.

Quin translated, "'I read your blog, the Pine Times'... 'I like you...

you tell the truth'."

Ivy wagged her finger and signed 'is', then spelled out A-U-D-R-E-Y, gesturing her confusion with both hands. Quin tilted his head, "'Where is Audrey?'"

Lim then signed back to her.

"Audrey is at the police station"

Ivy brought up her hand to her temple, as if about to salute, before bringing it down and sticking out her pinky and thumb to a W shape.

Amelia knew this one; she was asking why.

"She's fine, she's just checking on something."

Ivy pointed at her and the others, then rubbed the side of her hand against her open palm, which Quin translated to be "Are you okay?".

Pine smiled and nodded, "Oh yeah, we're totally fine."

But Ivy shook her head, as her expression got more serious, and she waved her hand horizontally in front of her chin, signing "Don't lie to me".

Pine sighed, knowing now she couldn't get away with much, if she was going to deal with a kid like Ivy. She shrugged.

"Sorry kiddo...I guess I'm acting like a sucky grown-up, huh? Bummer. Okay... truth be told? We three had a stalker. Not Quin, no one stalks him, but me, Gabe and Audrey. They snuck into our homes and took pictures of us. We think it's some creep who's trying to mess with us."

But Ivy shook her head, then grabbed her pen and paper that was sitting between her crossed legs, and she wrote on it. After a few seconds, she held the paper up and Pine read it, squinting behind her glasses. Her eyes then slightly widened.

It's them.

Gabriel cut in at that moment, peeking over at the girl.

"Who's 'them', Ivy?"

It was almost as if the child realized what she had actually said, and her eyes immediately fell to the floor to attempt at keeping quiet. She had said too much. But this did not perturb Gabriel.

He walked around Amelia and Quinton and sat down next to Pine, leaning in and talking to Ivy gently and delicately.

"You can tell us. We're here to help you."

Her eyes lifted back to him and she stared for a moment, before shaking her head only slightly, refusing to divulge anymore information. He sighed and leaned back a little.

"Ivy," Quin spoke, which caused the girl to look to him. He nodded one single time, before whispering his next words as he signed them, "Would you mind if we record you?"

Her chin lifted as she needed clarification, before he rose his camera up and explained further. "We need research for the case, to help us find out what is going on. Are you okay if we take videos of you?"

She held her hand vertically and pointed her thumb towards her chest as she signed "Fine". But then she continued.

Quin rose a brow. "It's fine... but I want to help find the... the... creatures?" His eyes turned to them.

Amelia perked, as Gabriel's expression turned defensive of the child. "You want to help find... Ivy, it's too dangerous. Besides, we don't have the authority to take you to something like that, not even Kathryn."

Ivy sighed in frustration, as she wrote something else down and held it up. *I have already asked Kathryn, she says it's fine as long as I stay out of the way.*

But Gabriel protested. "No, it's too dangerous. You could get hurt if something came at us, then you... besides, what if that thing that attacked you comes back? There's no way I'm letting that happen."

Pine turned her head to Gabriel, giving him a look she hoped he would soon take notice of. But he knew what she was doing and therefore avoided eye contact.

Ivy shook her head. She wrote something else.
You don't understand what's going on. I do. Let me help. Let me come with you.

Gabe and Amelia finally broke the uneasy silence, as their eyes lifted to Quin, who they saw was already taping Ivy. Their brows lowered at the boy.

"*Quinton.*" Amelia hissed.
She shook her head, trying to get him to turn it off.
It did not hinder Ivy. She wrote once more.
Let me come with you. And I'll show you how good I can be.
Gabriel sighed in mild frustration. "As what?"

Ivy signed the final blow.

Consultant   Uncanny

CHAPTER XIII
✦ RESONANCE ✦

Horrified by this revelation, and filled with paranoia all over again, Audrey raced to the entrance of the police station, looking over her shoulder in all directions. With Nelson
being checked out, the stalker could literally be anyone.

Her gaze was wild and distrusting, as her hold on her purse containing her weapon got just a little tighter. She quickly withdrew her phone from her pocket and went to text Amelia.

Hey, are you guys still at Ivy's?
She waited for a reply. She stood just outside the door, keeping an eye on her surroundings, as her body jittered in the cold. Pine was taking forever. She grew impatient after only a few minutes.

Amelia, are you done?
She waited another minute. Still no reply. She bit her chapping lips, shaking her head as she watched her own breath dispense into tiny puffs in the air. Her fingers were too cold for this. She typed again.

Amelia, Nelson wasn't the stalker. We were played. I need you guys. Now.

Her hands clenched, as she shivered under her coat. The air was growing colder with each passing day.

Her eyes kept darting towards every movement around her. She refused to live like this. She needed answers and she needed them fast.

That's when she got a chirp, alerting her to a text, and she perked as she clicked on the bubble. But her heart stopped.
It wasn't from Amelia.

Nice move with the hit on Nelson. Unfortunately, I'm one step ahead of you.

Her eyes enlarged twice the size. It was **him**.

The redirect was easy. Nelson was an obvious choice. Pity I had to destroy my previous phone to eliminate any chances. Cute boots, by the way.

She sucked in her breath and swirled around, eagerly eyeing

every single person passing her. Panic filled her mind and numbed her every sensation.

This was a bloody *nightmare*.

She looked back down, fear slipping into her psyche.

She hurriedly typed in with trembling hands.

Who r u? What do u want?

She hit send. He responded in seconds.

I warned you three not to proceed with this case. You should have listened. You may have a nice piece-- and by nice piece, I'm referring to the glock 38 you got from the safe, sitting pretty in your purse-- but that's not going to stop me.

Audrey gasped.

H o w?

Stay away from Ivy Rein. That's your last warning.

He was right. That was her last warning. Because she turned her whole body right around and ran back into the station. She sped past the many officers surrounding her to the counter, where Officer Martinez once again resided at.

As soon as he noticed her, he puffed with contempt. *"Not again..."* He muttered under his breath.

But she slapped the phone down before him. "He's texting me! He's texting me right now!!"

His face did not even change expressions.

"Who, Nelson?"

Martinez stuffed his mouth with Cheetos and waved a phone that sat a ways off on the counter. "Cuz this is his."

His words were slurred, but she could still make it out. And she huffed with irritation. "NO, you moron, the STALKER."

She held the phone up in front of his face. "He knows I'm freaking here and he's WATCHING me!"

Martinez strained to see.

"Huh...got chya. Well, what do you want me to do about it?"

"I DON'T KNOW, TRACK IT MAYBE?"

He held up his hands. "Whoa, lady, sorry. This isn't my field. Don't sue me, I'm poor."

He shook his head, having enough of Beckhart.

He rolled his chair a short distance away to grab a folder.

"You'll have to file for tha-"

Welcome to Hollowgrove

"Oh my god, I'll do it myself!"

She grabbed her phone and rushed further into the precinct, where she stopped at a random desk and turned the officer sitting in his chair around to face her.

He widened his eyes as she shoved her phone in his face, a piece of a bear claw hanging from his mouth.

"Figure out who this is, for god's sake, or I will cut off your freaking donut funds!"

He held up his hand and tried to take it, but she slapped his hand away, making him jolt.

"Not you and your filthy pastry hands! Have someone set up a device, hurry!"

Another officer approached the two,

"Sorry, Miss Beckhart, did I hear you say you need something tracked?"

Audrey stood up straight,

"YES, and we need to hurry before he destroys this phone too!"

Hearing the urgency in her voice, Officer King quickly gestured for her to follow him. "Come on over here, then!"

She ran to join him at a desk housed by a computer, and the kind officer went straight to work. He typed aggressively, as Audrey handed him her phone in order for him to do his magic.

"What's the story behind this number?"

"He's been stalking me, my brother and our friend Amelia Pine. Now he's threatening us and he even threw me off by redirecting his location and identity to Nelson Blum. And your colleague, Mr. Martinez, did not believe me."

There was venom in her voice.

His eyes darted to Officer Martinez, who had showed up behind the two... as well as the bear claw officer. King's face was filled with nothing but judgment.

"You over here not taking special care of Audrey freaking Beckhart and she has a STALKER?"

Martinez instantly grew defensive, "Hey man, she's a richie, I don't pay attention to nothing they say!"

"Fool, Gabriel and Audrey Beckhart are the only richies in this town you should be showing RESPECT!"

He shook his head in disappoint.

Audrey held her own hands, as she stood with a shaking body and riled up nerves. She felt a little safer with Officer King, as he was always a good friend to them growing up.

He kept trying, as he worked to pinpoint the number's exact information. Audrey feared they may have been too late and the caller automatically crushed another phone. Beckhart really didn't want to live at the precinct in order to wait for the next phone to be purchased and communicated with.

"Who drove you here, Audrey?"
She shrugged her shoulders, uneasily, as they felt way too tense. "Amelia."

"Have you been in contact with Amelia since?"
"No, she hasn't answered any of my texts. But I think it's because she's in an interview."

Martinez made a face. "An interview?"
Her eyes glared. "Yeah, we're sort've starting our own... kinda... private investigative service... I guess."

Martinez was shaken. And not in a good way.
"Seriously?"

But King was all for it, as he nodded his head in delighted approval. "Private investigator, eh?? Look at youuu. Well you got my business, miss lady."

She smiled, nervously, still a little unsure about the whole investigation thing to begin with. That's when King made a sound that caused Martinez, Audrey and the bear claw man to nearly jump out of their skin, and for all eyes to turn to the three. "GOT 'IM!" He declared.

He clapped and pointed at the screen.

"Your little stalker lives in Casper City and his name is-" Just as he was about to read the name, a chilling thing took place. The entire screen was overtaken by a deathly virus. And he gasped and yelled his lungs out, as his whole computer malfunctioned and went dark.

"NO NO NO NO, ARE YOU KIDDING ME?!"
He leapt up and tried to turn it back on, but the server was down. Audrey couldn't believe it. Who in the world was this man, that he had such resources to even trigger a virus on a cop's computer?

Then... her phone chirped. She quickly snatched it.

Welcome to Hollowgrove

Time to destroy this one now. That was a close one. You're good, Audrey. So good, you won't be hearing from me for a while. I won't underestimate you again. Watch your back.

And that was it. No more texts. Audrey breathed. King shook his head,

"I've gotta get to another computer, we'll keep trying!"

"Don't bother... he's gone."

She showed him her phone screen.

He deflated, shaking his head.

"Crafty little snake, isn't he?" Martinez uttered, munching on a bagel. Audrey's eyes rolled to him darkly, but she kept quiet. Her gaze eventually fell to the floor.

King put his hands on his hips. "I'm gonna give you an escort out of here. Who knows what this psycho will try..."

She nodded slowly, as she trailed behind him in a solemn manner. Her mind was disturbed.

"Where to, Audrey?"

She shook her head, not necessarily caring.

"Chapman residence..."

He nodded in acknowledgment, as he led her out. But even with him being near, she felt... exposed... like anything and anyone can now be a threat. But little did she know... the stalker wasn't all she should have feared. For anything and anyone *was* a threat.

- - -

Beckhart, Pine and Lim were stunned by the boldness of young Ivy Rein, to assert herself so dominantly in the investigative ranks, that she now appointed herself as their honorary consultant.

Gabriel needed proof. Solid convincing, in order to sway him. He wasn't about to let a child into an investigative team without seeing firsthand just how special she actually was. Or at least her intellect, anyway. And proof was exactly what Kathryn gave him.

Mrs. Chapman seemed overtly adamant that Ivy help them. Perhaps it was the pressure of therapy, or hopes of it being a chance for healing and growth, in order to confront her fears and trauma, moving past it all. He thought it risky, but Gabriel was a reasonable man when it came to negotiation amongst adults.

Kathryn had provided him with books filled with Ivy's thoughts and theories, that contained explicit details about the town. She was right in her words, that Ivy knew things that could get her in trouble. And as such, he took no risks and read them silently, trying to keep the book as covered as possible.

Kathryn sat across from him at the dining room table, as she watched him read through the books carefully, while Amelia and Quinton stood on the side, trying to wrap their heads around the case. Ivy remained in her room so that the adults could talk in private, Magnus keeping her company.

Gabe shook his head in disbelief, as he traced his finger across the page and took in each word with the utmost of concentration. His eyes briefly lifted to the light-haired woman across from him.

"How could she possibly know all of this?"

She shook her head. "She hasn't told me..."

"Why's that?" Quinton questioned.

Kathryn's lips pursed, her eyes falling to the wooden surface of the table. "She... says it's for my safety."

The three looked at the woman with mild concern. Amelia laced her fingers together, shifting uncomfortably.

"Mrs. Chapman... is there the slightest of possibilities that Ivy could be lying about what she went through? And that perhaps someone has been feeding her this information to reiterate to others?"

But Kathryn was stern in her response, shaking her head aggressively.

"No, no, not Ivy. I will tell you now, Miss Pine… that little girl... she is complex... she's guarded... she's filled with trauma... but she is the kindest and most honest child I have ever met in my lifetime. She would never break the trust of anyone she shares any of this with. Her character is better than I've ever seen from anyone."

Despite her suggestion otherwise, Pine nodded in agreement.

"I believe you both, Mrs. Chapman. I just want to weed out any possible doubts or holes in this case, so I can prove to the town that what Ivy says is true."

Gabriel shot his head at her, "We can't take her around people! They can't know what she knows!"

Amelia cricked her neck.

"Beckhart, trust me. Ivy needs this."

He was stubborn, however. He set the book down.

"Amelia, if she comes forward with any of this, it would make her a living target. She *has* to stay silent!"

Pine slammed her hand down on the table, as she leaned in close to Gabriel's face.

"When you know the truth about something, not being believed is the worst possible feeling. Ivy is alone, scared and desperate to move forward with her life, to warn other people about the things she has seen. You don't know what it's like, Gabriel. Being a believer is its own freaking hell."

The air grew silent, as all eyes focused on Amelia, whose own personal fiery passion for the matter burned bright in that moment. Kathryn looked away, as she shifted from the awkward and tense atmosphere. Pine didn't even flinch, however.

"Gabe... please trust me. I know what it's like to be Ivy. She needs this. *I* need this. We have to prove it to others. Before it's too late."

She let out a soft exhale, her posture easing.

"I know you're worried about her. I'm worried about her, too. But she's safer with us. We can protect her. If we stick together, we can fight through this. And we can help others, so no one else has to face what Ivy had to ever again."

Gabriel's eyes moved away from Pine's, as her intense gaze was making him uncomfortable. He sighed, rubbing his sockets from under his glasses. "Alright....you're right...let's do this."

Amelia stood back, as Gabriel closed the book and nodded to Kathryn, sliding the books back to her.

"Keep these somewhere safe..... in fact, *burn them*. Burn them until there's nothing left. We can't take any chances."

Kathryn didn't argue. She gently spoke her compliance, before she gathered the books in her arms and made her way for the fireplace.

"Thank you..." Gabriel heard in a quieted voice and his eyes glanced at Pine, who granted him a rare affectionate smile.
He smiled back, trying to dial back how much admiration of her he showed. "You're welcome."

Quin then gagged in the background, with no real context. They cut their eyes in his direction, but he dismissed their attention with a shrug and roll of the eyes. That was no doubt a discreet sign that they disgusted him.

Amelia's phone then chirped. She looked...but her face fell.
Gabe straightened his posture.

"Is it Audrey?"

"Yeah."

"What is it? Did she find him?"

"...It wasn't Nelson."

The two's gaze met once more, and Pine's blood ran cold.

"He messed with the tracker. Threatened her again. He's still out there... and we have no idea who he is."

CHAPTER XIV
✦ STRENGTH IN NUMBERS ✦

The growing concern over the stalker situation quickly became a clear and present danger, now that their stalker's identity not only was discredited, but proven to be someone of a much greater threat than they had realized. Whoever this was had resources, the likes of which even shot down the means that Gabriel and Audrey had the power to utilize.

Gabriel stared up at Amelia, as she gave a report on what Audrey told her; that the identity of their oppressor was not in fact Nelson Blum, but someone else entirely. Someone who was able to infiltrate their security system, sneaking into their homes, taking photos of them in the middle of the night, and was now demonstrating immensely chilling hacking skills of which he could even use on technology owned by the police force.

The worst part of it all was that even now, the intentions of this man were unclear. He simply was devoting himself to scaring them off without actually divulging what it was he was scaring them off *from*.

The Beckhart boy was overwhelmed by the scenario he found himself facing. This was becoming too unreal too fast. They hadn't even begun their work, and someone was already after them.

That's when it occurred to him... his mind flashed back to their conversation with Ivy... when she told them about ***them***. She was too terrified for it to be simple paranoia, or a straight up lie. Ivy knew things, they were all aware of that. But she seemed to know things beyond just creature existence and the town's history. She knew who was behind crimes of a far more sinister nature.

He looked towards the hallway leading to Ivy's room. Ivy knew their stalker was no normal man.
And she knew he wasn't alone in this. Whoever was involved... they had to be behind what was happening to Hollowgrove. Why it was getting worse with the attacks. Why the truth was being hid from the public. And Ivy, a seemingly harmless seven

year old girl with the mindset of a professor, had been attacked by a creature, ending up shaking the four to their core.

He realized now. It was no coincidence that they had come together, and Ivy happened to be their first case... she had planned this. She knew who they were. She knew they were coming. Ivy brought them there.

It was no wonder why Kathryn needed to heed Ivy's wishes, so desperate to give her what she wanted. The child had an effect on her, as she had an effect on everyone. There was something distinctly unnatural about Ivy Rein. Gabriel needed to figure out what it was.

The decision of letting her into the group was now transitioning into a crucial necessity. They needed to keep her close, to see what she knew, to see what secrets *she* even held. And no matter what motives the child may have, they most importantly *must* keep her safe.

Gabriel stood from the table, gathering his thoughts. It was time they act. The sooner, the better.

"What's the plan, Gabe?" Inquired Pine. "Should we proceed forward or... are you having second thoughts?"

The Beckhart boy's eyes gravitated to his friend's face, her glasses bouncing back his reflection, her copper red hair drizzling out from her beanie. His fingers ran through his own chocolate brown hair, as his mind deliberated his next move.

"I'm not walking away from this. Not now."
Pine looked away, trying to hide the proud smile she developed from Gabriel's refusal to back down. The Beckhart boy walked around the table and put his coat back on, as Kathryn walked back inside the room.

"It's done." She reported, to which he nodded in acknowledgment.

"I appreciate your hospitality, Mrs. Chapman. We have decided to move forward with Ivy's case and accept her as our consultant."

Her face beamed at that moment, her hands rising to her mouth, as she experienced bewildering amounts of relief.

"That's wonderful! Thank you *so* much!"
All three were slightly curious about why Kathryn was so delighted by this news. But Mrs. Chapman soon explained

it herself.

"I feel with you all watching her now, she'll finally be safe. And she'll have freedom and joy, and have the chance to be a normal child again. You have no idea how grateful I am, to all of you." The woman seemed to be on the verge of tears.

Gabriel laid a hand on her shoulder, to bestow some comfort.

"It's really no trouble at all, Mrs. Chapman. Ivy is truly an incredible child that I look forward to helping. It's you that we should be thanking."

She smiled warmly at the Beckhart boy, to which brought a rather positive feeling to a part of him that felt almost dead for a long time. It further proved to him that he now had meaning again, due to the changes taking place. Even if bad things happened in the future... it seemed worth it to bring peace to people like Mrs. Chapman.

"Mrs. Chapman... I have a feeling Ivy doesn't get out so much. Sooo, I was wondering if it would be alright if we could treat her to some pizza? Maybe ice cream?"

Kathryn nodded, as she wiped her watery eyes,

"Of course, she would love that."

Gabriel stepped back, as he stuffed his hands in his pockets.

"I'm going to speak with her now. See how she's doing." Without another word, Gabriel left Kathryn, Amelia and Quinton, and walked down the hall leading to Ivy's closed door. He knocked gently with his two fingers, before opening it and peeking inside.

There, he found Ivy standing by her window, watching the activity outside as Magnus sat next to her doing the same. The two were completely silent and did not bother to look at whoever came through.

Beckhart shut the door behind him and leaned against it, as he stared at the dog and little girl. There was a great disquieting sadness resonating from Ivy, as he noticed she was watching the other children. Children were playing and laughing, experiencing something it felt as though she could not relate to. She looked at those children as if they weren't even the same species, and there was almost an envy he could detect coming from the seven year old. An envy to be as carefree and naïve. But here she remained... an isolated child who knew too much, imprisoned by her own fear.

"You weren't just randomly attacked by that thing, were you?" He broke the silence.

She still didn't flinch.

"It was trying to bring you back. Back to where ever you came from. Back to *them*... wasn't it?"

Despite the lack of response, Gabriel went on.

"We've decided you can come with us. Be our consultant. I won't pretend I know what all this is about, or what you have went through, because I don't. That's why I- we- need you. And you need us… don't you?"

At last, he finally received a response from Ivy, as the young girl slowly turned her head to lay eyes on him. Magnus did the same, as if he somehow got permission to make eye contact with their visitor. Ivy then turned her whole body around and approached Gabriel gingerly, to which the Beckhart boy knelt down to her level.

"There is one thing I ask of you..." He laced his fingers together, as he briefly cut his eyes to the floor in order to silently construct his next words to the peculiar child.

"If we're going to do this… I need you to be open with me. I need you to tell me about everything. And I mean, *everything*. If there is only one person in the group that you should trust with this, it's me. I want to protect you, Ivy... but I can't do so, unless I know about these people. Even if it's a secret a day... or a week... you can't keep it inside anymore."

Ivy and Gabriel stared intently at one another, as he laid a protective hand on her tiny shoulder.

"I swear on my life, as long as I am with you, nothing will happen to you. I will do everything in my power to make sure they don't get you. Just please... promise me... promise me you'll do this?"

Ivy Reign had secrecy and distrust wired into her, that it was now simply as natural to her as breathing. But her opinion of Gabriel was pure and teeming with respect. She saw through him as if he were made of glass. There was no malicious intention of any kind in any part of Gabriel Beckhart. All that he said to her at that moment was truth. And all she could provide for him was a simple nod of the head.

Beckhart smiled. "Welcome to the family, Ivy Rein."

- - -

Amelia bent down and scooped Scrooge into her arms, the tiny dog having treated itself to the bowl of food and water Kathryn graciously set out for him, while Quinton reviewed the footage he had of Ivy thus far.

"You think Beckhart's gonna get the kid to talk more?" Pine glanced his way, reflecting on how she should answer that question.

"I don't know... she's pretty tightly wounded at the moment. We should give her some time."

"We may not have that with the 'them' people running around. Better count your days well, Pine. We might be getting our tickets punched early."

"God you're depressing." She sighed into the small dog's fluffy head. Quinton shrugged, completely unapologetic for himself. Amelia perked her whole body abruptly, when she saw that Gabriel was returning from Ivy's room, only with the little girl now in tow. Rushing past them was Magnus, of whom Scrooge let out a shrill growl at seeing the imposing German Shepherd. But Magnus paid the animal no mind, who was practically a munchkin compared to him, and walked right past him too.

Quinton eyed the enormous dog as he circled him, staring up at his face as if checking him out as the house's official security force.

"Let him smell your hand, Quin." Amelia suggested. Quinton shifted, "No thanks."

"It's how dogs learn to trust you." Gabriel added. "If we're going to work together, we need him to trust us."

"Work together? I thought we were only taking Ivy!" Quinton backed away as soon as Magnus let out an imposing woof at that second.

"You didn't get the message, Quin? Where ever Ivy goes, Magnus follows. No questions asked." Amelia snickered.
Lim deflated, "You've got to be kidding me."

"Honestly, I think it's a good thing." Gabriel enlightened, as he came and let out his hand for Magnus to sniff him. The dog did so, granting him the opportunity to pat and rub his large head. "You never know when a big feisty dog will come in handy..."

Ivy then reached in and tapped Quinton on the arm. He glanced down at her, to which she signed.

He rose a finger, "Oh, so now I'm her official translator?"

"Quin." Amelia scolded.

He sighed. "I know, I know… I'm honored, Ivy."

He knelt down and watched as she signed once again, to which he lifted his chin.

"What's she saying?" Amelia inquired.

"She wants to know if I like dogs."

Quinton sniffed a laugh.

"Yeah, I like them. They're just a lot of work."

Ivy then shook her head, followed by her clasping her palm in front of her face, and waving both hands in small circular motions to tell him "Don't worry."

She then pointed at Magnus and brought her fists together, while sticking out both middle and index fingers to sign "Takes care", and next signed "of" as she finished with extending her arm to her right, doing a thumbs-up, signing "himself."

"What's she saying now?" Gabriel wondered.

Quinton looked up at him. "Dog's a free spirit."

Kathryn then came up behind the group, holding Ivy's jacket out for her. "Ivy, our kind new friends are taking you out to celebrate with pizza, and perhaps some ice cream. Be sure to thank them."

Ivy gestured her thanks, by moving the tips of her fingers from her mouth. Gabriel and Amelia smiled at her, where Quinton signed "You're welcome."

"Now remember to stay with them at all times and use your manners, alright? I'm counting on you to be a good girl."

Kathryn snatched something from the dining room table and stuffed it in Ivy's pockets, who watched as the woman readied her up.

"Don't forget to use your notepad and pen, too, alright?"

The woman bent down and looked Ivy in the eye.

"Be kind, sweetheart. It's okay to have fun."

Ivy nodded, to which Mrs. Chapman gave her a loving stroke through the hair and kissed her forehead. "Good girl."

Welcome to Hollowgrove

The woman arose and tapped Ivy's back to move forward, as the others began to take their leave.

"Thank you again." Kathryn spoke gently, leading them to the front door.

Everyone waved their goodbye and exited, with Ivy and Magnus following right behind. The little girl turned her head and waved to her foster mother, who smiled as she laid a hand on her heart, watching the group leave for what would only be the first time in this blossoming journey.

Her heart was filled with warmth as she saw Ivy run to Gabriel and take his hand. Something that the Beckhart boy handled with extreme poise and delicacy. She knew then, Ivy's road to recovery had already begun.

~

The group advanced for their respective vehicles, as Ivy elected to go with Gabriel and Amelia, which automatically meant that Magnus would also be going with the two... meaning that Amelia's tiny car would soon be jam-packed, as Audrey would no doubt be joining them as well.

Gabriel was so preoccupied with the excitement of taking Ivy out to eat, that he completely forgot the general reason of why they were returning to the Pizza Shack to begin with. Which was to talk to Troy Brooke.

Pine had high hopes of recruiting Mr. Brooke, who she believed to be a valuable ally in what they all hoped to accomplish. Gabriel was a bit skeptical now, however. As upon reflection, Troy wasn't something he pictured to be a genuine asset to the investigative cause. Then again... anything could surprise him at this point. Given that their consultant was a seven year old girl.

Ivy and Magnus climbed in the back of the blue car, where Gabe handed the girl Scrooge to hold, in which the small dog quickly became a vibrating ball of fluff, completely hiding his face from the ignorant Magnus.

Gabriel was about to check his texts regarding any updates from his sister, when a police vehicle suddenly sounded off, causing the group to jump to the clouds. It then parked and the passenger window rolled down, revealing Officer King as the culprit.

Uncanny

The kindly man had large expressive and friendly eyes, his skin dark with warm undertones, his hair styled in a crew cut, and his entire upper body gorging with muscle build. His features were not only handsome, but also of a trusting nature, making him among the most well liked and well known of the officers.

He also happened to be a practical joker, so scaring youngsters with his siren was mere child's play, compared to his usual endeavors. He laughed, displaying the biggest grin a person is capable of making, as he pointed at his victims.

"Aw, you lot JUMPED! That was too rich! I got you good!" Amelia and Quinton made a face, but Gabe was the one to bend down and run a facial recognition scan. To which he soon enlarged his eyes. "No way... King?!"

"In the flesh, my brother!" King responded, as he stepped out of the vehicle.

Gabriel smiled wide as he saw his old friend.

"Wow, it's been ages! How have you been?"

"Ah, the usual rodeo that comes with this job. Town never sleeps." He walked around the car to the back door.

"By the way, I've got someone that belongs to y'all."

He opened the door, where Audrey soon emerged from within, her face drained of blood and any positive emotion. Gabriel knew why she was looking so glum, and he extended his arms for her to embrace him. Audrey ran right in for the offered hug, where she buried her face in her brother's warm shoulder. A welcoming refuge in the midst of the cold atmosphere.

Seeing Audrey climb from the back of a cop car was enough for Amelia to shake her head and mutter under her breath.

"I knew she had it in her..."

She lifted her chin to the Beckharts, leaning against her car.

"So couldn't get any more leads on the creepazoid, eh?" Audrey's eyes peeked at Pine and she softly shook her head.

Pine rubbed her temple, as her eyes departed from the richies.

"Eh, figured as much... oh well. We die, we die."

She then slapped the roof and started to jump into her seat.

"Anyways, get in! We got pizza to eat and a Troy to talk to."

"Just a minute now."

Pine looked, as King ran for the passenger window and leaned down. "Maybe I should I give y'all a police escort. It ain't been safe lately..."

"It's never been safe." She shot back, before bluntly rolling her window up in his face.

He rose a brow, as he stood back up and his eyes glazed over the Beckharts and Lim.

"Y'all be careful, then. And I mean it. It's dangerous and unforgiving in this town. I'd hate to see any one of ya get hurt."

That's when his eyes honed in suddenly on Quinton's face, and his expression grew serious as he pointed. "Hey... don't I know you from some place?"

But Quinton suddenly spun his body around and faced his car window. "*No.*"

King was skeptical of the fast-talking introvert. But he left it alone, nodding to the Beckhart siblings.

"Well... stay safe, Gabe, Audy... anything you need, you just come to me."

"Thanks, King." The two spoke simultaneously.

He did a two finger salute, before hurrying back to his car and heading out.

Audrey glanced over at Quinton, who was getting into his car to ride on his own, something of which made her feel guilty. She looked back at Ivy, noticing the presence of Magnus as he took up every ounce of breathing room. Then Scrooge, who was still trembling all the while. It was manageable riding with the three in the back, but it served as a good mental excuse to tap out from the riding arrangement.

"I'll ride with Quinton. He's all alone and that kinda makes me feel bad..."

Gabriel's brows furrowed at this. "Are you sure?"

"Yeah..." She started to advance to the strange spiky-haired fellow's vehicle. "I'll see you in a bit."

"Alright..." Gabriel waved as he got into Amelia's blue beetle.

Audrey walked around Quin's car, the latter of whom stared at her in confusion, and climbed in to the passenger seat.

"Uhhh, what are you doing?"

"Just drive, Lim." She replied curtly, shutting the door.

He looked away, in complete bewilderment, before starting

Uncanny

up his engine with a shake of the head, and proceeded to buckle up.

"So why'd you act weird when King asked if he knew you?"
Quinton was reluctant, but he answered her nonetheless.

"I... might have been at a protest..."
Her head shot at him. "*You*?! At a *protest*?!"
His eyes glared.

"I mean... I was filming it."
Her body deflated a little, "Oh... well that makes more sense."

"And uh... your buddy King there?"
He smiled nervously, before he put the car in drive.

"...He might have pepper-sprayed me."

CHAPTER XV
✦ TOGETHER WE STAND ✦

"Okay, it was totally *not* a big deal..." Amelia begun, right after Gabriel asked her about Quinton's call-out from Officer King. "Awhile back, maybe a year or so, Quin was asked by some fellow college students if he could film their protest. They offered to pay him and stuff, cuz he does freelance."

"He does?"

"Yeah." Amelia made a turn.

"So he gets there and it's a Save-The-Whales protest. Totally got out of hand, though. Nut jobs started getting wild and aggressive, and the police had to break it up, right? Then the protesters started swarming the cops. Over *whales*. Whales, Gabriel."

Amelia made another turn. "So in the midst of the chaos, Quin kinda sorta got pepper-sprayed by Officer King."

Gabriel clamped his hand over his mouth to keep from laughing. Pine grinned wide.

"Since then, Quin has completely written off attending protests. And is totally embarrassed by the whole thing, so please avoid with your life telling him I mentioned this."

The Beckhart boy shook his head, as he tried to contain his amusement. "Not a word, I swear."

Pine snorted like a pig, as she guided the car forward.

Gabriel looked behind them, seeing that Scrooge was still trying to hide from Magnus, and he sighed at the dog's timid nature. "Better get used to him, Scrooge... you're going to be outdoor buddies pretty soon."

Ivy stared at Gabe curiously before looking down at Scrooge, who was shaking like a leaf. She gently stroked his fur, which eventually started to calm his nerves. Magnus, at last, turned to the small dog and gave him some sniffs. Scrooge's eyes enlarged as this occurred, but before long, the large German Shepherd bestowed some friendly licks to the Pomsky's ear, and the small dog gradually made peace with what was transpiring.

When Gabe peeked at the backseat, his brows raised when

Uncanny

he saw the peace treaty take place.

"Holy smokes... that was fast."

"Mm?" Pine hummed.

Gabe pointed. She glanced at her rear view mirror and she laughed. "Ha! Seems the panic attack stage is over."

Gabriel chuckled in agreement and turned his head away.

Ivy's eyes lifted at the two as she sat in her eerie silence, before looking out the window once more.

- -

The group eventually arrived at the Pizza Shack.

It was already afternoon at this time, but the sun that was shining had no effect on the chilly air that nipped at their faces, as they exited their vehicles. They tightened their jackets, coats, scarves and sweaters, huddling together, hoping the close proximity would increase their body temperature.

"Well... we're back." Quinton muttered.

Amelia turned her head to Ivy, who held Scrooge close like a plush doll. "Have you ever been here before, Ivy?"

Ivy's eyes lifted to Pine's in acknowledgment, but she shook her head. Amelia smirked.

"Awesome. Best pizza in town."

Magnus looked around them, as if scoping out the area. Gabriel leaned in and pat him on the back, which made the dog jerk to look at him, but only in a startled manner and not in aggression.

Gabe pointed. "C'mon, buddy, we've got to get you saddled up." He looked at Ivy, but noticed that she did not wield any leash. "Um... Ivy... do you have a leash for him?"

She shook her head.

Gabriel blinked. "Then... how is he supposed to stay put?"

Ivy then exhaled deeply, before handing Scrooge to Audrey and pointing two fingers at her eyes as a motion to watch her, where she led Magnus over to the dog post. She looked Magnus straight in the eye, then pointed at the ground. On cue, he plopped his tail down and remained as she walked away. He surveyed the perimeter vigilantly, as if he had been put on watch duty. The others stared in complete awe, never before seeing such a well behaved pooch.

Audrey smirked, as she followed the others toward the shack's entrance, eyeing Scrooge's little face.

"Wow... Scrooge, take notes. He's doing it right."
She was about to hook him up to the side, before Magnus made a whimpery growl, grabbing her attention. She looked back at him, just as he pointed his nose to the ground, as if telling her to set the small dog down next to him.

She rose her brows, staring at him a moment, but ultimately decided to test it out. She set her fluffy child next to Magnus and stepped back, waiting for his reaction. She smiled in surprise, as Scrooge leaned against his new friend for comfort, his eyes wandering everywhere.

"Ok then... I'll leave you two to your male bonding time." She turned and skipped to the door.

Scrooge momentarily got mesmerized by a passing vehicle and nudged only an itch to go after it, but Magnus suddenly let out the loudest and most intense woof at the small dog, that caused his whole body to jolt to an immediate stop. Needless to say, he fell right back into position.

- - -

The Beckharts, Pine, Lim and Rein all entered the Pizza Shack. Instantaneous nostalgia hit the elder members of the small group, now convinced that the place had some sort of spell cast upon it to visually and mentally bring you back to a simpler and more carefree time.

Audrey smiled as she smelled the pizza, her hunger increasingly gnawing at her stomach in a begging attempt to be fed. She breathed deeply, before a tickle on her skin drew her attention to beside her, where she saw that Ivy was now taking hold of her hand. The gesture surprised her, as she wasn't expecting Ivy to be this openly friendly.

The sound of a familiar voice soon caused chills to run through her nerves, and she grit her teeth in reply.

"Wowhowww, welcome back to our casa, me amigos... *and* amigas!"

The group's attention settled on Spike, who rushed to them with a dirty apron, a notepad in his palm. The peculiar fellow grinned wide as he laid eyes on them, nodding his approval at seeing them.

"So glad to have you back with us, dudes! And dudettes!"
He winked, particularly at Audrey, before snatching the pencil

from behind his ear and jotting down on his pad.

"Lemme guess, you guys will be needing a radical booth and a menu for the ki-"

He stopped when he realized there was a child present, and he abruptly bent down, overly excited.

"FAR OUT, yo! I've not seen you before! You're part of the gang now, huh? Totally cool, miss dudette."

He proceeded to fist-bump Ivy, who tilted her head at him in a curious manner.

"*Spike*." Audrey uttered within a single breath.

Spike shot up, his brows raising, as his expression was replaced with one teeming with admiration. She huffed, her eyes closing as to avoid eye contact with her ex of one week.

"We need a table pronto, *please*, and an audience granted with Troy Brooke."

"Whoa whoa, audience granted?! Man, your wording is poetic, babe! I'm digging it."

"*SPIKE*."

"I'm on it, meeting with Troy, coming right up!"

He turned and pointed at the booth they happened to sit in from yesterday. "Have a seat, my guys! I'll be right back with the boss man!"

The group walked to the booth, where Audrey could hear distinct laughter coming from Pine. Her head swiveled to her and her voice dropped to a hiss. *"What is that?"*

Amelia chuckled, "I just can't get past the fact that you dated SPIKE of all people, like, omg..."

"Please refrain from talking now."

They all seated, removing their coats and scarves, tossing them in the corner, with Audrey proceeding to hide her face from looking at the others. Gabriel pat her on the shoulder, as he was squished in the middle of her and Ivy, where Amelia and Quinton sat opposite them. Much to Quinton's disliking.

"Where's the menu, I need a menu, something to look at." Audrey quickly snatched a menu to stuff her face into.

Pine couldn't help herself; her face soon buried into her arms in an attempt to stifle her laughter. Watching Audrey be this embarrassed was everything she hoped for.

While they waited, Quin took the opportunity to bring back

the topic of the stalker. Something of which Audrey seemed to be trying to forget, to a saddening fail.

"Amelia mentioned to us about what the stalker guy said to you. I think I'll state the obvious… this guy has cameras in your homes. Maybe microphones. Micro*chips*. Who knows? There's definitely no way he could have known you had the gun, unless he put a camera up."

The others were unsettled by the suggestion that their assailant was able to see everything that transpired. Everything they had done, and everything they had said. This added fuel to the paranoia fire.

"I would suggest doing a complete sweep when you get home, and I mean COMPLETE sweep. Every crack, every crevice. All the places capable of being a hiding place for your buddy's tech."

"What if we don't find anything?" Gabriel questioned. Quin shrugged. "...Then you got yourself a more supernatural angle to the case."

Audrey's face tightened. "Can we please not talk about this right now? Not where it's so... *public*."

Pine leaned her head against the wall. "Audrey's actually right. Not right now. Take no chances."

Quinton sighed, staring down at the menu below his nose.

"Fair enough."

Spike approached the group and handed Ivy her kids menu, as he set down a tray of the drinks they had previously ordered, beginning to distribute them.

Ivy, who had been intently listening to the group's conversation the whole time, graciously accepted the menu, and the chocolate milk Spike bestowed upon her. She immediately went to work with the activity page, using the provided crayon pack.

"Enjoy your refreshments, my dudes. I fetched Troy for ya, so he'll be right out momentarily!" He pointed. "And same as yesterday for the big pie, right?"

They all nodded.

He winked, clicking his tongue, as he finger-gunned excessively.

"Comin' right up!"

He skipped ahead.

Pine immediately darted her eyes to Audrey, smiling with

mischievous intent, but Audrey shot a finger at her with complete fire in her eyes. "DON'T."

"AMYYYY!! QUINNNN!!"

The party jumped for the second time that day, and it needed to end.

In came a tall, well-built man with tanned skin, golden blonde hair, dressed in a grey sleeveless shirt, worn jean shorts and brown sandals, whose arms extended happily as he saw his apparent favorite customers.

"DUDEESSSS, welcome back, man!!"

At long last, the fabled Troy Brooke.

Audrey and Gabriel stared with intrigue. He was exactly how Audrey pictured him, strangely enough... but there was something about him that still grasped her attention. Perhaps his instant impression of pure intent and carefree attitude. There was something undeniably, instantly likable about Troy, they could tell.

Troy soon took notice of the Beckharts and Ivy, and his face lit up like a Christmas tree. At once, surprise, bewilderment and excitement busted through his facial expressions.

"DUDDEEEEEEEEE, NO WAYYYYYY!!"

His hands shot towards the siblings,

"The frickin' BECKHARTS?! HOLYYY... IN *MY* SHACK, MAN?!"

His fist punched the air, making the two flinch. "Ladies and gentlemen, our distinguished guests; the Beckharts!!"

In that moment, the whole shack was filled with applause. The siblings wanted to slide under the table.

Pine covered her ears as the loud noise bothered her, but it thankfully only lasted a few moments before Troy gestured at them with glee.

"What brings you to my humble abode, my dudes?! You know what... I'm feeling generous tonight, especially now that I'm in such a good mood; tonight's meal is on me!"

"Oh no no no, that won't be necessary, please." Audrey tried, but Amelia tapped her hand.

"It's all good, let the man pay."

Audrey quickly leaned in to viciously whisper. "This man owns a simple little pizza shack, we're freaking rich, we can pay!"

Amelia leaned right back in. "So is he, dummy, he makes a killing off this place."

Beckhart's face fell, completely overtaken by this news.

"Wha-- ho-- then how come *we* get an earful about our wealth and not HIM?!"

"Cuz I actually *like* him!"

Out of the blue, Audrey and Amelia received an instant splash to the face by none other than Gabriel, as he took it upon himself to throw his water cup to quench their bickering, followed by a swift "PSH!", as if he were disciplining a cat. Understandably, the girls were shaken... and trying to catch their breath.

Troy's face dropped as he witnessed this, where Spike clamped his hand over his mouth, but Quin and Ivy only stared blankly at the hilarious occurrence.

"Gabriel... I am going to kill you." Audrey managed to utter through her gasps, as she attempted to dry herself with napkins.

"Same here." Amelia hissed through grit teeth, running her hands across her wet face.

Gabriel lifted his face, proudly. "And my militaristic strategy worked. You both found common ground in the midst of the chaos."

Amelia and Audrey both stared at him with murderous rage. Something of which Troy was not vibing with, and quickly tried to get past. "So! Spikey boy tells me you cool kids wanted to talk to yours truly... what can I do for ya?"

Gabriel laced his fingers together, propping his elbows up on the table. "Yes... we did... soooo... we actually came here to... talk business?"

Brooke did not follow. His eyebrows crinkled. "Business? You mean like... pizza business? Cuz I could *totally* use you two as actors for a commercial!"

"No no, not that." Audrey urged, shaking her head aggressively. Gabe puffed up his chest,

"No, actually... we were hoping that you'd uh, well, join our little-- **Sleuth Assembly.**"

Troy cocked his head like a confused puppy. "Huh?"
Pine honed her sight right on him.

"We're starting an investigative team for cryptozoological

and extraterrestrial phenomena."

Troy was speechless. His eyes focused hard on the Beckharts, as he obviously was trying to determine how in the world it could be true that the Beckharts were involved in such a scandal. Something of which Pine knew automatically how he was thinking and had to chime in.

"Yeah, I know. I had the same reaction."
Her eyes drifted to the two richies, grinning wide.

"You think they're feeling well? Something in the water? Think it's contagious, what they had? Will I succumb to their close-mindedness? Look at their eyes, you can tell by the eyes."

Audrey rolled her aforementioned eyes. Gabriel merely adjusted his glasses. "We're trying to cope with it... it's all so new and overwhelming."

"No, totally, man, I get it! That is SICK."
He laughed and hurriedly clapped their hands in a triumphant high five. "Welcome to the believer party, kiddos!! It's an honor!"

He then jolted with excitement and quickly grabbed a chair to whirl against the table, eagerly seating.

"Dude dude dude, I get it now! You guys totally came here to see me, cuz you want me to join the party, yeah?"

Wow... he wasn't as clueless as he appeared.

Audrey perked up, stunned. "*Exactly*."
Troy grinned excitedly.

"Oh man, you've no idea how long I've been waiting for this!" His eyes shot at each of them, "To be a part of a team? To put to actual use my monster skills and expertise?! This is a dream come true, bro!"

In that second, Troy turned in his chair to face Spike.

"Bro, how long on their pizzas?"
Spike straightened up. "Probably like, 15 minutes?"

"Excelente! Plenty of time!"
Mr. Brooke shot up and waved for them.

"Follow me, my dudes."

~

The party followed Troy out through the back.

They were curious as to what he was exactly up to, and what he had 'plenty of time' to show them. And that's when he halted and they all came to a sudden stop, where he jumped forward and presented like a showman a vehicle. A van, to be precise. They all gawked.

"I present to you, my sweet! The famous Valhalla!"

Audrey's eyes enlarged. "The Viking term for heaven??"

"Precisely, dude! She and I have traveled all over together and she has not once failed me! We used this little beauty for pizza deliveries, before we got our Ferrari!"

"You-- you use a *Ferrari* for pizza deliveries?"

Troy laughed at the confused female Beckhart. But she was genuinely seeking council for what she was hearing,

"Who ARE you?? *What* are you??"

He leaned against his trusty van, knocking on the door with grace. "She's still going strong, dudes... reason I'm showing ya is, well, she's perfect for the line of work we're gonna do!"

He then slid open the door to the backseat, revealing a marvelously set up display of special equipment. He reveled in their astonished reactions.

"Holy cow... Troy! You never said you were so loaded!" Amelia ran for the display, and stroked it all with immense love and care. "It's all so beautiful, I could cry!"

"That's right, Amy, I got video cameras, microphones, radio communications, lifetime supply of memory cards and hard disk backups, all the latest tricks and all the latest tools, and I got a hot piping amount of books, all loaded with endless info about any creature you can think of-- I've got it all, dudes!"

Gabriel swiveled his head at Troy, too shocked to accept the fact that Troy just happened to have all this.

"Literally why do you have this stuff?"

"I told ya, man, I've been waiting!"

"Yeah, but... it's all set up... for what?!"

"For when I go find the creatures, dude!"

He came close to Gabe,

"Why you think I settled in Hollowgrove, man? This whole place is a hot spot for mad crazy crypto and UFO activity! And more and more of these things are migrating to HERE."

Gabriel's eyes darted to Troy's. "Why??"

Brooke shrugged. "That's what we gotta figure out, man. That's what we gotta figure out."

Uncanny

  The Beckhart boy looked back at the van, laying a hand upon the sliding door. He contemplated something... something of which made him snicker. "...You missed an opportunity."
  "What's that, bro?"
Gabe tried to hold back his chuckles, "Instead of calling it Valhalla..." His eyes returned to the blonde wonder.
  "...You should have called it VAN Halen."
 As much as Troy appreciated such a name, and the fact Gabriel even knew about Van Halen... he already had enough of the Beckhart boy. "No that's it, man... you're paying for the pizza tonight."
  Naturally, however, he was messing with the richie and playfully threw an arm around his neck, as he ushered the group back inside, his face filled with happiness.
  "I think this is the start of a beautiful thing, dudes."

CHAPTER XVI
✦ THE TAPES ✦

Troy took the group back into the Shack, and the party talked for close to an hour as they ate their pizza. It was here that they told Brooke about themselves, explaining their backgrounds and reasons for approaching him about all of this to begin with... and they soon learned a little more about Troy.

At one point, he served as a cameraman for a news crew, and that is where he acquired his trusty van, Valhalla.

"I was hired by this big time news company, fresh out of college, where I landed a huge job as a camera man. The news lady was a bit of a mess and treated us like a bunch of dopes, but I put up with it in favor of having such a rad job. Things were good for awhile."

Troy laced his fingers together, as he rested his elbows upon the table in deep thought. "...That's when weird stuff started happening, man. I'm talking *freaky*."

He looked around at the few people sitting inside the restaurant, and cautiously leaned in as he pulled out a video camera. He laid it upon the middle of the table, where he pressed the play button. The video he played showed a news team walking across the road, the video presumably being shot by Brooke himself. They were hurrying towards something.

"We were doing a story about some missing people. Middle class people, you know, ones who everyone starts noticing going missing. It's only when we questioned other people, witnesses, that we realized it wasn't just those people. It was homeless ones, too. Missing by dozens. Business owners were noticing a drastic drop in the numbers hanging around the area. We couldn't make out what the pattern was. Why these dudes were being taken. Until we saw stuff... we couldn't explain."

He pointed at the camera, as the others watched intently. Brooke's news crew hurried faster. Faster towards a person who was on the ground, rocking back and forth. His entire body trembled. His eyes bloodshot. His skin a deathly pale complexion. All the vessels just underneath his skin were visible in a disturbing mixture of purple and red... almost like his very flesh was inflamed. What's more, he was talking to himself.

This sent chills down the party's spines. Especially when the lead news lady bent down to speak to the man.

"Sir, sir, are you okay?" She asked, as calmly as possible. The man did not respond to her. Just kept muttering to himself. She looked back at the camera with a frightened expression on her face. She had to keep trying to get through to the man, naturally. *"Sir please, I need to know where you've-"*

In that split second, the man grabbed her wrist and she screamed at the top of her lungs. His body heaved itself towards her, as he started to shout over her screams.

"IT'S COMING! IT'S COMING! WE'RE NOT SAFE! NO ONE IS SAFE!!"

He then grabbed her by the shoulders and violently shook her,

"YOU CAN'T LET IT TAKE ME AGAIN, DON'T LET IT TAKE ME AGAIN!!!"

The other crew members rushed to rip the man away from her, as he threw himself into a screaming, delirious fit.

The tape ended.

Brooke shifted, uncomfortably.

"...That was one of the missing homeless people. This man used to be... well... one of the best and brightest. He used to be a broker, until his wife left him, taking his daughter with her. He was a literal honors student in college, and was a highly successful dude. But everything fell apart when he lost his job due to a change in command, and he was left with nothing. Then this happened... poor guy was put into an asylum. He displayed extremely abnormal blood work, and there was clear evidence that *something* had tampered with his body, and still *was* tampering with it. He would have been taken seriously... if not for the declaration of a creature taking him."

He shook his head.

"But it didn't end there, man. Pretty soon... the news crew began experiencing severe doses of paranoia. Telling me they were seeing stuff. Their eyes were playing tricks on them or something. Stuff in the sky, stuff down here with us. I started looking into it. And man... the amount of people who reported strange stuff in the area was insane. Literally insane. None of them were taken seriously. People who saw stuff, people they loved going missing left and right. Most never came back. Some... they returned, but never the same. And 99% went where the homeless broker dude went... things got worse. Two of the news crew? They vanished. I looked everywhere for them. They weren't at their homes, they weren't answering texts or calls or anything. They just vanished without a trace... and then our lovely Janine, the news lady? She stopped showing up to work. Didn't answer our calls or texts, either. When I tried to visit her, she just screamed at me to go away. Like she literally did not want anyone to come near her. She was petrified."

Audrey leaned closer, "What was causing this?"

"No idea, man. I never got the chance to find out. I quit. And I left the city."

Audrey seemed appalled by this,

"WHAT?! What about Janine?! And the other news people?! And the homeless people?!" Troy looked away.

"...They never found them. The broker dude was the only one. The rest? Well, it's been years since... and still... no one knows. Janine? She quit, too. And moved far away. Changing her identity. All in hopes to keep herself safe."

Gabriel shifted, "So why did you leave? If you're so interested in the supernatural, why abandon such a goldmine of a situation?"

"Truth? I was scared at first. I had to leave, afraid I'd be next. But... something happened when I got to my next living situation. Traveling from Florida to Alabama... that's when I saw it."

Troy inserted another tape and pressed play.
The group was in shock. Through the video... they could see it.

"A full blown Skunk Ape, man."

A creature built like a primate trotted across a field, its dark fur covered in wet long grass, mud and moss. It was a good distance away from Troy, but the unsettling part about this was that its gaze was dead set on the man. A gaze that did not leave. It almost appeared to be stalking him.

"Oh my god... this... can't be real." Audrey's arms recoiled, as she raised a hand to her mouth.

Gabriel said nothing, just stared agape, while Amy and Quin leaned in with immense intrigue. Ivy appeared to be the only one unfazed.

The Beckhart girl looked back to the others, as her eyes fluttered in search of answers. "This had to be someone pulling a prank. It just..."

"Has to be someone dressed up? In the middle of no where?" Audrey shot Amelia a glare that cut like daggers.

"You take anything as gospel, Pine."

"It's real, man. I have countless other videos to prove I'm not crazy *or* lying." Brooke defended.

"Okay, but what if someone was following you? Or like... just knew who you were or something, and was trying to scare you."

Quin shut his eyes, shaking his head.

"Why would someone-"

"I don't know, this is just crazy!!" Brooke only held up a hand.

"It's okay, chica, I get your vibe. You're in denial." Beckhart sagged. "That makes me sound like a total close-minded skeptic."

"No, you're in denial because of how heavy it is. It's all good. That's why most people don't believe, anyway. It's not so much cuz of crazy stuff out there... it's because the crazy stuff terrifies them."

Troy turned off the camera, feeling as though he had shown enough for now. "And that's why the established order doesn't want you believing it's real, either. Cuz they don't want you in a panic, ya feel me?"

"Yeah dude, cuz like, how could you even sleep at night, knowing stuff like that is real, ya know? Most of 'em probably wouldn't even leave their house."

Audrey cut her eyes up at Spike, the party forgetting the boy was even there, before her eyes turned to Troy, Amelia and Quinton. "How do *you* people even sleep, knowing this stuff is out there?"

"Because our curiosity is more powerful than our fear." Quin shifted his glasses. "It's also not a question of fear... it's respect. We respect their power, but we know they're not raving lunatic monsters hungry to kill. Most of them are relatively petrified creatures, fighting for their own survival due to near-extinction."

"Near-extinction due to people's primitive fear of the unknown." Pine sipped her drink.

Audrey stiffened her back.

"Okay, but there's totally things out there that go bump in the night that aren't all peaceful like you say most of these are."

"That's why they said *most*, Audrey." Gabe cut in, rubbing his eyes. She cut him a glare.

"There are still evil, powerful forces, dude." Troy explained.

"That's the stuff you gotta be careful of. The things that play with your head and feed on your fear like leeches. You gotta use the right judgment between the scared animal and the psycho killer."

Gabriel turned his head, being particularly quiet about the matter. His eyes fell on Ivy, who at first appeared to be busy coloring, until he noticed she was gradually cutting her eyes every so often at the others, including him.

She was a suspicious child, and he couldn't quite read her most of the time. That's when he remembered... she was a child.

"Oh crap."

Gabriel looked down at his phone to check the time.

"We've gotta get her home!"

Amy's eyes enlarged.

"Oh geez, that's right, we've got a minor."

She sipped her drink again. "Have fun, I'mma hang tight here."

"You're our ride, idiot." Audrey ridiculed.

Pine's eyes stared into the distance. "Oh yeah."

"Allow me!" Troy suddenly interjected, shooting from the table. "I'll personally take our party to deliver the little miss, so we can head back together and keep talking!"

Audrey rose her brows. "Well that's kind of you."

"Ha, it's my pleasure, Beckhart!" He wagged a finger.

"Now you dudes hang tight, while I jump-start the van!" The blonde surfer walked off, his camera and tapes piled into his arms, while the others were left with his last words processing in their minds. This made Audrey lower her aching head and hold it. "Oh god..."

~

Day time soon left Hollowgrove, darkness now slithering into the cracks of the sky, eventually enveloping it to reveal a layer

Uncanny

of stars and thin patches of clouds.

Fog set upon the town, especially into the fields and relatively country part of the land. The fog seemed to be the heaviest at one particular farm, owned by a simple but financially struggling family. Such a family was away to visit relatives, leaving their farmhand Wyatt in charge of the property.

As the sky grew darker, Wyatt got to work herding the animals into the barn. So far, he was able to get the cows, horses and chickens safely inside their stalls. Now all that was left was the goats.

The chilled air grew bitter, as it reached the evening hours, and Wyatt was feeling the full effects kicking in. He breathed into his freezing hands, as he closed the doors behind him, a shotgun strapped around his shoulder in the event of predators.

He sighed heavily, his breath becoming one with the fog. He should have grabbed his jacket from the house, but he honestly did not account for the air to become that cold so fast. Not to mention the sky growing darker sooner, with each day that passed.

He shook his head, as he withdrew his flashlight from his pocket and clicked on the button. The infernal thing was losing battery or just had bad wiring, because it conveniently refused to work for him.

He gave it a few smacks and it glitched, but inevitably came on. This left him grumbling to himself about the accursed thing.... before a noise caught his ear.

His body swung around, shining the light ahead. The noise was coming from the goats. The normal, occasional bleat was to be expected. But not when the whole tribe was bleating at the same time.

Wyatt was instantly filled with a rather unsettling chill. The news had gotten to him. The news of so many people going missing and so many attacks. He was on edge.

With a shaky hand, the youthful man pointed his weapon forward, as he did the same with the flashlight. And with a cautious step forward, he advanced towards the noise. Maybe it was a coyote. A wolf. Mountain lion. Bear. Something prowling and spooking the herd.

More than likely, if he shot at the air, the beast would run off. He just needed enough time to get them safely inside the barn, after all. Followed by him retreating to a safe refuge, of course. His eyes stared wildly at every shape, panicking when his peripheral view played tricks on him.

He entered the pasture in which the goats all conglomerated. He noticed upon seeing the creatures that they were all in a panicked state. Crying loudly. Running from something. Surely nothing could have broken through the barbed wire fen-
He stopped, as his eyes laid on the side of the fence. They widened, as he beheld the unnerving sight.

Something had chewed right through the barbed wire... leaving a large gaping hole.

His breath became shaky, his hands now trembling. His whole body swung in every direction now, as he desperately sought out the culprit. That's when the goats got louder. And he could hear the loudest cry coming from the other side of the fence.

He didn't even think. He reacted. He ran toward the cry. His body grazed through the screaming goats, as he charged to the distressed goat in question. He didn't know what he would find. He just knew he had to stop what was happening.

These weren't his goats. And he'd be an unemployed man if something ever happened to one. Something he couldn't afford, naturally... but that was the least of his worries.

He cared about this livestock. The lives of these kind animals. He wasn't about to let an intruder get even one.

He was closing in on the end of the fence. He was getting close to the other side. But he skid to a stop, however. When his flashlight flickered off. He yelped and desperately hit it repeatedly, as he cursed the infernal thing for failing him at an inconvenient time.

The sound of the goat's cries rang in his ear. He whimpered. His heart raced, as he gave it a powerful jab that finally revived it. His chance of rejoicing was cut off, however, as he heard breathing. Breathing of a nature that was not human... and something he had not heard before in any other creature he had encountered.

His own breathing became irrational, as he slowly turned his body towards the breathing, the light traveling with him. And that's when his body froze. His own breathing deafened him. His eyes felt as if they would burst from his skull at what he saw.

One of the goats was thrown on its side before him, still alive, but its eyes pleading for help. What brought terror to Wyatt, however, was not the goat...
it was what was hovering over it.

A creature as black as the darkness around it, its eyes shining a bright green. It would appear to be canine, like some kind of dog, if it weren't for the lack of all hair, and ears that resembled a bat's, with *spikes* protruding from its spine in a grotesque but strangely natural formation.

What worsened the sight of this creature... was that it spotted Wyatt. Its eyes lifted at the trembling man. Whatever it was about to do to the goat was interrupted. Now that he was here, he now knew... this creature had turned its sights on *him*.

The creature arched its back and opened its mouth to growl a horrific snarl, that which revealed long sharp fangs that stretched past its chin. Wyatt was petrified beyond all reason. For before he knew it... the creature was stepping forward.

He did not even hesitate. He bolted. A screech left from his mouth just as a screech exited the creature's, and a terrifying chase ensued between the two. The goats all wailed at the commotion, especially at the presence of the creature, and soon the rest of the farm animals took part in sounding off, as the deadly pursuit caught their ears.

Wyatt was far too busy to hear any of it, as he raced through the field and jumped over the fence, making a swift break for the barn. Whatever it was, it was hot on his heels and a mere leap away from catching him. But a stroke of luck saw Wyatt reach the barn door in a split second, and he quickly, through his screaming, slipped through the barn door and shut it behind him.

As he did, the creature was met with an unfortunate blow to the head, as it rammed into the wooden door. Wyatt stood back and pointed his rifle in the direction of the beast, his entire body trembling. "GO AWAY!! LEAVE ME ALONE!!"

Eerily, it fell quiet as the spooked animals reduced their noise, almost as if a presence was commanding them to do so. They and Wyatt watched in intense anticipation.

The farmhand stared at the barn doors, as he realized they were still opened a crack, despite the lock he placed behind him. And through that crack, he saw it.

The creature had stepped into view and was peeking at him with one eye. It barred its teeth as it locked eyes with Wyatt, and casually tilted its head to slide in a fang through the crack.

And now...

   to Wyatt's horror...

      it was chewing off the wood.

The beast began gnawing off pieces and spitting it out, creating a gaping hole at the very edge of the door. It was eating its way to the inside.

Wyatt panicked. He fired. An atrocious sound came from the creature as it jumped away. Wyatt perceived to have shot it, but he was wrong. It wasn't wounded in any way. Only startled. Before he knew it, the creature was back to chewing.

Wyatt had enough. "GET OUT!!" He shot at it again. Reload. Fire. Reload. *Fire*.

He charged towards the beast and shot again through the hole it created, the creature snarling wickedly at him, as if it was rabid. It swiped at the gun in Wyatt's possession and roared at him, backing away in surrender.

"GET OUT OF HERE! YOU STAY AWAY FROM HERE!!" He shot a final time.

This time, the creature understood the message. It snarled once more before taking off, leaving behind a trail of absolute terror. Wyatt peeked through the hole, as he watched cautiously for several minutes. It appeared to be gone... but could he trust it?

He stepped through the door when he felt he had waited long enough, and he walked with ever watchful eyes. He gazed to the left, towards the outer fields and could distinctly see something running in the distance. He knew this to be his attacker. And he saw his chance.

He quickly ran and herded the goats, the first of which being the survivor of the attack, whom he treated special after all the poor animal had to go through. It was then that Wyatt blocked off the entrances of the barn, and fortified the house for good measure. And the young man fell into a chair, planted firmly at a window to keep close watch outside.

  For he knew...

    the more he thought about it...

      the more he put everything together in his head...

        he had survived an encounter with a **Chupacabra**.

CHAPTER XVII
✦ FENDER BENDER ✦

It was a rather tight fit, but the entirety of the party managed to compact themselves into Valhalla; Troy at the wheel, Amelia at the passenger seat, while the Beckharts, Ivy, Quin, Magnus and Scrooge sat in the back.

As eccentric as Troy was, he was a surprisingly attentive driver, following every road law as calmly and smoothly as possible. The group was in a deep, tired silence since leaving the shack, coming upon the road that led through a more barren area compared to the immensely green environment of Hollowgrove.

Amelia was busily typing on her laptop, no doubt updating PineTimes, while Quin had dozed off to sleep, huddling his body against the cold wall of the moving vehicle. Gabriel was undergoing a lesson in ASL with Ivy, creating innocent small talk to better communicate with the child, whom he was becoming quite fond of. The dogs were seated in the corner, Magnus closely watching the party with his intense dark eyes, while tiny Scrooge was curled into a cozy ball, his face buried into his fluffy tail.

But Audrey? Audrey was too busy for rest or relaxation of any kind. Audrey's mind was wrapped around monsters and the supernatural. And a touch of guilt over her handling of Troy didn't help, either. She was all new to this world, and it was a frightening place. But she couldn't turn away now. There was a large part of her that... through the fear... *desired* to find out more.

"Troy?" Her voice broke the silence.
All eyes immediately turned to her. Brooke perked up in his seat to peek at Audrey from his rear view mirror. "Yeah?"
Her head turned to him and met his gaze, her expression teeming with discomfort.

"About earlier. . .I'm sorry I disrupted things. It's just... a lot to process. I'm sorry for making it sound like I think you're crazy or lying, because you're not."

It was clear that Amelia was listening in on the conversation, as her head was slightly cocked to one side, her typing coming to a slower pace. Troy himself couldn't help but smile warmly at the Beckhart girl, his eyes glistening with gratitude for her consideration.

"Aw Audrey, you're totally cool! I dig the apology, but it's not necessary, man. This is a scary business, lemme tell ya." She shifted in her seat, her eyes glued to the floor, her head resting against the wall.

"I'd like to see the other videos...if that's okay. I'm ready." Brooke nodded with a grin, and pointed behind him with his thumb. "Cam's back there with you. Check it."

Audrey looked to her right where Gabriel sat, and he pointed to Ivy at the small box that contained the camera and tapes. The little girl proceeded to reach in and hand it to them. The Beckharts removed the device and inserted a new tape, where Audrey rested the camera on her lap and pressed the play button. She briefly glared over to the passenger chair, where she almost missed Pine's head quickly avert away, indicating full well that the strange red-haired nutjob was indeed eavesdropping.

But Audrey brushed her aside and put her full attention on the video. Said video, of course, containing footage of Brooke recording himself, traveling to a random location unlike the previous he had visited, and a chance encounter took place. Such encounters Audrey had trouble wrapping her head around.

Sea monsters, paranormal activity, suspicious figures in every type of lighting of the day or night, that Brooke had repeatedly caught on tape. A part of her wondered if he was somehow orchestrating these tapes as a way to deceive new believers, and witness their lives spiral out of control. The other was astounded by the things unraveling before her eyes.

It was rather fascinating. Something of which she never thought she would think. The scariest part of these videos wasn't just seeing the creatures... it was the idea that these creatures now resided in Hollowgrove. The very ones responsible for the disappearances.

Audrey looked down at the tapes, taking a peak at the labels. Lizard Man, Ghost, Thunderbird, Sasquatch, Mothman, Chupacabra, Mermaid, the list went on and on. She turned to her phone to look up the aforementioned creatures. Chills were sent up and down her spine.

These creatures were not only famous for their terrifying appearance... they were famous for what they did to their victims. Audrey never paid much attention to spooks and folklore. Not until now. And she was petrified. Troy was right. The thought of these entities being real terrified people.
So they closed their eyes to it.

She held her head, closing the laptop, feeling as though she were going to be sick. Amelia only smirked at this, gently shaking her head. "Newbie..."

Troy took the more compassionate approach, and peaked over at the Beckhart girl.

"Don't worry, man, I'm telling you, it's a lot to process! I had a hard first time, too!"

"What exactly is the goal..."
Their eyes turned to Gabriel, who turned his to them.

"Are we out to expose these creatures for their actions and reveal them to the world... or are we out to find them first, and put them into some kind of protective custody?"

His back straightened.

"Just who are we protecting? *Them* or their victims?"
Troy and Amelia both glared at each other, not exactly knowing how to answer that. Perhaps there was no real answer. Maybe they just didn't know. Maybe the truth of it all was far too self-intoxicating, than the overall outcome for the rest of the world. This could almost make one feel like a monster themself.

The party was a little too distracted, however. Too distracted to remember they were within a moving vehicle, and too distracted to pay any attention to the road in front of them. To where when Troy looked back ahead, the air was filled with a shrill shriek, as a blur of black leaped in front of the van, and a ferocious snarl could soon be heard... when the van rammed into it.

The van steered out of control, the entire group screaming at the top of their lungs. Troy struggled to put the vehicle to a halt, as quickly as possible, all while Amelia, the Beckharts, Ivy and Quin held on for dear life, their whole world literally going in circles. Scrooge and Magnus slid around as if on ice, yelping at the sudden change in conditions, their claws scratching the metal surface, as they attempted to plant their paws.

The ordeal seemed as if it lasted an hour, but in truth, it only lasted seconds. The van was finally put to rest, and the group was rattled to a heart-jolting halt. They all awaited, as if they now were entering the afterlife.

Scrooge's little body could not withstand the traumatic experience and he plopped to the floor. Magnus, however, recovered quickly and rushed to check on Ivy, licking her tiny face, as she rose from her side. The Beckharts snapped out of their shock and turned to one another, to make sure each other was alright.

Quin merely shook and held his aching head, having banged it against the metal wall beside him. Amelia scrambled to lift herself up in the enormous seat, trying to readjust her disarrayed spectacles. Troy was the slowest of the group to recover, no doubt having to do with the fact his company were all younger than he, but as soon as he did come to, he immediately turned his attention to the others.

"Is... is everyone okay?"

"If I say 'no', do I get a prize?" Quin grunted.

Gabriel shifted.

"What in the world... what *was* that?"

Just as these words were uttered out of the Beckhart boy's mouth, Magnus' head turned slowly toward the right metal wall of the van and a deep, intimidating growl progressed from his throat. Such a growl was made clearer when he opened his mouth, revealing his sharp barred teeth. It was almost as if he was honing in on something through the very wall.

This quickly drew the attention of the rest of the party. Amelia turned her head to the window and looked out. The very breath in her got trapped inside her lungs. "OH CRAP."

The others glared at one another; that is most obviously *not* a positive statement. Quinton shot up, grabbed the door handle and yanked it, until it slid open on its own. Audrey gasped and held her mouth, while the others widened their eyes.

On the other side of the road laid an animal, its fur black and mangy, and its body curled into a ball, which made it hard to identify just what it was. More than likely, it was a stray dog, as they could not spot any immediate identifying tags.

Quin widened his eyes, staggering from his unstable position.

"We're MURDERERS!!"

Gabriel averted Ivy's eyes away, but took quick notice that Magnus was still growling, and this made him suspicious.

In fact... Magnus' growls were getting worse.

Amelia did not give the others any time to debate the matter.

"GET OUT OF HERE BEFORE THE COPS SHOW UP, NOW!!"

"Why would the *cops* show up?!" Quinton exclaimed.

She swiveled her whole body around.

"I AM *NOT* GETTING CRUCIFIED BY PETA FOR THIS, YOU DO *NOT* KNOW WHAT THOSE PEOPLE ARE CAPABLE OF!!"

As much confusion as Amelia's fear of PETA brought the other members of the group, Audrey was not going to let this deter her. For she saw movement come from the creature.

"It's still alive!"

Troy widened his gaze, *"What?"*

The animal shifted its legs faintly.

"Oh my god, that's even worse, it'll live to file a lawsuit, DRIVE!"

"What the FRICK, Amelia, we can't just leave it!!!"

In that moment, Audrey threw herself out of the vehicle before anyone had the chance to stop her. Before she even had a chance to stop herself. This caused Gabriel to leap forward to try and grab her, "Audrey, wait!"

It was no use. She was already on the road, marching towards the stirring animal. Her actions were noble, yes, but ill timed. Ill timed, for... had she have waited only a moment before blazing out of safety to assist the creature... she would not find herself frozen in her tracks, only mere feet away from it.

The creature was recovering... its legs bent and coiled underneath it, as it began to unwind its body from its seemingly injured state... and from this, its arched back straightened, revealing long, grotesque spikes that protruded outwards.

Audrey's eyes bulged from within her skull, as she watched it rise from the ground and lift its head, presenting its strange bat-like ears... and incredibly sharp, petrifying fangs.

"Oh my god..." She uttered.

Amelia squirmed in her seat almost immediately, when she saw the event unfold before her. "Oh no..."

It finally hit her.

"Oh no, oh no, oh no, oh no, OH NO."

Audrey could not even move her body. She was much too shocked for that. "Oh my god... oh my god..."

The creature now stood before her... and opened its bright green, glowing eyes. In that second, Audrey knew exactly what it was. **"OH MY GOD!"**

"Hooolllyyyy craaaappppp!!" Troy exclaimed, as he pulled back his own hair, whilst Quinton uttered something under his breath, and Amelia struggled to unbuckle herself to rush out of the vehicle. Gabriel was having none of it, and he sprung his body forward.

"AUDREY, GET BACK TO THE VAN, *NOW!*"

His sister snapped out of her terrified state just in time. Just in time to narrowly miss the Chupacabra lunging towards her, which gave birth to a horrifying race to the van. The group all screamed, as Audrey ran with all her might back to them, the creature right on her heels.

Audrey feared she would not make it... until Magnus stepped forward and sent out a powerful bark, which made the Chupacabra briefly skid to a halt. It was just the split second she needed to leap back inside, before the creature jumped forward, right into the metal wall in front of it.

Audrey fell back, taking Quinton and Gabriel with her, all while Magnus was snarling violently at the fearsome being just on the other side of the door.

"TROY, GET US THE FRICK OUT OF HERE!!" Amelia screamed. Brooke, with a shaky hand, fumbled to turn his keys, but when he did... the engine neglected to start.

It did not help that he felt someone peaking over his shoulder, and looking toward it also did not help, as he saw it was only Quinton hovering beside him, taping the ordeal with his video camera. "Dude, *REALLY?!*"

"SHUT UP AND LET ME DO ME, FLORIDA."

Pine hung herself from her seat,

"Why is your van out to KILL US?!"

"I. DON'T. *KNOW!*"

Suddenly, a black blur landed on the hood of the van, and the culprit was almost immediately, aggressively, pressing against the windshield, which made all inside scream the highest they had ever screamed. The Chupacabra snarled madly at them, biting at the glass, and smashing its head in to break inside.

Troy desperately attempted to ward him off in the midst of screaming, which included him throwing notebooks at the windshield, and flapping the wipers into the already furious animal's face. Amelia attempted to shield her face by holding up her laptop, which was a smart move on her part, as Troy's attacks deflected towards her. Quinton... well, he was hiding his face behind the camera.

The chaos was only made worse when Magnus suddenly emerged from nowhere, shoving past Quin, and thrust himself into a screaming match with the creature, making everyone around them permanently deaf.

The arrival of Magnus added fuel to the fire for the Chupacabra, its eyes seeming to glow even brighter and more intensely. And from this fury, the creature lifted up its head and instantly came down, drilling its two fangs right through the glass. It proceeded to yank its head back, taking out shreds of glass with it, leaving a chilling, gaping hole as a result. All it had to do now was wedge in between that, as dedicated as it was, and it would be over.

"GET OUT OF THE WAY!" Screamed Audrey from behind. The others barely had enough time to look back before the Beckhart girl abruptly leaped forward, sticking her arm through the glass, and pepper-sprayed the Chupacabra in the face. The creature went from snarling to crying within seconds, and thrashed its head around, in a desperate attempt to guard its now burning eyes.

Without further ado... it sent out one final cry... and it bolted. The party was now left in silence. Complete, bone-chilling silence.

Ivy, who was eerily emotionless the entire ordeal, looked to the door. Before anyone could blink, she rushed for it and slid it open, making Magnus and soon everyone else snap their attention to her.

"*Ivy!*" Gabriel exclaimed, once again finding himself grabbing for an already bolting female. Audrey hurriedly ran after her, "Ivy, *wait!!*"

Audrey did not have to go far, as the little girl had stopped. Ivy stared ahead after the fleeing Chupacabra, which disappeared into the field, the last thing Audrey seeing as she joined the child's side. She looked down at her, noting how intent and grave Ivy looked... it wasn't fear, it wasn't shock. It was contemplation. Like she was studying its last images in her mind. Perhaps also the same realization that all of them had... the same wide-eyed marvel that overtook them.

Ivy's eyes lifted to the elder girl, her face just as stern and cold. Audrey did not know how to handle her. She merely put her arm protectively around the child's shoulders, and looked back in the direction of the creature, before changing her view to the others.

Gabriel was currently holding the dogs back, Quin was lowering the pointed camera at the two girls, and Amelia and Troy were leaned in, in total shock. Quinton ran his hand through his hair, shaking his head.

"What the crap just happened???"
Troy only turned his head to Quin, gradually snapping out of his shocked state.

"...Your first monster encounter, dude… your very first monster encounter."

CHAPTER XVIII
✦ SECRETS OF A SMALL TOWN ✦

The events of that chilling evening seemed to supernaturally make the residents of Hollowgrove even more skittish and paranoid than they already were. Many a Hollowgrovian flooded the church that night for sanctuary.

There has always been something about a church that brings peace, and a sense of security for those in distressing situations. Something one can't quite explain. It goes beyond the realm of the unknown. Beyond spirituality. Beyond the mysteries of this universe. And the church of Aidan Poe was no exception.

The Irish immigrant traveled years ago to the states, and had established himself firmly in the strange little mysterious town. His church had since become a staple for the people, and he himself was a highly respected, trusted member of their community.

Among the scared individuals pouring in were the families of the missing: spouses, children, parents, siblings, friends... so many came, fell on their knees, and begged for their loved ones to return.

It had been months. Months of waiting, the agonizing anxiety of the truth lingering in the back of their minds... that they were not coming back. No prayers or acts of comfort could quench that fear. That feeling of dread that at any day, news would reach them... and it would be the opposite of what they prayed and wished for. These were the times that Poe dreaded the most.

As a man of faith, he was bound to trust in his convictions and the teachings he so fervently stressed to others. But pretty words could only go so far when tragedy and the horrors of reality showed its ugly face. That is the stage of loss. When people are most susceptible to falling from their beliefs that once fueled them. He hated these times most of all. For he had lost many a friend to this stage.

The days were growing darker for him. He found himself many a night sitting alone in the sanctuary, and talking to the Lord in a completely empty church, for what turned into hours. He tried to rationalize how such terror and suffering could exist in a world lived upon by God's children. Tonight was one of those nights.

The people had went home and he was left sitting in a pew, clutching onto his bible firmly with both hands. Poe took deep, shaky breaths. The sadness and despair of his visitors remained, as an unwelcome presence, paralyzing the peace he worked so diligently to maintain. Such a large hole filled his heart. Such a loneliness he couldn't shake.

His eyes couldn't even lift to the ceiling. He couldn't find the words within him to come out of his mouth as he sat in a dismal, unbearable silence. His eyes were growing heavy, having not gotten any sleep for the past two nights. His dreams... his dreams were haunting him for a solid week. Disturbing his thoughts even in the midst of his duties, no amount of caffeine to keep him functioning. He was losing his grip on reality.

In the midst of the tears of his congregation, of the loved ones of the missing, all he could do was sit in silence. He could barely bring himself to utter a word. This was crippling his psyche, and it was showing.

"I see you're still too cheap to get a maid for this place." Poe's eyes then popped open. The voice behind him cut through the silence like a knife, down into his very core. A voice he so longed to hear from again. And that... that brought a spark of joy back into his soul.

He immediately stood up straight, turning right around to face who sneaked into his church without so much as a scuffle. He smiled wide as he saw his old and very dear friend; Talbot.

The scraggly man, dressed in his worn short-sleeved, blue button shirt and brown work pants, approached the pastor with both hands in his pockets. His bald head glistened as the candle light reflected off of it, which made Poe want to laugh.

Talbot nodded at the sanctuary, obviously trying to poke fun of the place to lighten the situation.

"I mean, honestly... look at these pews. Dust everywhere. And the light fixture is pathetic. You actually expect this place to get business. No wonder everyone's crying... that dust pile-up is enough to choke a horse."

Poe shook his head at his friend's rather inappropriate humor, trying to hide the snicker escaping his lips.

"I mean, you're welcome to come and help me out. I'm

known for my community status, not my financial status. Last time I checked, maids cost money."

The Irishman went to picking up a few things knocked out of place, Talbot's jokes seeping into his subconscious, which now turned into a paranoia.

"I'm good, pal, got enough to handle back at the shop."

"Tell me about it..."

Talbot chuckled. "You too, huh? I've got loads of idiots pouring in to get all the 'monster hunting' tools. Fools are bound to shoot their own selves in the leg."

Poe's eyes then shifted slyly at him, in a knowing scold that made Talbot uneasy. "*Speaking* of that..."

He pushed a pew in its right place.

"...I'd appreciate you not sending some poor misguided teenagers my way, armed with whole cases of bottled water. I'm not a bloody tourist trap gift shop."

Talbot rubbed his neck,

"Aw that....yeahhh... sorry, brother. They just... well... they hit my soft spot. Them kids were just so excited..."

"Yeah, they all are. They're so excited... so excited to chase after monsters and demons, and proving to the world that all those movies and TV shows were right, and it's all some thrilling adventure they get to brag about to their friends."

He shook his head.

"...When in reality, they're gonna get themselves killed..."

"We were no different at that age, Poe."

"Aye... we weren't." His eyes turned away.

"...Then look what happened."

At this, Talbot turned his head away.

"...We can't... we can't blame ourselves for..."

His voice trailed off, leaving Poe clutching the wood beneath his hands, as harsh memories flooded his mind. Talbot decided to turn both their attention away.

"Beckhart kids are back in town."

Aidan's interest was piqued, his eyes slowly gravitating to his friend. "...I see..."

Talbot bent down to pick up a bible that had dropped to the floor, where Aidan crossed his arms and turned to him.

"Have you spoken to them yet?"

"...No. I'm getting trusty young Lycan to take care of that for me."

"Heh, Lycan... that boy's been with you for years. Ever since he was... 12, was it?"

"10. Day his old man gave him a black eye the size of a football."

Aidan could sense great anger growing in Talbot's voice, which he felt just as strongly, as neither the two men could stomach the existence of Lycan's father. "Please tell me he's still in jail."

"For the time being... they gave him too short a sentence, though. He'll be out too fast for my liking."

Poe nodded his head in agreement, before eventually lifting his eyes to study his friend, seeking out an answer to a pressing question.

"...Why did you come here tonight, Russ? Surely it was about more than just the sanitary status of my church."

Russell rubbed his hands together, gently kicking the side of a pew. "...It's uh... it's those kids." He wrung his fingers, trying to collect his thoughts. "...I can't get them out've my head, you know? I just... I gotta talk to them... I've gotta."

Poe's eyes began to drift off.

"Talbot, you know we can't-"

"I saw them yesterday, Poe. I saw them. They were out, with that Pine girl and some other kid. And I know what they're doing... they're looking for them. They're looking for the creatures. They have no idea what they're getting themselves into."

Aidan's eyes narrowed. "So you think you can step in and act as their teacher?? Train them and show them the way, is that it?"

"*No.* I want them to stay as far away as possible. I'd *never* encourage it."

Poe didn't say anything at first... until he stepped forward, holding his bible close to his heart. "If they're as stubborn as you and I were... you won't have a choice."

Hearing this only brought even further despair to Russell's heart. He had hoped for some form of comfort or encouragement from his friend, coming to him that night... but instead, his quiet fears were only cemented in truth.

Poe was correct. If the Beckhart kids were motivated enough

in their pursuit, there was no force on the planet that could derail them from their path. And therefore, there was truly nothing Talbot could do to stop them.

Poe walked on, abruptly ending the conversation. Perhaps it was due to their brief chat already becoming too revealing, and who knew who might have been near to listen... or maybe because the past was still an open, burning wound for both of them, and allowing it to resurface would only make the wounds fester. It was clear Poe's walking away was his way of politely telling Talbot to shut up. So Russell pivoted the opposite direction, sighing heavily through his tired, aging body.

"So long, old friend..."

But that was when he halted. An immediate, paralyzing halt. One that a person does when they suddenly catch sight of an unpleasant, distasteful individual. Either one teeming with disgust or pure horror. Unfortunately for Talbot, that is the exact kind of person that entered his sights.

All the hairs on his body stood on end, as he locked his gaze on the one entering and drawing near.

A distinct clang broke the once peaceful silence, and echoed throughout the entire sanctuary. Naturally, this caught the immediate attention of Poe.

Both men now faced the visitor, a short distance away from each other, and watched the individual make himself welcome, stepping onto the glossy marble floor with polished oxfords, donning an incredibly expensive dark grey suit that was devoid of any wrinkles or imperfections in the slightest. The suit, complete with a black tie and glistening black leather gloves, only complimented the positively unnerving appearance of its owner. A weaselly, thin sort of man, with dark eyes and slender jawline. His irises were almost black, his hair even darker and just as thin as the rest of him, that stretched to his shoulders, and looked to contain all the conditioner Hollowgrove could afford.

His face... his face wasn't menacing, per say... it was just the look he gave... he was ageless and smug, and had all the characteristics of someone with an ounce of money and power to flaunt. His upper lip and chin were occupied by a well maintained mustache and goatee, while his skin was a mixture of olive and soft caramel, that only added to his dark and enriched appearance.

In his hand was a relatively beautiful, well crafted black cane with silver knobs on both ends, that he did not at all require to walk, but rather use as a symbol of his power and poise... and also as a weapon, if the time commanded it.

Seeing this man made both Poe and Talbot's every sense to recoil. The worst part was... they didn't even fully understand why. The man swaggered inside the church as if he owned it and was the stunning guest of honor. His putrid little smirk only deepened when his body halted, and his dark, mesmerizing gaze landed on the two men across from him. The smirk itself was unsettling. Now his stare only made them grow physically ill.

"Ah... Russell Talbot... and Aidan Poe!"
His smirk turned into a grin, revealing the shiniest and whitest teeth they had even seen on a man.

"I didn't expect to see a man like *you* here at the church, Mr. Talbot."
Talbot swallowed, trying hard not to take any offense.

"...I uh... accidentally stumbled in. Mistook it for a pub."
The man laughed at the obvious joke of a lie.

"I could say the same for you, sir..." Poe uttered as loud as his nerve-fractured throat could allow. "What's our esteemed and terribly busy mayor doing out of the city? And into my humble little church, no less?"

The mayor's eyes gained a rather alarming streak at that second, and his attempted charming grin turned to one fueled with mischievous passion.

"Oh gentlemen, I thought it was really quite obvious... I have come to pray for the dear, poor souls who are lost in this neglected little town!"

He walked so quickly and effortlessly past both Talbot and Poe, that they barely had time to register that he was already at the alter, staring down at the wall of candles and framed photos before him. He pointed with the tip of his cane at each of the photos-- ones of men, women, children-- who were among the many missing individuals from Hollowgrove and Casper City.

"I needed to come to a quiet, holy place for such an action. One I know I'll be welcomed and respected as a man and not... well, let's face it... those people worship me at times! You've no idea how suffocating it is."

He shook his head in a poor attempt to appear sympathetic.

Talbot and Poe both exchanged a glance that had the same knowing look of distrust and suspicion. Why the immensely self important and accomplished Ripley Ravenwood, mayor of their town and neighboring city, was wasting his time at a small church, when he could be... literally anywhere else? Trying to appear as if he actually cared about the citizens he had been leaving in decay for all those years.

Ripley's demeanor quickly became less sorrowful and more somber. As if he had changed masks in between the two's glance to one another. His back was turned, but the tone in his voice painted the picture of his current expression, as he poked one of the photos with his cane, "Tell me, Poe… how many came tonight?"

When Poe did not answer, Ripley grew impatient. He slightly pivoted his head in the pastor's direction. ***"How many?"***

Poe straightened his back.

"...Most of the families, I gather... they're desperate."

Ravenwood slowly nodded his head, as if satisfied with his answer. He then turned back around and walked towards the two men. His mask was changed once again, donning the one found on a wealthy man of extreme arrogance.

"I'm proud of the work that you do, Poe. You must bear such a heavy weight, to carry all these people for so long. Really, sir, you must be commended."

"That's not necessary, I merely do what I judge is best."

"Well the Almighty thanks you, I'm sure. Keep doing it and I'm certain you'll be showered with lots of riches and fine living."

Ripley chuckled, a chuckle in which made the men tense.

"Speaking of which... I'd like to make a contribution."

He then took two thin fingers, reaching into the inside of his jacket, and pulled out a small folded paper. A paper he dropped onto the ledge of a pew. "Just a small fund, nothing to become hysterical about."

He slithered past the two, tapping his cane against Talbot's arm in acknowledgment, before clanging it once again upon the floor. "Maybe get you a maid for this place..."

Talbot and Poe both instantly snapped their heads in Ripley's direction. Ripley did not bother to look back.

"Good night, gentlemen. Say hello to that boy Lycan for me, Talbot. I look forward to seeing you both again very soon."

Just like that, he was gone. His departure made the two gravely unsettled and weary. Why, well, his arrival was unexpected, his visit somehow intimidating, and his sudden exit brought more questions than answers.

There was a lot of mystery surrounding the man, and things said that sent their minds reeling... the most important thing they took notice of, however, was the reasoning of why he supposedly came.

Unless it was an incredibly condensed, silent version, Ripley never prayed to God. Which stated the obvious truth. He didn't come on behalf of the victims.

He came for them.

CHAPTER XIX
◆ EMOTIONAL RESPONSE ◆

It was rather difficult to put into words what they had just experienced. For Troy, it was nothing new to see such a creature, but being attacked by it? Now that shook him to his core. For the others, however... it was nothing like anything they had ever experienced. Being attacked by an animal already has its level of terror... but when you are attacked by an animal that is not supposed to even exist, that does numbers on your psyche.

   It took the group roughly 15 minutes to resume their trip.
Snapping out of their shocked state? 3 minutes
Fixing Valhalla? 5 minutes
Fleeing the scene as quickly as possible? 60 seconds
Arrival back to town? 6 minutes
Time it took Audrey to have a panic attack, and fling open the door of a moving vehicle? 0 seconds

   There was only a brief silence as they entered back into town, before the Beckhart girl snapped, screamed for Troy to stop the van, as she proceeded to slide open the door. Troy screeched to a halt, as she leaped out hurriedly, her breathing becoming irrational and intense.

   She ran a good distance away from the vehicle, fueled by anxiety, but she was quickly followed by Amelia, who launched from the van after her, zooming in front of her, and throwing up her hands in a desperate attempt to stop her.

   "Hey hey hey, wait a minute, listen, I know that was freaky, but this is actually a good thing!"

 This set Audrey off into a state of complete shock, her mouth hanging wider than a feeding pelican.

   "ARE YOU SERIOUS RIGHT NOW?! DO YOU EVEN REALIZE WHAT THAT FREAKING WAS?!"

   "YES! And it's BEAUTIFUL!"

The Beckhart girl flicked her finger in the direction they came from. "THAT was NOT *BEAUTIFUL*!"

   "Yes it is!! Think about it, we've got evidence! Quinton got it all taped, we can finally prove things now! They'll actually *listen* to us!"

"Amelia, they are *never* going to listen. *Ever!* Don't you get it? They don't want to believe! They don't want to accept those things are real! And why would they?! God, I mean, come on, that thing was out of a freaking nightmare! All these people will do is shut it down as some special effects spoof, and you'll be even *more* of a joke than you already are!"

Her head turned to Troy and Quinton, before it turned back to Amelia. "People have no respect for you three! They all think you're insane, or just plain idiots! You're never going to be taken seriously, so FORGET IT!"

"I, for one, thought the encounter went **really** well."

"Oh, SHUT UP QUINTON!"

"Okay." Quin retracted his head back into the van. She shoved past Amelia, who swirled around, trying to determine what the Beckhart girl was doing.

"Where do you think you're going?!"

"I'm taking Ivy home, away from you people!"

"Audrey, you can't run away from this! You saw it, too!"

"And I've seen enough! I'm getting that little girl and myself home and I'm-"

"-Just going to forget it ever happened? Close your eyes and pretend it's all just your imagination? Oh yeah, sounds *real* familiar, Audrey!"

At this, Audrey turned back around.

"Go on, do what you always do! Ignore the truth, ignore your friends, ignore what really matters, and get back to your cushy little worthless life! I'm done trying to convince you! Cuz I'm SICK of your crap!"

"You're sick of---" Audrey couldn't even finish her sentence. Her blood boiled, her heart raced, her every bone rattled with the urge to attack.

"Go and get yourself killed for all I care, you little freak!"

"I WILL! Ya know why? Cuz it'll be worth it! They'll finally believe me, and everyone else like me, and that's something I will *gladly* give my life for! For people to **wake up**! Like YOU!"

Audrey's urges led her to viciously run up to the red head and point at her with both fingers. "You are out of your MIND!"

"I must be for ever indulging being around YOU again!!"

"Ladies, ladies, LADIES!!" Troy came charging in, splitting the two apart like a grocery divider on a conveyor belt.

"I think we all need to calm down and take a big step away, dudes! We all got a little excited, that's okay, but I won't have you acting like two hungry hyenas fighting over a termite nest!"

He waved at the two, "Now walk it off, cool down! *We'll* take Ivy home, cuz I ain't having you bringing your bad vibes into the van!"

Amelia's mouth dropped at this, but Audrey simply grit her teeth. Pine couldn't believe she was banned from riding with her own. Audrey, however, expected a punishment. Things were getting out of hand, but the sad part was... she didn't care. She saw a chance to lash out. And she went for it.

She turned to her brother, folding her arms.

"Gabriel, come on. Let's go."

However... her brother did not budge. Her eyebrows crinkled.

"Gabe... home... *please*."

His eyes fell to the van floor, stroking Magnus' fur as the powerful dog stood guard over everyone inside. His silence said more than words ever could.

Her body sunk. "...You're staying with them?"

The hurt cracked in her voice, her eyes swelling with tears, as a slight sense of betrayal sneaked into her, without consent.

"...After what happened, you're staying with *them*? Really?"

Audrey's gaze scanned each member of the current party, trying her best to keep from shedding tears. Amelia could not look at her when the Beckhart girl's eyes landed on her, and her head faced down. At last, Audrey shook her head and turned to leave.

"This is insane."

With her own brother choosing the Assembly over her... after all the years of them vs. the world... her body still shaking from the terror of what happened... the cold creeping within her from the chilly air, topped with her own words ringing back into memory... Audrey could not fathom any more of this day.

She walked onward, leaving the group behind, heading towards the town which was in close proximity.

"Audrey... Audrey, wait!"

To her surprise...it was Amelia. But that did not stop her. She couldn't face them again. She was too filled with hurt and guilt.

She simply kept walking.

Despite the tension between the two, Amelia knew her too well. She knew how stubborn she was, and she knew with all the calling her voice could muster, that she would not be able to bring her back. She didn't bother another minute.

While she wasn't sorry for how she felt, she knew that they both had crossed a line and she knew that neither of their stubborn selves would ever apologize for it.

It was no use. Audrey was out. It was just the five of them now.

~

Valhalla drove through the now darkened streets of Ivy's neighborhood. Everyone inside was stricken with an awkward silence. Troy allowed Pine to come back, on the condition she did not argue with anyone. But she couldn't bring herself to saying anything, anyway. They couldn't talk about what had happened. Maybe they could have, if not for Audrey and Amelia's argument.

Perhaps in time, maybe even Audrey herself would have realized how extraordinary the encounter actually was. But no... the issue resided not with the experience. It resided within the group itself. They were far too emotionally damaged. Too filled with secrets amongst themselves to unite, as they had hoped.

They did not have the trust in each other. The loyalty to each other. Nothing strong enough to keep them as a team. And now with Audrey gone... they honestly wondered if they would even have the heart in trying anymore.

With a quiet "This is it" from Amelia, Troy stopped the vehicle. Ivy's home rested to their left.

"Okay, Ivy... it's time to go, sweetheart." Gabriel spoke gently, helping her up.

Quin opened the door for them as they crawled out, Gabe taking hold of her hand. Magnus jumped down next to them, and the three faced the rest of the group.

"Night, little rock star." Troy said with a genuine smile.
"You did awesome today."

"Night, Ivy." Quin and Amelia said, in humorous unison.
Ivy signed good night, a hint of gloominess in her expression.
Gabriel honestly could not bear to linger any longer, and he

quickly closed the door, hurrying for the house.

It appeared Kathryn was waiting for them, for she opened the door just as they had entered the property. Thankfully, she was not mad. She beamed when she saw the little girl and her new friend, with Magnus trotting happily back into the warm safety of their home.

"Welcome back." The kind woman greeted, as she held the door for the two to walk through.

As soon as everyone was inside, she shut the door and rubbed her hands together.

"Whew, it's chilly outside! Did you two have a good time?" While Ivy nodded her head yes, Gabriel was a bit more responsible in the case of the truth. He had always been responsible, and not really capable of hiding things. Which always made him a bad liar growing up. Even when he didn't say, you could tell something was eating on him from the inside. Such a look resided on his face at that moment, as his head lowered to the floor. "The thing is... something did happen."

Kathryn's body perked up, as Gabriel's eyes met her's. He shifted his glasses, nervously.

"And I honestly won't blame you if you keep Ivy away from us. But... we were attacked."

Kathryn's gaze immediately fell on the girl. Ivy herself looked stone cold as ever. "Dear god... is everyone alright? What happened?!"

"Everyone's fine, it didn't even touch us... we found a creature and it messed up the van pretty good."

"Van? You mean--"

"The old grandpa vehicle outside with the pizza logo, yes." Kathryn peeked out the side window at that moment to see the van herself, which made her raise a hand to her mouth.

"So Ivy... wasn't purposely put in danger, was she?"

"We didn't even expect it. It ran in the middle of the road and we thought we hit it. Then it attacked."

The woman turned and looked down at Ivy. There seemed to be an unspoken knowledge between the two whenever they made eye contact. As if they were somehow communicating telepathically. Gabriel was strangely fascinated by it.

"Ivy... is this what you still want?"

This made the Beckhart boy straighten his back quickly, in total disbelief.

"Wha- Mrs. Chapman, she's a little girl under your care! She's not even *your* child! Something as serious as this can't be decided by-"

"You're right, Mr. Beckhart. She's not my child. She has faced things you can't imagine, and has survived horrors beyond even my knowledge. She might not tell me everything, but the things she has, she has sworn me to secrecy. Therefore, it is not in my power to fight her decisions. If she wants to go out and confront her demons, there is no stopping her. I have no authority over her. All I want from you is to make sure she is protected in what she is doing, nothing more. If there is danger, you make sure you do your duty as an adult and stop the threat as quickly as possible. You understand?"

Gabriel could not believe his ears. Never had he seen a grown individual bow so heavily to the will of a child. It was as if Mrs. Chapman didn't even *see* her as a child. But he was too stricken with astonishment to argue. Not even to utter a single confirmation of her demands.

Kathryn nodded swiftly, as she took Ivy by the hand.

"Good night, Mr. Beckhart. We'll see you tomorrow."

Ivy gave Gabriel a final glare, before her foster mother led her away. Gabe's eyes fell to Magnus, whose intense eye contact made him feel strange. Like Magnus even knew things he shouldn't have and he was bending Gabriel the same way Ivy was. The dog turned after a moment, to trot after Ivy and Kathryn, leaving Gabriel alone.

There was nothing normal about either that little girl or her canine companion. And he couldn't figure out what. What effect did she have on Kathryn, he wondered. What effect did she have on the rest of them? Who was she? Where did she come from? And why was he still compelled to return the next day?

-

The ride home was eerie. The night welcomed a whole new level of unpleasant paranoia, now that they had faced a creature that primarily hunts at night. A creature of which now yearned to finish them.

Troy, Quinton and Amelia agreed to return to the hut after

dropping Gabriel and Scrooge off at their home in the woods. They spoke amongst themselves on what they needed to research, and observations of the Chupacabra. But Gabriel said nothing. He sat in the back, holding Scrooge in his arms, as the small dog slept peacefully. The dangerous excitement of the day obviously did a number on the pooch, which left him too exhausted to do anything, other than enter a deep, silent sleep.

The Beckhart boy laid on his back, staring up at the roof of the vehicle. His mind wandered, just as it had been wandering ever since he and his sister returned home. Something in him unlocked upon reentering Hollowgrove. He had lived here his entire life, so why was it suddenly different to be its resident? Why had the urge grown within him to find the truth about everything? Like something supernaturally came over him, and took over his very soul.

Such thoughts were interrupted when his leg jingled. He looked down, his hand fumbling inside his pants pocket, and pulled out his phone. Scrooge yelped at the disturbance, to which Gabe gave a few reassuring head rubs to calm him down. He brought the phone to his ear. "Hello?"

"Mr. Beckhart? It's Terrance."

"Terrance? What's wrong? Are you alright?"

"I was about to ask you the same thing, sir. I had to pick up your sister a while ago. She was sitting alone on a bench when I came. It had me worried for you."

"You just found her like that?"

"No sir, she called me. She's home now. Do you need me to come get you? I'll be more than happy."

"No, that won't be necessary. I'm on my way home now... thank you. For looking out for both of us."

"It's my pleasure, sir. Will you be needing my services tomorrow?"

"No... no, thank you, I have it covered. Enjoy your week."

"Thank you, sir, you as well."

Gabriel hung up. Terrance... another one of their loyal drivers. While he was glad to hear that Audrey made it home safe, he was struck once again with an overwhelming sadness that he had to face, upon returning to her. He had to look her in the eye, and attempt to explain why he needed to stay. Why he needed to continue. And why it made it seem as if she was less important than his new motivation for the truth.

He dreaded having to face her. He dreaded having to...

ringgggggg.

His heart skipped a beat, as his phone yelled at him once more from his hand. Scrooge's head lifted up, dispensing what appeared to be a mutation of a growl and a whine, his sleepy eyes shooting daggers at Gabe. Gabriel only smiled nervously, and brought the phone to his ear a second time.

"Hello-"

"Where are you?"

His brows flexed.

"Audrey?"

The other three's attention snapped to him in that instant.

"Get over here right now. Tell everyone to come in."

"Wha-- what's going-"

"Just get over here. Now."

She hung up.

CHAPTER XX
✦ WHEN THE DUST SETTLES ✦

Audrey paced back and forth. Her hands were tucked beneath her fuzzy lavender sleeves, as she rubbed the woolly material together nervously, huffing and puffing enough to annoy anyone; if anyone happened to be in the house at the time. If someone were there, of course, she would not be so anxious. Anxious to have another be in her company. Because being alone right then was not something she cared to continue.

At that moment, she jumped. A gasp exited from her lungs, and she held her chest tightly as if she had just experienced a heart attack. A knock at the door. Her eyes briefly squeezed shut, but she wasted no time in her next move.

"Wh-- Who is it?"

"Who do you think? Open the stupid-"

The door flew open, making Audrey jump all over again. But a sense of relief came over her nonetheless, as she saw who was beyond the door. Gabriel was at the front holding a key, while Amelia was beside him, pursing her lips back."--Door."

She scratched her neck.

"...I may or may not have forgotten he lived here..."

Gabe charged in towards Audrey. His initial instinct, whatever happened beforehand, was to hug his sister. And that is the instinct he rolled with, embracing her firmly, realizing just how terrified she actually was. Her whole body was trembling. This was not from had happened earlier. Something else was going on.

He stepped back, cradling her head in his hands like the concerned big brother he always was, his entire demeanor shaken from the disillusioned state he was in only moments before. "What happened? Are you alright?"

"You made it sound like it was emergency on the phone." Quin uttered, his eyes wandering the household he had never been in. Troy was just as spellbound by the Beckhart Estate.

"It was... it *is*." Audrey snapped out, shaking her head. She pulled away from her brother and ran for the door, locking it as tightly and securely as possible. That's the moment when

Uncanny

Gabriel and Amelia noticed what Quinton and Troy were noticing. Something unnerving. Something they were too distracted with Audrey's terrified state to initially catch.

The place was a wreck. Items were thrown off the shelves, and scattered all over the floor. Cushions were ripped from the couch and chairs, framed photos and paintings dismantled from the walls. Food and dishes were pulled out of all the cabinets. Even the fridge and freezer were not safe from the war path. Rugs were overturned, and all the curtains in the room were closed and held together with bag clips.

Gabriel was once again, for the repeated time that day, finding himself in a complete state of shock. "Audrey, what in the world happened here?! Did someone break in again???"
The female Beckhart rushed past him and peeked through a curtain, her hands still shaking beneath her sleeves.

"I came home… everything was as we left it. Everything. I checked all the rooms. Our desks. Our closets. Under our beds. The security system was on. Nothing had been touched. So, I was tired, things felt a little safe. I fell asleep on the couch."
She took a step forward.

"I woke up... to a flash. I got up, thinking it was morning. It wasn't. It was only 15 minutes since I fell asleep. Then I got a text… and it was him."

Amelia briefly looked to Gabriel. "...*Him*? You mean..."
It was then that Audrey lifted her arm and showed the group her screen. *A photo of her sleeping.*

The image left everyone stiff, a single chill running along their spines. Quin jumped forward and took hold of the phone out of Audrey's hand, and he brought it up to his face. Troy grabbed Quin's wrist in return and brought it close for him to see, too.

"The creep was inside your house *again*?" Pine exasperated.

"When I saw that, I panicked. Half asleep, I thought... the only way they would ever know anything... CAMERAS. It had to be! So I searched every part of the house. I tore this place apart, looking for any sign. Maybe they were hidden, maybe they were too tiny to see. I looked through the plants, every crack, every crevice."

"And you found the cameras and we have a happy ending,

right?" Quin half-joked.

Audrey swallowed.

"...There's nothing."

Hearing his sister's voice crack in absolute fear made Gabriel's heart sink. She had never been this scared. It was hard to console her. Even harder to watch.

"And it hit me... it hit me hard... I ran for my gun and... and my freaking gun is missing from my purse, it's *gone*!"

She held her head in that moment, as she tried to hide the panic slipping out of her. Troy scratched his forehead.

"So wait... if that flash came from a camera... and you woke up that quickly, then... how did the guy disappear that fast??"

"EXACTLY! He *couldn't* have! That's what I'm saying, he---" She took a deep breath, attempting to contain her anxiety. Right before approaching Pine. Pine, of all people.

"Amelia....is there... is there any chance that... is there any chance that a person can... be... *not* visible?"

The question left everyone's minds reeling. Even Amelia was stunned by Audrey's question. Her brows crinkled, as she blinked repeatedly behind her glasses.

"Ummm...... are we.... talking like.... H.G. Wells type of... not visible...???"

It took Audrey a second to recognize the expression within Pine, before she waved a finger at her.

"DON'T give me that look! DON'T! You are NOT allowed to give me ANY sort of look, after all the things you've raved about! Don't look at me like I'm making this up!"

"I don't-- I would *never*--"

Audrey turned from the Pine girl, grabbing her phone from Quinton's possession, leaving Amelia scrambling for words to defend herself with. But Audrey ignored her.

"When this started happening, I would never even consider any of this, but after that thing showed up, I just... I don't know anymore! But I'm *not* crazy!!"

"You're *not* crazy, Audrey!" Gabriel reassured, taking hold of her by the shoulders. "Listen to me... you're *not* crazy. And we all believe you, okay?"

He gently took the phone from her hands and looked at the screen once more. More closely. More intently. He scrolled to the previous image of the three of them. And he realized something... something in both photos... the reflection on the photo frames... the TV screen... there wasn't one... Audrey's theory must be correct. His eyes turned back to her and he let out a shaky breath.

"...Okay... here's what we're going to do..."
He handed the phone back to Audrey and shifted his glasses.

"Troy, I need you to take us back to the shack. We'll get our cars, and then we need to stay at another place tonight. Some place safe. In the morning, I'm going to the police station, and I'm going to show them this evidence."

"Gabriel, they didn't believe me and they won't believe you, either! And besides, he told me to-"

"That's exactly what he would say to make you scared. To control you through fear. And I'm not allowing it. If they believe me, if they don't believe me, it doesn't matter. They need to know, regardless. This is ending."

He laid a hand on her shoulder,

"Go pack your things, okay? We're leaving in a few minutes."
She rubbed her fingers together. "Where are we..."

"I can't say right now... we need to wait until it's safe."
His eyes shifted to the empty parts of the room. Audrey got the message. "...Got it."

She hurried to her room, while Gabe went to the safe. He covered his hand as he put in the code, and pulled the door open. There, he grabbed his pistol and shoved it into his coat pocket, before closing the door and wiping his prints away. He quickly made it back to the group, signaling them to go for the door. "Wait for us in the van, we'll be right out."

They nodded in compliance, Quinton scooping up Scrooge in his arms, and the three made for outside. Left in silence, Gabriel unloaded his weapon, checking the inside and the ammo within the magazine.

"I want you to know..." He spoke to the emptiness.

"...That I know you're there now. And my sister... she's the most important person in my life. I'll protect her no matter what. And your little game you're playing... I know it's to keep us quiet."

He put the mag back in and the top half of the gun slid back,

causing a loud, intimidating clap to echo. "But I don't scare easy."
- - -

    The Beckhart siblings raced outside toward Valhalla. Quinton slid the door open for them, which they jumped through immediately, and shut the door back up seconds later, leaving no gap for anyone to follow from.

    Troy started the engine and sped out of the property, into the pathway surrounded by trees. It was much more darker than before, as midnight was approaching. It felt unnatural to be up at this hour and on the road. They were all getting quite exhausted, despite the adrenaline pulsing through their veins. They just had to stay awake awhile longer. Focus on one thing at a time.

    "Okay, so, whose place are we crashing in?" Amelia spoke aloud. Before anyone could skip a beat, Troy threw in his own answer.

    "I crash in the van, dudes, so I'm not much use!"
Well, that answered the question of Troy's living arrangements. Gabriel's eyes shifted to the others, as all eyes seemed to fall on him anyway. He rubbed his temple in deep thought, as he considered things carefully. "...Quinton?"

 Lim's spine perked as he heard his name.

    "...Would you mind?"
Quin's head swiveled to every person, honestly quite confused as to why and how he got nominated.

    "Me? Why the heck *me*? How did I get involved in this?"

    "They know about my place, since the wonder twins put *me* in the cross-hairs... so your place is a bit safer... considering no one likes you, anyway."

 Quin blinked. "Thanks, Pine."

    "You're welcome, buddy."

    "*That* aside... you're not as loud in your beliefs as Amelia and Troy are, so I doubt they would have been paying as much attention to you. It just feels like a better place to go, based on a gut feeling."

    "Don't trust your intestines, they have a habit of playing politics on you."

    As strange as Quin's advise was, Gabriel thinking it oddly profound though, they needed a direct answer, and decided to look past his dodging to get it.

"Quinton, come on. We need your help."

"Oh, you have some nerve, YOU told me to shut up!"
Audrey's eyes quickly averted from his pointed finger. The other two awaited his response, which didn't take long to get.

"But yeah, I guess it's acceptable. Just don't burn the place down. We don't have house insurance."

"*We?*" Audrey inquired.
Amelia pat Quin on the shoulder. "Mommy and Daddy Lim. He stays with his parents, while he's away from college."

"Parents? They'll have a fit!"

"Not at all, they love company."

"But they'll be sleeping at this time."

"My parents are nocturnal creatures. They thrive on the moonlight."
He shifted his glasses. "Besides... tonight is bingo night."
\- -

After Troy returned them to the shack and bid them good night as they rode off in their own vehicles, the remaining members of the Assembly stood outside on a sidewalk of a new neighborhood, staring at a darkened town house. Plant life of various types was distributed all over the front lawn and windows, the house itself a dark blue with green trimmings.

"So, this is it." Quin presented in the flattest tone possible.

"*Voilà* and all that."
A tiny detail caught the Beckhart siblings' eyes of a small vintage looking sign hanging above the door, with gold lettering and red paint. Audrey peered to read the words from the distance they stood, though Quin saved her the trouble.

"The Afterlife Teahouse. They run their small business from home."
 The Beckhart girl chuckled, "Cute."
Quin's head rolled to the others.

"Listen, myyy parents areeee..."
Audrey smirked, "Traditional?"

"-Eccentric."
She nodded in acknowledgment, somehow getting over her previously panicked state rather quickly.

"He means they're sickly sweet." Amelia praised, grinning ear to ear in childlike excitement over going over to his house.

"They're alright." He dodged. "They're not normal. Nothing like me, just warning you."

"Oh so you mean they're actually friendly and approachable?" Quinton's eyes stared down at the concrete ground, as he tried to process Audrey's savage roasting as maturely and calmly as possible. Her shoulders jiggled, in intensely sarcastic glee.

"I think I like them already."

She left the boy staring into oblivion, as he continued to try and take that as constructively as possible. All he could do was smile through his wounded pride.

-

The four stepped through, the Beckhart siblings deeply intrigued, Pine clapping happily in anticipation, and Quin sighing his dignity away.

"I should be getting paid for this..." He muttered under his breath. "You're rich, you can freaking afford me."

It wasn't long before they were walking through the hallway, which was decorated heavily in framed family photos and paintings, the inside of the house being as red as a cardinal, and the distinct smell of herbs entered their senses. The carpet underneath their shoes was a soft plush material, and the temperature was set to a comfortable 65°.

A detail that lured them into wanting to find out more was the sound of frantic, ecstatic voices that cheered every so often, in the span of just a few minutes.

As they reached the other side of the hall, they were introduced to the rest of the small house. A bright orange fluorescent light shone in a large part of the room, while the other half was lit by lanterns or flickering bulbs from the old chandeliers. The aroma of herbs got even more intense as they entered the room, the kitchen sitting across from them at higher ground, that was encompassed by multiple hanging plants and leaves left to air dry. The furniture all looked to be antique in nature, but none of it matched. The walls were a mixture of brick and a white smooth surface, with what appeared to be real compressed leaves and flowers that had been mod-podged, to serve almost as a makeshift canvas.

A soft melody reached the ears of the party, that they quickly

Uncanny

traced to the vintage record player sitting next to the kitchen, tucked into a corner. The most interesting part, however, was the two individuals sitting in the middle of the room, at a red wooden table that normally would be housing food, but currently was at the mercy of an array of cards and tiny blue disks.

Just as the four had halted in front of the table, did the two individuals leap out of their seats and cheer as loud as their voices could allow, their arms waving happily in the air. They had little to no awareness of any other company but their own, the excitement of the game clearly clouding their better judgment. This made Quinton suck in a breath, as if he just got a splinter, and let his forehead fall into his open hand. Amelia only laughed at her friend's embarrassment.

The cheering couple ceased. Their eyes turned to the party at last. And in that second, they were both beaming, as if they were the very embodiment of joy itself.

"Quin Quin!!" The woman exclaimed. "Ddal!!"
The two ran around the table, with Amelia rushing to them and embracing them both tightly. Amelia was always known to give warm, tight hugs as a kid and young teenager, and it appeared this fact had not changed.

The redheaded girl stepped back, and immediately went for the kitchen to raid the fridge, asking them what they had for dinner and if there was any leftovers. Also asking how the bingo game was going, how much they made in sells that day for the shop, and how Mrs. Lim's poinsettia was doing. It seemed clear at that point that Amelia had officially adopted the Lim family as her own.

Quinton stepped forward, his arms folded.

"Eomma, Appa..."
Their attention was grabbed, just before he began speaking fluent Korean, which took the Beckharts by surprise, as they had not yet heard Quin speak any other language, but straight up English.

Gabriel, as it happened, had become quite educated in other languages over the years. Even the hardest ones seemed to come to him naturally. This being so, he was able to translate some of the hurried conversation.

What came out was...

Welcome to Hollowgrove

"Mom, Dad... my friends need to stay the night... it's been a long night of driving... why are you here so late?... you should have told us you were bringing company, we are a mess... are they hungry?... no, they just want to sleep... you look exhausted, like a nocturnal feeder... thanks, mom, I'll keep that in mind... do your friends want to... no, dad, they do not want to play bingo."

At that last part, Gabriel snorted a laugh, which he quickly concealed and darted his eyes away. He was still noticed, however, as Quin and his parents turned to him. Even then, the couple retained their huge smiles. And even more so, when they realized who the two were.

"Ohhh, you are the Beckharts!!" His mother delighted, before pointing to Audrey. "You are so beautiful!"

This made Audrey genuinely blush. It wasn't coming from some sleazy jock or a conceded reporter or crazed citizen just out to please for an autograph. It was coming from a kind, real person who actually meant it. And this made her smile. Really smile.

"*Thank you.*" She sung, as she scrunched her shoulders up, peeking over at Gabriel, "I knew I'd like them."

Quin's father pointed at Gabriel with an excited nod,

"And you, you are such talented writer! I remember play you did, for high school. You wrote script?"

Gabe was bashful at the thought, stuffing his hands into his pockets, as the memory returned to him. But Audrey seemed to have trouble recollecting.

"Wait... when was this?"

"You were in play, too. You were lead actress!"

"And your brother was the tree!"

After a good minute, the Beckhart girl's mouth fell.

"Oh my gosh... *yes*... you were the dancing tree, and I was the princess... and you *wrote* that?"

"Yeeeep. I was 15, and had a crush on... never mind..."

That's right. Her brother didn't like to talk about his one-sided feelings for girls. Thought it inappropriate. She giggled at first, but her mind fluctuated to a question she felt compelled to ask.

"Were Mom and Dad..."

"No." Gabriel quickly, but quietly, answered with a shake of the head.

Audrey's nose crinkled, nodding in anticipated disappointment.

169

"Figured."

Quin's mother leapt forward, grabbing hold of the two's hands, "You hungry? We will make you food!"

"Oh no no, it's so late, Mrs. Lim, we couldn't impose."

"No be silly! You tired, you hungry, we will make you tea! Play bingo." Mrs. Lim ran for the kitchen.

"Eomma, no, we just wanna SLEEEEP!"

"PLAY BINGO!"

CHAPTER XXI
✦ A WARNING ✦

Mr. and Mrs. Lim were quickly becoming the Beckharts' favorite new people to be around. They couldn't decide what they loved best... between the completely accepting nature of the couple and their willingness to open their home to the siblings. Or the couple feeding them with unexpected delicious homemade pastas and boiled all-natural teas. Or maybe it was their immediate jump into enthralling, but innocent conversations about the simple things of life.

   Hearing Quinton's parents talk was like going back to a time where things were more pure, and less muddled with complications of the modern world. Almost as if they had preserved a world all on their own from that small household. The Lims made the siblings forget about their troubles, at least while they sat at that table. And that was good enough for them.

   Quin and the Beckharts sat with Mr. Lim, while Mrs. Lim prepared them a meal and hot tea. Amelia circled the area while eating a chicken leg, listening in on the conversation with a playful smile. It was evident that she loved being there at the Lim house, maybe even more than her own. Perhaps it was because, they were not a broken family. It felt complete here. Like the image of what a family should be.

   She loved her father, she truly did. But... Pine felt empty. For a long time. It was hard growing without both parents. Even harder when you are constantly reminded of it by another family's happiness. But here... she did not feel that prejudice. She felt welcomed, loved, accepted... at peace. Those are things Gabriel noticed heavily, as he watched the Pine girl wander in circles. There was so much he missed about Amelia. So much he wasn't able to witness or learn, because of the unspoken feud between her and his sister. Now... now he felt he might actually get that chance again.

   "Mrs. Lim, where are you all from originally, if you don't mind me asking?" Audrey's question pulled his mind back to the table, and his eyes returned to Quin's parents. Indeed, he too was rather interested in finding out more about the joyous couple... and their quirky son.

"Korea!" Mrs. Lim chirped, getting out the cups. "Jii and me, we come to America many years ago, before Quin was born."

"Aera and me, we come for American dream!"
Audrey's eyes grew a little, as she maintained the best smile she was capable of. "To *this* house??"

While the reference of the house being, well, not in the best of neighborhoods, in the best of towns for that matter, went over their heads, Quin caught on to what she was saying... and was in complete agreement of it. He smiled back at her, nodding his head in sheer sarcasm. "It's a piece of crap, right?"

"EY!" His mother smacked him upside the head. "You be grateful! We have nice house, roof over our heads. You go to nice college!"

"Nice colle-- eomma, it is a HOLLOWGROVE college! That place is even more haunted than the *town*!"

"Aye-ya!" She hissed, shaking her head.

"We work hard for our life, Quin Quin." His father soothed, calmly. "You work hard for school. And be big producer! Make lotsa movies!"

"Why can I totally see you as a film maker?" Audrey acknowledged, which made Quinton shift his glasses and his position in the chair. He was still uncomfortable talking for so long to people, it seemed. His social anxiety was kicking in.

"So what you doing out so late?" Questioned Jii, who put his bingo cards aside for his plate of food.

"Yeah, what you all doing today, being so tired?"
Gabriel didn't even consider what he was about to say should probably be kept secret, so when it did come out, it took him a minute to notice the reaction of Jii and Aera.

"Monster hunting."
His head lifted. Audrey's face fell. Quin's eyes darted to the Beckhart boy. Even Amelia gave a pause.

Quin's parents stared at him for what felt like the longest, most uncomfortable silence. Their smiles completely vanished. Their positive energy seemed to be swept off by an unseen thief, and the room grew cold. Were they trying to process what he meant? Were they confused as to the meaning? Or did they know right off the bat... and were stricken with an unnerving knowledge?

Eventually, even Quinton began to look at his parents in a manner that wrote confusion all over his face. He had no inkling what had gotten into them, for them to be so dreary and soundless for so long. It took far too long... but eventually, Mrs. Lim forced out a chuckle. And her smile cracked open, her breathing a little irrationally. Her husband soon joined her in laughing the awkward moment away, as Aera soon poured tea into the cups.

"You funny. You joking, yeah? Or... I know... you actress, you writer, he producer... you making movie! Yeah?"

Gabriel could not bring it in him to make matters any more cringe-fueled than they already were. He slowly nodded in agreement, smiling nervously.

"Yeah... we're making a movie."

"Exciting!" Jii mused. "You do awesome!"

Jii bent over and gave the Beckhart siblings a gentle fist bump.

"You rock at it!"

"Please stop." Quin pleaded in a hushed, dying voice. Mrs. Lim turned around, carrying the dirty plates to the sink, while Amelia helped her with the dishes that had not yet been washed. "Oh thank you, ddal!"

Ddal... further proof of Amelia's adoption into the family, with Mrs. Lim calling her 'daughter' in their language… it was one of the most wholesome things he had ever witnessed regarding Amelia Pine.

"You stay the night, leave in morning, yeah?" Jii questioned.

"Yes, if that's alright." Audrey checked.

"Good. We make breakfast, go for morning walk. Drink lotsa tea." He shifted his cards, adjusting his discs. "Play bingo."

"Appa, for the last time; NO bingo!"

"Quin Quin hates bingo."

"I have valid reasons."

"Quin Quin afraid of being real man."

This made Quinton curl his lips back, and slap his hands on the table. He started to rise,

"You know what? Play your bingo. Revel in the American dream of tea and chicken legs. I'm going to bed."

Jii watched his son start to walk off, before his eyes fell back to his cards. "Lady Quin Quin need his beauty sleep."

Uncanny

Audrey slapped her hand over her mouth, which caused Quin to cast his father a venomous glare, a fire in his eyes of which could not be quenched. He eventually walked away. But what he uttered, Gabriel dare not repeat. What he could tell you... was it had nothing to do with bingo.

- -

It wasn't much longer that Quin went to bed, that the rest of the party grew too tired to function, and called it a night. Mrs. Lim prepared the spare room for the girls to sleep in, while Gabriel took the floor of Quinton's room on a nice soft bedding.

Audrey and Scrooge made good usage of the area granted to them. It was in subtle hints of soft greens and pinks, a beautiful flower pattern located everywhere. The wallpaper, the sheets, the pillows, the curtains, everywhere. Entering inside such a room almost made Amelia dry-heave. She had never actually been in this room before. And the sight of it made her panic. Far, far too girly for her tastes. The pink alone was enough to give her an ulcer.

Audrey laid down upon the soft sheets and plush pillow that felt like laying on a cloud. Scrooge was glued to her arms, and sunk right into the mattress, as much as his human mother did. The Beckhart girl forgot about the fact that she was literally still wearing her baggy lavender sweater and white pajama bottoms from the house. But it didn't matter. It's not like anyone was judging her for it.

She kept her suitcase sitting on the chair at the foot of the bed, taking only what was necessary for her. Why she had to take an entire suitcase for one night, she was unsure. Then again... Gabriel might have been right to have her do so. Maybe they couldn't go back home for awhile... maybe things really were different now. In more ways than one.

Amelia's mouth puckered into duck lips, as her eyes scanned the room, in a fashion that was not unlike an interior decorator who was getting ready to mentally fire a room from existence.

"This won't do... I can't stay here."

"You're just saying that cuz I'm here."

Amelia's eyes shifted to the Beckhart girl with that comment, who opened her own eyes to look at her. The two girls stared for a moment in a tense, unpleasant showdown of sorts. Both girls were at their last straw with the other. Pine didn't know how much more she could take from her.

"I'll be inside my car."

She placed her headphones over her ears and began walking herself and her laptop bag through the door, shutting it behind her.

Pine did not need to tell her anything, Audrey didn't care. But now? Well... now she felt loneliness all over again. And when conditions are quiet, peaceful and perfect as that, with her bed feeling like cotton candy and a satisfied Scrooge sleeping heavily in her arms... it was hard not to feel that way.

~

A vile stench hung in the air, one teeming with rot, overwhelming Gabriel's senses. His eyes opened, his head having been melted into his pillow... but the room he fell asleep to was not the same as he left it. Quinton was missing.

The purple fluorescent lights that shined from Lim's fish tank, even the pet itself, had also vanished. The room was filled with darkness... until a faint light now trickled in from outside.

Gabriel arose from the floor, and looked around. Things did not feel real. This didn't feel like his body. This didn't feel like his mind. Everything was overloaded with a surreal sensation. One he could not put into words.

When he walked, it was as if he was moving through water. Like he had to fight against an unseen force. His legs felt heavy, as he took difficult steps towards the window. He finally reached it, but had not the energy to celebrate such an exhausting task. It drained the life from him just getting that far from such short a distance.

He reached in to get the blinds, wondering what in the world was going on outside. But whatever discomfort he was feeling now... something in him told him it was about to get worse. Much worse. As he opened the blinds, something suddenly lunged at him with a demonic snarl, that made his very breath suck back into his lungs through a loud gasp.

He jumped back instinctively, as the creature's head wiggled through the window, broken glass flying everywhere, the monstrous being struggling to get to the Beckhart boy. It took him a minute, but he recognized now what it was. **The Chupacabra.**

Uncanny

It had found him. And it was trying to kill him. Gabe had only seconds to act. He knew there wasn't any other weapon effective enough except his pistol. He ran for it. Ran so fast, he tripped. He came colliding with the floor, but thankfully landed on his hands and not his face.

His pillow was just in reach; he crawled over to it, and slipped his hand underneath, the Chupacabra viciously snarling behind him, still trying to get in. With a flick of the wrist, and a spin of his body, he swung around back towards the creature. He was prepared to fire....but he froze.

The Chupacabra was no longer moving. No longer making a sound. He was motionless, silent... and he was watching Gabe. Watching with intensely glowing green eyes. Gabriel's eyes widened as he stared back at the creature, his finger resting on the trigger. His body trembled, his teeth chattering together.

The beast cocked its head at Beckhart, as if... **studying him.** Waiting for his next move, perhaps? Snapped out of his mur-derous rampage? He did not know. But he wasn't going to make any movement until the creature did.

Yet the creature did not appear to be as determined to kill him as he had thought. For it suddenly withdrew its head, just as quickly as it busted in, and retreated out of sight. Gabriel released some of the tension built up in his muscles, and he eased his posture, but only a little.

What game was this beast playing... why did it turn away for no reason? Or was it simply afraid of his weapon? No... it couldn't be... not that quickly. Something here was not right.

After a few uneasy moments passed by, he emerged. The beast had left behind shards of glass scattered everywhere, a great hole gouged through the window. Wind pulsed from it, whistling and blowing violently, bringing in a bitter cold that repeatedly took Gabriel's breath away.

He slowly leaned in to see through the hole left behind, cautiously holding himself against the wall with one hand, while his eyes peered beyond the glass. His fluffy brown hair fell over his glasses, which would normally be fogging up at this point. But he paid no attention... for the sight he saw left him stricken with a feeling he couldn't even find the words to describe with.

The strange light he had been seeing flicker from the window was the strangest lightning he had seen. Lightning bolts striking the earth in blinding neon purples, reds, greens and blues. The air outside was filled with ash that rained from the sky above. But the sky itself did not even give home to day or night... it instead gave home to the blackest, most petrifying clouds, that spawned the sporadic lightning bolts that dispensed in unpredictable directions.

The clouds themselves were teeming with fire. A fire that raged across the horizon. And beyond that fire lay shapes. Shapes of fearsome shadows that moved like giants behind the clouds, producing sounds that almost made the hearing in Gabriel's ears go out. For reasons he could not explain, the storm clouds and terrifying, monstrous shapes no longer concerned him. Not when he heard a horrifying, shrill scream come from the distance.

His head immediately snapped to it, his face wiped clean of all emotion, the blood within him drained from his head. Without hesitation, he threw open the window and jumped through, running across the road ahead of him. The scream came from the woods.

He needed to hurry. He needed to hurry as quickly as possible. He reached the trees, just as another scream occurred. He didn't have time to breathe. He didn't have time to think. He kept running. Deeper and deeper he went, rushing past trees that whistled the faster he pushed himself. And he heard it...

"GABRIEL!!!!!!!!!!!!!!"

His heart pounded. Ivy. Something was coming for Ivy.

"IVY!!" His voice screamed through the darkness.

He continued to run towards her echo.

"GABRIEL!!!" Her voice pierced the silence once more.

"IVY!!!"

At that moment... something reached in and grabbed him. He flew forward with a gasp, and landed right on his face onto the ground, covered with dead, muddy leaves. His body landed with a thud, and knocked the wind out of him. He groaned as he squirmed. He tried to move his legs to continue running... but he found himself restrained.

He couldn't feel his leg... he couldn't feel anything... he whipped his head behind him. His eyes enlarged. A vine was wrapped around his ankle. Tight and growing tighter. Cutting the circulation off. It was trying to pull him in.

He quickly looked up, as he heard a noise. His heart pumped even faster. Before him was the Chupacabra. Walking past him, paying him zero attention. In his mouth, he was dragging something... a person... a small person.

Ivy.

She was in shock; unable to speak or move, but fully conscious.

The creature ran her against the filthy earth beneath them, towards a collection of trees, where it finally dropped her. Gabriel struggled to move, but he could not break free of the vine's grasp.

"IVY!" He exclaimed.

It was useless. She did not hear him. Neither did the creature. It was almost as if he were invisible now.

Just then, something strange happened... instead of attacking Ivy, the Chupacabra **bowed**. Bowed before the darkness before him. Ivy lay in front of him, staring up at whatever visible parts there were of the sky. Her hands rested on her stomach, her face cold, her body motionless.

Her head turned, as it happened. Something... something was coming from the darkness. Something of which made Ivy's eyes enlarge wider than what her skull could allow. Her breathing immediately increased, growing louder.

"IVY, NO!!!"

The being approached Ivy, its body completely made of shadow. It reached in for her, getting closer and closer. Gabriel fought with all his might. He fought and fought and couldn't break free.

"IVY!! IVY, RUN!!!!"

Just as the hand hovered over her face...

Ivy screamed.

-

Gabriel rolled off his mat, hitting his head against the floor. He grunted in pain and huffed, leaping up, his eyes wildly zooming in on everything around him. His breathing quickened, as he braced for whatever might have been waiting for him. But that was just it. There was nothing. Just him in a mostly dark room, Quinton's purple light shining over the fish tank, as a small dragon fish floated around inside without a care in the world.

   The window was intact, not a trace of broken glass in sight. He hurried to it, and wedged his two fingers between two blinds. The only thing on the other side was a quiet road, the faint sound of wind humming from the distance, swaying the far off trees ahead.

   He stepped back. Another nightmare....but this one... this one wasn't at all the same as before. He bent down and checked under his pillow. Below was his pistol, as he left it. A shaky breath left his mouth and he sat back down, running his hand down his face. His fear was far from quenched, however.

   His same hand came back down and grabbed hold of his phone, sitting next to his glasses. He dialed in a number. A number given to him by Kathryn Chapman, in the event he needed to contact her. Well... that event arrived. After what he just saw, he had to make sure Ivy was safe.

   It was only a few rings before it was answered, with a tired voice on the other end. "H- Hello?"

"Mrs. Chapman... it's Gabriel."

"Mr. Beckhart... wha-- what's this about? It's late."

"I know, I'm so sorry... but I need to know that Ivy is safe."

"Safe? What are you-"

"Please just go check on her. Make sure she's in bed."

There was hesitation. Kathryn sighed on the other end.

"Okay... give me a minute."

And he did. He waited very patiently. His hands were still shaking, one of which he stared at, as he held his phone to his ear, before he closed his eyes. He attempted to rationalize his breathing, get his heart to slow down, and calm his muscles.

   He felt as though he really did just endure the events of that dream, and at the last second of a terrible thing he was forced to watch, he was transported back.

"She's perfectly fine. Asleep in her bed, safe and sound."

He opened his eyes. "...You're sure?"

"Yes. I promise you. Magnus is on the bed with her, nothing's happening to her when he's around."

His gaze wandered the room, trying to determine what was real and what was not.

His mind was spinning.

"Mr. Beckhart? Are you there??"

"...Yeah... I'm sorry, Mrs. Chapman, I... I just wanted to..."

"I know. I get it. Are you okay?"

"...I will be. Good night."

He hung up and dropped his phone onto the bedding below him. Despite Kathryn's assurance that Ivy was safe... he could not shake the awful feeling that all was not right... that dream was far too vivid. Far too intense. He found himself trembling again. Ivy was still in danger... he knew it.

His concentration was broken, however. He jolted and swiveled his head towards the window. His body darted to it faster than his mind could process, and he pulled the blinds back. He scanned the outside, expecting something terrifying waiting for him on the other end.

He swore he heard rustling, followed by a loud bang. A trash can, by the sounds of it. He peered through the darkness, up and down the street. *There*... there was a blur... he was sure of it. A blur whizzed by from the shadows. Something was there... or was there?

He kept watching... waiting... waiting... nothing. Nothing further. No attack. No snarling creature... was he just imagining? Was his paranoia kicking in? Was he losing it?

He couldn't watch any longer. His eyes fell heavy, and he let go of the blinds, turning defeatedly away. His eyes cut to the fish tank, at the tiny dragon fish that just happened to be facing him at that moment. The small creature stared at him, with its frightening little face filled with sharp teeth, the light reflecting off of its cloudy eyes. He knew it was secretly judging him. He felt attacked. He was being bullied by a fish.

His brows crinkled, and he walked away. "Shut up."

CHAPTER XXII
✦ BLOOD FEUD ✦

It might have been currently freezing outside, and Pine's broken heater was not making things any better, but the small red-headed cryptid enthusiast would rather take the cold and tight space of her vehicle, over spending a night alone in the same room as Audrey Beckhart. At least she had Gabriel to distract her the previous night, but it being just the two girls was out of the question.

Besides, the silence and seclusion would do her mind better. Clear it of all distractions, so she could focus on her work. She busied herself away typing, surrounded by nothing but darkness. While she typed, she listened to podcasts of fellow believers. She often got a significantly large amount of juicy details on creatures and strange happenings from said podcasters, but that day's scoop wasn't all that impressive thus far. When she got bored with one, she skipped to the next. Some were stretching to keep listeners, sadly, as all they ever relied on was the news they heard from others, rather than seeking out the information themselves.

She sighed as she skipped her sixth podcast, adjusting her headphones. She then saw there were a couple that were currently live, die-hard night owls, one of which was only an occasional podcaster, as they only came on when something big happened. Her faith in humanity was possibly about to be restored. She clicked on it.

"Good evening, **beautiful creatures**." A rather unnerving robotic voice spoke through the silence.

SleeplessInHollowgrove.

They never came out with a real name. Only a username they carried on from the creepypasta website, which now famously became their alias. No one knew if it was a boy or a girl. They had no identity to speak of, only a voice that sent chills to all, and was very minimal in what they said.

Their name was a play on Sleepy Hollow, which they once mentioned was their favorite book. It made many listeners compare their own town to the one in the book, as both held secrets and supernatural elements that no one had the guts to

Uncanny

confront.

It wasn't clear where Sleepless got their information. But they always knew things no one else did. Or at least before everyone else found out. They had thousands of followers as a result, Pine including. Sleepless was personally her favorite podcaster, as they shot out straight up facts and never tried to impress anybody.

"We have a new Chupacabra sighting."

Amelia perked.

"Police received a call just hours ago from a local farm hand, who reported an attack on the livestock and himself. After firing at the creature multiple times, it finally fled the scene. Time of said attack was between 6 and 9 PM, based on the time the call was made. The following will be the 911 dispatch recording. This is SleeplessInHollowgrove, signing out."

Pine jerked upwards, as she held her headphones tight against her ears.

"911, what is your emergency?"

"H-Hello, my name is Wyatt *beeeeep*, I'm at the *beeeep* farm at *beeeep* street. I was just attacked by a wild animal! It almost killed our goats!"

"Yes sir, is the animal still present?"

"No, it ran off! I shot at it a bunch of times and scared it! I don't think I hit it..."

"Is anyone else with you?"

"No, it's just me."

"Did the animal attack you?"

"Y-Yes, I said it did!"

"Are you injured?"

"...N-No... it didn't touch me."

"It didn't touch you, but it attacked you?"

"Yes! I mean, no... it tried! I... hey, I'm not making this up, I swear!"

"Just trying to understand the situation, sir."

"The situation is, you need to send the army!!"

"Over the animal attack, sir?"

"I don't like your tone, ma'am!"

"Are any of the livestock injured, sir?"

"No."

"The animal is gone, sir?"
"Yes."
"Can you describe the animal?"
"Um... it... it's..."
"...Sir?"
"...IT'S A CHUPACABRA, OKAY?!"
"......"
".........."
"..............."
"................................."
"I'm hanging up, sir."
"No! Don't! Please! What if the thing comes b-"
The call ended.

Pine threw her headphones in an instant and jumped out of the car, taking her laptop with her. Her excitement was too great to contain.

- -

Beckhart laid on her side as she stroked Scrooge's fur, staring at the wall across from her, as the faint light from the lantern nearby flickered against her face. The twinkle in her eye, and the soft warmness from her demeanor, was deceptively tranquil.

Much was on her mind and if she had to explain it to anyone, she wouldn't even know what words she could begin with. Everything was confusion. Her emotions were muddled and her beliefs, her certainties, were slowly caving in underneath her. But the thing was, she didn't even know if she *had* been a skeptic all those years.

Honestly... she hadn't even paid it any mind. Almost like a dish you have one time and store into the fridge, but forget about for a month, leaving it to decay in some far back corner, until you finally clean house one random day. It was an idea that was controversial to so many, but merely a small existing thing tucked in the back of her brain, easily avoidable.

Sure, her initial response was explosive. Complete denial. But only, she realized, because of how scared it made her. How life changing it truly was. She came to wonder, at that moment... as easily as Gabriel and her were transformed by this... seduced by it... in fact, hungry for the truth... were her and her brother actually believers the whole time, *and they just didn't realize it?*

Her thoughts were cut short. Her door was thrown open, and she jumped up with a jolt, Scrooge fidgeting with great complaints.

"I'm here, accept me." It was Quin.
He charged in, carrying an open book with him, and he sat on the edge of the bed, making Audrey stare at him with absolute bewilderment. Quin's eyes lifted briefly, just to look around the room. "...Wait, where's Amelia?"

Audrey opened her mouth to answer, but it was to no avail.

"Whatever. It's *you* I really wanted to see, anyway."
The Beckhart girl's brows lifted in surprise. "*Me?*"

"Yeah, I mean, I could leave and discuss these important observations with myself, but I'm arrogant, and I gotta look good to someone."

That didn't explain anything. That was strike 2 for Quinton and his nonsensical replies. But Audrey allowed it. She sighed and shifted. "Kay, what you got?"

That was so street sounding of her. Her stuck-up parents would have her head. Quin adjusted his glasses.

"Your brother's an annoying sleeper. Kept talking in his sleep. Walking over to the window and laying back down. One point went up to me and put his hand on my head. Then laid back down again. I had enough of that. I don't appreciate being sleep-harassed."

"Is he okay?"

"This isn't about him, this is about *me*!"
She tightened her lip.

"I simply can't go to sleep tonight with him around. God help his future wife. I need to work elsewhere."

"Work? You've been *working* this whole time?? You told your parents you were going to sleep!"

"And you tell your boyfriends you actually like them; we're both sinners on this rock, Beckhart, don't play games with me."
Her head jerked back. "...God, your attitude's gross."

"Your mom's attitude's gross."

"That joke died with your social confidence. Now what do you want, I have to get back to staring at the wall."

Quinton's eyes turned into mere slits, as he briefly stared at Audrey. He quickly looked back at his book.

Welcome to Hollowgrove

"There's no actual historical evidence of any Chupacabra attacking humans. It's always been livestock, right?"

Audrey stared at him, and it forced him to glare at her.

"...I'll take your word for it, Quin."

He blinked. "...Right... so why did it get so- forgive the term- *bloodthirsty* with us today?"

"I mean, it might have had something to do with us hitting it with our vehicle."

"Most animals would try to run away, though. Not murder you, no matter what it takes."

"So you think, what? Something *drove it* to coming after us?"

"Something made it go crazy. Something is making *all* of the creatures go crazy. There's too many missing people in this town, there's too many sightings, ghost stories, attacks, for there *not* to be a source of the craziness."

"Like... something's **influencing** them?"

Quin glared. Audrey suddenly got up, walking towards the wall ahead of her. "Something *controlling* them."

She turned back around. "Like a presence."

Lim's eyes darted back and forth like a game of ping pong.

"What, you think there's a big bad Big Brother somewhere, pulling the strings?"

"Maybe. Or something bigger. Think about it. There's too much being hid in this town right now. I mean, for god's sake, me and Gabriel are being *stalked*. The BECKHART children. One of the richest and most influential families in the town, and some invisible creep is harassing us? Trying to intimate us? Somebody is trying to cover all this up. It may not be them, but I have no doubt... all of this... it's all connected."

Quinton shifted his glasses, trying to hide the fact that he was impressed. "You've literally been a believer for *three days*."

Audrey smirked, her arms folding, as her eyes couldn't help but sparkle at the idea.

"...Actually, I was reflecting on that before you came busting in… maybe, I really *was* a believer for all those years. Maybe the seed was in me, it was just... *dormant* until now."

He cocked his head.

"...What changed?"

Her eyes fell to the floor.

"I don't know, exactly... maybe... maybe the presence, whatever it is in this town... maybe it's affecting **people**, too. Awakening us."

Quin nodded slowly, his eyes trailing away in thought. Beckhart's own eyes lifted back to him.

"About the creatures, though? You're right, they haven't had a history attacking humans. But the thing is... we know next to nothing about these things. *Anything* is fair game. So, we gotta take whatever info we got. And we gotta be prepared. For anything."

Lim sat in silence, slowly nodding his head once more. He never thought in a million years that he would be having a deep conversation with Audrey Beckhart about *monsters* and the *supernatural*. It's like this was a fever dream from a temperature of 120°, he was overdosing on jello, and Teletubbies was playing in the background-- all at once. He more than likely would have to seek out therapy by the end of the week, for clarity.

At that moment, the both of them jolted and tensed their whole bodies as the door was thrown open, this time by Amelia.

"Quin, *there* you are!"

She eyed the two with a crazed, widened gaze, holding her laptop with one hand.

"Having a slumber party without me, are we?"

Audrey peeked in her direction,

"Does that door have a lock, cuz if not, I'm installing one."

"CHECK THIS OUT."

The spastic nut plumped down on the floor, spinning the laptop to face the two. "*This* was just released!"

Her finger tapped on the button. The recording of Wyatt played. Making Lim and Beckhart perk their bodies in suspense, as they listened. As soon as it finished, Amelia closed her laptop.

"It was on the rampage tonight!" Quin exclaimed.

"It wasn't just us!"

"Exactly! We have our first witness, ladies and germs!"

"But they cut off his name and address, we have no idea where to find him!" Beckhart lamented.

"SleeplessInHollowgrove does that, for security reasons. BUT, here's the thing... *we have clues*."

Amelia shot up, pointing a finger at the two as she began to pace, a cunning look of mischief in her eye. Audrey knew that look all too well. Pine was scheming.

"The attack was said to have taken place between 6 and 9. But... what do we know of Chupacabras?"

"They harass goats."

"They should go on a diet?"

"I hate you both."

Audrey smirked. "They hunt at night."

"Exactly!"

"Which means... it would have attacked the farm when it was getting dark, like it was when we were on the road?"

"And about what time was that?"

Beckhart scratched her neck. "Uhh, say, 7 or 8ish?"

"*Right*. The attack must have happened prior to this for the Chupacabra to be so worked up, and distracted enough to run across the road like that. Remember, Wyatt shot at it several times, and it finally left. Which would explain why it was so vengeful towards us during the attack, cuz it was already hyped from the experience."

She wiggled her pointed finger at them.

"Now, what farms do we know of in that area?"

The two did not respond. Pine sighed. She pulled out a map on her laptop and tapped at the area.

"There are three farms in the general parameter of our sighting. I personally know one, and they don't have any farm hands, it being just the man and his daughter. So that leaves us with two families."

"He has to be by himself right now."

Quin and Amelia swiveled their heads at Audrey. She cut her eyes at them, feeling almost guilty for thinking.

"...I mean, *he* called 911, right? Not the owner? Why would it be *him* calling 911 when it's not his property? He must be watching it for them."

Pine pursed her lips. She had no desire to praise Beckhart for her good observation skills, and she was angry she was even tempting her to do so. "Mm, right, I guess..."

"So tomorrow, we check out both farms and interview this Wyatt dweeb?"

Amelia nodded slowly, her eyes wandering.

"Yeah, tomorrow... got a big day ahead of us. Gabe is visiting the station, and we gotta interview Wyatt. We have to make sure we pick up Ivy first and get an early start."

"Oh, that sounds great." Audrey's attention was already longing for the bed ahead of her.

"Now can you two, if it's possible, **actually** go to bed so that *I* can sleep?"

Lim shrugged, "It's possible."

Pine bit the inside of her cheek.

"Fine. My car is better company, anyway." She made for the door and blazed through, "Later, losers."

Quinton glanced at Audrey before standing up, shaking his head. "I'm halfway convinced Pine is not of this planet, and she's just trying to get back to her people."

"I was actually convinced of that about you."

"That's not a lie."

"I mean, you *are* a pretty different species from your parents."

"Also not a lie."

Quinton grabbed the knob, turning his head back to her.

"Night, Beckhart."

"Night, Quin."

He started shutting the door,

"Please seek help for your brother. I'm serious."

-

The hallways were so quiet, it made one feel guilty for making any sort of noise. Even to go to the bathroom. But this was something Pine had to venture in doing.

Before she went back outside, she needed to take care of herself. Starting with her hoodie. Something in the back of the collar was irritating her skin through her shirt. She walked through the doorway and shut herself in, rolling over to the mirror.

She sighed as she looked at herself, before going to take her jacket off. Holding it with both hands, she began to look around for the cause of the irritation. Her slender fingers ran across the soft material, trying to find anything that would be poking her. So far, she wasn't feeling anything until... *"Ow!"*

She hissed and gawked as she held her hand up, fresh blood now traced across the side of her palm. She turned her jacket around to find that a decent sized shard of glass stowed away inside, obviously from the attack earlier. She grit her teeth, as the blood started to run down and she quickly turned on the water, placing her hand under the faucet.

In bitterness, she tossed the hoodie away from her on the floor, shaking her head at the dumb situation. Injuries this late annoyed her, especially when she was about to go to bed. She didn't even know if the Lims had what she needed for this type of cut. It was bad. She needed to apply pressure, as soon as she washed the blood off.

However... something was distracting her. Something felt a little uneasy. While her attention was still mostly on the cut, there was something... not quite right. Coming behind her.

Her eyes narrowed, as they slowly lifted to the mirror. It was a nice, clean little bathroom. The curtains were drawn on the window and the door was locked, so she had her privacy.

Just... she couldn't shake the feeling... that something... was....
CRASH!!!
Amelia screamed and jumped back, as something tore through the window, glass flying everywhere. Her mouth hung, her eyes enlarged to saucers, and she was left frozen in terror, as the thing that now attacked her had ripped its head through the curtain and revealed its sneering face.

The Chupacabra.

CHAPTER XXIII
✦ A LONG NIGHT AHEAD ✦

Amelia slammed back against the wall so hard, she nearly fell through it. The creature of which plagued the fears of the Assembly was at that moment crawling through the hole made out of the smashed glass, and snarling mindlessly, dead set on coming after her.

Pine screamed and desperately clawed at the doorknob to unlock it, but never took her eyes off the creature. Its glowing eyes drilled holes into her, as it wiggled wildly through, its long fangs protruding from its drooling mouth.

"What's going on?!" Someone shouted from the other side of the door.

"GABRIEL!!" She exclaimed. "I'M IN HERE!!!"

She then heard rustling, as someone tried to get in from the other side and began beating on the door.

"AMELIA! OPEN THE DOOR!"

"I'M TRYING!"

The Chupacabra was almost through, literally forcing himself through the shards of glass which cut into its skin. Pine's eyes widened, as her attacker was almost free. She tugged on the knob like a spaz. "GET. ME. OUT!!!!"

At last-- the knob jerked. Her every sense went on alert. She flew the door open, long enough to get through, before slamming it back within seconds. As she did, the Chupacabra could be heard screeching on the other side.

Pine held the doorknob, pulling it towards her as tight as possible, in the event the creature would try to break through. Next to her stood Gabriel, Audrey and Quin, the three huddling close to Amelia, all four equally as worked up as the next. Amelia's whole body shook uncontrollably, as she leaned her head against the door frame, breathing sporadically. The other three drew close, and listened for the creature.

That's when Gabriel pulled out something from his pocket.

"Everyone get back."

They looked, but were shocked to find that Gabe was now wielding his pistol. "Amelia, get out of the way."

Her eyes shot at him.

"Gabe, *don't*!"

His face fell and his eyes squinted at her. *"What?!"*

"We can't kill it!"

"Why the heck not?!"

"It's a bloody Chupacabra, you idiot! One of God's most elusive creations!"

"I think God's gonna have to forgive us!" Quin shot back, just as Gabe shook his head and pulled back the slide.

"We don't have time for this, Amelia, it's us against that thing!"

"I don't even LIKE you people!" She squealed, just as Audrey grabbed her and pulled her back, just in time for the Beckhart boy to swing the door open and point the gun.

"GABE, *NO*!"

Gabriel gasped. Everyone peered in.

"That's impossible..."

They looked all around, looking up and down. It was gone. Again. They hurried to the window and looked out, a gaping hole left behind, glass everywhere. They squinted through the darkness. It had completely vanished, without a single trace.

"You've gotta be kidding me." Audrey muttered, shaking her head. "I just... I just feel like we're never gonna be allowed to sleep tonight, guys. There's a campaign against it."

They all stood up straight. The Beckhart boy rolled his shoulders. "Must have heard my gun... spooked him."

"Or he was called back."

He looked at his sister with suspicion, and she couldn't help but look at him back. There was nothing to say to her, however. But he had plenty to say to someone else. He turned to Pine.

"What did you think you were doing back there?"

She straightened her back.

"My main objective, Beckhart, is to *save* these creatures. Not gun them down like everyone else before us has. I'm on *their* side here."

"And what about the side of the victims?"

She paused as she heard this. Gabe shook his head,

"The victims who are more than likely dead right now? Whose families are hoping and praying they will come back? You know, the ones that THING out there probably took!"

"Took?"

The three now stared at Gabe. He realized what he said... the confusion was justified and he knew it. He swallowed, as he felt his face begin to flush.

"We... we should all stay in the same room tonight... it's safer." Saying what he needed to, he started to walk away... until Audrey's next words caught the attention of everyone.

"Amelia, you're bleeding."

Both boys turned their eyes to Pine, who looked down at her hand, blood trickling down it all over again.

"Oh..." She held it, instinctively. "Yeah, I cut myself on some glass before it...." She perked up. *"...Attacked."*

Her eyes grew in realization. The other three were catching on. Gabriel's gaze drifted to the window.

"It honed in on you like a shark..."

But Audrey folded her arms, "It wouldn't have found her that quickly, though… it had to have already been in the area."

Pine's eyes were glued to the floor.

"...It was tracking us."

The party stood in silence, as they exchanged uneasy glances. They were too stunned to say anything more. Except for Quinton.

"You guys are lucky my parents were out for a walk."

He pushed past them.

"Get to my room and wait for me. I'll clean this up."

He grabbed the small dust pan and sweeper from the corner to start scooping up the glass. "I'll tell them a wild animal tried breaking in. We'll get it replaced tomorrow. Just go to sleep."

"I'm not sleeping here with that thing out there." Audrey argued.

"We really don't have a choice right now. It's too late to go anywhere else."

"Quinton's right." Gabe stepped in. "All we can do is fortify things right now and prepare ourselves... maybe it's best we keep watch tonight. We'll worry about tomorrow when it comes."

The girls glared at Gabriel and Quinton, but knew they were right. It was best just to do the best they could... at least for that night.

"Quin, where's your first aid kit? We need to tend to her hand." Quinton turned to Gabe and pointed at the cabinet.

"In there."

The Beckhart boy nodded. He hurried and grabbed it, before him and the girls set back out into the hallway and made for Quinton's room.

-

As they discussed, they fortified the room. Gabriel and Audrey patched up Amelia's cuts, while Quinton cleaned and sealed up the bathroom, placing a chair against the door to block it off from the creature.

Mr. and Mrs. Lim had gotten back by the time Quinton was finished and went off to bed, having no clue what had taken place. This was a bonus for Quin, as he was too exhausted to explain about anything. He returned to his room and helped the group close off the window, by rearranging the furniture to block it off. Feeling a little safer, they all sat down.

It was decided that Amelia and Gabriel would take the first watch, as both were the most awake out of the four. Audrey and Quinton would be next. Scrooge cuddled close to Audrey, sighing tiredly into her arms.

Quin allowed Amelia to sleep on his bed, resting her arm atop a pillow, even though she insisted it wasn't as bad as they were making it out to be. She almost felt like a wounded soldier. But it was nice to get some positive attention.

They were settled at last. They all sighed heavily, and prepared for the long night ahead. Hoping and praying that by the morning... things would finally get better.

- - - - - -

"*Don't.*"

Ivy's body jerked and tossed on its side.

"*Don't do it.*"

Her closed eyes squeezed shut. Squeezing in the physical, but widening in the subconscious.

She watched in horror as it happened.

"*Stop it! Stop it!!*" Her little voice began to whimper.

The shadows. The endless shadows. They all converged and consumed. They consumed the town. They swallowed everything in their path.

"*Please!*"

Ivy's face teemed with hurt.

"IVY!!!"

She ran towards the ones ahead of her. The ones being chased.

"No!" Her voice actually broke.

Ivy ran as fast as she could to the group ahead of her. But the shadows... the darkness... it blocked them all off. She froze, eyes widened, as she watched helplessly. The group turned... she saw their faces... Gabriel... Audrey... Amelia... Troy... Quinton. They all stared at her, unable to move. Pleading for her help.

*"No! Not **them**!"*

That's when she saw it... the thing chasing them. Not the shadows. No... the one the shadows were assisting. There it was... the Chupacabra. It found her new friends.

"Don't!!"

It barred its teeth, approaching them slowly and menacingly. They all screamed as it came. They couldn't move. It all happened so quick... too quick... too quick to realize it suddenly leaping forward. Leaping right at the others.

"NOOOO!!!!"

Ivy gasped, her eyes popping open, as she was pulled out of the nightmare, thanks to Magnus whining heavily and sniffing her face, giving it a few concerned licks. She yanked her body upwards, her breathing unsteady, as her tiny heart raced. Her eyes drifted around the room wildly, trying to wake herself up to make sure she was all alone. She swallowed, licking her lips.

Her face turned to Magnus, who turned his away a little, but still resting his sights on her. It was as if the two had the same thought at that moment. She hesitated no longer. She pushed the covers off and leapt out of bed, walking quickly to the hallway.

She made her way to Kathryn's room. She wasn't allowed in here, naturally, but she had to do this. She crept over to her foster mother's night stand, and silently took hold of her phone. There, she sneaked out of the room and into the dining room.

Kathryn was not the best in cyber safety, as Ivy had found out many times from borrowing her phone. No password to speak of, therefore it made things easier for a seven year old to take control of her tech and use it as she pleased. This time was different, however. It wasn't for research. It was life or death.

She peered into the contacts. She scrolled down the list. She

found the name she wanted. She clicked it. She waited only a second... then began texting.
"Gabriel. **You're in danger.**"

CHAPTER XXIV
✦ SURREALISM ✦

Light flickered gently through the cracks of the blinds, signifying that a new day had arrived in Hollowgrove. Gabriel's eyes fluttered open, as the light hit his face. He shook his head gently, as he forced his body to sit up. His first instinct was to check the others; no surprise, they were all asleep.

They were good at taking turns on watch for awhile, until they found the task to be too great, becoming too comfortable with the lack of any activity in the room. Amelia was crashed on the bed, her hair a completely tangled mess. She must have fallen asleep before she could take her glasses off, which couldn't have been very comfortable. Quinton did, however, which probably meant the boy simply called it complete quits, and plopped down for well deserved rest.

Nothing seemed to be out of place in the room. The barricade against the window remained, and he imagined if the house was attacked again, that they wouldn't even still be alive. It was day now, though... they were safe.

He arose, cricking his back and neck. His eyes gravitated to the clock next to Quinton's bed and saw that it was pushing to 10:30 in the morning. As much as he sympathized with the others for their need to sleep, he knew they shouldn't be wasting any more time. There was work to be done. And a creature to stop.

He bent down and gently nudged Audrey's shoulder, who curled into a ball upon contact, Scrooge's tiny body buried under the covers with her. "Audy." He poked Quin. "Quinton."
He turned his head and poked Amelia's beanie-covered head.
"Amelia."
The three stirred, grunting in their half-asleep states.
"Whatever it is, forget it." Quinton grumbled, throwing his blanket over his head.
"We need to go." Gabriel stressed.
"Or do you three want another night of getting attacked by a bloodsucking monster?"
Audrey nearly launched from the floor at the sound of monster, throwing the blanket into the air, while Scrooge's entire expression

was one of horror, as he was woken up so chaotically. It appeared that his sister recalled the experience.

"No thank you, I choose coffee instead."

The Beckhart girl immediately bolted for the bathroom. Quinton crawled from his blanket cave, snatching his glasses from the floor, while Amelia quite literally rolled out of bed, onto her back. She stared at the ceiling with half opened eyes, her tired breathing mixed with disdain for life in general.

"I'm ready to die now."

"At least wait for nightfall."

Gabriel took her by the hands and dragged her backwards against the carpet, until she squirmed like an eel and hurried up on her own. "Alright alright, I'm up!"

Gabriel smirked and hopped to his bedding to retrieve his phone.

"Might as well leave everything here." Uttered Quinton, doing some stretches.

"Don't know if you idiots will have to come back."

Gabe shrugged, "Fair point."

At that moment, he checked his phone content. And at that moment, he saw the text. Left early, when he was already asleep. His blood ran cold when he saw *who* it was from.

Kathryn Chapman.

"Gabriel. You're in danger."

He swallowed hard, standing completely still. His eyes motioned to Amelia and Quinton, who paid him no mind as they shuffled around to gather this and that for the morning.

His attention returned to the phone... he began typing.

"Kathryn? What happened?"

He didn't expect an immediate reply. Kathryn would no doubt be busy with other things since sending him that. Why she would even send him that and not call him, he wasn't sure.

His heart jumped, however, when his phone dinged.

"It's about time you woke up."

His eyebrows crinkled.

"I've been waiting for hours, using the phone for 'games'."

Gabriel was so confused. "Kathryn? Is this you?"

"Why would this be Kathryn?"

"Who then?"

"It's me."

He shook his head. Until it hit him...

"Ivy? Why are you on Kathryn's phone?"

"If this is the height of your skill-set as a detective, then I will have to find better."

His mind was spinning.

"Why did you send me that text? Are you okay?"

"I'm fine. It's *you* that has problems."

He was about to reply. But another text came through.

"Don't tell Kathryn about this. This is between me and you. I'm deleting this conversation as soon as we're done here."

"You are not sounding like a child at all. Are you really Ivy?"

"Are you calling me stupid? *Someone's* being ageist."

If this really was Ivy, he was surprised. Ivy seemed like she would be a completely sweet and well behaved child, if she were talking verbally. Maybe she just had a bad night and was a little... crabby. He shifted his glasses,

"What happened, Ivy? Tell me. How am I in danger?"

There was a delay. His facial expression was one of worry and contempt. He was getting frustrated. "Ivy."

"Come pick me up. We'll talk more then."

"The others can come. I can't."

"Why not?"

"I have to go to the station."

"The police?"

"Yes. To show them evidence."

"...Don't go to the police."

He jerked his head back as he read her text.

"...Why not?"

The delay between texts was making him nauseous.

"Just don't go."

And that was it. No other replies.

He attempted to call, three times. All straight to voice mail.

He kept texting. And texting. And texting.

None of them were even read.

It almost seemed like he talked to a ghost.

He squeezed his nails into his palms, as he paced the hallway outside Quinton's room. Now he questioned the entire plan... what he should do... where he should go... who he should see?

Why was Ivy being so enigmatic, warning him, baiting him,

but never giving him any answers? It felt as though this little girl was luring him further into all of this, becoming part of the conspiracy, but still trying to protect him from learning anything further. What secrets was she so afraid would endanger him if the full truth was discovered? What in the world was this girl really involved with?

But the fear of the unknown was honestly starting to turn into irritation. Ivy might have meant well, but Gabriel had lost his patience with her by now. He couldn't let his life be ruled by fear. Fear of monsters, fear of dreams, fear of what could be or what couldn't. He had to make his own decisions, even if they turned out not being the right ones to make.

-

So... they got dressed. Gathered their belongings. And they left. Quinton wanted to depart before his parents awoke, which would be before noon, as he knew they would no doubt desire to make a big breakfast...and play bingo.

Quin and Audrey rode in his car, while Gabe and Amelia rode in hers. The four wasted no time in getting Gabriel to the police station.

-

Beckhart crawled out, holding his coat together and tightening his scarf, as the wind had decided to be against the world that morning, blowing violently through the streets, as if summoning a storm. His eyes lifted to the sky for but a brief moment. And his mind... his mind flashed to that dream. That terrible dream where the sky was consumed by a black massive cloud, which distributed terrifying bolts of multi-colored lightning.

The images of the shapes within the clouds and the chilling, inhuman sounds they made echoed through his head. He held the door with his open hand, his muscles quivering. He could almost see the clouds above him. The lightning. The shapes. He could almost feel the fire burn into him, as he nearly went cross-eyed staring deep into the atmosphere hovering over the town, expecting one of the bolts to strike him down where he stood.

With those horrifying images and sounds came the chilling screams of Ivy, as he remembered her tiny flailing body being dragged through the woods by the creature.

She was trying to warn me. She is trying to reach out to me. Gabriel's fingers pressed hard against the edges of the metal of the car door. *But I can't get through. Why won't you let me get through?*

"Gabriel."

He jumped, his eyes zooming down on his sister. Audrey leaned over, staring up at him with the utmost concern.

"What's wrong with you? I said your name like, seven times."

"I-I'm listening..." He adjusted his glasses, swallowing hard, as his body shifted.

"You're listening, alright, but not to me."

"I swear, I'm alright, I'm listening, it's fine."

Her eyes flexed a bit before lifting her chin.

"Maybe I should go with you."

"No... no, I'm fine. I can do this."

He shut his door as Amelia took his place, climbing in the back of Quinton's car. Pine rolled down the window and tossed the Beckhart boy her keys.

"Bring it back safely or I'll sue."

Gabriel said nothing. Just stuffed the jingling handful into his pockets. Audrey shut her door, sticking her head out the window afterwards.

"Remember, stick to the evidence. Don't back down. And *don't* let them make you feel crazy."

Gabriel shook his head, sniffing a small secretive laugh.

"You've had one run-in with the cops, and suddenly you're an expert?"

"That's Audrey for you."

Audrey gave the backseat a painfully venomous glare.

"...Just be cautious. Text me when you're out, okay?"

"I will. Be careful."

His sister gave a quickened nod, before ducking her head back in, just in time for Quinton to speed away, leaving the Beckhart boy behind. He swallowed once more, stuffing his hands into his pockets.

It felt as though he and his sister, though joined in the same complicated tangle of an assembly, were now spending even more frequent gaps apart than they had ever had since they were children. With that separation, there was an unspoken sadness.

They practically felt like twins, with the bond they shared.

Watching her now ride off, including when she walked away from the group the previous day, displaying only a sliver of the anxiety he was feeling from the departure... it honestly made him feel isolated. His eyes were glued to Quinton's car, which grew smaller and smaller to the eye, as each second passed. And he let out a shaky breath, rubbing his freezing hands together.

Gabriel finally took notice of the station beside him. Various citizens passed it, walking right by him on the sidewalk. Lost in their frivolous conversations, or deep nonintellectual thoughts, as they mindlessly went about their dull, silly lives, chasing after all the things that didn't truly matter.

Gabe was beginning to become aware of the way things really worked. The way things people tend to ignore or become part of. A way in which Amelia strongly advocated against.
Accepting the 'bubble' society placed them in.

The Beckhart boy's terrifying encounter with a bloodsucking creature was weighing too heavily on his mind to care about the latest social media trends, or who was dating who, or which sports team was conquering the news. None of that mattered now. Not anymore.

Gabriel wasted no more time. Fighting against the ferocious wind, Beckhart rushed inside.

- - -

It didn't take long before Quinton, Amelia and Audrey arrived in Ivy's neighborhood. The group agreed to meet up with Troy upon arrival, the party deciding to go find Wyatt from there, to conduct their interview. As they pulled up next to her house, they spotted Valhalla in all its banged up glory, looking like a pizza van ready for delivery.

Exiting out, the three peered over at where Troy was parked. It didn't take long for the blonde-haired surfer to notice them, roll down his window quickly, and wave excitedly at his new posse.

"DUDESSS! A good morning to you!"

"And a good morning to you!" Pine called back, with a chipper attitude. "Have you seen Ivy yet?!"

"Not yet, think she's still sleeping! Poor kid must be wiped out!"

"Can we please stop shouting across the street?" Audrey uttered aloud. Amelia completely ignored her.

"We're gonna go get her! Stay put!"

At that moment, however, something lunged at the Pine girl. Something that made her scream, even causing Audrey and Quinton to shout in surprise, and jump back. Something in which made Amelia swing her body around and attack the thing that lunged at her. Attacking something of which was laughing with pure wicked delight.

"LYCAN, YOU IDIOT!"

She hit him so many times against the chest, it successfully knocked the wind out of him. Normally he wouldn't be so easily fazed, but Amelia was the one exception. She was deceptively strong within that geeky little body.

"Don't freaking do that!! After the night we had, you're lucky I didn't shoot you!"

"Wow, that's a little dramatic!" Lycan managed to get out through a half-laugh, half-pained groan.

"And man, your fists pack a punch..."

He rolled his shoulders in exaggerated motions.

"Excuse me, hello?" Audrey said with a wave, drawing the attention of the other three. She then pointed at Lycan.

"Who the heck is this?"

"Thanks for looking me in the eye and asking that." Lycan poked with a hint of irritation. Before pointing at her.

"Lemme guess.... mmm, spoiled rich girl who lives in a fancy mansion, who treats people like the scum of the earth, and thinks she's above any and all consequences. Am I getting warm?"

Audrey's brows crinkled. Lycan's arm fell limp to his side.

"...Thought so."

With his other hand, he pat his chest.

"I'm Lycan. Not that it really matters to you."

He turned back around, leaving Audrey feeling just a little bit embarrassed.

Even with just Quinton next to her, who was rolling his eyes at the presence of Lycan, she felt her face swell as if she were in a room full of staring people. Another one of Amelia's cohorts, it seemed. There to simply stir up the pot and drive her further down the rabbit hole.

Welcome to Hollowgrove

Just as Lycan had turned, Amelia leapt close to him. *Very* close to him. A closeness that is not the standard distance you stand to... well... **just a friend**. And it made Audrey's eyes grow in size just a bit. In both surprise and curiosity.

"What are you doing here?" Pine hissed in a whisper, trying to be discreet. "Now is not a good time, I have work to do!"

"I know, I know, you texted me that already, but there's something important I have to tell you!"

"I don't have time! You gotta wait!"

Audrey couldn't help herself. She strained her ear in the most nonchalant manner she could muster, trying to listen to every word regarding this new and intriguing development. Their hushed conversation continued.

"Why can't I come along?"

"Because!"

"That's not a real reason!"

"Just trust me, we're barely getting by with the team we have right now! Just wait, okay?"

Lycan huffed, shaking his head from the rejection.

"Will I at least see you tonight then?"

Audrey perked. Especially when Amelia bit her lip, trying to hide a smile. Which she naturally failed to hide.

"Maybe. We'll see..." She rubbed the back of her neck. Audrey remembered that Amelia often did this when they were young, when she was embarrassed or uncomfortable in a situation. And by god... Pine was *blushing*??? It truly was the end times.

"We're going to interview that Wyatt guy now."

"Alright... text me when you're done. It's important."

Pine broke eye contact.

"I will..."

Lycan smirked and poked the middle of her glasses, which she scrunched her face at, before turning to leave.

"See ya, pretty lady."

He gestured at Quin with a jerk of the head, but completely passed Beckhart without saying a single word or even acknowledging her general direction.

Sadly, the reputation of Audrey Beckhart was not one she was proud of. While many former classmates of hers either wanted to befriend or date her, there was a large number of them who despised her simply for her social status. The abrasive treatment of Amelia's 'friend' only reminded her of that.

"What did *he* want?" Quinton venomously spoke, Audrey now distinguishing to be unlike his usual droll, sarcastic tone. It appeared he did not much enjoy Lycan's company.

Pine shifted her glasses, clearing her throat, as she tried to rid herself of the lingering smile the young man caused her.

"He just needs to talk to me about something important, that's all. I told him it's gonna have to wait."

"*Good*. We've got work to do. He can take you out some other day."

"He wasn't asking me-"

"I knew it! *He*'s the one you got your eye on, isn't he?"

This made Amelia instantly straighten up and go completely stiff. Her smile had vanished, replaced by an expression that teetered between anger and embarrassment.

"Shut up, you don't know what you're talking about."

"Oh yeah? Is that why your face looks like the inside of a volcano right now??"

Pine did not just look like a volcano. She was about to erupt like one. Both her fists were curled so tight, her veins pulsing with violent adrenaline, her every molecule ready to charge at Audrey and tear her to shreds.

Amelia did not admit intimate feelings aloud. She was not the type. Audrey was putting her on the spot, right in front of Quin, who was the only peer she did not want to appear silly around. Thanks to her, she felt like a weak, silly little school girl. Oh, how she loathed Audrey Beckhart.

Audrey could sense the rage emanating from Pine. Even Quinton could feel the tension between the two start to grow, and he ever so slightly backed away, in the event of a fist fight happening. Fortunately for both of them, the day was saved by the sudden arrival of a blurry creature, that pounced Amelia to the ground, and wasted no time showering her with sloppy canine kisses.

Pine pleaded for help, as she had been pinned to the ground by Magnus, in between eventual giggles and humorous screeches.

"Magnus, stop! Get off me, you hulking goof!!"

Audrey tried to stifle a laugh, as she watched Pine get attacked by the enormous German Shepherd, but a quick glance beside her made her own breath suck back into her lungs with a loud gasp, making her literally choke on air. Her hand clasped over her heart as a result, and she bent down a bit too dramatically.

"Ivy, holy *crap*!" She exclaimed to the silent little girl who appeared next to her and Quinton, as if out of thin air.

"You can't be doing that!!"

The Beckhart girl shook her head as she tried to catch her breath, her hand squeezing her chest, her heart throbbing from within.

Quinton peaked at the little girl from behind Audrey, whose eyes only glared at the two beside her for a brief moment, and he waved without saying a word. Ivy was serious, however. Very serious. More serious than what they had seen of her thus far.

It was almost as if she did not wish to look at the small group. Not out of resentment or fear... but out of an unpleasant knowledge of something. Something she was keeping from them.

She stepped forward past the two, her eyes glued to her canine companion. Lifting up her tiny hand, she snapped with two fingers. Magnus immediately ceased and jumped back to her side, leaving Amelia wiggling on her back like an upside down beetle. Ivy watched as Pine scrambled up to her feet, the little girl's expression ice cold.

When Amelia regained her composure, she looked down at the child. Her own expression started to sink and implicate concern.

"What's wrong, kiddo? You okay?"

Ivy's eyes fell in the direction of Valhalla. This drew the attention of the others, where they noticed someone fast approaching. Troy.

He grinned wide at the small group, which was not an unusual expression for him, being such a relaxed and care-free human being. "Sup, dudes! Are we good to go yet?"

He rustled the top of Ivy's head, turning her hair into a bird's nest, before scratching Magnus behind the ears. If looks could kill, Ivy would have struck Troy where he stood, from the amount of poison she cast him through her intense little eyes.

"You guys good?"

"Something's wrong with Ivy."

Brooke glanced at Pine, whose own gaze was glued to the child.
"Oh yeah?"
But Ivy suddenly signed something, of which made Troy's brows lift in curiosity.
"Yeah?"
He shrugged, as he turned his head back to the others.
"Said she's fine, just tired and thinking about yesterday."
"Tell her that's a straight up lie. She was perfectly placid last night with what happened. Something else happened."
"She can hear you."
"Well, whatever." Amelia folded her arms, getting agitated.
"We're not leaving until you tell us what's going on, Ivy. I can promise you that."
 The little girl glared.
Amy was being stubborn. She was always stubborn, but now she was impossibly stubborn. When she got this way, it was futile to resist her, something only Audrey knew best. She would not let down, even if you caused her physical pain. It's what made her a relentless activist. It's what made her a fighter. It's what made her such an irritating, but passionate human being. One had to at least admire that aspect of Amelia Pine.
Ivy swallowed as her and Pine locked eyes, neither one backing down from the other. It appeared Ivy was just as stubborn as she. This was quite the turn they did not expect from a seven year old.
The other three's heads bounced back and forth between the two, waiting to see who would break first. It was a humorous, but tedious moment, as if watching a game of chess with the players dressed in bunny costumes. A tug of war for power between an adult woman and a child was equally as entertaining.
 Eventually the silence was too much for Troy to take.
"Dudes, please, can we go now? We're burning daylight, man!"
While Troy was right, it changed nothing. Audrey and Quinton's eyes drifted to Amelia, then Ivy. They were smirking. This brought them a much needed inner laugh, after the previous night's harrowing events.
"Amelia, please?" Troy pleaded.
"That's up to Ivy."
Ah... another power move. Pine was leaving the ball in Ivy's

court. Leaving all the pressure of the investigation on an obstinate child. Even Ivy seemed surprised.

Suddenly, a phone rang. Everyone jumped. It was the X-Files theme. All eyes pointed to Amelia.

Feeling personally attacked, Pine turned her body away, as she buried her hand into her pocket and brought the device up to her ear. "Speak."

Is she a mob boss? Audrey mentally questioned. *Who answers the phone like that?*

Amelia listened intently, as did the rest of the party. Even Magnus seemed as though he was joining in, as his head turned in curiosity, his large ears pointing straight up.

"You're kidding me."

They all perked.

"Seriously?"

The anticipation was making them anxious.

"Okay... I'll tell them."

She hung up abruptly, and her body swiveled.

"We've gotta watch the news right now."

CHAPTER XXV
✦ TURN A BLIND EYE ✦

At the mention of 'news', Troy was struck with a spark of urgency. He rushed to the van, adjusting the antenna on the roof, before sliding back the side door, and burying into his equipment. Compelled by their curiosity, the others followed him on his sudden energetic venture.

Audrey was the first to break the awkward silence.

"What are you up to, Troy??"

"Amy said we need to watch the news, well... *voila*!" Brooke pointed with pride at the powered television screen, of which was tuned to the local news.

Pine's face lit up.

"Troy, you're an absolute *beauty*! This totally beats my phone!"

The group climbed into Valhalla, Troy shutting the door behind them, as they all huddled around the TV screen. The dogs laid on the floor, feasting on the bowls of food Troy had prepared for them.

Despite the heater not being on, it was still relatively warmer inside than out. They were thankful of Brooke's quick thinking.

"I hooked this baby up on my travels as a source of entertainment, but also to keep up with the news the old-fashioned way. I'm not much of a social media guy."

He turned up the volume, as the news anchor spoke to the audience. A woman with medium length red hair, a blue blazer, staring into the camera with intensely bright green eyes, as she sat within the studio.

Audrey recognized her from the parties her parents attended, dragging the siblings along against their will. She was amongst the only genuinely nice people in the social group, not faking to everyone's face, and trying to impress them. She seemed real. Audrey liked her.

"*Good afternoon, I'm Karen Neill. Thank you for joining us today, as we prepare for a special press conference from our very own mayor, Ripley Ravenwood. The conference is set to address the police investigation, regarding several attacks last night on local livestock, including one where a farmhand claimed* *the animal responsible chased and tried to attack **him**."*

"Oh my gosh, they're talking about Wyatt!" Audrey exclaimed.

"Listen to that, though." Quinton noted. "Chupie was on a rampage last night. There were other attacks."

"Oh god..."

"Y'all, be quiet, I'm trying to hear."

The two fell silent, as Pine leaned in closer to listen.

"-Where several goats and cows were found. Some were not even finished, leading investigators to wonder if this is a cruel hoax, or a rabid animal on a spree of violence."

"Spree of Violence, that's a good movie title."

"Quinton, *hush!* I already missed the first part!"

His lips curled back. Amelia's eyes narrowed.

"However, police encourage citizens to remain calm, and to not go out searching for the culprit on their own. Sightings of a creature have multiplied within the last two weeks. This has led many to believe that the string of recent disappearances may be connected. Disappearances dating back several months just this year. When asked about the missing Casper City and neighboring Hollowgrove citizens earlier this week, Mayor Ravenwood assured the public there was nothing to worry about, and to get on with business as usual."

"I remember that from the report about Melony." Audrey whispered. "I couldn't believe he said that..."

At the mention of Melony, Pine glanced at her. An expression of sadness grazed her face for a brief moment, that went unnoticed by those around her, who were all glued to the TV screen at this point. Except for Ivy, who sat back against the wall of the van, her hands crossed atop her lap. She watched the news, as if she was already aware of every single word they were about to spew out. Nothing shocked her.

Amelia's eyes turned back to the TV, softly shaking her head, as she tried to clear a memory flashing back to her. A memory of when Melony had come over, terrified. She had just gotten into a heated argument with her controlling and emotionally abusive mother. Her father, as usual, did nothing to stop it.

Melony arrived at her house in tears, and Amelia could barely make out what she was saying. That's when Melony tried to tell her something... tried to tell her that something was following her. She didn't know what, though. But Melony... she had never seen her friend so petrified. It was as if she knew she was going to be taken. She knew her days were numbered.

If only Amelia knew what would become of her friend… she never would have let her run off in a fit of blinding desperation. Like Melony didn't even know where she was going anymore. Like something compelled her mind to run off into the darkness of the night and be taken.

Pine swallowed. Her mind forced itself to leave the chilling last moments she had with Melony Martin, and get back to work. She was distracting her own self now.

"-Martin's mother commented."

Her eyes widened. ***No.***

"The family continues to hold out hope their daughter is alive."
What did she say?!

She missed it. But she couldn't ask the others what it was, or else she would miss more. Just the mention of Melony's mother made Amelia's blood boil. She couldn't help it... she hated that woman.

"If you are just joining us, we are now tuning in on the press conference right here in Casper City, where Mayor Ravenwood is to address last night's strange attacks on local livestock. Let's listen in."

- - -

Gabriel stepped through the halls of the police precinct.
It was crowded. Various officers were moving in every direction, scrambling in the hustle that demanded their attention, even if they didn't even know what they were getting themselves into. Majority of them didn't.

The Beckhart boy proceeded with caution, unsure of how to handle the chaotic environment.

A part of him was ready to retreat back to the quiet, calm confines of his home. Where he was safe, and he knew he was safe, and he didn't have to think about anything or anyone else, because everyone knew who he was and where he was, and with that came a sort of invisibility.

No one bothered him, because they didn't have to. They didn't see the right him, because they already had their own image of him. He was just another stuck up rich boy. Perfect. Keep thinking that. Leave him alone.

However, the other part of him... the part that forced him to look into those news reports. Those police reports. Those missing people. The mysterious creatures. The strange phenomena that enveloped his town... that part made him take every step forward.

Despite the horrors he already had a glimpse of... the horrors he knew that he was bound to face. The part that made him keep walking. The part that made him not care anymore what anyone thought.

He had a duty now. A duty to find out the truth.

"You freaking *moron*!"

Gabe's eyes snapped at an officer to his left, from within a small room. He knew this one... he always had a short temper and berated other officers for the slightest thing. He could only imagine how the recent strain on the department had worsened his behavior.

"Get your butt over here and fix this! This is utter crap!"

His language was much more colorful, of course. Gabriel elected to mentally censor it, as he hated needless profanity. The thing upsetting the officer was a broken coffee machine. He made a further point to stick his tongue out and make a face like a Chinese guardian lion, before pouring the presumably bitter coffee on the floor, and throwing his paper cup at the back of the one who was cleaning the mess.

"Don't tell me you fixed the freaking thing, if it's still tasting like raw sewage! Good for nothing piece of garbage!"

What a tasteless man...

Beckhart's eyes venomously followed the man, as he passed the room slowly. The officer noticed the magnetic presence of one so famous as Gabriel Beckhart and he looked to him, his expression changing to one almost sheepish in nature.

The other officer, the one cleaning the mess, sat up and pushed back his glasses as he saw Beckhart. The appearance surprised the humble fellow.

"M-Mr. Beckhart!" The cruel officer let out in a hurry. "I, uh-"

Gabriel didn't give him a chance to finish. He kept walking. This was the nicest way of embarrassing the brute in front of the others. Not giving him the time of day. He could do much worse.

But for now, this had to do.

Many officers took a moment to pause and greet Gabe, elated to see a celebrity walk into the precinct.

I wonder if they do the same for everyone of power... He wondered.

Or is it just rich celebrity nobodies that everybody else praises on cue... because they have to?

His thoughts were cut short, as he arrived at the front desk. Ah yes... Officer Martinez. The one whose brother had an enormous crush on his sister.

As he recalled, the Martinez brothers were from a dirt poor family in the trailer park. Social services forced the parents to send them to school, or else they would strip them away into the foster system. Did no good in the end for the one brother... as he was already in prison by the time he was the siblings' age. But Officer Martinez, he did make *something* of himself... even if it was being one of the most incompetent policemen Gabriel had ever met.

Martinez, he never liked Gabriel. Upon making eye contact with Beckhart, his face displayed obvious signs of annoyance and irritation. Almost the same as when he saw his sister the previous day.

"Not the other one." He heard the pudgy man utter under his breath.

He rubbed his forehead in clear frustration, before he looked up at him properly, straightening his back against his spinning chair.

"What is it now, Thing 1? Thing 2 already wasted our time yesterday with that stalker stunt."

"First of all, that's my sister you're talking about. You're *going* to address her with respect."

Martinez's eyebrows lifted in surprise. Gabriel was never an aggressor... this was new.

"Second of all, it wasn't a stalker stunt. After the week we and others have faced, the last thing I have patience for is your unwillingness to take us seriously. I don't care what you think of me. I am *going* to tell you things and you are *going* to listen. I am *going* to show you evidence and you are *going* to examine it. Is that clear? Or do I need to repeat that more slowly for you?"

Martinez could do nothing but blink in the blankest way possible. Beckhart just took his mind on a trip he did not expect to go. Was this even snooty old Gabe Beckhart that everybody made such a big deal out of for no reason??

"Uhhhhhhh, okay?"

He stood up from his chair, the furniture creaking uncomfortably to the ears, and he walked around to the side door, soon going through it to lead Gabriel along.

"C'mon, I'll take you to the boss man."

Gabriel wasted no time. He followed.

"Nelson Blum wasn't the stalker."

"Yeah, no kidding."

"He was set up by the real one."

"Obviously."

"The real one, who was able to feed false results to Audrey's search engine and frame someone else. The real one, who entered our house again last night and stole my sister's weapon from her purse."

Martinez skid to a stop, his shoes squeaking loudly through the hall, and his eyes darted at Gabriel. Gabriel, in turn, gave him a look of soft triumph. He finally was able to faze him.

"He broke into your house again?"

"And took pictures of my sister, yes. As he took pictures of us the night before. The thing is..."

He scrolled through his gallery and lifted up his phone.

"There's a problem with the way this guy looks..."

"You got a picture of him?"

Beckhart pushed the phone screen closer for Martinez to see.

"Look at the TV screen, at the reflection."

The deputy's eyes squinted.

"...I don't see no reflection."

"That's the problem." Gabe pointed.

"There is none. *There's no one there.*"

Martinez scrunched his entire face in bewilderment.

"How can a man take photos and not be seen in a reflection?"

"He can, if he photoshopped himself out."

Both the young men turned, as another officer approached them. Beckhart slumped defeatedly as Sergeant Spiel came close, nodding at the phone.

Uncanny

"Gotten reports of other break-ins. Same thing happened. Pictures taken of the people, personal belongings stolen. Some thought they saw no reflection of the culprit. Until one realized he was doctoring himself out of the photos. That's it. He's trying to scare you lot."

Martinez's head turned back to Gabriel. He couldn't make out his expression while facing another person, but Gabe just knew it was a smug one. Mocking him for being seemingly silly and paranoid.

Don't let them make you feel crazy...
Audrey's words rung through his head.

This is what she experienced when she came here. She felt the same embarrassment, and disheartening moment of feeling like she was losing her mind. But he knew they were right. He wouldn't let them make him feel crazy.

"You got names to those so-called victims?"
The sergeant lifted his head up. Gabe shook his head in disappointment. "Don't even bother. Of course you don't. Because there are none."

"Now hold on, Gabriel..."

"It's Mr. Beckhart, thanks. I'm not going to even bother with this anymore. You won't do anything about it. Why, I don't know, maybe you're just trying to cover this all up to save your own skins. Or maybe somebody's got you in their pocket. I don't care. We'll handle that ourselves. In the mean time... we were attacked yesterday. Both in the middle of the day, and last night. And I think you know by what."

Spiel's face tightened. Gabe couldn't tell if it was from growing irritation, or simply the discomfort of Beckhart seeing right through him. Maybe it was both.

"...The Chupacabra attacks."
Gabriel nodded. Spiel cut his eyes to Martinez. They shared the same look, as if they knew some great truth. A truth they were about to unveil to the Beckhart boy.

"Follow me." Spiel commanded.
He turned and began striding down the hallway, of which now made Gabriel feel vulnerable. Where was he leading him...

- - -

The group watched in anticipation, as the news cut to a

spacious, well-lit room filled with reporters and journalists, wielding notepads and pens, awaiting the arrival of the joint mayor of Hollowgrove and Casper.

The media fed on the presence of Ripley Ravenwood. He was a sensation. Handsome, smart, charismatic. He fueled them with his speeches and playboy-like appearances, sucking the media dry like a vampire.

It didn't matter what trials the town and city faced, what creatures appeared to terrorize the people. When Ravenwood showed his face, it all went away. He had the people in the palm of his hand. And they liked it.

Just as quickly as the camera had switched to the conference room, Ravenwood walked through the back door. He was all instant smiles, vigorously waving at his audience. They cheered for him. With all this suffering and fear, they were cheering for him, as if he were the messiah. It was enough to slowly turn the small group's stomachs into knots, as they felt a growing sickness.

The whole event happening before their eyes briefly made them dizzy, dissociating themselves from that particular reality. These were times of loss, times of sincere turmoil. This was no time to worship an ignorant politician.

Ripley reached the podium, grinning ear to ear at his citizens.

"People of Casper... people of Hollowgrove... my beloved, beautiful citizens!"

His arms outstretched. One side would take this as him embracing the people's presence. The other would take this as him shamelessly basking in the praise. And the way he spoke... it was more like a theatrical performer, than an appointed leader.

"It came to my attention late last night... by our diligent law enforcement, who bravely guard this city and the town of Hollowgrove without rest... they told me that terrible attacks were committed upon the livestock of the town. Innocent animals perished. Some were senselessly wounded and never finished off. One such attack left a defenseless young farmhand rushing toward a barn to barricade himself, as he was chased by what he believed to be... a mythical creature."

Ripley straightened himself, licking his lips. It was almost as though he were stopping himself from laughing. He was really mocking Wyatt, on live TV.

"...But I can assure you. These attacks were orchestrated as an **elaborate hoax**."

Audrey's jaw dropped.

"You've gotta be kidding me."

- - -

Gabriel was led through a cold, damp feeling hallway, that no other officers were present at. They walked until they reached a room, of which Sergeant Spiel had to unlock with one of his keys.

The lights were flickering above the three. Beckhart cut his eyes to it. It was as if something were trying to tell him to turn back. This felt wrong... he felt almost sick. Gabriel's skin was growing cold, as his blood was draining from his face. He felt his eyes swelling, his body becoming so stiff, he could feel his own heart beating. Every one of his senses were on high alert.

They're about to lie to you.

Don't believe a single word they say.

Spiel and Martinez went first, leaving Gabriel to reluctantly follow along. It was another hallway, but the lighting was terrible here. The flickering persisted. It was also dirty. He did not expect this, as the rest of the precinct seemed to be quite clean and maintained.

It smelled... oh, did it reek. It was the first thing Gabriel noticed, as he reached the middle of the hall, and his nostrils were infiltrated by one of the most putrid smells ever to reach your senses. **Death**. It smelled like **death**.

Gabriel's breathing quickened. There was a door ahead of him and the officers. The closer he grew to it, the worse the smell became. *Where are you taking me?*

Something in him wanted to run the other way. But he was in a building full of armed officers. If Spiel wanted him to stay, he very well had the man power to keep him there. How far would he even expect to go? Spiel could snap his fingers to arrest Beckhart, and no one would hesitate. He figured as long as he complied with him... the better his chances would be.

"We're here." Spiel's husky voice announced, as they regrettably arrived at the end of the hall. He placed his hand upon the knob and turned it. "Hold your breath."

Gabriel indeed held his breath, as the door opened. As if even possible, the smell was now stronger. Martinez brought his arm up and covered his nose and mouth. Beckhart couldn't hold his breath for long. And when it escaped him, he coughed horridly. He soon had to cover his nose and mouth as well, using his scarf as an emergency face mask.

They were in the morgue. And before them were tables used to examine bodies. In this case, the tables were lined up together. A total of three. Something was laying on those tables. Covered with sheets. Gabriel's eyes focused intensely, dreading what this could mean.

"What is that?" His voice broke in a whisper.
Spiel cleared his throat, as he placed a surgical mask over his head, shielding his airway.

"The truth about what attacked those animals last night." Beckhart's heart raced. Spiel wasted no time. He waltzed right up to the table, briefly glanced at the young men, before throwing off the sheets. Whatever it was beneath was now revealed.

It took everything in Gabriel not to throw up. Before him were three recently deceased animals...but not just any animals.

"Meet your Chupacabra."

- - -

"The police unveiled the horrific predators to me just this morning, but they are nothing of any supernatural properties. These were ordinary beasts from the forest that were sighted, that went rabid and attacked the livestock. And a cruel individual decided to exploit the unfortunate occurrence, and orchestrate a hoax of a mad Chupacabra terrorizing the area. But I assure you, citizens, the threat is over! The animals were captured and put down. And the fiend behind these crimes **has been apprehended**!"

"There is no way... absolutely NO way!"
Audrey's blood boiled. She was filled with such shock and fury, she didn't know what to do. "THIS IS ABSOLUTE--"
She bit her own tongue, remembering Ivy was sitting right next to her. "--Words I can't say in front of a child!"

"Go on and say it, Ivy can cover her ears." Quinton joked. As Ivy actually did go to cover her ears, even through staring at the others with mild confusion, Troy stopped her.

"No one's saying anything, sweetie."
He lowered her arms back down, before looking back at the others. "You see now, Audrey? You see what they do? What they

always do?"

Audrey looked back, but still couldn't believe.

"I can't believe this! This is ridiculous! We literally were attacked by this thing twice; he isn't some mangy, rabid animal!! We saw this thing with our own eyes!"

Pine was unfazed. In fact, the mayor's words made her almost smirk. She was expecting this. She knew they would pull the hoax card. *Predictable.*

Audrey gasped.

"Gabriel... he went to show them the evidence!"

"Won't do him any good." Amelia spoke. "They got the cops in their pocket on this one..."

"Don't say that. We'll need the police!"

"Politicians own law enforcement, Audrey. Yes, they are a crucial tool for justice, but they can't help who their boss is. Governments rule them, the media, even the regular people. If they say jump... all of them must ask how high."

Audrey tensed, wanting so desperately to do something.

"They can't do this."

"They've been doing this for decades, Audrey. Probably even longer."

"Weather balloons... satellite wreckage..."

Quin sighed, deeply.

"Man in costume... coyotes with mange... drafty houses... bad lighting... too many movies..." His eyes rolled to Audrey.

"There's always an excuse. Always an answer to the madness. And there's two ways to handle you, the truth seeker: you either end up in the crazy house... or your reputation is forever destroyed."

"You forgot the third option." Pine uttered.

"You have an unfortunate 'accident'."

Something then dawned on Audrey. Her eyes widened, as the thought became more clear inside her mind.

"That thing… it followed us last night. It tracked us down."

Quin, Amelia and Troy all directed their attention on her. She blinked through her cold, darkened expression.

"...Do you think they....."

She didn't have to finish. They knew what she was saying.

"...We've gotta get to Wyatt, dudes." Brooke let out.

"We've gotta get to Wyatt before they do!"

He scrambled for the driver seat, where Ivy, Audrey and Quinton all positioned themselves in their respective seats, and buckled up.

Amelia reached in to turn the TV off. As she did, Ripley's face looked directly into the camera. He smirked, making it feel as though he were looking right at her.

"So don't you worry, Casper... Hollowgrove... there's nothing to fear. I'm taking care of you. **All of you**."

His eyes peered into Pine's from within the television, making her mind and heart race. *Including you, Amelia Pine.*

She grunted in disgust and slammed the power button.

- - -

Beckhart stared at the remains of the three creatures spread out on the tables. Their fur was stolen by the obvious presence of mange. Their tongues were sticking out, their eyes closed forever. It appeared to be a fox, a dog, and another animal he couldn't make out. Perhaps a bear. Regardless of what they were, the sight of these poor sick animals disturbed his very soul.

"We found these last night. Close to the attack sightings. We put them down, out of their misery."

Gabriel was seeing it, but he couldn't believe it. Not this...

"They're the ones responsible for the attacks. Sick creatures exploited by a freak, who wanted to turn them into the little Chupacabra fantasy. We caught that guy, too."

Don't listen to them... He warned himself. *These are roadkill they dragged in off the street to deceive you.*

"The guy we caught was Nelson Blum."

Gabriel swiveled his head at Spiel. His eyes were saucers. Spiel rose his brows.

"Blum confessed. Questioned him for two days, and when we found out about the creatures, he admitted everything. It was all a hoax, Mr. Beckhart."

Gabriel stepped back. His eyes fell to the floor, as he tried to process this. This... this made him... sick.

Lies... blatant, outright *lies*.

What made him feel even worse was... if he hadn't seen the truth for himself... horrifically, he would have *believed* them. This horrible, cruel, disgusting cover-up. And the scariest part was... he didn't think it was even Spiel's idea. No. Spiel was being used. They all were. *Someone was making them do this.*

Martinez was silent the entire time. He looked ill from the sight and smell of the animals. In fact, he looked like he didn't even want to be there at all. He was no longer smug. Just repulsed.

If it was all a hoax... Gabriel thought. *Then why was the creature we saw covered in fur... with spikes protruding from its back? If it was all a hoax... why did its eyes glow?*

He held his head.

If it was all a hoax... why did it track us down and attack Amelia by the smell of her blood? The way not many other animals can?

He stepped back even farther, staggering. Like he was going to collapse. *If it was all a hoax... then why does this feel so* **wrong**? *So sickeningly* **wrong**?

He forced himself to swallow. He couldn't even look up at the two any longer. He slowly made his way to the door. He was going to show the officers the video proof of their encounter... that idea was now long buried.

"Thank you for your time." He managed to grog out, before stumbling toward the exit out of that dreadful room.

Out of the presence of Spiel and the animals, Gabriel found new life in his legs, as he walked through the door and moved fast for the end of the hallway. He could hardly breathe and he refused to do so anyhow. Not until he was out of there.

Gabriel had developed a paranoia since that fateful day of returning home. Now... he no longer felt safe anywhere.

-

Talbot leaned against his own counter, standing in a currently empty store. He had decided to close shop for the day, giving Lycan a day off, and giving himself time to process things. He took short, deep breaths as he drank from a bottle, squeezing his eyes shut.

Memories... memories flashed in his head of a life that seemed as if it were a mental fabrication. The people he knew, the things he had done... the battles he had fought... it was all too much for him to handle sober anymore.

He shook his head, as he tried to shake the thoughts creeping up on him. That's when a voice cut through his thoughts like a serrated blade. His eyes flashed up at the TV, his expression teeming with mild irritation.

Ripley.

Making another infernal, self-glorifying public appearance, in the wake of a tragic event. Just the sound of that man's voice made Russell's skin crawl. ***You disgusting pig. People are dying.***

"But I assure you, citizens, the threat is over! The animals were captured and put down. And the fiend behind these crimes has been apprehended!"

He straightened his back. ***A hoax, huh?***
He chuckled to himself... not of a comedic reason. Just over how desperate this man was to appear believable.

"I promise you, citizens, there are no supernatural, malicious forces out there working against our community... only the evil forces of man! We must unite to fight against the hysteria plaguing Hollowgrove... plaguing Casper! We are all one and the same, and we must not fall into the temptation of backwards thinking! No! We are beyond that! We are the future! The glue that holds everything together! Never fall into the lies! These people will deceive your hearts and minds... trust in your appointed leaders... trust in the justice, and what you see with your eyes! Trust in ME!"

Rip held a pause, as the crowd cheered for him.

Russell's eyes narrowed. Before he fully realized what he was doing, his hand had already reached for the phone and had dialed a number. The phone was at his ear. It was ringing. It was too late now. It wasn't long before the receiver picked up.

"'Ello?"

Talbot furrowed his brows. He leaned back in.

"...P--Poe... i-it's me...."

He held his aching head.

"Russell?"

"Yeah. I just... wanted to call."

"...You're drunk again, aren't you?"

Talbot's eyes looked elsewhere, as if looking away from Poe's holy judgment. There was a sigh from the other end. A sigh of sad disappointment. But never of judgment.

Poe knew... he just knew.

"Talk to me, mate. What's on your mind? I'm here."

Talbot took a deep breath. It was painful for him do so, as every muscle in his body was screaming at him in pain. Pain from years and years ago, that resided in him like a caged beast.

His eyes lifted at Ripley's annoying face.

"Bud... run it by me again... assure me it wasn't just a fever dream… wasn't Ripley in town last night??"

He could sense the suspicion from Poe, even when they were only present through their voices.

"Yes. Why are you asking?" He soon corrected himself.

"What are you *thinking*?"

Talbot rubbed his jaw in thought.

"Huh… just a weird coincidence... that's all..."

"Russell... don't even think about it. We've been careful all this time."

"Yeah? Well... maybe that's the problem."

He sat down in his chair, his eyes thinning into slits, as he stared at the TV screen.

"We've been careful... and now the monsters have taken over."

CHAPTER XXVI
◆ REFORMATION ◆

The Assembly was shaken to its core. The more they learned about this case and every other case of the slightest bit of similarity, the more disturbed they were of just how deep and how chilling the mystery of the unknown truly was.

The creatures, the otherworldly forces, they were scary in their own right. It was the idea that people were purposely trying to cover them up that scared them even more.

Nowhere is safe. Amelia kept thinking. *I've lived in this town my whole life... and it's not safe anymore.*

Just a few days ago, Pine was updating her blog, feeding her pet guinea pig. Going about her every day life, as a conspiracy nut. An advocate for the weird. An outspoken ufologist. Besides the typical backlash from the normal folks, she was never in any real danger. No one was out for her head.

Then the Beckharts came knocking on her door. And ever since, she has been on the move. Until she found herself being attacked by one of the very creatures she supported. And racing to a man whose life was very well in danger by a malicious force working behind the scenes.

Her eyes fell on her bandaged arm, that still stung from the cut she received. Pine no longer felt in control, as she always had. She felt powerless.

"We need to get to safety." Pine let out. All those in the van paid attention. "We need to get Wyatt and barricade ourselves somewhere."

Audrey's eyes narrowed. "Seriously? You, of all people, running away from this?"

"This isn't a joke, Beckhart!" What displayed from Pine was not anger. It was fear. "This isn't some silly little adventure you can turn off with a switch! They're after us now!
We aren't safe anymore!"

Audrey felt herself drifting to Ivy and putting a defensive arm around the child's shoulders. A maternal instinct emerged from her to protect the little girl from a fearful situation. What she did not realize was that Ivy was completely calm. *Audrey* was the scared one.

Amelia's words only made her concerns more real. Where were they going to sleep? Where were they going to hide? They couldn't stay anywhere, unless it was a fortified facility. Her own house wasn't safe. Neither was a friend's.

An invisible stalker was after them. A legendary creature was after them. Now it appeared even their own *elected officials* were after them. They had rattled cages they had no business rattling. And now it was costing them their very sanity.

"There has to be somewhere we can go." Audrey spoke with hope, in her slightly husky voice.

"Someone we can trust in this town that will take care of us."

"What was your boyfriend saying earlier? Sounded like he had a plan."

Amelia glared at Quinton. He wasn't talking against Lycan. In fact, it sounded as if he actually trusted him.

"He... he wants to help us. With supplies."

"Supplies from where?"

"His boss' shop. Talbot's Den."

"*Russell* Talbot?" Audrey said, with a slight laugh.

"Isn't he a--" But she stopped herself. When she realized what tone, what implication she was about to let out. A kook. An eccentric. A crazy old man. The type you hear ghost stories from. The type everyone whispers about and mocks. The type that believes in things no one else does. The stuff of gossip. Name calling. Finger pointing. The very type of man Audrey never would have believed... until now.

"Okay." She spoke firmly. "What does he have in his store?" Amelia was surprised at the willingness Audrey had, to put her faith in such a man.

"Things for traps... hunting equipment..."

"Weapons?"

"...Weapons. Tons of stuff. People go to his shop all the time. Lot of believers. To prepare."

Beckhart's eyes fell to the floor.

"...Then that's where we need to go."

"Sounds like a plan." Troy spoke from the driver's seat.

"Talk to Wyatt. Protect Wyatt. Go stock up on supplies. And

set the trap."

The others nodded. Ivy then tapped Quinton's leg. He looked to her. She signed to him. He watched intently.

"Ivy says... we can't kill the Chupacabra." He sat up straight. "She says it's not its fault."

Audrey looked down at the little girl, a hunger for knowledge in her eyes. "What do you mean, Ivy? Whose fault is it?"

Ivy looked up at her. She continued to sign.

"The Chupacabra is just like any other animal." Quinton interpreted. "It hunts to survive. Doing so the way he was created to do. He is being made to be this way. Attacking random animals and people."

She paused a moment, before her eyes became dark and somber.

"Coming after us, especially."

Seeing Ivy this way brought a chill down Audrey's spine. She breathed.

"Ivy... I promise you... we're not going to hurt it... our goal is, and always has been, to **protect** creatures like him. We'll do everything we can to make sure *everyone* is safe after this... even him. Okay?"

It took the little girl a minute... she finally nodded her head.

"Thank you." She signed, bringing out the tips of her fingers from her chin. Audrey smiled a soft smile, as she brought Ivy close to her. She did not know how feasible it was to protect themselves *and* the creature trying to kill them. But she made a promise to a little girl, who trusted her... and she intended to hold on to that promise.

-

Gabriel rushed through the halls of the precinct, running like his life depended on it. His coat and his scarf floated behind him, as if caught by a wild wind. The surrounding officers looked at him like he was mad. Running through a station, as if he isn't safe? The very idea boggled their minds.

But Gabriel knew he wasn't safe; Spiel was not on the side of the truth, clearly. And he didn't know who else was in on the cover-up. He didn't even know if he was being let go so easily. He very well could be tackled just at the door by a slew of officers, dog-piling him and handcuffing him. Dragging him back to lock him in a cell. Gabriel was stricken with fear. A fear that possessed him to escape as soon as possible.

Don't stop. He huffed internally.

Don't stop until you're out of here!

CRASH!

Beckhart's mind was spinning, as he found himself flying through the air, directly on his back. He had collided with another. And he was now laying on the floor, in pain. He groaned and stiffened his body, as he clenched his teeth. His spine was experiencing swift and sharp pains running all along it. A severe swelling grew from his head, throbbing. He hit it, he knew it. That would explain why he was now so dizzy.

As he crawled up to his feet, he removed his glasses. He couldn't see straight, even with his corrective lenses. By god, if now, of all times, he was to receive a concussion... because of some distracted oaf not properly dodging his speeding body...

He shook his head. He had to hurry... but instead, he was staggering.

"Mr. Beckharttttttt..." A woozy voice said from behind.

The world was spinning for Gabriel. All sounds and sights were distorted.

"Arreee youuu okaayyyyy?" The same voice dragged.

He kept squeezing his eyes shut, hoping the sensation would end. He was lightheaded... too lightheaded to function.

"Get....away from... me..."

He held his skull, his face displaying obvious signs of pain.

"My my..." A voice spoke. A voice incredibly foreign to him. Then again… also wasn't? That's when a pair of hands slapped his shoulders. And it made him jolt.

"Get a hold of yourself." The voice cut through his mind-boggling experience. "Come on, kid... snap out of it!"

One of the hands waved something under his nose and... Gabe snapped up right. He could suddenly see clearly. Hear clearly. Stand clearly. The pain remained, but it almost felt like someone shot him with morphine to wake him up.

Before him stood a man, a small vile between two of his gloved fingers. And he was one of the strangest looking fellows he had seen in person. A slender man, dressed in a long black trench coat. His skin was pale, his hair a raven black that stuck up in a way similar to Quinton's, except more eccentric. And his eyes... his eyes were concealed by thick spectacles, that almost resembled goggles.

"You okay, kid?" The man asked him, with a peculiar voice. Gabriel squinted at him.

"Here, you might need these."

The man handed him his glasses. Beckhart took them without a word. The man then slapped his arm.

"Be more careful next time. Next person you run into might not be as forgiving and handsome as me."

He chuckled, grinning. Beckhart only stared at him, with a suspicious glare in his eye. He wasted no time. He was too disoriented for his usual manners. All he could think about was... keep running. So he did.

He ran for the exit, having no intention on coming back. But the thing that bothered him was the man... the man was watching him leave. Every lasting second of him being in that precinct, and the man was observing it.

Maybe it was just his paranoia... maybe it was his still ringing ears playing tricks on him…

but he could have sworn he heard the man say to an officer...

"What's that kid's name?"

Gabriel could not run any faster. He slammed against the door, pushing it with all his surviving might. And he sped for Amelia's car. The keys fumbled in his hands, as he couldn't get them out at all gracefully.

He staggered right into the driver's side and practically fell into the seat. He shut the car door with violent force, and immediately locked it. He was surprised that he still had the alertness to make his next move; checking every seat to make sure no one unwanted was inside with him.

As soon as he felt a sliver of security, he laid back his head and took a breath. The breath he promised himself he would not make until he was out. He got this far… now to regroup with the others. He was already tired of being alone. Facing all this himself. He needed Audrey. He needed Amelia. He needed Quinton, and Troy, and Ivy. He even needed Magnus and Scrooge.

With that, he started the engine and bolted out of there. His phone was pulled from his pocket. He held it up, calling a number, putting it on speaker.

No more secrets. He decided. *I'm telling them everything. I'm telling them about that dream.*

-

Audrey's purse buzzed. She jumped. It was becoming a habit for everyone to pay attention when one of them received a call or text. It obviously meant by now they were reporting bad news.

Audrey swallowed, holding her breath. She brought the phone to her mouth, as she put it on speaker. "Hello?"
She said it with such uncertainty... like it might not have been her brother on the other end.

"Audy."
A sigh of relief. From everyone in the van.

"Gabe... you're okay."

"Okay? You had your doubts, me going into a police station?" He was joking, but Audrey knew, the sound of his voice... he was trembling. Something happened. Something shook him.

"Are you alone?"

"Yes." He didn't even bother questioning it.

"I can see we both found out stuff that scared us straight..."

"Gabriel, the news... Ravenwood got up there and told everyone it was a hoax. The police are convinced of it."

"The police showed me the bodies. Told me Nelson Blum was the one behind it all."

"*What?!*" She exclaimed a little too loudly.

"Yes... they also told me that others have reported break-ins. Claimed they were being stalked by an invisible man, who took pictures. Nobody could see his reflection. Until a guy realized he was just photoshopping himself out."

"That's a bald-faced *lie*." There was a poison in Audrey's voice as she hissed this. It made the rest of the party see that for the Beckhart siblings... there was no going back from this. They were too far involved now. Too disgusted by those that opposed the truth.

"I hope to God you got out of there and aren't calling from a cell."

"I did. I'm on my way to Wyatt now, to meet you all. We aren't separating again. Not after this."

"Gabriel... no one will believe us now. Not after what Ripley said."

Audrey had no fond memories of Ripley Ravenwood. She knew him best from the parties she and her family attended. Social events where he was present. He always gave her looks... looks that made her feel uncomfortable. Like he was watching her. It made her skin crawl.

Everyone tried to portray him as such a handsome bachelor who women adored. That wasn't what she saw. All she saw was a sleazy, suspicious creep... who looked at her as if he knew something about her. He screamed it at her. And it was as if he was telling it to her in a language she could never understand.

"It doesn't mean we should stop trying."
Gabriel's words encouraged her. They encouraged everyone listening to the conversation.

"Gabe!" Troy called out from the front. "Hang in there, dude! I promise you guys, this ain't over! Not by a long shot! We're gonna win this!"

It was Gabriel's turn to feel encouragement. Audrey could tell he was smiling from the other end. "Thanks, Troy... I'll see you all at the farm."

"Okay... I love you."

"I love you, too, Audy."
Disconnected. The party rode on in silence.
- -

It wasn't too much longer a drive before the group reached the beautiful farm land, which gave them a momentary state of calm to witness. As far as they could see, the earth was covered in grass, with trees and mountains peeking in the distance. Even with the windows rolled up, they could smell the nature just outside. Soon came the animals. Horses, goats, cows. They all seemed to lift their heads up to watch the pizza van roll by, staring with their kind and innocent eyes, almost as a way to greet the party.

Pine lifted her phone up, staring at the screen. Her GPS arrow pointed in a direction, and she perked up. "Right! Go right!"

Troy made a hard right, the tires squealing, a cloud of dirt kicking up, as they entered a path leading to a farm. It stretched a moment, before the van finally came to a stop and the group jerked forward.

As the dust settled, the party crawled out from the back to gaze through the windshield upon the farm before them.

"There it is." Quinton observed.

At that moment, he pulled something out from beneath him and lifted it upwards, invading just a little too much of Audrey's personal bubble, which made her grimace at him.

His camera.

Inches away, Quin grinned in sarcasm at her, as he pointed the object her way. "Show time."

He was off.

"Quin, hold on a bloody moment!" Pine exclaimed, just as he slid the door open and jumped out.

"QUIN-" She hissed. "Get your butt back here!"

Her growling voice came out in such a way that made her seem like Quinton's fed up sister ready to scold him, as she leapt after him. Ivy was the next to climb out.

"Ivy, wait!" Audrey exclaimed, running after her.

Only Troy and the dogs remained in the vehicle, as the doors hung wide open. But soon Magnus made a sharp woof and bolted, he too now chasing after them.

Scrooge stared after the departed members, before his head turned to Brooke to see what his move was going to be. Troy simply sighed and pulled out his sunglasses.

"Why is this starting to feel like a dysfunctional family road trip?" He opened his door and stepped out. "C'mon, boy, let's follow the kids."

Scrooge was the last to leave.

The party ventured forward, the animals in the surrounding area announcing a foreign presence to one another. As they approached the house ahead, something could be heard from inside. It sounded faint, metallic in nature... something rather unsettling.

"Wyatt??" Pine questioned, the others looking in all directions in the event he was tending to the animals outside. But their hearts soon all skipped a beat. As something bolted through the front door in a flash, and stormed onto the porch.

"STOP RIGHT THERE."

They all instantly froze, their faces in complete shock.

It was Wyatt. And he was pointing his shotgun right at them.

"WAHOHOHO!" Amelia exclaimed, as she jumped back. Quinton ducked, but remained dedicated to filming the encounter.

"Wyatt!" Audrey yelled, ducking behind a wagon.

"Wyatt, Wyatt, you're Wyatt, right?!"

"What is this?" Wyatt interrogated. He was referring to the camera-wielding Quinton.

"Are you reporters?! Are you recording this?!"

"No no no, dude, it's cool, we're independent investigators, man!" As Troy said this, he shoved his hand behind him into Quinton's face and pushed it back, making Quin fall clumsily backwards to the ground, along with the camera.

Wyatt did not budge. "I don't know what that means." Amelia's eyes cut to the others, her face straining for options, and paining over the lack thereof.

Magnus, meanwhile, was growling intensely at Wyatt, stepping forward in a most intimidating posture that made Wyatt uneasy. Ivy stood behind the canine, completely emotionless.

"Dude, come on, how many reporters do you know that brings dogs and kids?!" Quin chirped from the ground.

"Then you're *tourists*. This is private property, *get out!*"

"We *are* out." Audrey sassed, as she emerged from behind the wagon. Amelia curled her lips back at this; Wyatt ought to shoot her just for that.

Typical bad timing... another car was approaching. Wyatt instantly pointed his firearm in its direction. It was a blue beetle. The others held their breath. Amelia's mouth hung. *Oh no.*

"WHAT?!" The farmhand exclaimed. "WHAT IS THIS?! WHAT'S GOING ON?!"

The beetle froze. Wyatt charged after it. Out came Gabriel, who instinctively held his arms up.

"Get out, get out, put your hands up!" Wyatt said a little too late, as he trotted up to him.

"Gabriel, make a break for it, this guy is off his hinges!" Pine exclaimed.

"I am not!" Wyatt argued, as he grabbed Gabe by the shoulder and pushed him forward.

"Yes, you are." She snapped back. Audrey and Amelia clearly were not well verbally equipped for a life threatening situation.

"What are you punks doing here?! Leave me alone already! I

got enough stress trying to protect myself and the animals from that dratted monster!"

"That's why we're here, Wyatt!" Audrey exclaimed.
His eyes darted at her.

"We're here to help you!"
He still did not budge, as he had the gun pointed at... well, a bale of hay. He wasn't much paying attention to his aim at the moment.

"We're the Sleuth Assembly, newly formed, and we're here to solve your case." Amelia explained. "We heard your call last night, then saw the report this morning, and rushed here before anything else could get to you."

"We're aiming to catch the monster, dude!" Troy backed up.

"And clear your name!" Audrey added.

"And... *not* get shot..." Gabriel included with overconfidence.
Wyatt stood a moment, trying to reflect on his options. His eyes were bloodshot, his body was twitching and shaky as an obvious sign he had barely gotten any sleep, no doubt fueling himself with caffeine to keep going. He looked exhausted and terrified.

After getting attacked by a mythical creature, and appearing on the news as a whack job, there was no wonder why he was so paranoid. There was good reason for being weary of strangers, anyhow.

"Please, for the love of God, put the gun down." Quinton was growing impatient remaining crouched on the ground. His legs were getting tired.

Wyatt let out a trembling breath. In addition to the exhaustion and paranoia, he also had to deal with the bitter cold air. He squeezed his aching eyes shut, taking in the sweet sensation of them not feeling dry and strained for two seconds, as he aggressively rubbed his face.

He lowered his weapon in the process. The others let out a sigh of relief. "I'm so sorry... gosh, I probably seem like a psycho to you! I just..."
He shook his head, holding his face with his open palm.

"I haven't slept all night... they had me on the news this morning and... and the mayor and police turned me into a sham! The family I work for won't get back until next week, and that creature is still out there..."

He groaned loudly, as he shook his throbbing head in his hands.

It was here that Wyatt began to cry. He was only a young man. A good-natured one, at that. His encounter the night before was the most traumatizing thing he'd ever experienced.

Magnus had eased a few minutes before, stepping back and taking a seat, as the threat had died down. The others relaxed, Audrey rushing to Wyatt's side to comfort him. She put a caring arm around him, as he sobbed in absolute defeat. He couldn't hold back his emotions anymore. He had been strong all this time, especially for the animals, to be on alert. Now around positive company, he was forced to release.

"That thing... that thing almost killed me! It was hellbent on doing so... its eyes... I'll never forget its eyes. They were glowing! A bright green... and its teeth. It had long fangs... it was the most terrifying thing I'd ever seen!"

"We've seen it."

Wyatt snapped his gaze through his tears at Gabriel. Gabe had turned to him and nodded in acknowledgment.

"We were attacked yesterday, twice. The second time it followed us into town, and went after Miss Pine after she started bleeding."

"It appears if it smells blood, it goes crazy." Quinton included, straightening his back as he recorded the young man. He cocked his head. "Were you bleeding at all?"

"No sir..." Wyatt sniffed.

"Were any of the animals?"

"No, not that I know of."

"So why did he attack you?"

"He... it... I... I don't know! I just... I heard one of the goats cry out, and I ran to help it. That's when the thing saw me and it chased me."

The party glanced to one another. Gabriel rubbed his chin.

"Why would it come after you just for seeing it??"

"New prey?" Quin theorized.

"No..." Audrey spoke up.

The others glanced. She nodded in Ivy's direction.

"It was forced to do these attacks... someone is making it go crazy."

Wyatt's eyes enlarged.

"Why would anyone do a thing like that?!"

"I'm afraid there's a bit more here to the situation then you're really prepared for, Wyatt." Pine stepped to him and pat him on the back. "We might want to sit down."

~

Amelia, Audrey, Wyatt and Quinton sat inside the house, as Wyatt drank a cup of hot chocolate Audrey made for him to warm up and relax his nerves. He had a blanket around him, as he was seated in a chair at the dining room table, taking slow sips from his drink, as he listened to everything Amelia Pine was telling him.

His eyes, still swollen, were staring down at the wood floor beneath him. He was taking everything in, very carefully, his shaggy dark hair falling over half of his face.

"...And that's why we came to you as quickly as possible. I don't trust what these people plan to do."

Wyatt said nothing. Just kept drinking. Audrey leaned in and gently laid a hand on his shoulder.

"Is there anything else you can tell us about last night? Anything that might be useful for the trap?"

Wyatt finally responded, shaking his head ever so slightly.

"...All his characteristics... were that of any basic predator... but.... the way he came after me... it was unlike anything I've ever seen. Nothing fazed him. I kept shooting. He kept coming. He pulled that wood apart with his teeth like paper. And he woulda kept at it, if I hadn't kept shooting at 'im."

The three reflected.

Quinton, still recording, sat back in his chair.

"Interestingly enough, he was doing the same thing to us when it attacked. Except this time, he was tearing apart glass from the windshield."

"When he attacked me in the bathroom, he smashed through the window, and was literally driving the broken glass into himself trying to get to me."

Amelia shook her head, staring up at the ceiling.

"Nothing was fazing him at all. Not even pain. It's as if whoever is doing this is overwriting his ability to think straight."

Quin jumped, with a chirp. "MIND CONTROL."

The other three snapped their heads at him.

"Are you serious??" Wyatt doubted.

But Audrey and Amelia took this into heavy consideration.

"Could this even be possible?" Audrey wondered. "Someone literally controlling the minds of the creatures to attack Hollowgrove citizens? What would even be the point of that?"

"To create panic." Amelia concluded.

"Controlled chaos." Lim added, nodding his head as if impressed by this, before rotating the camera to his face.

"Using creatures that aren't *supposed* to exist to stir up the pot, so anyone attacked thinks they're going crazy. That's brilliant. Side-note; Quinton Lim original theory, copyright in progress."

"Quin, shut up... but yes." Amelia rose from her chair.

"Alright then... we've gotta get down to business."

"What are you all planning to do?" Wyatt spoke gently.

"We need to gather supplies to capture it."

"The creature? Oh gosh... that's way too dangerous!"

"You need to trust us. We're the only ones that not only believe you, but are also willing to help you."

Wyatt was a little reluctant, but he was coming around to the idea. "O- okay... what do you need? I might be able to help you."

"We need weapons and various traps, ones I don't think you can provide here. But there is something we *can* use from you..."

He shifted, uncomfortably. "...What's that?"

Pine walked over to the window and pulled back the end of the creamy lace curtain with her pinky, as she peered out at the field. The herd of goats fed on the grass, completely naïve to her scheming mind. Her gaze trailed back to Wyatt, as a smug little smirk traced across her lips.

"...Bait."

~

"I can't allow this!! Absolutely not!!"

Wyatt struggled to run after Pine, as she advanced to the others out on the field.

Ivy was standing near Gabriel, petting the goats, while Troy ran after Magnus and Scrooge, the two dogs vigorously harassing the cows; Magnus was being the worst of the two, as he barked obnoxiously at the poor unassuming animals, and chased them in broad circles. Troy was getting too exhausted from running and yelling for the canines to stop it. Rowdy pair, those two were becoming.

Gabriel turned to Pine, his scarf flying in the wind, as Amelia approached him, stuffing her hands into her pockets. Wyatt scrambled after her.

"Please, Miss Pine, I can't let anything happen to these animals! I care about them, and they're my responsibility! If even one gets taken by the creature, I'll lose my job!"

Ivy clapped. The three directed their attention to her. She looked them straight in the eye, and began signing something. Something that made Gabriel stand up straight.

"What... what is she saying??" The farmhand questioned.

"She's saying... none of the goats will get hurt... because... this one..." He glared at the goat standing closest to Ivy, who she had been petting and whispering to the most. His brows crinkled.

"...This one is willing to volunteer."
Wyatt's face was full of confusion. "That one..."
He took note of the detail of the goat... the fur, the ears, the eyes, the structure... he recognized it. He blinked, as his mouth ran agape. "That's the one that was attacked!"

"She knows." Gabriel deciphered. He cleared his throat, his eyes drifting to the two through his lenses.

"...He's out for revenge."

CHAPTER XXVII
✦ WITNESS PROTECTION ✦

I should tell them... Gabriel internally reflected, as he stood in the middle of the field, watching Ivy drift between each goat. His freezing hands were stuffed inside his coat pockets, his scarf wrapped tight around his neck.

He marveled at the fact that young Ivy was standing out in merely an old looking grey dress and jeans, and yet displayed no signs of being cold. That wasn't the only thing he marveled at. He marveled at the fact she was leaning in to certain goats, as she stroked their fur, staring into their innocent eyes, and *whispered* to them.

Ivy had not spoken a word to anyone since her attack some time before... and yet here she was, telling secrets, and bonding with random farm goats. He wondered if Ivy spoke to Magnus in this way. Maybe animals were the only ones she could trust enough for now...

His thoughts of Ivy and her secrecy now brought back the thoughts of his own self.

I should tell them about the dreams now...
He pondered, as he played with a random coin in his pocket.

Those weren't just dreams... maybe Ivy will know something... maybe she can tell me what it means...

He hesitated a moment, as he watched the little girl before him continue to play with the small group of goats munching at grass. Even now, she was barely smiling. And even then, it seemed fake. Like she was incapable of experiencing actual joy. Like her trauma was literally preventing her from feeling what every child should feel.

Because of this, he felt guilty for even entertaining the idea of approaching her about this. Burdening her with talks of terrifying apocalyptic dreams. Dooming her further, after all she had experienced. He wanted so much for her to have the privilege of being a normal little girl. Putting behind her the world of monsters and conspiracy. She was far too young to be worrying of such things... but deep down, he knew. She was compelled to know. She felt a responsibility to find out just as much as he.

This is what he used as a final decision.

"Ivy..."

The little girl cut her eyes at Gabriel. He cleared his throat.

"...Ivy, we need to talk about something..."

But she did something that dumbfounded him... she turned her head away and refused to acknowledge him. His brows crinkled.

"Ivy."

She did not bother to turn. Already being a silent child, with the silent treatment thrown in the mix, was the most torturous thing to Gabriel. He swallowed hard.

"Ivy, please… this is important."

That's when a thought traveled across his mind, one that felt almost foreign to his own brain cells, but ricocheted through it nonetheless.

You went, anyway.

Gabriel stepped back. His face demonstrated signs of shock, hesitation and bewilderment. He went...yes...now he remembered. He went to the station, even though she told him not to. He swallowed through his dry throat once more.

"Ivy... I'm sorry about going. I should have listened to you." He got closer to her and knelt down beside her at her level.

"You were right. I should have come to pick you up and talk to you instead. But it's just... I thought they would be on our side. I thought they would help us. But, maybe it was a good thing I saw for myself what they were really thinking. How far they would go for a cover-up."

In that moment, Ivy swung her body around. She signed aggressively, her facial expression teeming with irritation and hurt. Gabriel's eyes narrowed, as he watched her and mentally interpreted her words...

You don't understand... the more they hear what you think... and what you believe... the bigger of a target they will put on your back...

Gabe was becoming unsettled.

Going to them today only marked yourself as a threat... it doesn't matter what they showed you. It's that they showed you... and now they know you are a believer.

Ivy continued.

Your wealth and power gave you a cloak. We were supposed

to keep this knowledge from them. Now I'm scared.

Gabriel instinctively grabbed her shoulders.

"Ivy, don't be scared! It's going to be alright, I promise you. I won't let anything happen to you!"

But she shook her head.

I'm not worried about myself.

As she signed her next words, his eyes enlarged and his mouth hung low.

*I am scared for **you**.*

His eyes were hurting now from how much they outstretched. He stood back up and paced, trying to determine how he should process that. Ivy would not lie to him, nor would she exaggerate. She wasn't the kind. So when she told him she was scared for him, and his actions that morning only put a target on his back, then he knew there was cause to be nervous.

He shook his head. What was the point of even saying anything about those dreams, when he very well could be assassinated in due time? He took a deep, long breath, trying to relax his steadily increasing heart rate.

Keep calm...

Gabriel turned and faced Ivy. She was glancing up at him from stroking a goat.

We'll work something out...

Were these his own thoughts...

or was Ivy somehow...

***getting** inside his head???*

He shook the thought away. No... *no*, he was imagining things. Ivy was a normal girl... *just a normal little girl.*

His attention was drawn behind him, by Amelia Pine, being trailed by Wyatt. And he shrugged off the pressing concerns that had been plaguing his mind.

Now's not the time... just wait. Wait until this is over.

He breathed as she drew near.

Just survive the night.

~ ~ ~

"Someone has to stay here with the animals."

The group had all gathered at the porch, where they found they had to decide who was going to Talbot's Den, and who was staying behind with Wyatt... something that made Gabriel uncomfortable.

"Wyatt has to stay inside the house and barricade himself." Wyatt's eyes gravitated to Pine. "Say what now?"

"It's for your own safety. The Chupacabra already went after you once. He's sure to finish you off when the darkness returns. Not to mention we have the men in black after you... just stay in the house."

"I mean, okay, can't argue with you there, good plan..." He proceeded to sit in one of the porch's rocking chairs.

"Then I'll stay with him." Brooke volunteered. "I'll have Spike deliver a pizza."

"You darned fool, this isn't a sleep-over!" Amelia barked, as she waved a hand at Wyatt. "This man is practically under witness protection! He can't be happy about it!"

"I can't?"

"You can't."

Wyatt sagged, defeatedly.

"That's why I'll text him now." Troy rebelled, now scrolling through his contacts. Amelia sighed.

"Whatever... I'll go to Talbot's. Gabriel, you come with me. And... you, too." She was directing her attention to Audrey, who scrunched her mouth to the side.

She felt seen, *she felt heard.*

"I suppose I'm staying behind with Brooke and co.?" Quin verified, as he stood at the edge of the porch and filmed around the field at the various grazing animals. The sun was going down. Fast.

"That's actually not a bad idea." Amelia thought. "You and Troy can scope out things from here, while Wyatt's inside. Be each other's eyes."

Audrey glanced over at the little girl standing next to Quin, her arms dangling off the rail.

"Ivy... do you want to stay here, or come with us?" Ivy turned her head to face Audrey, her eyes hinting at heavy activity working within the child's mind. She did not blink, she did not sign, she did not give any indication at all. Yet Gabriel knew the answer.

"She's staying here. It's honestly the safest place, anyway." Gabriel did hold some truth. They did not yet fully know whether going back to town was the best decision. Especially with Ivy's words to Gabriel looming in his head.

What if returning got them arrested? What if the creature singled them out, and attacked them on the road? It didn't matter at that point, as they needed supplies. But he just knew endangering the child like that would be a dumb move, and he already made one too many that day.

Gabe glanced down at his watch,

"It'll take us 15 minutes to get there. If we leave now and hurry in getting stuff, we'll be back before it gets dark."

Amelia nodded. "Let's go, then."

She said no goodbyes. She just bolted for her beetle. Audrey sighed as she crawled from the porch, her eyes rolling back into her skull. She was tired already, and now she had to endure another car ride with Pine. Things were growing more and more lovely by the day.

Gabriel gave a two finger salute to the remaining party members.

"I know I said we shouldn't separate, but-"

"Don't sweat it, dude, we got this!" Troy was overconfident. Troy didn't seem like he fully understood the concept of danger half the time. But he trusted him in this case.

They were capable. They were smart. They could always barricade themselves, if the creature attacked again. They also had Magnus, who was the fiercest guard dog he'd ever seen... not to mention, he had unfinished business with the Chupacabra himself.

He walked away after Pine and his sister, leaving Wyatt sitting in his chair, Troy standing next to Ivy and the recording Quin, and Magnus and Scrooge sprawled out on the porch, painting a scene as if this was a typical, friendly visit to the country.

No... it was fine... it was fine... they would hurry. They would get back in time. They would face this together. They still had the light. Nothing could go wrong.

They were safe.

CHAPTER XXVIII
✦ SUPPLY AND DEMAND ✦

The car ride to Talbot's was a fast one, thanks to Amelia's hasty driving. Their trip was cut down a good 6 minutes, with no other cars being on the road. Audrey had channeled out her brother and Pine, turning to her music player for council. This left Gabriel and Pine sitting on the front lines in complete awkward silence. It was strange, being technically alone together a second time. They hadn't talked much at all on a personal note.

How have you been?
What have you been up to?
Seen any great movies recently?
Is your favorite food still your favorite food?
How's your dad doing?

He had been spending so much time with her that week, but he still felt like there was still so much he didn't know about Pine anymore. So many hobbies and favorites she had to have acquired in that time gap. Things they could have been telling each other to pass the time, and ease the nerves. A brief distraction from what they were about to do.

Gabriel sighed, deeply. Unable to come up with anything else as an ice breaker that wouldn't sound tacky, he turned his head to her. "How's your arm doing?"

Amelia gave her arm a quick glance as if confirming, ah yes, she did have an arm, before returning her intense gaze on the road. Beneath the strong leadership vibes she was exhibiting, Pine seemed incredibly tired and drained of life. Certainly no condition to be in when catching monsters, but she had zero time for a nap. So she made due.

"It's fine. Stings a bit, but I'll be alright. Gotten worse. Thanks." See, that. That right there. 'Gotten worse'. He never knew Pine to have received any serious injuries when he knew her.

She was the wildest child amongst the children of Hollowgrove several years back, but she hardly ever got hurt in the process of her own shenanigans. Despite all the adventures she embarked on, often dragging her two best friends along for the excitement. That goofy, care-free little redheaded tomboy. So stuck on believing anything and everything. She was a stranger to him now.

Gabe adjusted his glasses. "I'm sorry..."
Amelia thought the statement a little peculiar. All she could do was smile a bit.

"Don't be. You're not the one that smashed through glass in pure murderous rage."

"No, I mean... *I'm sorry.*"
Pine's smile faded. She gave him a quick glance, seeking answers to his apology. Gabriel looked away, turning his gaze to the window.

"It's been so long... and I just... I should have called you. Texted. Something. I never should have stopped. I'm sorry for just... vanishing. No matter what happened between you and Audrey... it never should have ruined things between *us*."

Amelia's turn to adjust her glasses, as her eyes fluctuated to the oblivious Audrey, sitting in the back seat.

"...She never told you what she did, did she?"
Gabe's face crinkled. "...What she did?"
Pine paused. She pondered whether she should even bother... if it would even matter. But she realized... it didn't.

"Nothing. Forget I said anything. It doesn't matter now. I don't want to dig up the past, to be honest."
Gabriel bit his lip.

"...Why can't we just... start over?" His eyes slowly moved to Amelia. "...*All* of us?"

Pine swallowed, as she now drove into town. Her facial expression indicated turmoil. A turmoil she could not speak about. "Listen, Gabe... let's just get through tonight first, alright? And then, well... we'll talk about the rest. Deal?"

Gabe was not so sure she meant this. It appeared she was dodging the topic. Pine loved to deflect. But he submitted for now. "Alright. I understand."

"Made it to town unscathed." They heard from the back; Audrey had taken out an earbud to report this.

"Astute observational skills, Watson." Amelia sassed.
Audrey ignored her and went back to her music.

Gabriel only smirked.

Uncanny

Darkness had come quicker than any of them had anticipated. There was a hint of blue still hovering within the darkening skies, but it wasn't enough to bring the group back at the farm any peace. It had already been 15 minutes since their three friends left for Talbot's. But the light the party once had pretty much departed with them.

Now Wyatt was in a panic. He scrambled to get all the animals put into their pastures with the help of Troy, finally barricading them, so that no living creature could get in. He finished any remaining tasks for the next day within the short time they still had daylight.

The only remaining animal left on the field was the survivor goat, of whom was seeking revenge. He stood close to the house, munching on some grass, bleating every so often to voice his impatience.

Wyatt did not believe that the goat was out for pay back. But he went along with the idea anyhow, even though it was risky gambling on the animal's life based on overconfidence. Their encounters with the Cabra thus far left them narrowly escaping certain death. How they planned to just catch such a ruthless creature... well... Wyatt was nervous. Very nervous. He was just getting to like the group, too.

"This is insane." Wyatt uttered, as he chugged down a bottle of cream soda. "I'm just a stupid farmhand; I have no business trying to help catch a monster! I got no training of any kind! Heck, I can't even shoot straight!"

"That's why you're gonna be in the house, bro, and leave the rest to us!"

"You ain't got no training, either! You almost got killed last night!"

Troy didn't let Wyatt's fear deter him from his good vibes. He simply gave him a half smile and pat his shoulder,

"Don't worry, man... my main dude Spike is bringing the pizza. Pizza will fix all our problems, man. Just you wait."

"Maybe we should serve Chupie some pizza. That'll calm him down." Quinton was still recording the field, leaning against the railing in front of him, cricking his stiff neck from standing so long.

Wyatt and Troy both turned their heads at him, amazed at how he never left that spot the whole time.

"Don't you have a stand for that or something?? Aren't you film maker types more prepared than that?"

Quin cut his eyes to the side, but did not bother rotating to look at him. He only breathed an annoyed sigh.

"Sorry, forgot my movie kit back at the house. Ya know, when we were clambering to hurry and save *your* country butt."

Wyatt went quiet. He rolled his shoulders, taking another swig of his soda. "No offense, but that kid kinda gives me the creeps..." He stared at the swinging door in front of him like it was a closet that housed a monster.

"She freaks me out... talking to goats and giving me these *looks*."

It was the 'she' that helped Quinton deduct that Wyatt was not actually talking about him. He was less offended now.

"Don't worry, she has that effect on everyone." He defended.

"Yeah man, she's a bizarre kid, but ya gotta love her... she's been through a lot."

Wyatt thought about this a moment... the effect the Cabra had on him, for instance. It had already made him panicky and paranoid. Drove him to losing sleep and his own sanity. Now he felt guilty for speaking of such things about a child.
Lord only knew what she went through, and the fear it instilled in her. He shook his head, holding it with the tips of his fingers.

"Oh man... I'm sorry. I keep saying horrible things. I'm so insensitive now..."

"*I* think you're still sensitive." Quinton mocked. Troy snapped his head at him and shushed him. That's when a car horn alerted the three men.

Their heads swiveled in its direction, witnessing a sedan approaching them from the blackness ahead, its headlights temporarily blinding them. Troy held his hand over his eyes to block some of the light, while he grinned from ear to ear.

"Aw yeah, here's Spikey boy now!"

He stepped off the porch and jogged over to the now parked car, as Wyatt gazed in somewhat excited anticipation, while Quinton simply looked away, back to his filming.......*but Quin jerked.*

He saw something. A trick of the light, maybe. The wind

rustling some trees. He swore he saw something shimmering from the woods ahead, past the field. And he swallowed. He couldn't play back... not now... he might miss something if he stopped for one second.

So he kept watching. Kept standing. Kept recording, as the beaming Spike got out of the car and greeted his boss, his arms full of pizzas to last them the entire night.

"Here you are, dudes, a beautiful array of pies, all set for the stake out! A monumental night like this calls for us feasting like kings!"

"Dude, you closed up nice and tight, right?" Troy checked. It was surprising to hear whenever Troy touched serious topics like safety and responsibility. Spike nodded.

"Yes sir, all locked and loaded! Ready for business tomorrow!"

If we even make it to tomorrow.

Quinton was starting to lose just a little bit of the boredom that was entering his brain, standing there for so long. Now he was a little more on edge...

Troy slapped his back, laughing about a joke Spike made that Quinton didn't even bother to overhear.

"Quin, man, you coming in for the pizza?"

"No. Thank you."

"You gotta eat, bro!" Spike insisted. "Can't do proper monster hunting if you don't have the sustenance!"

"I said *no*. **Thank you**."

The boys got the message. Spike held up his open hand as a gesture to chill, smiling nervously, as Wyatt held the screen door open for him. "Alright man, sorry."

Brooke watched Quin for a moment... Lim could tell, as the tall blonde-haired wonder lingered for a moment on the porch, before following the others inside, leaving an unsettling silence behind.

He felt like Troy was perhaps looking at him with pity. Because the fear and paranoia had gotten to him... not the wonder, the thrill of the experience. Even Amelia was falling prey to this. Their passion for the unknown was being overwritten by the primal, instinctive, intoxicating sensation of basic survival. They didn't want to die... and now they were losing their principals to that goal.

Troy was different. Troy had seen countless creatures at this point. This was nothing new to him... and yet he still retained that childlike desire to keep searching. To enjoy the hunt. To embrace the find. And to live like there may not be a tomorrow. Hence why he ordered pizza, before setting a trap for the Cabra. He just didn't care. So why couldn't Quinton feel this? Why was he getting so scared?

Troy was gone... Wyatt was gone... Spike was gone... Ivy was gone... even Magnus and Scrooge went inside; Magnus because of Ivy, Scrooge because of the cold.

He was all alone. All alone, except for the vengeful goat sitting below him, of course...*and whatever it was glistening in those trees.*

-

Talbot sighed heavily as he sat in a chair now, his face buried into the counter in front of him.

"Talbot, get some sleep already." Poe negotiated, still on the other line. "You're in one of your awful states, and I have service in the morning. We both need rest."

"There ain't no point no more, Poe. I ain't got no meaning to be here..."

"Stop talking like that. Just sleep. You'll feel better in the morning." Aidan sighed, no doubt sitting in his office, his hand still hovering over paperwork that needed to be done two hours ago. Talbot could hear the slight frustration in his old friend's voice. "You always do."

But Talbot was being stubborn today.

"Not this time, bud. Not this time..."

"For bloody goodness' sake, get your filthy rear into bed this moment, or I will stop blessing that bloody bottled water you have your customers shove at me!"

"That's no language for a pastor to be using... and cheap threats are beneath you. This is why the churches are dying."

"I'm serious, Talbot, you are drunk and unhappy, and these two qualities about yourself *scare* me."

"Don't be... you know I can't die. No matter how hard I try."

"Shut up already. Or else I'll come over and beat it out of you." Talbot chuckled.

"Ah, I *would* like the company..."

Poe's turn to laugh.

"You old fool... trying to trick me, as usual."

Talbot jumped. **A knock at the door.**

His eyes zoomed right on the door across the room, bolting his half-drunken body up to see who may be standing outside of it. The roller shade was concealing the identity. The sign said closed. Who could even know if anyone was still here...

His eyes squinted.

"What is it?" Poe questioned.

"...I don't know..." Talbot whispered, gruffly. "...Somebody knocking on the door..."

"I thought you closed up shop."

"I did."

"So ignore it. They'll go away in a minute."

So Talbot did. He waited. He moved a little to see if his view would change, and it didn't. But he could now hear voices coming from the other side. There was more than one person. He held his breath.

"...They're not going away, I think... it's a group of them."

"Why are you still whispering?"

"Cuz I don't want them to know I'm here!"

"You're acting like a hermit that turns off all their lights to hide from trick or treaters."

"They keep talking!"

"Stop it."

"They keep knocking!"

"I will preach an entire sermon against you tomorrow, mark my words."

"They won't leave!!"

The door suddenly unlocked. *The knob turned.*

Talbot immediately fell to the floor, and ducked behind the counter. Russell held the phone at his shoulder, his eyes widened with panic.

"Russell." He heard Poe's voice keep saying.

But he dared not speak.

They got in, they actually got in. They were after him now, this was it. They came to kill him. They were finally going to kill-

"Mr. Talbot?"

His brows raised. **Lycan**. His mouth ran agape.

"Mr. Talbot?!" Lycan's voice got a little bit louder.

Russell eased. He suddenly sprung back up, like a flower in spring time, and now faced the group ahead. Lycan stood before him, accompanied by Amelia Pine and... *the Beckhart siblings.*

All of them jumped when they witnessed him popping up out of no where, their eyes glued to him. He held his head high, before bringing the phone back to his ear.

"I'll call you back."

He slammed it down. Lycan cocked his head.

"Sir? Where'd you come from?"

"I uh... tied my shoe." He nodded.

"I see you, uh... got friends."

He started to walk around the counter, running his hands down his shirt and pants to tidy himself up a bit... his eyes did not leave the sight of the Beckharts.

"Mr. Talbot, you know Amelia-- and this is-"

"Of course, Gabriel and Audrey Beckhart, seen and heard a lot about you!"

He hastily shook their hands, as if he were doing something he shouldn't have, but did it before anyone would see. The siblings cut their eyes at one another, a little weirded out.

"We um..." Gabe cleared his throat. "We actually don't have a lot of time, Mr. Talbot." He ran his hands through his hair.

"See, this is going to come out a bit insane and unbelievable, but..."

"We encountered a Chupacabra last night." Audrey finished for him. Talbot froze.

"...You mean... the uh... the animals they found?? They were debunked this morning... remember that?"

"No, that was a cover-up. This is for real. We have actual footage of our encounter. Then Amelia was attacked in the bathroom, after it tracked us down and reacted to her bleeding. He went crazy."

"This isn't a hoax, Mr. Talbot, we swear. And we were hoping you'd be the one person who would openly believe us..."

It was Pine's turn to talk now.

"You know I'm a big fan of your's, Russell, and I heavily respect you in the believer community. Right now, we really *do* need your help."

Lycan stood up straight, "They're going to set up a trap for the Cabra, boss. They need supplies, weapons. I thought we could-"
But Talbot suddenly pulled him aside, grabbing him by the collar of his shirt. He took him in the farthest corner, before leaning in to whisper as quietly as possible.

"What are you doing, boy? We can't help them."
Lycan's face dropped.

"What? Sir... we... we help people hunt for things all the time! All the believers we see coming in here every day... this is the actual real deal!"

"Yeah, because those fools can't do squat even if they tried! I humor them, I give them the right info, but they ain't catching nothing. They ain't *seeing* nothing. They're tourists, kid. Movie buffs. Spectators."

His eyes briefly landed on the three behind them, who were trying not to stare, but failed. He shook his aching head.

"...These kids are the real deal, Lycan. They actually *believe* in this. They actually have a chance. That's why we can't help them... it's too-"

"-Dangerous?"
Talbot's eyes lifted at Lycan, whose face was displaying obvious signs of indignation.

"Sir, you took me in, when no other business in town would tolerate me. You gave me chances, when no one else believed in me. You took care of me, when my father would kick my teeth in. You've been there for me all this time, and have taught me everything you know. All my knowledge, all my passion for this line of work, is thanks to **you**. I wouldn't be the man I am if not for you. I'm *better* because of you. I even have that incredible girl standing over there, because of the passions and morals *you* taught me. And there is one thing I am certain of... you have never backed down from the opportunity to chase the supernatural. You crave it. You thrive on it. This is your life's work, sir. And *they're* your ticket to go after it. We finally have a chance to embrace it. We can't waste it."

Lycan raised his hands,

"And with all due respect, even if you say no... I'm still helping them. You're just gonna have to fire me."

Talbot stared at the boy with the greatest admiration he had ever had for anyone. No one looked at him the way Lycan did. Not even Poe. No one blindly believed in him like Lycan. No one trusted him. No one put him on as high a pedestal.

He took the lad in for a moment... the medium built, black clad young man in his late teens, his jet black shaggy hair falling over his dark brown eyes, his skin touched with brown from his Native American ancestry. His good looks, his good nature, came from his mother. Who was indeed a remarkable woman. Unlike the monster who regularly abused such an innocent, special child.

Talbot... Talbot was proud of who he was looking at. Of the privilege of being able to watch him grow. To become such an amazing, fearless man.

It was a moment that everyone reaches at a point in their life, when witnessing new life develop over the years... and you realize just how mature and unique they have actually become. Against his better judgment... he smiled.

"...Alright, boy...let's get to work."

--

They're not back yet. Why aren't they back yet??
Quinton was getting worried. Quinton, of all people. *Worried.* Even he was surprised. He wanted to check his phone, to text or call them, but after what he thought he saw, he did not want to take his eyes off the woods.

His arms and back were getting so tired. His legs felt like lead underneath him, like they were about to cave in at any minute. If only for a second, he wanted to look down and make sure the goat was still there. He could hear it rustle and make a noise, yes, but at this point his mind could just be replaying sounds from hearing it so much, and it'd turn out not even being there anymore.

What if it wandered, or something grabbed it by the throat to stifle its screams, before dragging it into the darkness? And what if he was staring in the wrong place all this time?? What if something were to climb up those stairs behind him and go for the kill? Talk about a typical horror movie character cliché. And that's what he felt like. Cliché.

You're better than this, Quinton.
Or was he? He didn't really think so. In fact, he didn't at all care for himself. Thought he was far too broken, and possessed a

million flaws and issues that were honestly downright shameful. Far too much to dislike.

If you were normal, you'd be in there with Troy and the others...
He shifted, trying to wake up his aching legs.

If you were normal, you'd be partying with all the other college kids at the beach...
He had to gently shake his head to keep his eyes from fluttering too much. The sleep he required... it was coming after him again.

If you were normal, you would not be here standing on a porch for an hour, watching for signs of a Chupacabra...
Memories began to creep back up on him.

F r e a k

The most common name he received growing up. From the lowliest of human beings: Bullies. People who made Quinton feel less of himself. A small seed of self loathing. Of self doubt.

No matter what he did, he would never be good enough for anyone. Except Amelia, it seemed. She was the only one who really understood him as a person. He loved her like a sister. He was blessed to have found her. And honestly, it made him jealous when Lycan was around. Stealing all her attention.

Quinton was selfish, but he would never admit it. He missed the times when it was just him and Pine, researching and theorizing, and putting together patterns like a puzzle. He missed his youth... and the innocence that it provided.

Now... now he was just sad. Lonely. Depressed. All the time. And the saddest part was that his personality came off so dry... so vicious... so heartless sometimes. And he didn't mean to.

His breath quivered. His body trembled. The temperature had dropped. He was freezing.

Please hurry. He pleaded, but he meant it for anyone.
Either for the others to get back, and he wouldn't have to just stand there anymore. Or for the Chupacabra to just show up, and get it over with already.

The others laughed inside. He let out another shaky breath. Soon his hands could no longer keep still. It now pained him to force himself to stay alert.

"Just. Freaking. *Kill me.*"
His voice was dangerously close to breaking. He had enough.

I'm about to go Amelia Pine and bleed too. This is ridiculous.

His blood then ran cold. The animals could be heard from the barn... making the biggest ruckus. So loud, it made his ears ring.

His breathing quickened. He saw nothing in front of him... nothing. If he could just look for a brief second... he could make sure there was nothing behind him. Nothing trying to get to the animals. His breathing now became irrational.

*Just look, just look, just look for **one** second!*

So he did. He looked quickly. There was nothing there. Nothing at all. His head snapped back. **He screamed.**

In the middle of the field, there it stood. Its black fur merging with the darkness. Its long fangs glistening in the moonlight. Its green eyes focused solely on Quinton.

The Chupacabra stared right into the camera.

Quinton's eyes enlarged into saucers, as he jumped backwards towards the door.

"OH! OH OH OH OH OH OH!!!"

His free hand beat violently against the wood of the house. Real words could not even escape him. Just screeches, grunts and the inability to move, as the deadly creature ahead of him drew nearer and nearer.

"OHHHH!!!!!"

The swinging door slammed open; Troy and Spike stormed out. Wyatt followed right behind, despite his being told to stay inside. Their mouths all hung open.

"OH MY GODDDD!!!" Wyatt screeched.

"IT'S *BACK!!*"

"HOLY COW, MAN, HOLY COW, THIS IS ACTUALLY HAPPENING!!!"

Spike held his mohawked head in disbelief; the others realized that this was indeed the first time he had ever seen... well, anything. "DUDE.... DUDE!!! DO SOMETHING!!"

Something *was* done... just not the right something. Confirmed as Wyatt grabbed a watering can, and threw it with all his might at the creature. It bounced off the railing, narrowly missing the goat, and tumbled down on the grass.

"YOU IDIOT!" Quinton screamed. "GET INSIDE THE HOUSE, *NOW!!!*"

Wyatt's legs went in all directions as he tried to turn, which inevitably caused him to tumble backwards in a state of panic,

Uncanny

knocking over the furniture behind him. This commotion only temporarily delayed the Cabra. He kept creeping up seconds later.

Troy, thankfully, took over in this situation. He already had his phone in his hand, calling Amelia, while he grabbed Wyatt by the collar with his other, to pick him up and push him inside.

"Get inside with Ivy!!"

Wyatt grabbed the door, violently shutting it, and barricaded it.

"PINE! It's HERE! We need you back NOW!!"

The Chupacabra's booming snarl forced Troy to hang up. He pocketed his phone, throwing his hands up. He had to act, **fast**.

His eyes scanned the area for an emergency plan, breathing heavily. "Quin!! Spike!! We gotta buy the others time and distract this thing from the goat!"

Spike's head nodded vigorously, as he tried to snap out of his freaked out state. "O-Okay, boss!!"

"Now Spike, on the count of three, I want you to-"

What he was *going* to suggest was that Spike run to his car and go for the Chupacabra, literally driving it away from the house and animals.

What Spike *instead* decided to do...

was jump over the railing, and land in front of the goat...

directly in the path of the snarling creature.

The Cabra's eyes sparked with new life.

A grand feast was in store.

"SPIKE!!" Troy exclaimed, lunging forward in shock. Just before his faithful employee began running with all the life in him, leading their assailant away from the screaming, vulnerable goat. "WHAT ARE YOU DOING?!"

"I'M DISTRACTING HIM FROM THE GOAT!!" Spike hoarsely screeched behind him.

"NOT *THAT* WAY!!" But Troy was too late. Spike was already on the move, in the complete opposite direction of everywhere he needed to be.

Quin and Troy watched in complete helpless horror, as they witnessed the boy practically kill himself in this chaotic act. The Chupacabra took the bait... and was now in hot, heart-pounding pursuit of the young mohawked Pizza Shack employee.

And the two ran... right into the darkness.

"SPIKE!"

CHAPTER XXIX
✦ VULNERABLE ✦

It had grown so quiet at the house. Quiet enough for Ivy to sit on the couch in the living room, and open up her drawing pad to continue working. Magnus sat below her, while Scrooge had moved for the fireplace.

Soon the quiet was stripped away, as Troy, Spike and Wyatt all barged inside in a fuddled fashion, making Ivy pause, her crayon-wielding hand hovering over her sketch pad, where she let out a deep and disapproving sigh.

The boys feasted on the pizzas Spike had brought for them all in the kitchen, popping off more cream soda caps, and laughing up an obnoxious storm that made Ivy's ears ring.

She was starting to grip on to her crayon so tight, she almost broke it. Just a little peace... that's all she asked. She was still angry at Gabriel. She understood his actions and his apology, but she was still angry.

None of this was how it was supposed to happen. She was growing increasingly frustrated with the group. The only one following up on their original role to the letter was the dog. Magnus deserved a raise.

Finally growing too frustrated with the noise, she closed her book in a huff and threw her crayon to the floor, where it bounced and bonked Scrooge on the nose. The sleeping dog peeked with one eye to find the fool that dared assault him.

Ivy sat in silence, both her arms at her sides. The only sounds that previously accompanied her were the ticking clocks, and Scrooge's snoring. Now both were drowned by the chaos. The little girl heavily considered migrating outside with Quinton, who she knew to be a loner, and much too concentrated on recording to be as talkative as this lot.

Besides, Ivy and Quinton didn't have much of a reason to talk yet. It would have been the perfect opportunity to sit in awkward silence, while doing their own things. And honestly, Magnus needed to be outside in the event of--

Her posture straightened. Her muscles tensed. Her eyes bulged. Magnus' ears twitched, and a soft growl escaped his lips, as his head began to move back at the window behind Ivy's head. The two were in sync, feeling the same chill that darkened their spirits, and broke the silence.

No... She mentally gasped. *It's too soon.*

As if on cue, an abrupt and haunting sound came from outside, followed by a series of violent knocks against the walls of the house. Quinton had seen it. And he was alerting the rest of the party.

Ivy's eyes shot to her right and watched, as the three men all instantly dropped their drinks and pizza slices to the floor, fumbled from the kitchen, and out the door.

Her heart raced. *They're going to get themselves killed.*

It wasn't long before the sound of laughter and immature jokes was replaced with crashes and ear-splitting screams, as the four men outside entered a complete state of panic at the unforeseen early arrival of the Chupacabra.

It took only seconds for Wyatt to charge back into the house, nearly falling to the floor, as his legs kicked wildly underneath him, trying to move furniture in front of the door.

"Oh my god, oh my god, oh my god!!" The farmhand exclaimed, rushing away from the kitchen, and into the living room. "Ivy, honey, get away from the window!! It's not safe!"

He made for his shotgun, which was sitting on the other side of the room. Ivy swung her body around, and immediately looked out the very same window she was told to stay away from.

Her tiny eyes enlarged. The creature was in sight, approaching the house, as he stared the others down that remained on the porch. The goat was standing before him, bleating wildly at him. He, too, did not expect the Cabra to arrive so quickly. *No one was prepared.*

*Run. You need to **run**.*

She pressed her forehead against the glass at what happened next. Spike had jumped down in front of the creature.

What is he doing?

She couldn't believe the foolishness transpiring before her.

Especially when he began running, his body zipping past her view, as the Cabra wound up right on his heels in lightning fast pursuit. Spike was trying to lead him away from the others.

He's going to die.

Ivy was confident now. She was surrounded by imbeciles. Everything was falling apart. Her heart nearly launched up into her throat as Magnus leapt beside her, barking psychotically at the creature from the other side. He clawed at the glass, pressing against it with all his weight, snarling without mercy.

"Magnus, get down!!" Wyatt exclaimed, loading his gun with as many bullets as he could insert. Which unfortunately was not enough. "Ivy, get back!"

He grabbed her arm and hurried her away from the couch, attempting to guide her towards the stairs.

"Go on up, into one of the bedrooms, it's safer up there!! And no matter what you hear, *do not* come back down!"

Ivy wished she could argue. But the words… the words were still stuck in her throat.

She swallowed hard as he let her go and rushed back to the window. Magnus turned and gave Wyatt a brief look of confusion before he, too, got booted from the couch.

He knelt down on the soft piece of furniture, and proceeded to lift the window up. Ivy held her breath. He was going to try and snipe it from inside.

He said it himself… he can't even shoot straight…

Her fists curled, as her mind ran in a million directions at once.

Someone's going to die.

Wyatt leaned against the back of the couch, sticking the barrel through the open crack. His arms were still trembling. His eyes insinuated strain, with the occasional twitch. He was in no condition to be playing hero now.

Between both dogs barking in everyone's ears, the goat screeching a short distance away and the horror unfolding outside, Ivy and Wyatt were living a nightmare.

"I'm not running away this time." He switched the safety off.

"I'm not backing down from you."

He gulped, as he closed one eye and looked out into the darkness.

"Hold on, Spike. Just hold on."

As noble as this moment was, Wyatt could not be allowed to pull the trigger.

*You **will** get your chance to show courage…*

Ivy crept up behind the farmhand, as he was about to take the shot. Her hand reached in, her fingers ever-so-slightly spreading upon his forehead. Wyatt's very breath then sucked up back into his lungs, and his body instantly fell back on to the floor with a rattling thud.

Ivy stared down at the man, as he now lay unconscious.

Just not now.

CHAPTER XXX
✦ TARGET ✦

Talbot couldn't help himself. He took the three visitors around the shop, endless facts and recommendations flowing out of his mouth. Amelia herself could not contain her excitement, to be indulged by such an esteemed member of the believer community... while the Beckhart siblings were fascinated, absorbing the information being spoon-fed to their amateur believer minds.

This world was still so new and strange to the Beckharts; they couldn't help but respect this community, however, as their strong beliefs were never crushed, no matter what was said to or about them. They held on, and that was admirable.

Russell stood beside the three, making the mistake of looking just a little bit too enthused with his explanations. He was enjoying this, Lycan observed. He was enjoying it, but he didn't want anyone to know.

The older man grabbed a shotgun, and held it up.

"This is a classic, double-barrel shotgun. A preferred oldie of mine back in the day, developed in the early 20th century. Haven't used it since... well... I was younger."

"What'd you use it for?" Audrey inquired.

Talbot hesitated.

"...I've kept it polished and in good maintenance."

He handed it to Audrey.

"Never failed me then, shouldn't fail you now."

"Whoa, hold on!" She gasped, as he handed it to her. It made her arm bend awkwardly in order to catch it.

"I've never shot a gun this big! I'll be blown back into the century you got this from!"

"That's right, Audrey has very weak muscles." Pine aggressively teased from behind.

Audrey's eyes glinted in an unflattering manner.

"Actually, this will do just fine."

Her pride getting the best of her, she lifted it up and did a confident pose, despite the fact her muscles were screaming at her. She did not work out. Things would have to change if she wanted to keep up appearances.

Talbot smirked. His eyes turned to Gabriel now, who was gawking at the fact such a weapon was handed to his sister, and not him. Not in a jealous manner. Just sheer surprise. Talbot did not play around. He obviously did not see gender when it came to weapon operation.

"For you, Mr. Beckhart... I have an exceptional piece. A real beauty."

He pulled a glistening crossbow from the wall, of which looked to be another relic from the past he was bestowing upon the group.

"A vintage crossbow, owned by a friend of mine many years ago. He treasured this old girl like it was his own child."

He handed it to Gabriel, who instinctively positioned in a shooting stance towards the door.

"It fires quicker than any other crossbow I've operated. While it is lethal depending on where you strike, this is good to wound a threat, compared to the shotgun. So try to use this as a means to stop your assailant from attacking, without the risk of killing them."

"We'll only be going after the creatures, though, so we should be good."

Talbot's eyes drifted to Audrey, then Gabriel, then Amelia.

"...If you three are serious about this line of work... you'll have to come to terms with the facts." He turned and walked to one of the shelves in the middle of the room. "...It ain't always gonna be creatures you'll have to fight against."

The group exchanged glances. While the thought might have crossed their minds a few brief times, it never actually came into serious consideration that they very well would have to combat forces beyond animal status. They would have to protect themselves from people, too. At this point, they didn't know which was worse.

"Now... for Amelia."

Pine's head snapped in attention at the sound of her name.

Russell turned to her, holding up a pair of handguns.

"You seem like a fiery sort. With good aim. For you, a pair of semi-automatic 9mm pistols. These beauties are a special from the 90's, a personal favorite of another old friend of mine."

He handed them to her as she adjusted her fogging glasses, a widened smile planted on her face. She was getting giddy all over again. She held them up, pointing towards a corner of the room, closing one eye as she aimed.

"Golly... thanks, Russell. These are stellar."
He nodded.
"Take good care of these. I'm trusting you."
The three nodded their heads in a unison 'we will' fashion.
Russell stared at them a minute...
They're just kids... He thought to himself.
They're so eager... they have no idea...
He remembered when he was that young. How ready he thought he was… he shook and rubbed his bald head, with a trembling hand. He was reminded of the fact he had been drinking before the four came. While he could still operate well enough, he was still mentally delving into places he had no business going.

"Those will do for now... I'll give you more as time passes, in the event you wanna keep doing this. Now we gotta talk traps."
He paused. His head turned to Lycan.
"You wanna help me with that, boy?"
Lycan perked from standing in the corner, uncrossing his arms.
"Yes, sir!" Lycan glided over to the trapping aisle.
"Now you need to make sure you get the appropriate equipment, depending on the animal. For a Chupacabra, based on the size you said this thing was... I'd recommend items used on a large dog." Amelia smirked, as she watched him. He was so adorable, running around, being a little salesman.
Lycan pointed over at a row of cages.
"That'll fit him. But based on the facts you're telling me, this thing don't scare easily, and won't hop into a cage like some mouse coming for peanut butter."
Lycan held up a pack of cord. "Tripwire. If you can get it to chase you, this will help in knocking it down."
"And that's where you use *this*."
Russell appeared out of nowhere, and was shoving an item at Gabriel's chest. Gabe flinched, as he involuntarily took hold of it.
His eyes fell on it.
"A tranquilizer gun??"
"Has sedatives just enough to take down a creature that size. You wanna take down bigger, you'll need stronger brands. This

should do the trick."
 "And then what??" Audrey questioned. "We'll just drag the dangerous blood sucker when he's unconscious over to the cage?"
 "Exactly."
Audrey's eyes shot to Lycan.
 "And what idiot is gonna let this thing chase them?!"
Amelia's phone suddenly rang. Her heart stopped. All eyes turned to her. She quickly drew it from her pocket, and put it on speaker.
 "Troy?"
 "PINE! It's HERE! We need you back NOW!!"
Everyone in the room jolted.
 "Are you serious?! Troy? TROY?!"
Disconnected.
 Her eyes wandered the room, wildly.
 "We have to go, *right now*!!"
She started to speed towards the door.
 "Amelia, wait!" Lycan exclaimed. "You need the equipment!"
 "Then hurry and get 'em in the car!"
Lycan's mind was swirling, He quickly grabbed the items they needed. Russell wasted no time loading the group up with ammo, stuffing them into a duffel bag, which he hooked around his shoulder, as he made for the cage.
 "Gabriel, give me a hand with this!"
The Beckhart boy rushed to the cage, and both took hold of it.
 The two men ran through the shop and slid it through the exit, with Audrey trailing along, shutting the door behind her. The group ran to Amelia's car, Pine already starting the engine, as the three men loaded it with the weapons and trapping equipment. Pine jumped out from the driver seat, as her phone rang again.
 "Troy!! Talk to me!"
 "WHERE ARE YOU GUYS?!"
 "We're coming!!"
 "HURRY, IT'S AFTER SPIKE!!"
Audrey gasped at this. She rushed to Amelia, her eyes widened.
 Pine's hands were trembling.
 "WHAT?!"
 "SPIKE DISTRACTED IT, BUT IT'S CATCHING UP!!"

"SPIKE, YOU *IDIOT*!" Audrey screeched.

"Troy, you have to stop him!! Get inside right now and barricade yourself! Do you hear me??"

There was no reply. Only uncontrolled breathing, the unmistakable cries of the vengeful goat, and screaming that sounded distant and frantic. This could only be from Spike. It was literal chaos from the other end.

"TROY! ANSWER ME!"

"JUST HURRY!!"

What came next sent chills down the group's spine.

"QUINTON, *NO*!!!"

The line went dead again. Amelia's entire face went into a state of panic. "Oh god no... no no NO!"

She jumped into the driver seat.

"GET INSIDE RIGHT NOW, I DON'T CARE *WHO*!"

Audrey and Gabriel leaped into their seats. Lycan swung around to Talbot. "Come on, sir, we gotta go!"

"No, boy."

Lycan's mouth hung open. Talbot pointed.

"This moment is for you kids. Go."

Lycan went to argue, but Talbot grabbed him by the shoulder, and pointed even more firmly. *"Go."*

There wasn't much he could say or do. Not that it mattered, anyway. They didn't have time. They needed to leave. He sadly, but understandably, nodded his head in respect as he backed towards the car.

"Yes sir... thank you."

Russell lifted his chin. He watched, as Lycan opened the passenger door and shut it behind him, the blue beetle soon flooring it in a straight line down the road, determined to get to their destination as urgently as possible.

He swallowed. He knew he made the right decision. This was their time... their first case... they needed to learn. He would only be a nuisance. An old relic in a battle he had no business fighting. His time was over.

He shut his eyes, taking a deep breath, which came out more shaky than he cared to admit. And he uttered words of an old tongue... a language of Native American origin...

"Go with God."

Spike was screaming at the top of his lungs. The mohawked blunder ran in uncoordinated circles, as the Chupacabra was growing closer and closer.

Troy watched in terror, just waiting for the heart-stopping split second moment to happen, where the creature got close enough to finally *leap* and tackle him to the ground. And that'd be the end of Spike.

He had to do something. He was just too freaked out, too shocked to begin to know exactly what. He fumbled for his phone again as a result. His unsteady finger pressed Amelia's contact photo. He brought it up to his ear.

"Please tell me you're on your way!!" He exclaimed, the ringing sound making him nauseous. She picked up.

"Troy!! Talk to me!"

"WHERE ARE YOU GUYS?!"

"We're coming!!"

"HURRY, IT'S AFTER SPIKE!!"

There was a pause on Pine's end.

"WHAT?!"

Troy's eyes followed the event unfolding before him. His breathing quickened.

"SPIKE DISTRACTED IT, BUT IT'S CATCHING UP!!"

*"SPIKE, YOU **IDIOT**!"* He heard in the background. It was Audrey's voice. But that is the last thing he heard clearly. For the connection began to jumble.

"Tell them to get over here, RIGHT NOW!" Quinton let out.

"I'm trying!!" Troy cried.

"They don't have a freaking *option*!"

The goat was bleating loudly below them, helplessly, more confused than he had ever been. And the screams coming from Spike's blurred, running body were getting louder, and gradually injected with uncontrolled doses of fear. Troy and Quinton were sure by now they were going to be deaf.

"TROY! ANSWER ME!"

Troy did not know what else to say or do.

"JUST HURRY!!"

It was in that second... in that moment of complete stupidity and madness... that Quinton did the unthinkable.

He held tight on to his camera and leaped over the edge... he started running after the two. The goat was giving up hope of survival at this point. Troy could not believe his eyes. **Everyone** was losing it.

"QUINTON, *NO*!!!"

It was meaningless. Quinton was running headlong towards Spike and the creature. Troy's hands clasped both sides of his own head.

"WHAT IN THE--"

Quinton lunged himself forward, until he was close enough. He then held his arms up. "*HEY*!"

The Chupacabra's attention was stolen, instantly. His eyes zoomed right on Lim. It almost appeared to *smile*. A most twisted, heinous smile.

"Remember me?! You know me! Come and finish the job, *sucker*!" He ran the opposite direction.

As to be expected, the creature followed right behind. Spike could not believe it; Quinton had put himself in the line of fire to save *him*. Now *he* was the one watching, as the Chupacabra chased its prey. It was in that moment, Spike realized what they had to do.

"Hey!!" His voice did not carry far. He tightened his fists. "HEY!!!"

The creature skid to a stop. His eyes wandered wildly, now conflicted about who he should target. Troy caught on. His horrified expression now transformed into a smile.

"HEY!!"

Its head swiveled as Brooke hurried down the steps, rushing around the corner to face the creature's direction.

"Over here, dude!"

Quin couldn't help himself; he smirked.

The three men formed a widespread triangle, performing a strategic 'Mexican stand-off' on the animal. The move caused immense confusion on the beast, leaving him snarling and flashing his fangs, his eyes glowing even brighter and more intensely.

He no longer knew *who* to target.

CHAPTER XXXI
✦ FISH ON A HOOK ✦

Hold it off. *Hold it off. All they had to do was hold it off. Long enough for the others to get there and set the trap.*
But what if it was too late for that? What if this creature was too angry, too vengeful, too motivated to kill, to stop and fall for such a simple trick now? The others had been gone 30 minutes, but it seemed like an eternity at this point.

The three men were standing off against the creature before them, their adrenaline pumping, a wicked mixture of fear and excitement clouding their rational thoughts. Distracting the Chupacabra was one thing... distracting the Chupacabra with their own selves was another. They could confuse it so far... but this tactic might not last very long. Its gaze fluctuated between Spike, Quinton and Troy.

They held their ground, drawing closer and closer towards it.

"Is this really the plan, man?!" Spike shouted across the field.

"We're really challenging this thing?!"

"We gotta do what we gotta do, dude!" Troy exclaimed.
He then bolted, his fist shooting high into the air.

"FOR THE PIZZA SHACK!"

Quinton's eyes grew wide as he watched the tall, blonde surfer rush through the field, his long hair flying in the wind behind him. As if taking this as a cue, Spike was the next to take off, in the opposite direction, rushing with speed only a man his age could reach. Together, the two men screamed at the top of their lungs, as if releasing a battle cry, as they ran like wild men in sporadic directions.

Quin found that him, the goat, even the Chupacabra, were staring in a completely traumatic state. *This is madness.* Eventually, the bizarre, slightly humorous, scene came to a swift end. Because it didn't take long before the creature before Quin snapped out of its confusion.

Just as they feared might happen... the creature worked out what they were doing. And his head slowly turned to Quinton, its glowing eyes narrowed, its fangs barring, as a chilling growl escaped through his teeth. A growl that Lim felt travel through every single one of his bones.

He couldn't breathe. He couldn't move. He couldn't think. He was completely frozen, at the mercy of the creature who now set his sights solely on Quin. He needed to run. He needed to run right now, or he would be dead in seconds. All the Chupacabra had to do was take a few steps, and he would have him; that's how close the two really were.

The terrifying creature seemed even closer through the lens of the camera. Something which further shook the aspiring film maker. Soon to be *dead* film maker. He held his breath.

"Don't you dare... I'll press charges... **I know my legal rights!**" Humor did not save his plight. The Chupacabra was not amused in the least. And Lim did not feel any better.

Before he could even take another breath... the beast lunged forward. He screamed. Until...

WAM!

~

"Amelia, *step on it!!*"

"I am going as fast as this car will let me!"

Audrey was sitting up, frantically beating the back of Lycan's headrest. Something that irritated him greatly, but felt would be inappropriate to mention, as everyone in the car was panicking in their own right.

Troy sounded petrified. Confused. Desperate. They hadn't heard Troy Brooke, completely chill, carefree surfer and Pizza Shack owner, talk in such a tone. The way a man speaks when he feels death is imminent. Hearing him enter such a state of terror did not bring them any ounce of comfort, especially being so far from the incident taking place. Quinton, Troy, Spike, Wyatt, Ivy, the animals... they were all at the farm.

They thought they would be safe, if they had just barricaded themselves. The three were only going to be gone for a little while. Just a little while. Until the sun went down. That's how much time they thought they had.

The ones responsible... whoever was behind all of this... there was no question now. They were out to kill the group. By any means necessary.

With one hand, Amelia operated her phone, repeatedly trying to reach Troy again. There was no answer.

"*Frick it!*" She hissed, lifting it in a manner that implied she was about to throw it.

"Amy, calm down!" Lycan attempted, but she instead let out an aggressive growl, and banged her elbow against the center console multiple times. Everyone in the car, including Amelia, knew that she was going to regret that later.

Gabriel winced. His nerves were inflamed, his mind racing too fast to keep up with. All he could think of was Ivy, being dragged through the woods by that... *thing*. Being offered up to... who knows what.

He felt just as helpless now as he did in that dream. He was stuck in a car, which he couldn't move any faster. He wanted to jump out and run, but he would be no better off. What made this experience even worse was the undeniable level of guilt. Regret filled his consciousness. He cursed himself for leaving. He never should have left. Never should have left *Ivy*.

He should have known this would happen. He should have been there to protect her. He vowed he would not separate from the group again, and sure enough, *something went wrong*.

He felt sick to his stomach. He was holding it as a result, his breathing quickening, which he attempted to silence to the best of his abilities. He did not want to appear so terribly weak to the others, especially his sister who depended on him so, though she would never say. No, he refused to be a burden. He refused to invoke such negative emotions upon them.

To bring further panic.

He tensed. His eyes squeezed shut. His mind was swirling. He felt just as dizzy as he did in the precinct. His mind started channeling out, his thoughts returning to the dream...

to the sky...

to the shapes...

to the woods...

to the darkness...

to the figure trying to take Ivy...

He felt he could almost make out details about the figure... if he just... **concentrated**...

Oh god, please... please, be safe...

"**Gabriel!**"

The Beckhart boy nearly jumped up right into the roof of the car.

His eyes flashed to his sister, who was looking towards him with the utmost worry. Her eyes were the size of saucers, her mouth hanging open wide enough to catch flies. He blinked repeatedly at her, waiting for comment on why she shouted at him.

"W-what??"

"*What*? Seriously?? You were just babbling absolute *nonsense*!"

His eyes narrowed into slits.

"*What* nonsense? What are you talking about??"

"You were spouting out some kinda language, bro, but it wasn't English!" Gabe's eyes turned to Lycan.

Even Amelia glared at her rear view mirror to check on him. Audrey reached in and placed a hand upon his forehead.

"Are you okay? This is getting out of hand... first back at the house, then the precinct, now this... what's gotten into you?!"

Gabriel pushed her hand away,

"What do you mean back at the house?"

Audrey sagged back.

"You didn't think I noticed? You made terrible sounds the other night while you were sleeping... and you've been acting strange this whole time. Gabriel, what's happening? *Tell* me."

Gabriel was about to answer her... he truly was... or maybe he couldn't. He didn't know. He didn't have the chance to find out.

"HOLD ON!!"

The car was suddenly swerving a hard right, causing everyone inside to hold on for dear life. The Beckharts knew what this meant. They made it. They were at the farm.

~

Quinton gaped. His eyes enlarged behind his thick framed glasses. He held his camera with unsteady hands, pointed at the beast before him. The beast that was now laying on his side, struggling to recover. Standing proudly before him was an unexpected savior; **the goat.**

"*Holy crap!*"

The goat's head turned to Quin, its eyes full of a furious bravery that put all three men to shame. His chin was lifted to Lim, as if expecting praise, its horns glistening in the moonlight. The goat had enough. Its revenge was inevitable.

"GOAT!" Spike yelled, as he and Troy ran for the two.

"You're the *GOAT*, man!"

"Nice one, dude!!"

The impact was so hard, it knocked the Chupacabra down, disorienting it for several seconds. Long enough for the others to regroup and praise the goat for its brave act.

Goat really wanted revenge...

Quin's brows lifted. Not even *he* had the guts to do that.

But the moment was short lived. The three men and the goat all swiveled their heads toward the rising creature. The spikes protruding from its back seemed to make it appear even larger in the darkness. The moonlight and the green of its eyes were the only means of light the four could now focus on. A snarl came from the beast. A snarl so loud and blood-curdling, it struck the small group where they stood all over again.

Their muscles froze. Just by the Assembly, the Chupacabra was hit by a van. Slapped in the face by windshield wipers. Pepper-sprayed in the eyes. And now rammed to the ground by a *goat*. He was out for blood. Literally.

The creature bent down, ready to pounce. It opened its mouth and roared. The goat's eyes enlarged and its mouth dropped, sending out a single bleat.

"NO!" Quin exclaimed, already foreseeing the doom come upon the defenseless creature. But a force drove itself between the Chupacabra and its prey once more. For a snarling blur suddenly appeared as if by magic, causing the creature to recoil in alarm. A figure appeared behind them. The twist was one the others screamed at, "IVY?!"

The little girl slowly approached the group, her hands curled into fists, her long brown hair falling over her face. The moonlight made her appear almost like an unearthly apparition. It sent chills down everyone's spines... but the sight of Magnus, as he drove himself between the Chupacabra and the goat, his paws planted firmly in the ground, his normally fierce face turned into one just as terrifying as the cryptid itself... they no longer knew who to fear most.

It was a stand-off. And now the men felt outshined by this stupid arrogant canine, that acted tougher than anyone else on the property. Even the goat was awestruck. Magnus growled intensely, his eyes and fangs glinting under the moon. Show-off.

They knew, though... Magnus was not playing around. This

was not a mere threat. It was a warning. The only one the cryptid would get. *Magnus had unfinished business.*

But what concerned them most in the moment that followed wasn't that the Chupacabra was not backing down... it was that it turned its attention to something else. *Some*one else. Someone that had no one in between her. The three men's mouths fell in heart-stopping realization, as the creature's gaze rested on his next target. *Ivy.*

It looked at her not in a way it should have... it was almost familiar... clarifying... calculating... as if it was... realizing something. Working out a key secret. And it hit Quin... it hit him so hard, he wanted to scream.

This wasn't about them. It was never about them. Never about Wyatt. Never about the goat. Never about the Assembly. Wyatt was an inconvenience. The *Assembly* was an inconvenience. The goat was merely food. This was about Ivy. It was **always** about Ivy. *They sent it to kill her.*

"Ivy, RUN!!!" The spiky haired young man shrilled. For just as he said this, the creature had turned. Reeling its body. Ready to pounce at her. Its fangs joining the rest of its teeth to form a wicked, unnatural smile.

It found her. It finally found her.

But Magnus... Magnus was having none of it.

The Chupacabra leaped... and so did the canine.

The cryptid was tackled, violently and brutally.

The two creatures merged as one, rolling upon the ground.

And thus, an all-out battle had begun.

CHAPTER XXXII
✦ IMPROVISED ✦

The air was filled with ravenous barks and screeches, enough to turn one's blood cold. The group initially watched the battle commence before them, the very second Magnus took down the Chupacabra and initiated an all-out assault, keeping the cryptid back by any means necessary.

The canine bit into the creature's black covered flesh, of which caused the beast to cry out in an unnatural shriek. Magnus did not stop there; once having a hold on his opponent, he used the greatest muscle power the group had ever seen come from a dog, to fling the beast effortlessly with just his teeth. This launched the creature several feet away, out of the path of Ivy.

The beast was not deterred, however... he scrambled back up to his feet, disregarding its own grizzly wound, as it roared and charged back in Magnus' direction.

Quinton did not wish to stay and find out the outcome. He started to run, just as the Chupacabra made impact with the dog just inches from where the young man whizzed by. The two beasts collided and rolled on the grassy ground, biting at each other's throats, snarling in terrifying volumes. Quin's eyes flashed to the little girl, before returning to Troy and Spike.

"Troy!" Brooke returned the gaze, as he watched his friend point. "Get Ivy! We gotta get outta here!!"

Troy nodded in compliance, and at once rushed to the little girl's side. Instead of grabbing her by the hand and risk her protesting, he quickly scooped her into his arms and started to make a break for it.

"C'mon, kiddo, let's get the heck out of here!!"
Quin turned to Spike next, as he ran. "SPIKE! *GOAT*!!"
Spike jolted, his eyes zooming to the screaming goat before him.
"COME ON, GOAT, RUN FOR YOUR LIFE!!"
He snatched the animal by the horns and sped like the wind, the creature complaining the whole way, but quickly moving its legs to catch up nonetheless.

The five whirled away from the frightening scene of the two beasts continuing to try and kill each other, Magnus doing his job well in protecting young Ivy Rein.

Quinton swung his body back around, pointing his still filming camera at the commotion behind him. His eyes widened, as he watched the Chupacabra attempt to dig its long fangs into Magnus, as the cryptid had the current advantage.

"MAGNUS, GET UP!!"

Magnus deflected the attack; he tossed his opponent right off of him, slamming his body into it, which successfully knocked it down, before rushing to its head and stomping on it. The amount of pain Quin felt in his ribs watching this battle made him nauseous. The German Shepherd that had been accompanying them thus far was a fighter Lim did not expect to see. If only they knew how fierce and dirty this dog really was in a fight... they would have opened the van doors the previous day, and avoided this hardship.

The viewing of this assault alone did not last long... for Quin heard a familiar set of voices.

"MAGNUS!!"

"OH MY GOD!!"

"ARE YOU GUYS *SEEING* THIS?!"

He tossed his head in the direction of the four running towards them, before they skid to a stop, their mouths hanging open in utter shock. Their gaze was naturally glued to the battle taking place on the field, just mere yards away.

Audrey held her mouth as she watched helplessly, Gabriel beside her looking whiter than a sheet of paper... Amelia and Lycan stood, their faces teeming with amazement.

"Magnus, no!!" Audrey cried, her eyes swelling up with instant worry. "Oh god, no... we have to stop this!! He'll be killed!!"

"Killed? He's *butchering* that thing!" Lycan exclaimed, in wild excitement. "I'm more worried for the Cab!"

"Ivy, where's Ivy?!" Gabe's eyes wandered the field, searching frantically, until he caught sight of the four shapes running in the opposite direction. His heart stopped. They were running toward the woods.

"NO!!! *STOP*!!!"

The others came to a hard break, and swirled around to face behind them. They perked in relief.

"About time you bloody made it!" Quinton finally exclaimed.

"DUDE, WE GOTTA RUN!" Troy yelled.

But Gabriel hurried forward, waving his arms.

"NO! DON'T TAKE HER IN THERE!"

"WHAT?!"

"I SAID DON'T. TAKE HER. IN TH-"

"GABRIEL, LOOK OUT!!!"

Gabriel's eyes flashed to his right, but they soon widened, and the very breath inside him sucked back into his lungs. He was then pounced... by the Chupacabra.

"GABRIEL!!!" Audrey cried, her voice hoarse and filled with horror.

So distracted with each other, they did not look to see that the Chupacabra had knocked Magnus on his side, just long enough for him to charge for an attack on another. And the one closest to him just happened to be the Beckhart boy.

Gabriel was now fighting for his life, as the black-furred creature, with eyes that burned into his soul, fangs inches from slicing into his chest, was using every force within itself to try and kill him. It was mad, delirious. Fueled with the urge to take a life. It did not care who or what it killed... as long as *someone* ended up dead.

Gabe screamed. The only thing he could do. For whatever words he might have been able to say were refusing to leave his mouth in that present moment. His last moments.

"Get away from my BROTHER!"

Something whizzed by Gabriel's head... a long, whistling dart... and directly hit the Chupacabra's shoulder. It was sent back, flying; flying so far, it slammed to the ground.

Gabriel gasped, huffing and puffing, sending out sounds of pain and terror, as he struggled to get as far from it as possible, inching back towards the others.

"Oof! *Ivy*!!" Troy recoiled.

The means, Quinton did not know, but Ivy had somehow escaped Troy's hold on her, using painful means against him, and was currently rushing in the direction of the others. Quin did not know how a giant man like Troy could so easily lose a fight to a little girl. But here they were.

Audrey stood behind her brother, still pointing the crossbow she just shot the creature with. Gabriel soon hurried up.

"Ivy, STOP!" He found the strength to let out, as he saw Ivy charge right in the direction of the Cab. The Chupacabra started to recover. Its eyes gravitated in an instant at Ivy.

*It wants her... it **wants** her. I knew it!*

The little girl did not yield. The creature started to stand. Amelia's eyes shot at the others, before finally turning to the woods. A wicked smile instantaneously traced across her lips, her red hair blowing in the wind. *Trap.* She bolted forward.

"Lycan, c'mon!"

Lycan did not hesitate one second; he ran after Pine.

"Where are you GOING?!" Spike squealed, only for Amelia to point her finger at him, as she ran for the woods.

"We need more time; just keep him distracted!"

Spike felt as if he could level the field with his fury.

"I'VE *BEEN* KEEPING HIM DISTRACTED, YOU FREAKING TOMATO!!!"

Despite being wounded in two separate places, the Chupacabra was not quitting. It faced against Ivy, saliva dripping from its mouth, as its heart raced faster than it could bear. It wasted no time. It darted towards Ivy.

Everyone screamed in that instant... until a voice demanded for all their attention.

"Hey there, big boy!"

The Chupacabra swung its head around, just in time for an object to smack it in the face. It shook its head, its snout throbbing, when at once, a blinding light came from the object. It squealed in confusion, its ears now ringing, blinking its eyes repeated times.

The rest of the group struggled to see clearly, working their stiff jaws, as the ringing in their ears persisted. What they saw made them gawk. **Talbot.**

"Talbot!" Audrey exclaimed. "You came!"

"No time for talk, kids!" He snapped.

"BECKHARTS, get your weapons and help Brooke get that cage! MOHAWK, get the kid back into the house!"

There was a loud bleat.

"And the goat, too!"

There was an edge of sarcasm in the gruff man's voice, but Spike, trying not to feel offended by being addressed as 'Mohawk', did as he was told. He grabbed the goat and ran, snatching Ivy by the arm, as he made it for the house. She tried to fight him, but Spike was surprisingly strong enough to resist her.

The Cab turned in Talbot's direction, before looking back at Ivy, who was being dragged back into the house. It growled, attempting to follow. But Talbot, his shotgun pointed in its direction, was now in the clear to shoot, with the child out of the equation. He shot at its paws, which stunned it enough to snarl in fury. Which only worsened when he saw that Magnus was now charging towards him.

"LIM, keep that camera pointed on the creature and NOTHING else!"

"Got it!"

Talbot watched as Magnus once again collided with the creature. He took this welcome opportunity.

"GO GO GO!!"

Everyone leapt into action.

CHAPTER XXXIII
◆ SOME ASSEMBLY REQUIRED ◆

"Where's the tranquilizer gun?!"

In the heat of the moment, under the pressure of everyone scattering in different directions, to do different things in order to beat one single creature, Audrey's mind was scrambling for answers, as she ran by Talbot's side.

"The *gun*, Audrey, where is it?!"

She blinked several times, trying to force her mind to work faster.

"It's in Amelia's car!!"

"We need it! Grab it, NOW!"

Audrey did not argue. She ran straight for Amelia's blue beetle to retrieve their much needed item. As Talbot ran, he scanned all around him on the field to account for every single member of their makeshift monster hunting team. His heart raced even quicker when he realized that two were unaccounted for.

"Where's Lycan and Pine?!"

"The woods!" Troy answered, as he and Gabriel trotted backwards from the beetle, the cage in their elevated possession. They set it down, quickly.

"They told us to distract the Chupacabra, so they could run to set a trap!"

Russell's eyes flashed to the woods. All the hairs on the back of his neck stood on end. *They need to get out there **now**.*

"We need to go after them! Right now!"

"Shouldn't we lure it into the woods??" Audrey inquired, as she returned with the tranquilizer gun.

"*No!*" Gabriel cried. "You don't--" He took a few short, exasperated breaths in between his words. "We don't know what's in there! It could very well be the leader trying to kill us!"

"I think that's why she went in, dude." Troy spoke.

"To find the leader! Chop the Hydra!"

Talbot's brain was going a million different paths at once. It was hard to think clearly, with a pair of animals viciously brawling behind you, and the very real threat of actually dying lingering over your head.

The group did not leave their back turned in one direction for very long. They all looked around, deliberating their next moves as fast as their minds would allow.

"...You're right, Brooke." He nodded at last.

"You're right... let's go."

Gabriel's eyes snapped to the old man, widening in growth behind his glasses. He couldn't believe the words coming from his mouth; now Beckhart was the only one against the woods.

"What?!"

"We need to go after those two, anyway... better us than the kid being put on the line. We can lure the Cab there. Finish this thing."

"Are you serious?! This is crazy!"

"This is monster hunting."

Talbot quickly pivoted towards the Cab and Magnus, who were still fighting brutally.

"Magnus is keeping that thing distracted... we need to move. *Now*." He then sped for the woods. "Bring the cage!"

~

Amelia and Lycan raced through the trees, only trickling doses of light scattered from the night sky above to lead them on their way. Their minds and hearts were too consumed by terror and adrenaline to realize just how unnerving these woods actually were. Unnerving in the sense that a presence resided here. Not animal in nature. Not human in nature. Just a presence... something was waiting for them. Watching. Calculating the results. Trying to determine what made these two enter an obviously poignant destination... for a trap.

They needed to find a spot open enough to set the trip wire. That would knock the Chupacabra down, and give them the advantage they needed. They couldn't be too picky. Couldn't go too far. They were in high hopes of capturing the beast and actually getting to walk away from this in the end. The capture of Chupie needed to be swift. Needed to be safe. And needed to happen, before something else was unleashed upon them.

Lycan suddenly screeched to a stop. He scanned all around, moonlight resting upon the surrounding area.

"Amy!"

Pine stopped hard in her tracks and hurled her body around to face him. He pointed where they stood, as the light peaked through the trees, and shined upon his soft brown skin. That's when Amelia noticed the environment, catching on to what Lycan had to tell her, before he could even speak a word.

"Right here!"

Her eyes gave the spot a few more quick glances, as a smile traced across her lips. She approached him quickly, lowering the bag of supplies from her shoulder.

"This is perfect!"

Indeed, it was. An open area just large enough to set up the cage, and have enough breathing room to run if need be. There were trees lined up in a row, with gaps large enough to hang the trip wire.

The objective was as they discussed before; lead the Chupacabra here, where it would trip on the wire, fall down, and whoever stood at the post would shoot it with a tranquilizer dart, then the group would proceed to transport the tranquilized animal into the cage, and the day would be saved. A simple enough plan, with a simple enough solution. There was just one complicated scenario they needed to face.

"Whoever's controlling Chupie is here."

Pine looked around her, as she pulled out the trip wire, her eyes peering into the darkness in great suspicion.

"Someone's watching us. Wanting us to die."

At the sound of this danger, Lycan's eyes honed in on her, with what appeared to be a mixture of anger, intimidation and overprotectiveness. He instantly drew out his rifle that had been strapped to his back, and pointed it out into the same darkness that Amelia was eyeing. "Whatever it is, I'll keep watch of it. You go. Get things set up."

Amelia looked back, her red hair glistening in the moon's bluish light. Lycan cut his dark brown eyes to her, just as she leaned in and planted a kiss upon his cheek. She stepped back, her face beaming in a delighted, endearing manner as she smiled wide. "I adore you."

She turned and hopped off to prepare the trap. Lycan's eyes returned to the darkness. And a charming, boyish grin slipped through his serious expression.

~

Spike ran up the steps, and charged through the door of the

Uncanny

house, Ivy's arm held tight in one hand, the screaming goat in the other.

"C'mon, c'mon, hurry!" His voice had went hoarse from all the yelling, his face as red as a cherry as a result. And he was reacting quicker than his mind could process, simply going on basic instinct at this point, in comparison to his laid-back personality under normal circumstances.

The goat cried out one last time, before retreating further into the house, into the warmth of the living room. Spike huffed and puffed, as he barricaded the door that had now been barricaded a second time that night. He held his hands against it, using all the force his muscles could muster, as if he had to hold it off against the beast itself.

His mohawked head fell to the floor and he closed his eyes, his body heaving unevenly. Ivy stood behind him, staring at him with an intense gaze, her small body completely motionless. There was no expression on her face... the stare she gave him would make anyone else in the room uncomfortable, had it have been noticed.

"You're safe, Ivy." Spike let out between heavy, recovering breaths. "You're safe... I promise... I won't let that thing get to yo-" As he turned, he jolted. His eyes widened, almost to the size of plates. "IVY?!"
His head whipped in every direction.
"IVY?!"
The little girl was no where in sight. He ran forward, out of the kitchen, and into the living room. His eyes glazed over the environment in search of the child, to no avail.

"Ivy, come on, this isn't funny!!"
That's when something caught his eye. Not the goat and the barking Scrooge cowering next to the fireplace. But the one laying on the floor before him, completely unconscious.

"What the-- *Wyatt?!*"
He leaped ahead and fell on his knees, as he extended his reach to shake the farm hand's lanky shoulders.

"Dude! Duddeee!! Wake up, man!"
He tapped the man's face. It took him a moment, but at last, Wyatt's eyes started to flutter open.

"Uhh... uh.... ohhhhhh..."

He immediately held his head, his face scrunching up.

"My head..."

"Dude, what happened?! Who did this?!"

"I...I..."

Clear signs of Wyatt's mind trying to search for the answer were there... but something just couldn't put it into words.

"...I... I... I fell. Yeah... I fell... I hit my head..."

He gently shook his aforementioned head.

"...Ivy... is Ivy... safe?"

"No, man, she disappeared!"

"...Oh... oh no... Spike, we gotta… we gotta find her!"

The farm hand quickly sat up, still holding his aching skull and groaning in obvious pain. "We need to save her before-"

Suddenly, there was a loud, blood curdling screech outside. One which made the two men nearly jump out of their skins, as their heads swiveled in the direction of the window above. Their eyes widened. Their mouths dropped.

It was the Chupacabra. *And a cry of sheer, absolute pain.*

~

Magnus had enough of this fight. Neither he or the Chupacabra were backing down. So he took things to the next level. He jumped in and bit down. Bit as hard as his jaws could bite. Biting into the throat of his opponent, of whose own fangs had been itching to sink into something as well.

This attack caused the creature to cry out. Cry out the loudest and most brutal they had ever heard from the cryptid yet. A sound that echoed across the field. Deafened all ears surrounding the property. Imprinting itself in their memory for several lasting minutes.

Magnus did not wait for the creature to stop; he pushed the attack even further by shaking his head, which drove the Chupacabra past the point of pain, and now entering the realm of straight-up torture. Magnus was intending to end him. With little to no regard for the others' plans for it.

Talbot, Troy and the Beckharts halted in their path, turning their bodies to look behind them, in the direction of the two creatures. Audrey, for one, felt her skin developing goosebumps.

"What in the word is Magnus *doing* to him?!"

Russell's eyes drifted back and forth between the field and the woods they had just crossed the threshold of. He bit his lip.

"...Keep going. Bring the cage to the others."

He started to turn back, now pointing his gun up in front of him.

"What do you think you're doing?!" Audrey hissed.

"You can't leave us alone!"

"I have to stop that dog before he kills our fine specimen, yeah?" He didn't even look back at the group; didn't even give them enough time to answer.

"I'll be the bait. I'm gonna lure it right to you."

The three gawked. This man... *this man was crazy.*

"You're insane!! It'll catch you and kill you!"

Gabriel backed up his sister in this,

"Audrey's right, let one of *us* be the bait... *I'll* do it!"

"Y'all kids are in over your heads. I ain't as old and frail as you think. Been at this game longer than you been alive."

He buried his open hand in his pocket, digging something out, of which he handed to Troy. Troy took it, looking down with instant curiosity. It was another flash grenade.

He breathed, his voice entering a gasping whisper.

"*Dude.*"

"Throw it in case things go wrong. Audrey, you shoot that tranq gun, and you shoot it good. Don't miss. Y'all signal me when I'm about to reach the wire. Gabriel..."

His eyes met the Beckhart boy's. Gabriel's back straightened, as he saw what was behind Talbot's eyes. *Trust.*

"The others are looking to you. I see it. You helm this wheel. You captain this crew. You don't let them down, you hear me?"

Gabriel swallowed. Was this an observation of Talbot's... or was he assigning a role for the boy? Putting him in leadership, placing the others in his care.

Naturally, Troy had been a mentor in his own right, the oldest of the assembly... but Gabriel. Gabriel had qualities that Talbot recognized. Qualities needed of someone to take charge... and protect the rest of them.

Beckhart did not know what compelled Talbot to say this... but he would have been a fool not to acknowledge it.

"I won't."

His eyes fluttered behind his glasses. He shifted them, nervously, as his head bobbled in a nod. "I promise."

Talbot nodded one single time, before turning his head back around. "Good."

He took a deep, calculating inhale... then exhaled.

"*Go.*"

The three wasted no time. Audrey bolted ahead of the other two. Gabriel and Troy immediately grabbed hold of the cage once more and they waddled past the trees, their legs bouncing comically, as they proceeded further into the woods. Despite, of course, the urge to turn back.

The growing sickness Gabriel felt in the pit of his stomach. The screaming voice in his head, telling him not to take a step further, reminding him of the dangers by replaying his dreams over and over, the disturbing images flashing before his eyes. Images that would forever haunt him. Something in him wanted to cry, and he did not know why. Something terrified him.

He was still worried about Ivy. Even though she was safe. Safe in the house, with Spike and Wyatt. But wait... where *was* Wyatt?? Why did he let her go out alone to begin with??

His blood ran cold. His eyes turned back to the open field, where he saw an armed Talbot advancing back to Magnus and the Cab... Quinton, filming the fight... and an image of Ivy, standing in the middle of the field, hands clenched, brown hair flowing in the wind. Imagining the child staring after them, waiting to be seen, as she had outsmarted the rest of them, refusing to be kept cooped up inside the house.

It's an image he now was unsure was real or fiction... something he no longer could find out. For they had delved too deep in the dark... it was hopeless now. Gabriel knew it to be true.

Something was pulling them inside the woods.

\- - -

Lim kept the camera right on them. Refusing to look away. Refusing to move a muscle. He watched, breathlessly, as Magnus brutally attacked the Cab. He wondered, for a split second, of maybe putting a stop to it. Considering they needed the creature alive and all. But he continued watching. Especially when a presence walked up from behind. And a gruff voice spoke in his ear.

"Quinton... *run.*"

The spiky-haired young man jerked his head up. Talbot. He

stood next to him, his gun pointed right at the two ahead of them. Judging by the passing seconds of silence, Quinton now determined that Talbot was not going to repeat himself. He sucked up his breath, "*Okay*." And he ran.

Talbot was grateful for a crew that listened. Now it was time to see if their canine companion would do the same.

"Quinton! What's the dog's name?!"

"Magnus!" Lim yelled over his shoulder.

The man did not skip a beat.

"MagNUSSS! *STOP*!"

Magnus froze, instantly. His eyes quickly skipped to Talbot. The old man perked up, his gun pointed right at the Cab's head. Talbot's eyes narrowed. *Magnus nodded.*

As if on cue, as if understanding the situation completely, Magnus whipped his head to the side, taking the Cab with him, and he let go. The creature flew forward, landing aggressively upon the grass and dirt, kicking up a cloud upon impact, which distributed into the air.

It took it several seconds to recover. To regain its strength, its composure. To realize it was still alive, and it still had a mission. To open its eyes, and lift up its head, and gaze upon Talbot. Talbot... who fearlessly stood mere feet from the blood sucker, pointing his shotgun right at the creature's head.

The old man and the Chupacabra at last locked eyes. Russell formed a wicked grin. "Hey there, handsome."

His arm then retracted. He extended both high into the air, as if he were a showman at a great circus. And his face displayed uncanny signs of pure unadulterated *fun*.

"Come and get me, big boy."

The Chupacabra... it got its spirit back. Regained its wits. It stood up once again. And an unearthly growl exited its mouth. It charged forward. Right after the now fleeing Talbot.

CHAPTER XXXIV
◆ SNARE OF THE FOWLER ◆

The undeniable sound of a screeching Chupacabra brought chills down Lycan's spine. The terrifying cries of pain that echoed through the woods, reaching his ears at such a loud volume, broke his concentration on the darkness before him.

He found himself looking back, for only a moment, his gun still pointed ahead. He was still as a statue, trying to determine whether that sound meant the creature was still preoccupied, or that it was coming after someone.

His eyes finally turned from behind him to his left, where Amelia was still setting up the trip wire a small distance away. Knowing something or someone else was in the woods with them, the two had to stay close. They had to. Or it would no sooner pick them off like stems from a fruit.

But soon... Lycan had his own problems.

"Lycan"

He lurched, his head spinning back to the front of him. His eyes, instantly expanded, honed in on the darkness. Where he awaited further incident. Was that just his own head... or was someone.... *talking* to him?

He found that staring at the nothingness before him only made matters worse. He had no clue if something was there or not. The question alone petrified him.

Lycan was never one to shy away from a fight. He rarely ever got scared doing dangerous, rather typical boyish things. But now... in this scenario... this was a whole 'nother level of primitive fear. For in his near constant disturbing dreams, Lycan had always heard something calling to him. A voice of such inhuman quality. Riddled with fury and hatred. Malice and blood-lust. Something of which made him feel like a scared, vulnerable child.

Was it trauma? Was it memory? Was it his own dark imagination? Or was it something darker... something much worse? And now, awake... this voice called to him once more. A voice that upon hearing it, made Lycan tremble where he stood.

He tried not to. He tried with all his might. Especially with Amelia Pine standing near, a woman of whom he had been infatuated with since childhood, but never thought he would get the chance to know personally. A welcome light in his darkness.

His eyes repeatedly glanced over at her. This person, this thing... was it trying to distract him? Was it trying to prevent him from protecting her? If his attention was off of her, would that be the moment the thing struck?

His breathing became irrational. Regardless of how much he tried to control it, control his body, his muscles, his thoughts. Regardless of how he took deep breaths, and tightened his grip on his weapon, as he stared back into the black hole before him, licking his dry lips, trying to get his mind off of the fear...
it didn't matter. None of it mattered.

For the paralyzing fear came right back.

"You don't want to do this, Lycan."

Lycan gasped.

"You don't know the power I have."

Lycan dared not look to find Pine. He *knew* this wasn't his mind any longer.

*"You don't know the power that **you** have."*

Without a second passing by, Lycan fired. Pine shouted bloody murder as she fell backwards, right on her back. She scrambled to get up again, to look at the crazy gun-toting punk ahead of her. Her face was brimming with confusion.

"WHAT THE ACTUAL *FRICK*?!"

"AMY, IT'S HERE!"

Amelia's brows lowered as she stared at him, ever so slightly approaching.

"What??"

"IT'S *HERE*! I heard him! It's talking, it's in front of us!!"

Amelia ran to him. She grabbed on to his shoulder, and turned her gaze upon what he was shooting at.

She swallowed.

"Lycan, I didn't hear anything... are you sur-"

"*Yes.*"

He still wasn't looking at her.

Pine knew Lycan. She knew he was no coward, nor was he unjustly paranoid. If Lycan believed he saw or heard something, she believed it too. "Okay... we're almost done... the others will be here... just... wait."

But Lycan, still experiencing tremors in both his arms, rattled his head. "No. This isn't gonna work. We have to get out of the woods right now."

"Lycan!"

"I'm serious, Amy, we need to leave NOW! This thing is out to kill us!"

"What did he say to you?!"

"It doesn't matter what he said!"

"Come into the dark, Lycan."

Lycan screamed. This made Pine jump.

"Come into the dark and join us."

Another shot fired. Amelia instantly looked ahead, holding both her ears from the ringing the gunshot caused.

"YOU IN THERE!"

She leapt forward,

"WE KNOW YOU'RE THERE! AND WE'RE BRINGING YOU DOWN!"

"AMELIA, *STOP!* DON'T PROVOKE HIM!"

"Says the man SHOOTING at it!"

Amelia looked back at Lycan... his terror... his tough guy exterior washing away... the side of him that she always admired, because she knew it was a result of what he made himself into.

He *had* to become a fighter. He *had* to be strong, after years of oppression. Whatever this voice was saying to him... whatever it was trying to do... it was bringing him back to the time he was not strong. The parts of himself he hated and wanted to bury. Those parts were resurfacing because of it.

Back into a scared little boy. And for that alone, hatred for it filled her heart. Her eyes returned to the darkness. The darkness of which seemed now to be its own entity.

"You listen to me... you've been in power long enough. You've taken lives... you've killed, you've destroyed, you've ruled by fear and possession, and keeping everyone in the darkness you're hiding behind. But I promise you... that's all about to change. *We're* going to change it. Your empire is about to crumble down. Your minions will fall. Your evil little roots will wither... and *we* will take back the power. We'll set all your slaves free. This is the end of you. It starts *tonight*."

She then drew out both her pistols, raising them both in the

same direction she locked eyes in. "*Got that?!*"
   Bang.
A simultaneous shot from her pistol pair sent a wave of echoes across the trees, and through the air. Sounds of which caused birds to cry out in a panic, the wind blowing violently through the leaves.

   Despite firing from two small weapons, Amelia managed to make more noise and commotion than Lycan's rifle. And Lycan could not be more proud. As usual... Amelia took all his fear and pain away in an instant.

   Pine lowered one weapon, but still held the other, smoke flooding from the barrel.

   "Now *get out!*"
They did not know whether the unseen entity was still there or not. All they knew was, it did not speak again, if it *was* still present. And that, at least, brought some comfort to Lycan's mind.

   "*What* are you two shooting at?!"
They both spun on their heels. Running towards them were the Beckharts and Troy Brooke. In Gabe and Troy's hands was the cage. In Audrey's, the tranquilizer gun. Seeing the three brought relief to Amelia and Lycan's hearts. Even if they were not indeed safe, it was the illusion that only a group of people brought in which calmed their minds. The feeling of being safe was enough for them.

   "I repeat," Audrey persisted. "*What* are you shooting at?!"
The Beckhart girl could not take any more bad news. If another creature happened to now be in the equation, she was turning in the tranq gun, and going home.

   "The one who's controlling the Cab, it was here!"
Pine pointed in the opposite direction.

   "It was talking to Lycan!"
Gabriel's eyes glazed, drifting ever so slightly toward the shrouded trees. "Did *you* hear it?"

   Pine hesitated a moment, as if unsure she should answer truthfully to that or not. "No... but I know it was there. I felt it."

   "*It?* That's it, I'm quitting."
Audrey lowered the tranq gun, and held her increasingly aching head.

   "We don't know what it was..." Lycan tried to explain.

"We just know it was talking to me, getting inside my head... and then we both shot in the voice's direction, and it stopped."

"Okay, you killed it, fantastic, let's celebrate after we trap this other stupid thing."

"I don't think we killed it, Audrey." Pine swallowed.

"I just think we shut it up."

"Why do we keep referring to it as 'it'?" Troy inquired, in great confusion. "You guys are freaking me out... if it was talking, it had to be a person!"

"Or an entity capable of speech." Gabriel breathed.

Audrey thrashed her free hand.

"Oh my god, why are we discussing this?! Talbot is leading that thing back here as bait! We don't have time to stand around!"

Lycan perked at the mention of Talbot. He would have celebrated, but the pressure was on.

"She's right... quick, bring the cage over there! We gotta get to our posts!"

Troy and Gabriel quickly grabbed hold of the cage once more and ran it a close enough distance away, carefully climbing over the wire. They set it down, and proceeded to prop the entrance up using a large stick.

Lycan turned to the Beckhart girl, pointing sternly at her.

"Beckhart, are you taking the shot?!"

Her brows lowered, *"Excuse me??"*

"Are *you* taking the *shot*?!"

"Heck no!"

"*I'll* do it!"

The gun was grabbed by her brother, who proceeded to position himself behind a tree. He looked a little hesitant about what he was signing himself up for, but if his sister was not ready for such a task, he would gladly take the helm in her stead.

"You better not miss, preppy."

Lycan's eyes gravitated to Audrey.

"And *you* find something useful to do."

As harsh as it seemed, it was something that Audrey needed to hear. She needed the motivation. Not to prove herself to them. But prove herself to *her*.

It took Lycan's words, the unmistakable sound of Quinton's incoming screams that 'it' was coming, and Troy walking back to the small group, for Audrey to realize something. She lifted her chin. "Whatever was controlling the Cab is probably still here, right?"

The others looked to her, obviously in need of clarity as to what she was on about. She smirked.

"Well we can't have it messing our plan up, now can we?"

Her arm reached out, as she heard heavy footsteps come from behind her, and she grabbed hold of someone's jacket. Her head turned to a stunned and confused Quinton. She gestured at the camera in his hand.

"That thing's on night vision mode, right?"

His face scrunched up. "Y... yeah??"

Her blood pumped faster, as a surge of wicked delight overcame her anxiety of the situation.

"Quin, Troy, come with me. We're going on the hunt."

Her head turned back to Lycan, whose face lifted in surprise of the Beckhart girl.

"We'll take out the operator. *You* take out the grunt."

She stepped forward and pat his shoulder, a glare in her eye that he didn't find at all appealing.

"Find something useful to do."

Gabriel smirked... he couldn't help it. He knew full well that his sister was an absolute savage when you pushed her too far. And now that her limit had been reached, there was no doubt about it; Audrey would do everything in her feasible power to ensure they succeeded in their plan, and make it home that night.

Your move, entity, your move.

- - -

Despite Talbot's age, he ran fast. Faster than even he thought he was capable of. But the Chupacabra was also fast. Just as fast, if not a little more, as all the standard animals he had come across in his life time. But Russell was no stranger to this. After all... this Chupacabra was not his first.

He breezed past the trees for several seconds, hoping and praying that the kids had everything set up by the time he reached them. He made sure to keep a vigilant eye on the ground, for the trip wire that he hoped would already be prepped.

As soon as he saw it, instead of jumping it, he would bolt in another direction, at just the opportune moment, so that the Cab would lack any time to prepare itself. It would slide right into the wire and come tumbling to the ground. Giving way for the wielder of the tranq gun to fire. The plan was foolproof. All he needed now was timing. And that was something he knew he had no problem with.

A small flicker of a minute, though, he got worried... how far did they go into the woods? Did they even make it past a certain point? Did something happen to them? Were they okay?

But no...
  there they were...
    he saw them.
He saw Gabriel peeking from a tree, Lycan from another. He saw Amelia waving her hand at him, and pointing at the wire's location. He looked down and saw it. The wire was set up perfectly. Just the right height to trip the Cab.

...However...something was wrong. Something ate at his mind. Ate at his stomach. The plan was going perfectly. Nothing could possibly go wrong now. Except... he felt it... a presence... another pair of eyes was watching them. A sickening feeling crawled into him. And he didn't have enough time to do anything about it.

He quickly dodged, right before he made contact with the wire, and he leaped away into a hard tackle with the ground. Through the pain of his landing, his ears awaited the sound of his pursuer making violent contact with the wire, flipping high into the air, before slamming on to the earth...but he heard none of that. Just silence. A silence that brought him great dread.

He was forced to look back. Forced to see what had happened. And his fears were true. The Chupacabra had come to a halt. A small cloud of dirt surrounded it, but not dense enough to shroud its face, as it stared down at the wire before it. Its eyes glowed and studied the wire, its expression teeming with an unnerving calculation. As if it had just worked out their plan.

Its next move brought chills to Talbot; it looked at him. Its eyes were narrowed into a slit. As if it were looking with betrayal... disgust... insult... and a growing fury. One look and Talbot knew what it was thinking.

This *is what you were planning to do?*
  I don't think so.

The others stared in shock. Their mouths hung open. Their gaze focused on the terrifying creature before them. How? How did he know??

That's when it hit Amelia. The entity... **it told him.** The three screamed internally, as the creature turned its head to Beckhart. And with one unprepared stretch of its neck, the Chupacabra opened its mouth, and *chomped the wire in half.* Pine gasped, "NO!"

"GABRIEL, SHOOT IT, SHOOT IT *NOW*!" Talbot's command made Gabe's heart leap, and jolt his mind into action. He instantly pointed the gun at the Cab, that snarled at him.

His finger found the trigger. He breathed. But he did not press it. He wasn't given the chance to. For he suddenly felt his arms bend. Bend against his will. He yelled out, as they twisted the object he wielded in the complete opposite direction... now finding it pointing right under his chin.

"GABRIEL, WHAT ARE YOU *DOING*?!" Amelia screeched. "IT'S NOT **ME**!!!"

His scream was followed by his finger relocating the trigger. He had lost all control of his body.

Lycan leapt forward. He quickly took hold of the gun in the split second window of time he had, and he jerked it away. Just as Gabriel's finger was forced to pull the trigger. The dart fired out of sight, high into the air.

The Chupacabra charged at the two, but Pine was having none of it. She shouted at the creature, immediately drawing out her pistols, and began shooting a series of bullets in the creature's direction. *Each shot was deflected by an unseen force.*

Her eyes enlarged, as if she had just witnessed a performance of a magician. The entity was protecting the creature. And turning their bodies against themselves.

"HEY!" Talbot exclaimed, leaping up. He went to tackle the creature himself. He didn't care if it would kill him in the process. It didn't matter, as long as the kids would be safe. His heroic intentions were futile, however. For he had been beat.

The Chupacabra stopped suddenly and swiveled its head around, the sound of a loud bark drawing his attention away

from the group. Everyone else turned their heads.
And their hearts sank.

Ivy and Magnus stood a short distance away.
The little girl's hair blew in the wind, her eyes honed in on the creature. Magnus stood by her side, growling threateningly, but calmly. The Chupacabra was entranced by the child's arrival.

Gabriel's heart raced... for Ivy gave him a look. And he knew what that look was.

"IVY, *NO!*"

Her gaze turned back to the creature. She bolted.

And the Chupacabra chased after her.

CHAPTER XXXV
◆ LEAP OF FAITH ◆

The instructions of Audrey were simple. Disperse in a small area, and flesh out possible hiding spots of the entity. Stay in communication with one another via group call. If Quinton saw something through his camera, tell Audrey, and she would open fire.

And so, they crept through the moonlit spot of woods, their eyes adjusting now to the almost nonexistent lighting. Audrey's shotgun was strapped to her back. She, like Quin and Troy, was holding her cell phone up to her mouth.

There were no updates to give yet. They just kept searching. Searching as quickly as their eyes could move. They knew they were pressed for time. They knew danger was imminent.

They had to find this entity. They had to find it, before it was too late.

"You guys see anything??" Beckhart inquired.

"Negative." Quin muttered.

"Nada, mi amiga." Troy responded.

Audrey sighed, deeply. She didn't know whether to be worried nothing had turned up, or relieved. Her eyes drifted to the emptiness around her, cloaked in blackness.

She felt vulnerable.

A primal, instinctive fear swelled within her. One that only shows its ugly face when one is in the presence of an open, dark area. Where even the shadows threaten to consume you.

Anything could be waiting for her here. It could even be behind her. Beside her. Above her. Under her. Who was she kidding... after learning of the nature of her stalker, the entity could even be standing *in front* of her.

She swallowed as she kept her gaze fixed ahead, backing closely against a tree.

"Still nothing?"

"Audrey, shut up. I'll let you know when I see something." Quinton's attitude was not appreciated, but it was understandable. They were all anxious. Waiting in heavy anticipation for something that might not even happen anymore.

The three had hopes that the others would call out to them,

telling them that the Chupacabra had been captured, and the threat was over. That would be the biggest relief. For it would put to rest their concerns and fears, and would be one less danger the Assembly had to face.

But no, instead... the sounds they heard stiffened their backs. Their muscles tightened. Every hair stood on end. For the sounds they heard were not ones of victory. They were screams of panic.

First Audrey heard Talbot... then her brother... then Amelia... then Gabriel again. She couldn't breathe from the words that reached her ears.

"Ivy, NO!"

She was about to run. Run to save the child, wherever she was. Until Quinton's voice stopped her.

"IT'S THERE, IT'S THERE, AUDREY, IT'S RIGHT THERE!"

Her eyes flashed to her phone.

"Where?!"

"IT'S RIGHT THERE *WITH YOU*!"

The very breath in Audrey's body sucked into her lungs. Before she even knew it, before she could even scream, something grabbed her by the throat, and violently threw her into the tree she had depended on for comfort.

Her oxygen was further cut off when another hand slapped over her mouth. She did not have a chance to fight back. The hand that held her lifted her high into the air, her legs now dangling, kicking to make contact with something. In the attack, she had dropped her phone. And now, with both free hands, she was aggressively trying to free herself. Fighting against her attacker.

What she saw before her was no man. But not a creature, either. She could not make out any details of what was slowly killing her. It was a shape. A shape that was physical, but at the same time, she felt she could almost see through. This shape was choking the life out of her.

Her mind was dragging itself. Her eyes felt like they were about to burst. She felt her lungs screaming at her to be released, the surviving oxygen in her trapped and becoming poison to every other organ within her.

Her cries were stifled behind the entity's hand, who held it tighter and tighter, as if it were critical that no air be let out, even through a crack.

"Hello, Audrey."

The voice. The entity spoke... and its voice... a voice that instantly haunted her. It was so inhuman. So calm, yet so venomous. This was no human's voice. Whatever it was, she didn't know... but she knew it was not human.

"I'm very sorry it had to happen this way... but I can't allow this to continue."

He tightened his grip around her neck, making her squeeze her eyes shut, as fresh hot tears made their escape.

"I have worked too hard... and too long... for you and your friends to tear it apart now."

Audrey kicked her dangling legs, hoping to hit something. But it felt just as pointless as kicking at nothing at all. Whoever, whatever, this was... he was much too strong.

"I can not allow you to shed light on my work. Not now. I'm much too close."

The entity turned his head to the side, as he stared at her with unseen eyes.

"A pity, truly. To snuff out one as beautiful as you."

He brought his head closer. Even as close as they were, Audrey could barely make out any distinguishing details.

"You hear those sounds?"

As he said this, Audrey could hear it. The snarls of the Chupacabra. The panicked screams of the others, as they ran to save Ivy. Audrey could only guess what was happening...

Ivy was being chased.

"Our fine bloodthirsty specimen will soon catch up to the child. After all this time, you have finally led her back to me. I thank you for that."

She couldn't see it... but she could sense a disgusting, sadistic smile in the entity's voice.

"The child will finally be mine. And it will all be over."

Audrey's eyes expanded at the sound of this. What did this freak, this *monster*, intend to do to Ivy? There were zero explanations in her mind. No possible reasoning whatsoever.

Then she remembered. In a flash of a memory. Ivy survived a monster attack. Ivy was running from something. Something that Magnus saved her from.

This thing...
  whatever it was...
   there was no question now that it was the one responsible.
"AUDREY!!"
The voice, either from Troy or Quinton, Audrey couldn't even tell anymore, it pulled the entity's attention away. For a single instance, it turned its head. And that's when Audrey found it in her. The chance she needed.

She sucked up whatever air, whatever energy, was left in her body, and she launched it all into one single arm. Just as the head turned back, she went for it. Her arm swung and punched him square in the jaw.

Her body fell to the ground as the entity let go, letting out an angry cry of pain. Beckhart landed on her knees, the impact sending out sharp signals of agony to her recovering brain. She felt like coughing until she passed out. But one thought overran her every other instinct. Her hand reached behind her in that second, and pulled out her shotgun.

With a quick spring, Audrey was back on her feet, and began mercilessly firing her weapon at the entity. Each shot made chased him away from her. She shot until her eyes lost sight of him. She did not know if she successfully hit him or not.
She just knew she was no longer on the verge of death.
And he was running for his own life.

When she knew for sure he was gone, she bent over, proceeding to cough and gather back her ability to breathe.

"Audrey!!"

Her swollen eyes lifted. Troy and Quinton had found her. Brooke was reaching in to check on her, concern written all over his face.

"Dude, are you okay?!"

But the concern, to her, was pointless. She slapped his arm away, as she staggered forward.

"Don't worry about me, we've gotta find Ivy, QUICK!!"

- - - -

Ivy's mind was flooded with memories. Memories of when we first found her... running... crying... screaming. Chased by a creature. Only this time, she had Magnus by her side. Her faithful canine companion, ever since he saved her that night. When he charged at her attacker, before it could take her. And the dog led her to safety, to salvation.

She wasn't crying now. She wasn't screaming. The others were underestimating her. Underestimating the intelligence and capability she actually possessed. She wasn't being chased by the Chupacabra. She was leading it precisely where she wanted it to go. *Into her own trap.*

She didn't look behind her. Didn't even need to. She knew he was right on her heels. She knew he was closing in. Which was exactly what she was counting on.

Her lips moved, ever so slightly, to form a tiny smirk. She snapped her fingers towards Magnus. The canine lifted up his eyes to the little girl. She nodded at him. He looked away.

At once, the two screeched to a sudden halt and quickly rebounded, swiveling on their heels in the opposite direction. This caused the Cab to slide. Its paws shuffled underneath him, as he scrambled to go after them. He nearly fell in the process, but he soon recovered. He was on the trail once more. Not questioning why the two had done what they just did.

Ivy and Magnus were heading back to the others. The sounds of their voices came into earshot. The child did not know how close they were, but she knew they were soon bound to run into each other. But Ivy... she felt it... she felt something unpleasant. Something which drew her attention to the shadows surrounding her.

Her eyes wandered, seeking out the one of whom she felt so strongly. The one behind all this madness. Magnus barked. It broke her out of her thoughts.

Her gaze snapped to the dog. But she looked too late. His legs were sliding underneath him, as he struggled to stop himself, yelping in the process. When Ivy looked, it was only made worse. She soon collided with another. Magnus tumbled, and rolled over her and the other victim of the crash.

All three landed upon the ground, knocked out of the chase. Sadly, luck was not on Ivy's side at that moment. For the one she ran into was not of the Assembly. It was the Cab.

The little girl lifted her head up quickly, toward the creature that was recovering faster than the other two. She quickly lifted herself up from the ground, and she faced the creature with an intense gaze.

Magnus slowly emerged, shaking his head from the dizziness the impact caused, and he rejoined Ivy's side, soon entering a deathly staring contest with his opponent once again.

The three did not budge. They did not even blink. Just remained, still as statues, as they awaited on one another's move. It was clear that the Cab received help from the unwelcome presence to pull such a trick. And now, he had Ivy right there in front of him... ready to be taken.

"IVY!"

Ivy did not bother to look. The others had found her.

All of the Assembly, now reunited, were standing behind the child. They cautiously approached, but dared not move too close. The creature before them was remaining still. Which was uncharacteristic of him. Gabriel stepped toward the girl, reaching out his hand for hers.

"Ivy... come on... I'm taking you out of here..."

She did not look at him. No acknowledgment of any kind. She just kept standing. Even when Audrey tried to do the same thing.

"Ivy, listen to us...we need to get you out of here!"

"Listen to them, kid, you're in more danger than you realize!"

Even Talbot's words, as a seasoned monster hunter, made no difference to the child.

But no... Ivy would not leave. She wouldn't run. She was winning. This was still *her* plan.

As Ivy stared into the influenced eyes of the Chupacabra... she smiled. A satisfied, self-praising smile. One that screamed victory. One that indicated... she had gotten away with outsmarting the creature. Because she had. It was right where she wanted it to be. At the precise timing needed to end this showdown.

The Chupacabra's back recoiled, its spikes spreading apart. Its eyes lit up the darkness, as its long fangs glistened, its mouth opening wide to let out a petrifying snarl. And then...

Its body jerked. Its expression entered an instantaneous state of absolute shock. The others peered to see what had happened, still frozen in place. *A tranquilizer dart.*

The Cab did not know what to do.

Its eyes fluttered. It shook its head.

It staggered, swaying back and forth.

Its body was now becoming groggy.

A hum came from its mouth. As if unsure what noise to make. Was it angry? Was it frightened? Was it relieved? Its mind was clouded.

The others gawked, as it finally happened. The creature fell to the ground before them. Lycan leaned in, staring into the eyes of the Cab. The eyes of which seemed to actually be diminishing in brightness. And the pained, intense expression of anger on the creature... melted away.

"Are you kidding me??"

His head jerked to every single person around him.

"Just like *that*?!"

The Assembly turned their attention away from the creature. For at long last, they didn't have to look. Their eyes moved to the right, into the darkness... where a figure stepped forward and revealed himself.

Gabriel's mouth hung even more in that moment. Armed with a tranquilizer gun of his own, the figure came into the light, staring down at the creature. **The man from the precinct.**

His long black trench coat fluttered in the wind, his sunglasses reflecting the moon's looming image, and his gelled pompadour hairstyle sparkled in the vague light shining overhead.

He rested the gun against his shoulder, before his head finally turned to the group.

"You!" Gabriel exclaimed, with almost an accusing finger.

"*You*." The man shot back in sarcasm, pointing at Gabriel's face with a blinding flashlight, instead of a mere finger. The Beckhart boy covered his eyes, shaking his head.

"Who the heck are you?!" Pine demanded at once... until Talbot leaned in.

"*Falcon*?!"

The group swiveled their gaze upon the old man. The man smirked, as he shifted. "Talbot."

"HOLD ON!" Audrey yelped, as she stomped over between the man and Talbot. She pointed at both.

"You two know each other?!"

The man did a single fingered salute.

"Agent Falcon, at your service."

Russell rubbed the back of his neck, as he began chuckling softly.

"Falcon's an old friend from... back in the day."

He rolled his shoulders.

"For god's sake, Falcon, why didn't you tell me you were back in town?!"

"That would defeat the purpose of my profession as a *secret* agent, Russell."

He set the tranq gun down upon the ground, then put both hands on his hips.

"I was brought in for the very reason you cool cats banded together. To investigate the increased mysterious activity."

He stepped over to the Cab, tapping its paw gently with the tip of his boot.

"Little did I know, it was worse than any of us imagined."

Troy's eyes narrowed, as he stared at the man who seemed to have walked straight out of a hokey 90's show.

"So wait, you're like... here to help us??"

Falcon's head lifted.

"More like, help each other."

"You're here to kill them." Pine let out, defensively.

"Or take them to experiment on them."

Falcon's covered eyes rested on the redheaded girl.

"...Let me ask you something... if I were here to kill the thing... why would I tranq it?"

Pine did not appreciate his tone. She marched over to him and shoved a finger into his chest.

"Then you're here to take him and *dissect* him."

"Wrong again. I'm here to take him, yes... but not to run experiments on him. On the contrary."

"Falcon would never, Amelia." Talbot spoke in the background. He then approached her, and laid a reassuring hand on her shoulder. "He's here to *protect* the creatures."

Amelia perked. Her head cocked to the side to look at Talbot, before her gaze fell back on the agent.

"...Protect??"

Falcon shrugged. "Think of it as like, uh... an organization, aimed towards exotic animal preservation."

He turned, looking down at the Cab.

"This little guy here... we're gonna bring him, and keep him safe. Take care of him. Make sure he's out of the line of fire. Until we can relocate him where he won't be taken advantage of again."

The group was silent, taking in this new information. Unsure of whether to accept it or not. Pine, however, gained an expression that indicated she had just found her new best friend. She was grinning ear to ear, exhibiting an excited energy. It was as if she just met a famous celebrity.

"This sounds sketchy as crap." Quinton was glared at for his comment. He shrugged a little too casually. "I'm just saying."

"I don't blame you for doubting me. There's not a whole lot of people you can trust in this town anymore. Lots of secrets. Lots of cover-ups. Lots of liars."

Falcon bent down and peeled back an eyelid of the Cab, who was at this point fully sedated.

"What I can promise you is... I'm not here to hurt you."
He stood back up, staring at each member with heavy concentration. As if by doing this, he was proving his sincerity.

"...And I'm not against you."
Talbot's word alone was not enough to fully convince all of them... but for now, at least... they felt less threatened.

"What about the entity?" Gabriel remembered. "He's still out here!"

"Entity?" Falcon inquired.

"The guy thing controlling the Chupacabra." Lycan answered.

"It tried to kill me, and take Ivy!" Audrey added. "If it's here, maybe you can help us-"

"*Wait.*" Gabriel let out.
They paused. He was staring down at Ivy... who was shaking her head. She looked up at the group and began to sign.

Gabe breathed. *"He's gone."* He looked back.

"She says he's gone."
Audrey laid a hand on the girl's shoulder, "Are you sure?"
The child nodded her head. She continued signing.

"When the Chupacabra was shot, he let go of his control. We're safe."

Each member of the Assembly turned their heads to one another. Finally... they all sighed in relief.

"It's over, then." Lycan spoke. "We did it."

Talbot held his aching hip. The excitement had put a strain on his aging body. "...You kids... you were incredible."

His hand rested on Lycan's back, who beamed at his mentor's admiration.

"I couldn't be any more prouder."

"Okay, cool, but how did you know we were here??" Quinton, forever suspicious and eternally disgusted by mushy situations, quickly deflected the attention back to Falcon. Falcon sighed at Lim's distrust.

"The answer to that is simple. I followed you from Talbot's Den." His finger quickly wagged at Audrey,

"And before you start accusing me, no I'm not your stalker! We're currently working on that."

The Beckhart girl's mouth fell,

"How did you know about that?!"

"I went to the precinct, *moron*."

His insult made Audrey jerk her head in offense. He continued, regardless.

"I learned what I needed about you twerps."

Troy turned to Quinton to speak in a hushed voice.

"This dude's too mean to be a mole, man."

"I'm starting to agree, he's a bit of a troll." Quinton whispered back.

"I heard that, porcupine."

Falcon's loud tone made both Quin and Troy jolt.

"DUDES!!!"

The Assembly could not take any more excitement. But they looked, nevertheless, where they saw two men running towards them. Spike and Wyatt.

The mohawked pizza guy and the farm hand collapsed to their knees, and held tight to the trees beside them, completely out of breath. Their lungs heaved, as they tried to recover as quickly as possible, for they needed... needed so desperately...
to get something out.

It was Spike now that pointed with a trembling hand.

"...IVY'S ON THE LOOSE!"

The Assembly bowed their heads upon hearing this... they didn't know whether to laugh or... well... laugh.

"QUICK! WE GOTTA FIND HER BEFORE-"

"Spike."
"No, LISTEN! Ivy broke ou-"
"Spike."

Spike's face fell as he saw what Audrey was pointing at. Ivy peeked from behind. Looking as innocent as she was capable of. Never mind the fact that she had outsmarted both men, and caused Wyatt to still have a splitting headache he wasn't quite sure he was going to recover from...

At this, both young men deflated.

"Well crud."

The agent took a deep breath, as he drew out his phone and began taking photos of the Cab.

"Now that we've got *that* out of the way..."

His eyes briefly glared at Spike and Wyatt, who sagged in embarrassment, attempting to hide their faces behind the trees.

"I think it's time for you kids to be getting back home."

"Home??" Audrey quipped.

"Chupacabra or not, the guy responsible is still out there and *still* wants us dead!"

"She's right, man, we've got like a serious death squad after us now. We totally have a target on our backs."

As much of a point as Audrey and Troy had, both Falcon and Talbot's eyes turned to one single person in response; Quinton.

"I think your friend here has the answer to that."

The Assembly members beheld their friend. Still wielding his camera, he lifted his face to his companions, looking pleased with himself that he was the center of attention, for once.

"What are they on about?" Lycan questioned.

Quin's eyes briefly fell on the camera.

"...Well... what does a film maker do best?"

He pressed a button and released an SD card, of which he presented to the Assembly, with a wide grin, and pride that he now saw they had caught on to his cunning plan.

"...*They capture stories.*"

EPILOGUE
✦ COME BACK SOON ✦

A new day shined upon the town of Hollowgrove. To the amazement of the Assembly, they woke up. Alive. Safe. In their own beds. In their own homes. Nothing had tried to kill them. They slept hard and soundly, without a single worry on their shoulders.

So much of this was due largely to Quinton Lim. The young Korean born film maker had carried out the plan he had been carefully constructing that entire time... he released the footage of the Chupacabra attacks.

The shocking videos streamed on his channel. In a matter of minutes, he received thousands of views. The footage now became the talk of the town. The rage of the believers. Even the skeptics were scrambling to understand what it all meant. And they weren't the only ones scrambling. The videos were enough to get another special press conference, this time from the police *and* the mayor.

"...We understand that the footage depicts a creature of unknown origin." Amelia Pine read from her phone... reading the very article she wrote.

She sat at the table, which Gabriel and Kathryn Chapman also sat at, as the two listened to her voice recount what Ripley Ravenwood told the public.

"...But we encourage the residents not to take it seriously. For hoaxes and conspiracies are still a very clear and present danger in this town. We wish to unite the community to fight this extremism."

She shook her head.

"Ugh... I swear, that man says things solely for the love of his own voice."

"Knowing him personally, I can 100% verify that." Gabriel took a drink from his coffee.

Kathryn sighed contently, as she brought her own cup to her lips. "Well it doesn't matter what they think anymore... it's what the public thinks. And the public is itching to find out who all was involved in that video."

"I thought Quin didn't cut us out?"
Pine smirked at Gabriel's inquiry.

"He didn't. Falcon did. He says we need to wait a little bit before we reveal ourselves to the public..."

"So the Assembly is basically a secret??"

"For right now, yeah... he says it's for our safety, until we can stand up to bigger fish."

Chapman nodded. "He sounds like a smart man... he's right, though. Give it some time. I think in a few cases, you all will be ready to come out and step into the spotlight."

Gabriel and Amelia both nodded. Kathryn smiled at her two welcome guests. "How are the others doing?"

"Quin has his hands full with the videos. The popularity is kinda going to his head, not gonna lie... Troy and Spike have been getting slammed at their shop. Talbot and Lycan, too. People are on a monster rampage now, since we pulled the curtains on this thing."

Gabriel brushed some strands of hair out of his eyes, and adjusted his glasses.

"Agent Falcon took the Chupacabra to his base near Casper City. They're treating it, and making sure it fully recovers. Besides that, he told us he'll contact us when something else turns up. So we're basically on the look out for our next case until then..."

"What about that Wyatt boy?"

"He was praised by the family he works for. They gave him a raise, and are hailing him as a hero. The vengeful goat... well... Spike gave him a name."

"What's that?"

Gabriel cleared his throat, and went to sip his drink.

"The Mad Goater."

Kathryn laughed out loud.

"Well, he *did* sound like a crazy goat!"

"I never want to see that goat again as long as I live."

Pine shuddered. Mrs. Chapman tilted her head, still grinning.

"And what about you two... and Audrey?"

Pine and Gabriel's eyes met for a moment, before Pine looked back at the woman and shrugged.

"Getting by, I guess... not much to tell."

Gabe then leaned back, swallowing hard.

"I'd like to speak to Ivy before I leave, if that's alright."
Kathryn smiled a gentle smile. "Of course."

And so he did... he went into the living room, where Ivy sat at a coffee table, drawing. The TV played cartoons, but it was only background noise at this point.

Magnus laid beside the child, sleeping soundlessly. After watching him in battle, Beckhart had a new respect for the canine. And a slight intimidation. Gabe sat at the couch behind the girl, cupping his hands together.

"Ivy..."
Her head turned and their eyes made contact. Gabriel breathed.

"I just wanted to say... I'm really proud of what you did back there. At the farm. But you need to be more careful... for next time."

He lowered his head.

"...I've got to ask... the Chupacabra... it... it was the one who attacked you... wasn't it? Before you came here? The one Magnus saved you from?"

Gabriel was asking, even though he had fully convinced himself that this was the truth. And he knew she would respond so. It would ease his mind and heart to know that the threat of the child was over for now. That the thing she was so terrified of, that she kept drawing over and over, that haunted her dreams every night...was subdued.

That's when his heart sank. For Ivy shook her head. His facial expression melted. Melted into a state of pure shock.
She signed,
"He wasn't the one. Neither was the entity."
She swallowed hard.
What she signed next made Gabriel sick to his stomach.
"The one who attacked me is still out there."

~

Still out there...

Gabriel stared into the mirror of the bathroom. His mind raced with terrifying thoughts... his dream... it came true. But to an extent. The Cab did not get a hold of her, and did not offer her to the entity he saw controlling it.

However, the door to the unknown had now been opened.

The Assembly had only just begun. He knew that now. And with that, the all-consuming reality that the group did not necessarily want to think about started to show its ugly face; the Cab was only the first of many.

There were more monsters. More horrors and oddities waiting to be discovered. More secrets and conspiracies waiting to be uncovered. At this point, Gabriel did not know if he should be ecstatic or terrified.

"Hey, you kids want to go to the movies tomorrow?!"

The Beckhart boy shook his head, shaking the thoughts from his consciousness. Their parents had returned home. Something that brought the siblings a bit of relief. Not to see them again, necessarily... just the knowledge that with them back home meant the stalker would not touch them. At least not for awhile.

"Sure." He called back.

They had not told them of the stalker. The Chupacabra. The Assembly. Nothing. As far as their parents were concerned... the kids were simply thriving on their much anticipated vacation.

The sad part was... even if they did tell them, it wouldn't matter. They would still be just as emotionally distant as they were now. That was the sad fact of the Beckhart family.

The Beckhart boy walked back to the hallway, where he peaked into Audrey's room, her door wide open.

She laid on her side, facing him, her eyes staring down at the floor. Scrooge was laying on the bed with her, sound asleep. Both were glad to be home, in their own beds again.

"Hey." He spoke gently.

She lifted her gaze up at him.

"You okay?"

She forced a smile. A soft, stifling smile. That indicated much more than she was willing to reveal.

"Yeah, I'm okay."

He curled his lips back, as he studied his sister for a minute.

"...Listen... if you need to talk about..."

"-I'm okay."

Gabriel got the message. He nodded, smiling warmly.

"Okay... good night. See you in the morning."

"Night, Gabe..."

Her brother left. Leaving her alone in the darkened room. Even though she felt a bit safer... she still felt a sense of dread. Like something was coming. Something was still not right. Something that made her-

Ding.

Audrey's body perked. Her eyes flashed to her charging phone, sitting upon her dresser. She sighed. She stood up and ran to it. She took hold of the small device, expecting it to be a text from one of the girls, or a pathetic ex... but her heart stopped.

She let out a gasp.

"Impressed by your exploits.

Still watching.

Good night, sweet Audrey."

Her every muscle tensed, as she stared down at the tiny screen, in a completely darkened room. Suddenly... the illusion that life in Hollowgrove had returned to normal was shattered in seconds.

All with one simple row of texts.

"See you again soon."

✦✦✦ The Assembly Will Return in *Belief Is Half The Battle* ✦✦✦

⋆⋆ CHARACTER GALLERY ⋆⋆

Gabriel Beckhart

Audrey Beckhart

Ivy Rein

Amelia Pine

Magnus

Quinton Lim

Troy Brooke

Lycan

Russell Talbot

Ripley Ravenwood

Spike

The Chupacabra

ACKNOWLEDGMENTS

With all the trials that I had to overcome, this book honestly was so close to never seeing the light of day. In truth, there are so many people who helped make this dream a reality. Such as my wonderful and incredible mother, who supported me for so many years, from the time I was a stupid, starry-eyed child to a clumsy, struggling starry-eyed adult. She was with me from day one, and I would not be half the woman I am now if it wasn't for her.

To my dear and closest friends, the first being Hannah. The beautiful soul who I have known since I was 15, being with me through thick and thin, fueling my passions and encouraging me to go after my dreams. It was she who helped me make the wonderful cover you see now on this book and continues to assist me in beautiful creations inspired by the series.

To Zack and Vedant, two other dearest of souls who helped me through the darkest points of my life. Listening to all my ideas and refusing to let me quit. I love you three immensely and am so very proud to have the privilege to know you, and watch you grow.

To Noah, Susan, Andy and Vivi, and my incredible family, for helping me build my new life and supporting my growth as a person and artist. You helped make this possible by supplying me with all the books and tools I needed to get it all going.

To all the incredible, hard-working men and women at the job that changed my life. To "Commander Cool", who gave me a huge chance by hiring me, and blessing me with a job I love coming to, and people who truly became my work family. To Amanda, Tyler, Gabi, Jess, Brian, Taylor, Jules, Grace, Neha, Fiona, Cody, Ben, Doris, Zohra, Payton, Ruben, Alexis, Travis, Pre, Keith, Marian, Maryam, Tuul, Alex, Sasquatch Alex, Gideon, Nathaniel, Ryan, Isaac, Kaitlyn, Dani, Abigail, Angela, Nevaeh, Mahza, and everyone else that touched my life there, including my favorite customers... you know who you are!

I love you all, and am truly grateful for your encouragement of me, and the thrill you had of the entire process. This journey was made better by such supportive coworkers and friends.

To Michelle M Bruhn, a darling old friend of mine...I would not have gotten this far without your patience and advice. I'm so proud of you and your own journey as a published author of *Songflight*. Thank you for your patience and wisdom, as you answered all my persistent questions. It was a rough process, but it was made more bearable with you as my personal expert in authorship.

To Sam Cudney, author of *How to Publish Your Book For Free*, that gave me so many helpful tips and aided my painful quest in formatting.

To all my loved ones, you are dear to my heart and I couldn't be more grateful for your presence in my life. Above all, I am grateful to my Lord and Savior, who blessed me with the idea of Uncanny and all its inhabitants. Who held my hand through every trial and helped me achieve my goals, becoming the storyteller I always dreamed of being.

Finally, to my inspirations... the dozens of pioneering authors and filmmakers who paved the way for me to get this far. To all the classic monster movies and gems of science fiction. And to you, the readers. Thank you for giving me a chance. For inviting my world to join yours, and shaking hands with the inhabitants of Hollowgrove. I would be nothing without the people who got me here...but I would be even less if it wasn't for YOUR support, and fascination of the unknown.

I breathlessly look forward to continuing this journey with you, from here on out...

✦✦✦ ABOUT THE AUTHOR ✦✦✦

A strangeling whose lifelong dream of writing and film-making led her to the creation of a tale such as Uncanny, a personal love letter to the world of monsters, aliens and supernatural elements alike. When not writing, you can find her brain-storming, movie-binging, gaming, eating or gushing about dogs. Or, perhaps, all five at once.

I wrote this book for such a huge audience...

for the believers nobody believes, for those poor souls alone in their search for the truth...

for the lovers of the monster and cryptid genre, craving for a combination of sci-fi and supernatural...

for the sheer nostalgia of the 80's-90's time period and all the campy, glorious gems it left behind for us.

Most importantly, for everyone who needs strong, flawed, but passionate characters fighting for what's right.

There is so much I have to tell and show you from the world of Uncanny. From the inhabitants of Hollowgrove.

And that adventure has only just begun.

Visit me at
www.sarahdemens.com